THROUGH THE WINDSHIELD

MIKE DECAPITE

red giant +books

www.redgiantbooks.com
First Red Giant Books edition 2014
ISBN: 978-0-9883430-7-8

This is a work of fiction.

Mike DeCapite would like to express his gratitude to Richard Hell,
who was the first to publish excerpts from *Through the Windshield*,
in three issues of *CUZ* magazine in the late 1980s, and to the
following editors, who also published excerpts: Charlotte Pressler
and Steve Wainstead, in *Ragnarok;* Robert Griffin, in *Seven: Scat
Records Quarterly;* Robert Gordon, in *Asymptote;* Ivan Suvanjieff,
in *The New Censorship* and *In This Corner;* Ruthie Singer, Barbara
Schultz, and Andrea Beach, in *Kingfisher;* Jim Ellis, in *CLE;* Cindy
Barber, in *Cleveland Free Times;* Bonnie Jacobson, in *Cleveland in Prose
and Poetry;* Ron Kolm, in *Evergreen Review;* and Rob Jackson, in *Great
Lakes Review*. DeCapite would also like to thank Dave Megenhardt, the
editor of Red Giant Books, for the care he took with this edition.

The author would like to thank the writers and publishers of the
following songs for lyrics quoted herein: "Big Chief," "Down South
in New Orleans," "Got the Water Boiling," "Long Hot Summer
Night," "Strange Relationship," and "Tipitina." The quote from
Charley Patton's "Moon Going Down" is based on a mishearing
of that song.

Cover design by Whitney Highfield

THROUGH THE WINDSHIELD

Driving through the iron landscape of early winter, early December: black and white and monochrome: dust of snow on slanted tar roofs, wide plains of iron, gone numb under a hard low sky, driving blank, gone frozen coasting the lines of longing, slowly scattering all invisible ghosts—even that of loneliness which usually follows all around and as close as a good friend: powder, asphalt, cement and steel, merging brown and purple into black and back, spread across wide distances and rising up into the ash and smoke of bare trees: grey gone silver, gasping in silence, gone stoic in silence: ash and smoke and the wide sunk mud-iron landscape of forever.

THE ENVELOPE DAYS OF FEBRUARY

I

I woke one morning lying on my side . . . the clock said nine-thirty. I had driven the cab till after three, but I knew I wouldn't get back to sleep now. The apartment felt empty as I pulled on my clothes and boots and jacket.

Outside, the world was warmer and more intimate. The sky was crouched and darkly white, and the snow had begun to melt into itself. For days I hadn't zipped my jacket.

I got into the car and started the engine, sat cold behind the wheel while it warmed up. Then I coasted slowly down the hill to the river.

Ernie's was a concrete box under the black trestles of a railroad bridge. Behind it was the Yellow Cab lot, with leftover Checkers along the fence. A hundred yards away were gravel mounds and the river. Inside, Ernie's had a counter and a few booths, a couple slits of window for ventilation, a calendar from a trucking company, workgloves and aspirin for sale at the register . . . walls painted an institutional green. I sat at the counter. There were two other customers: a guy in a booth reading the paper over coffee, and another at the far end of the counter, polishing off an order of French toast. Both looked as though they saw the dark before dawn every day. The place was quiet.

A woman came out of the back and asked what I wanted. When I spoke, it seemed like the first time in days that I'd opened my mouth. I asked for two eggs with ham and potatoes and coffee. She brought the coffee, and then took the pot to refill the other guys' cups.

I took my time eating. I had plenty of time to think and no reason not to. It was good to realize that I wasn't thinking about Marie. After a six-month diet of blues and greys I was back to white. I was an empty plate.

The man down the counter took a last swig, left some change, paid at the register and walked out. The guy in the booth was done with the sports and wondering what to do next. The woman came and filled my cup. I lit a Lucky Strike and settled into another day . . . wondering what to do next.

I left her a buck, paid up, and walked out to the Buick. It was spattered with salt and mud. The air felt damper now.

I drove up the hill and into downtown. The streets were wet with melted snow. I pulled into the YMCA lot as a few raindrops hit the windshield.

From another row of lockers came the booming voice of Carl. He was a big old Jewish guy who insisted on talking to me about the racetrack. I had the impression he had been there once, thirty years ago. He shouted questions and didn't listen for answers. Usually he asked if I was working, and for some reason I felt like I had to explain what I was doing here in the middle of the day. He had decided my name was Pat.

I grabbed soap and towel and started for the stairs.

"Pat, my boy! How are you!" He was shouting at the top of his lungs.

"Hi Carl. How's it going?"

"Yeah, you'll be going out to the track soon, eh!"

"Track don't open for another month, Carl."

"Yeah, yeah . . . But I mean! You'll be going out there, won't you?"

"Oh yeah."

"Yeah, me, I—aah . . . No luck, Pat! How'd you like to hit

one of those BIG TRIFECTAS! Hah, Pat? Never happen! Hah? Better save your money! You working today?"

"Oh yeah, I'm going in around n—"

"That's good, that's good—Make that MONEY!"

"Okay C—"

"Forget about the horses!"

"Okay. See y—" And he was turned around already, shouting at someone else.

I sat in the steam room. Someone else was there . . . an old man, barely visible through the steam. He was shaking. When I broke a sweat I stood and loosened up a bit and then went out to the showers.

Pretty soon the old man came shivering into the cold tiled room, hunched over, with arms hanging dead. He had the look of a man being led without hope of mercy through one torture after another. He came to the shower next to mine, and with a hand swollen and twisted like a flipper he managed to get the water on: full blast, ice cold. It splashed onto me like needles and I jumped out of its range. He stood riveted, as though unable to let go of an electric wire—shaking violently—staring upward in a frozen gasp with that icewater blasting all over his bald head and in his eyes and running out his mouth . . .

Only two other guys were in the basement weight room. There was the clink of weights. Up near the ceiling a couple windows were tilted open, and from the street came the slush of traffic and an occasional pair of heels. I worked with the weights awhile and then did pull-ups and sit-ups.

In the boxing room I shut the door behind me, took a chair from the corner and sat by the windows. I liked it in there. It was a small room, empty with a winter light. The wooden floorboards worn smooth . . . two windows of frosted glass . . . Between them hung a set of weights with cables; on the opposite wall was a short wooden bar, worn dark, for building up the wrists and forearms. Against the back wall was an old red mat. In the center of the room the heavy-bag hung still, in a kind of quiet conviction. There was a silence about the room that seemed never to have broken.

I got up and hit the bag until I was breathing hard, and then went back to sit by the windows.

An older black guy came in and closed the door. A big guy—big gut on him, but solid, wearing a white T-shirt and blue shorts, carrying a gym bag. He glanced at me once and then paid me no mind. He had the scarred and grizzled look of a bull walrus.

Moving with care, as though this were a daily ritual of many years, he put the bag down, unzipped it, took out a pair of bag gloves and set them aside. He did a series of quick perfunctory exercises to loosen up. After stretching, he came to the cables on the wall and I moved to the other side of the room.

When he was done with the cables he picked up the gloves and began working the bag. He hit like he was hitting an old friend: as though it were no more than necessary. His movements were deliberate; he didn't move his feet much. He didn't break much of a sweat and he wasn't breathing hard, but he came to this place every day, and went through the old motions. I left him to himself.

After another few minutes in the steam, I took another shower and washed my hair. When I was dressed I combed some grease into it. I slipped into my jacket and walked out of there feeling like a hundred bucks.

I felt calm as the day outside. My footsteps were certain below the neutral sky. I wished there were someone watching.

. . . envelope days of February: a blind sky and the white wet snow. I was driving somewhere not particular, but anyway there was nothing doing at home. So I stayed away from there and kept moving, driving as though hypnotized through the long howling sprawl of East Side streets, in an afternoon where the light never changed: past the campus of Community College, the grey cluster of downtown standing blind in the distance

5

. . . past the shut-down Woodland Food Terminal, place of dogs . . . detecting undue motion in the parking lots of fast-food joints—the heroin trade on Fifty-Fifth . . . guys lined up in twos and threes or alone, moving through the hive of projects . . . a fat woman limping home with a bag of groceries . . . a dim-lit superette selling single cans of beer to guys with one or two things to do today, a gang of kids hanging around a video game . . . another group walking home from school . . . Jack's, Mandingo, The Native Son/ Vel's Quarter Century, The Smoky Pig, The Suave Buzzard/ Bible Meetings, Checks Cashed, Party Center/ Food Stamps Accepted, Fish Dinners, Red Devil Lucky Number Picks . . . Around Seventy-Ninth a big woman in a rabbit-fur jacket, short skirt and boots, wading through slush into traffic—blowing kisses and shivering . . .

Driving up Central a stray handful of rain fell across my windshield and pocked into the snow of long vacant lots . . . past a block of burnt-out stores, down sidestreets of big old houses built for nobody-remembers-who . . . sidestreets that curved deeper into nowhere, with fenced-off junkyards forgotten under snow, past a looming brewery and a few factories running at minimum capacity . . . over a short bridge that spanned railroad tracks and weedbeds . . . I had the feeling that if I kept driving I'd drive off the edge.

I found my way into pockets that were Polish and Slovenian, Appalachian: hidden streets of small frame houses dirtied by winter . . . silent against the opaque sky . . . cars at the curbs, waiting for some hillboy to drag himself off to a third-shift job . . . A Christmas tree on a tree lawn, left for garbagemen who probably wouldn't take it this week like they hadn't for the last six . . . Five minutes of rain like something left over from an earlier draft, and then the sky would seem to brighten, almost, but wouldn't . . . only the same bedroom light as before . . . soft swish of tires on the street, and my face in the mirror came as a dark surprise. I felt like I hadn't spoken in months.

And in the final moments of that sunless day, as the colors

of the world sharpened, and deepened with significance, the sky came like a trout's belly, and the snow on the ground came red, with a hint that seeped up from within. I looked up and the sky was blank as before—deadpan, and the snow as white . . . but when I focused on the street again the trout swam back above, a hint of red played to either side . . .

Night filtered down.

And then night was here, after a day of measured breathing, and I could forget about breathing because the waiting was done.

I pulled into the taillight stream and headed home, took the freeway bridge over the river: the mills were a black winking pool, and from a distant smokestack there was fire. I coasted off the exit ramp, back into the Southside.

Fast Eddie lived next door to me.

He'd moved in a couple months before, and I'd see him on the street, or coming in and out of the yard we shared, or at Feef the bookie's. Once I'd given him a jump. He insisted on giving me three bucks for the trouble. Something in his brusqueness cheered me up. More, something in what I could glean of his existence fascinated me. I found myself going over to spend a few minutes with him on my nights off.

I stepped onto the porch and rapped on the door.

"*Yes?*" came the weary voice. This was just another in a series of irritations to which he was resigning himself.

I stepped into his kitchen. He was against the heater, his gut too big for his T-shirt. His hair was going, but he had a wisp of widow's peak . . . a thin moustache-and-goatee: he looked like a slightly overweight Western badguy. He was waiting to hear what I wanted from him. All four burners of the stove were on, as well as the heater.

I said "What're you, growing orchids in here?"

"Fucking *freezing* in here man I—out in that truck all day my *bones're* frozen."

"Just get back?"

"Just walked in before you come pounding on my door . . . phone was already ringing when I walked in, assholes calling about a card game. Now: what's *your* story? What do *you* want?"

"Nothing. I dunno."

"Possible card game tonight."

"Oh yeah?"

"Talked to this buddy of mine Ronny last night: Ichabod. I just fell asleep: I went to bed early—lost a fucking two-teamer I had with the Celtics, got beat in the last thirty seconds, after being ahead the whole game. I said Fine, shut the TV off at ten o'clock and went to bed—ten-thirty the phone rings, it's fucking Ichabod, says he talked to the Villain and Jones—possible emergency game at the Finn tonight. I told him I'm broke but the asshole won't let up—keeps me on the phone for half a fucking hour because he's lonely, telling me about some broad he seen in a bar, how she's giving him the eye. Some stripper. This guy's so pathetic, Danny—He goes to these bust-out stripper joints, and these women sit on his lap, he buys 'em a drink . . . He thinks they like him. He thinks some drunk, bust-out dancing girl's got the hots for him—"

"Yeah."

"Goofy guy with his—big hands and his—long, gangly legs, his red face . . . Tells me how he turns on the charm . . . He really thinks he's some—suave macho guy, with his gold watch, his gold chains . . . I wish you could see this guy."

"You gonna play?"

"I told him I was broke—These guys're all the same, they all got good jobs—Ichabod and Villain both work in the steel mills for twenty years, they don't do a fucking thing down there, they make twenty bucks an hour . . . Jones owns two beverage stores, TJ works at the post office . . . They all got nice houses, nice cars—they got a ton of money to play with . . . You need a hundred to get in the game. I ain't even got the hundred, these guys all got five hundred, a thousand bucks to play with—They know I'm playing tight, and they just hammer me till I'm out. It's a no-win situation."

"What time you going?"

". . . Nine o'clock, nine-thirty, if I go. I got forty-nine from Coke today, plus twenty I beat 'em for on the empties is sixty-nine, plus a couple bucks in change lying around here . . . I got about seventy-five, plus whatever you'd like to contribute. You drive the cab last night?"

"Yeah."

"Driving tonight?"

"No."

"You bum. Why not?"

"I dunno."

I took a seat at his table. He was moving around . . .

"So uh . . ."

"I can give you ten."

"Okay, that's a start. How 'bout twenty?"

"Yeah, I can give you twenty."

I pulled out my money and peeled off a twenty. His eyes widened and he let out a whistle.

I laughed. "Forget it."

"Okay buddy, I'll have it back to you tomorrow. Possibly Wednesday."

"I'm gonna cook some pasta. You hungry?"

"You gonna make it now?"

"Yeah, it'll be ready about an hour."

"If you got a few extra noodles throw 'em in the pot. I might take a walk over to Feef's and put this twenty on the Cavs."

"How you gonna get in the game without the hundred?"

He pulled out a roll: "I got all singles here, they won't ask to count it. I've gone with a lot less than this, believe me."

"Come on up when you're ready."

"You eating up there?"

"—Well—Yeah . . ."

"Why don't you bring it down here? I gotta be here in case one of these idiots calls."

I unlocked my place and poured a shot of Ancient Age, drank it. The whiskey was cool from the cold of the apartment, but it burned going down. The next one burned less.

I covered the bottom of the frying pan with olive oil and cut in six or seven cloves of garlic. The smell of garlic frying brought me back to where I lived. I threw together a quick tomato sauce and let it simmer, drank another shot and boiled water for pasta. When it was done I threw the water off, mixed the sauce with the pasta and threw in some Romano cheese. The windows were steamed. I took the pot to Ed's. Going down the stairs it occurred to me that whiskey in the evening was the perfect answer to all those questions that bother you during the day.

"Whattaya want to drink?" he said. "I got rancid lemonade from Abdul, half a liter of Coke's been flat for three days, the last dregs of a carton of skim milk, and two cans of Pabst."

"Coke."

"I got no ice, unless you want me to chisel it off the side of the freezer."

"Skip the ice," I said. "You go to Feef's?"

"Yeah I took a two-teamer for twenty, took another shot. That's my backup bet, in case I tap out at the Finn."

"Who you got?"

"I took Cleveland with Boston again, even though Boston fucked me last night."

"Cleveland on the radio?"

"Yeah—Tune it in. See what you can do."

We finished eating and I poured a last swallow of Coke.

I said "Spaghetti okay?"

"Excellent. Better than I make it."

"How do you make it?"

"I boil noodles and then I pour ketchup over them."

I got up to go.

He said "What're you doing, later on? What's the story?"

"I dunno. Nothing. Why?"

"Stop down at the Finn, you're not doing anything around eleven o'clock."

"Well I don't wanna piss them guys off—"

"Nah, fuck 'em. Just tell Mandy the barmaid you're looking for Fast Eddie. You should see these guys."

"Yeah alright. Maybe."

"Check in back first to make sure my car's there. I might already be tapped."

I went to the drugstore to get a number. Actually I went to get a look at the girl who worked the number machine. She had black hair and pale blue eyes and Ed claimed she was crazy about me. I waited in line behind a smoky old man who looked like the idea of winning anything had never crossed his mind. Maybe he was there for the same reason I was. I gave her two bucks for a dollar backup on 721, and she gave me the same tired flicker of a smile she gave everyone else.

Dark had settled and nothing had changed. The sky was white as before. Darkness was just a trick of habit.

I walked up to the Greeks. Light from inside gave onto the sidewalk. The door was locked, which meant there was a poker game in back. Mihale saw me and came from behind the counter to let me in. There was no one else in the room; I sat by the windows. From the next room came the sound of the Greeks arguing over pinochle and anything else they could think of. From the room where the poker was dealt came no sound at all.

"Coffee, Mihale. Sweet."

He nodded, gravely, and started making it. He looked like Buster Keaton. The closest he ever came to a smile was once in a while when he'd ask if the coffee was okay and I'd tell him it was perfect. He thought that was funny. He wore the same blue paisley shirt every day, like it was the only one he deserved.

He brought the little cup of black sweet coffee and set a glass of water beside it. I let the grounds settle and lit a cigarette.

The windows were greasy with smoke, and the light looked as though it had been left on overnight. I sipped the coffee. The Greeks always seemed like a good place to sit and think, but usually once I sat down I found I had nothing to think about, so I just sat and watched the Greeks. The Greeks, having already thought of everything twenty-five hundred years ago, argued and played cards and waited for their lottery numbers to come in.

Just before seven-thirty I went into the other room to watch the drawing on TV. In the center of the room was a circle of men playing pinochle, and another table involved in a mystifying Greek game in which each player is dealt thirty or forty cards which he throws in at the end of each hand so that he can receive thirty or forty more. Old Tony the Pinochle King was in the corner alone, gazing out the window and chewing a twenty-year-old cigar . . .

Lea was at a table near the TV. He was a white-haired bear of a man, in a checkered hunter's cap and jacket. Lea spent his days getting lottery tickets for the others . . . back and forth in a fog of possibilities . . . walking slowly . . . eyes cast just above the horizon, numerals whirling round his head. I sat across from him and nodded. He leaned toward me, unfolding a list. He hunched over it, muttering and pointing to each number: there was a story behind each one. He was speaking in Greek, so his secrets were safe with me.

A blonde in a bikini picked three ping-pong balls from a barrel of popping balls and set them before the camera: 2 . . . 7 . . . 4. I'd just missed the box, as usual. I shook my head to reassure Lea I hadn't won and showed him my ticket so he wouldn't be suspicious, left half a buck for the coffee and walked out.

*

About ten o'clock I went back into the night, driving through the same streets I'd gone through earlier: dark now, and shiny with rain. From the foot of Broadway, the white smoke billowed slowly up forever, the mills like broken castles . . . I switched the radio on and listened for the sports. Ed had hit the Celtics game but lost with the Cavs. I switched the radio off.

The Dragon Court was one small room lit like a dentist's office. A counter and three booths. I'd never seen anyone eating in there. Open till four. The few places open past dark were like oases of hoarded light on the curving back of the long city streets. I got a pint of soup and ate in the car, and then drifted down to the Finn Cafe.

Ed's car was out back, so I parked and went inside.

I asked the barmaid for a shot of Windsor. She brought it and I drank it, paid.

"Ed around?"

"Who?"

"Fast Eddie."

"You supposed to meet him here?"

"Said he was gonna be in back. The party room or something. Said I should ask you."

"He's there—that door on the back wall. Just knock."

I did.

Someone yelled "Who is it?"

"Ed!" I called, over the juke.

"Oh yeah, 's a buddy of mine. Let him in."

Someone flipped the hook on the door and I pushed my way in—could barely get the door open. The "backroom at the Finn" was a storage closet. Stacked against the four walls were cases of beer and pop, and squeezed into the middle of it all were six guys—big guys, all of them—around a card table just about big enough for solitaire. A naked bulb above, shrouded in smoke. There was no oxygen in the room, it was ninety degrees, and so tight it looked as though the six had taken their places and had the table lowered from above, and then, with careful maneuvering, one of them had managed to get a deck of cards out of his pocket. They were knee to knee.

Ed was to the left, still in his jacket, with a switched-off transistor radio in the pocket.

"Glad you could make it," he said. "I wanted you to meet these assholes I been telling you about. You got the cab?"

"No."

A guy to my right was peering, owl-eyed, through bottle-bottom glasses. "You a cab driver?"

"Yeah."

"Yeah? I went down there once, but I failed the eye test."

"This TJ," Ed told me. "Pretends he's a friend of mine, but he's been hammering me all night."

TJ smirked and reached a hand across, almost capsizing the table.

"What's your name?"

"Danny."

"You come to get in the game?" snapped a guy with a pointed beard.

"Don't look like there's room."

Ed said "Aah they hadda use the backroom for something else tonight, so they stuck us in here."

"Oh. You mean this ain't usually where you play?"

"Fuck no."

The guy with the beard was ready to deal. He looked like a greying Satan. "You playing or not, Eddie?"

"I'm in, Villain."

"Nigger Monte," announced the Villain.

Ed looked at me. "This, Danny, is the Villain: the cheapest motherfucker here."

Villain glanced up at me and opened his sweater to reveal a

T-shirt with THE VILLAIN in black letters across the chest. He gave me a wary, defiant look, in case I questioned his right to the title, and then he began to deal.

The guy who dealt next had a face like a crab apple. He sat hunched and folded over a neat stack of bills he kept weighted down with a silver lighter. He looked like he was under tremendous pressure—not only to win this hand, but to remain conscious. This was Ronny: the guy Ed called Ichabod, after Ichabod Crane. He wasn't saying much. Of the six, he looked the most uncomfortable with the accommodations.

"Whiteman," he announced.

"Rich fucker," Ed was saying: "Just comes here to hammer me. Fucking guy's got a thousand bucks in front of him. Look at this suit he wears to the game—"

"Please," Ronny told him. "I just came from a funeral."

"Whose funeral?" asked a man named Wade.

"Old buddy of mine, I used to work with," said Ronny as he dealt.

"You got no fucking friends," Ed reminded him.

I said "Ed, how you doing so far?"

"I got no friends either."

"I mean tonight."

"I's doing fine till you showed up, Doctor Doom. You listen to the Cavs game?"

"I heard the score."

"See? You didn't listen to the game and they lost. Then you show up and doom me and I lost the last two hands here."

"There's no way you were gonna beat me on that last hand," the Villain informed him. "I know you too well, Eddie."

This opened a discussion of the last five hands: who had fucked whom—accusations, insults . . . explanations, threats . . . gloating, over hands played with such finesse you'd think the game was all skill, until the next hand was lost.

TJ took out a bag of grass and a pipe. He lit a bowl and took a couple hits, held it toward me.

"Naw, thanks."

Wade won the pot, and now it was Ed's deal.

"Vegas," he said. "Danny, go get me a double Windsor with a little ginger on the side. Get yourself something too." He handed me a few singles from his pile.

"Anyone else?" I asked.

A grumpy guy in a cap said "Yeah, I'll take a Velvet-and-Coke," and handed me three quarters.

Ronny said "Ooh, yeah: bring me a rum-and-Coke, wouldya?" He slipped me a buck and said "Get yourself something with the change."

I went out to the bar and got the drinks, plus a double for myself, and Mandy gave me a tray to carry it all back. They were discussing the hand when I walked in, and Wade was dealing.

"Murder," he said.

I set the drinks and Ronny said "Did you get yourself something?"

"Yeah," I told him. "Thanks."

I leaned against the door to watch the game. The guy in the cap shot me a look. Ed won the next hand, and gathered his money like a man disgusted that it'd taken so long for him to get what he deserved. I asked if he wanted me to hold some of it.

"You taking off?"

"No, not yet."

"Alright. Good idea, buddy. Here:"

He gave me two twenties and a ten; I put them in my shirt-pocket.

"Don't go yet: I might need it back."

After while I went out and got Ronny another drink, and another for myself. I sipped it and watched a few hands.

That third shot punched everything in and I could feel the whiskey running through me like blood. All of a sudden there was something I had to do. I stepped out of the backroom into the bar. The juke was playing . . . a table of guys laughing over Liar's Poker . . . four five guys at the bar . . . I walked toward the payphone as though on a tightrope: my heart was pounding lightly and my hands went cold. Without thinking twice I dropped a quarter in and dialed her number, like blood. I hadn't talked to her in a month.

Her phone rang once . . . twice . . . three times . . . four—I knew it was late, but—five times, and she picked it up.

"Hello?" she said, half asleep.

"Hello? Marie?"

"Oh. —Hi."

"Hey. How you doing? Everything okay?"

"Yeah . . . ?"

"Yeah? Good, I uh . . . I dunno, I just figured I'd call."

"Yeah?"

"Everything okay with you? You need anything?"

"No . . ." She wanted me to know she was being patient. "Where are you?" she asked, as if changing the subject. She was leading me away from something. From her bedroom. She had a guy there. Sheets rustled.

"I'm at a bar, Ed's playing cards in the back."

"Oh yeah? Is he winning?"

"Yeah, he's doing okay . . . He didn't have much to play with, but he's hanging in there . . ."

I wanted to tell her about the people in the bar, about the Villain and Ichabod . . . about driving around all day under that white wet sky, and the way the night looked outside . . . I could tell I was making her nervous.

"Yeah?" she said.

"Yeah, well . . . I's just calling to say hello, make sure you're okay."

"I'm fine," she said. "Are you okay?"

"Yeah, I'm alright."

"Good."

"Yeah . . . Okay then—I'll talk to you, sometime. Take care of yourself."

"You too."

"Goodnight . . ."

"Goodnight."

I set the phone down lightly. In that moment I wanted to be at home, in bed, in the dark: asleep. I felt myself shrivel up. I decided not to call there anymore.

I went back to the game. It was good to sit with men who weren't thinking about women, breathing smoke, and listening to their harsh insulting talk. The pressure in that room was like the pressure deep under water: the room was like a diving bell. I watched without paying much attention. When I had fed the whole fifty back to Ed and watched him lose it, I took a swig of his ginger ale and told him I was taking off.

"You shoulda left when you had that fifty."

He pulled out his wallet and produced a credit card.

"Alright," he said, showing it around. "Forest City: anything you need, twenty percent off. Color TV, lawn mower, chainsaw—we can pick it up tomorrow, no problem. I'll take the cash right now."

The Villain tried to jump: "You pull that card one more time I'm gonna cut it up, Eddie!"

"I'll see you tomorrow, Ed."

"Uh—Yeah, okay: stop over in the morning, around ten. I'll probably be broke."

I cut the engine and sat in the car in front of the house. Minutes passed. The keys dangling from the ignition swung tinier until they hung, still. From the bare tree above a drop of water hit the roof. Another fell onto the windshield and trickled, catching, down. There was no one on the street. I decided to go for a walk.

. . . Wooden houses lined up dark below a sky glowing orange . . . houses that bobbed, sinking, downhill to the river, and sagged along the crest of the valley . . . I turned down a road that sloped along the edge of that crest. The strung march of telephone poles . . . the strung vigil of streetlights . . . the blacktop covered in a moisture like soot, showing tire tracks from hours before . . . A secret maze of backalleys: plastic on the windows, a room lit by the blue glow of a television . . . two houses gutted by fire, giving off a damp charred smell in the night . . . sideyards of old sprung furniture and toys . . . a vacant lot with four cars sunk in snow . . . The neighborhood felt like the set for a play: street-lit: silent: suspended: My footsteps made the only sound in a long alley leading down to the projects: a cluster of brick barracks with a smoke-damaged look and screendoors hanging loose. And squatting at the edge of those projects, overlooking the mill valley, were the onion domes of St. Theodosius Russian Orthodox Church. A lot of churches left behind . . . changed hands . . . half-remembered denominations . . . And old bars, too: Hotz's, and the Friendly Inn . . . Lemko's, and the Jefferson Tavern . . . or Flo's, down the hill by the tracks—a rough joint fed by the projects . . . Now, late at night, the neon beer signs were dark. The whole neighborhood was closed up . . . quiet . . . huddled against the damp in a sleep where nothing is forgotten, enclosed below a winter sky.

I walked into Lincoln Park. It lay open and empty . . . a few trees . . . some swings at one end . . . a sidewalk crossing through . . . I sat on a bench. There was no breeze, and the night was warm. I was thinking about Marie, at home with someone else. I glanced around at the wet snow, the black trees . . . Every few minutes a car wished by, down West Fourteenth.

Across the park was the building where we'd shared a place. They were up there now, top floor, corner windows. I searched for an attitude toward those windows, but they were only two in a brick wall of black windows. I remembered her head on the pillow, as she lay listening to her dreams, lightly. I remembered lying awake, nightly, consumed in fears that something would happen to her. Aware that even with me beside her, she was alone in the world. I remembered leaning in doorways:

our kitchen doorway, our bedroom doorway . . . leaning, and watching . . .

Smoke was rising, rising from behind the houses that bounded the park. I was thinking about Marie and I realized I didn't care. Pain was just a trick of habit. I felt as much a part of the night as the benches in the park. I stared up at the sky: it was like looking into nothingness: a vibration. I unzipped the jacket, found cigarettes and shook one out. Struck a match; it flared, briefly, yellow and near, lighting my cupped hands and part of my face. I tossed the match off and inhaled. A silence spread within me.

II

rolling tripping smacking drums—log drums, under steady
dreamlike motion/ i stand: numb and watching, as my spirit
glides . . . pulled and pulling forward . . . / and water moves, beneath the ice. now is almost time—soon will be time—or, i can
see a time (when i awake i will plant new seeds. all the bills are
paid./ . . . the city rolls past, as though on film . . . the outlying
flatlands as though in dream, covered still in snow. snow comes
and goes and turns to rain and comes again. the tunnel of day
into night: a sprinkle of lights—a handful of lights, across a dark
distance/ the sound of silver, the blush of suspended hope: col-
lide, calliope . . . a moon, reflected in a tin ashtray, a brief pale
sun, shrouded and without heat . . . the peripheral glistening of
trout's-belly colors—like personal laughter, beside me/ and the
buick rolls onward, ever forward: the slow cascade of a ferris
wheel that's always turning. on film . . . in dream . . . / and water moves, under ice, and i am completely detached: behind the
wheel, beneath a mask of skin, muteness is no longer new, and
might be forever now . . . through wet city streets . . . on film
. . . in dream . . . trickle and streaming . . . a sparkle at the base
of the skull and something is released: flicked and sprinkling
outward—

    and i am cast out among the taillights . . .)

III

. . . Rain came and went. The snow melted into the grass and was washed away, and morning broke white again on a time between seasons: a softness before the hard ass-end of winter came belting back/ broke white again to reveal debris that had lain soaked underneath: a branch or two, one mitten, a bicycle tire . . . washed up. I cut loose an anchor one night to find myself afloat in a sad limbo the next day. The world felt dirty, wet, and lonely . . . swallowed in mists and puddles, and touched with a strange sense of loss.

Ed was at his kitchen table with a deck of cards.

"What's up?" I said.

"What's it look like?"

"Looks like you're broke."

"Exactly. I went bust at the Finn the other night, got home around three o'clock, dead fucking tired, with a splitting headache—somehow I managed to drag myself out of bed at six and go down the hall. Waited there an hour and a half and didn't get out, so I came back and sat at this table all day hoping my buddy Danny'd show up with a few bucks—Does he show? Nope. So I sat here all morning and all afternoon playing solitaire, the phone rang twenty-seven times . . . finally around five-thirty I answered it, thinking maybe it was you with some extra cash—Fucking TJ: he's having a game at his house. I told him I'm broke, Don't call me no more. I spent the rest of the night watching TV. Where the hell were you?"

"Drove the cab."

"And didn't try to get ahold of me? From now on you re-port to me at least once a day, in case I need anything."

"I'll keep it in mind. You go the hall today?"

"Yeah, they still didn't send me out . . . fucking Fat Jerry eating his Polish sausage with onions at seven o'clock in the morning . . . I came home and sat back down at this table, without one cent in my pocket. Not one."

Cigarettes were lined up on top of the heater.

"What's with the cigarettes?"

"Aah, fuck, I—scraped a few coins from inside the couch . . . I went out to my car, found another thirty-seven cents down in the seats . . . had two pop bottles to cash in—I man-age to scrape up enough for one pack of generic cigarettes, I go to Abdul's . . . Going crazy with boredom here, so I get a rag and a bucket of water, get down on my hands and knees and start scrubbing the floor—I ain't cleaned it since I been here. And I'm crawling around with my fat belly on the floor: cigarettes fall outa my shirtpocket and into the water bucket. The whole pack. So I's tryna dry 'em out. That's what I get for tryna do something constructive."

"I can give you twenty."

"I can sure use it."

That night I was sitting in the dark at the window, it was late. A little tin ashtray was balanced on my knee. I finished the cigarette and squashed it out, and there was light reflected in the ashtray. I looked up and saw the moon, and realized the sky had cleared.

The next day the hard ass-end of winter came belting back.

I'm out in the cab around one in the morning, cold as a bitch outside. The cab is full of drafts; I've had the heater on all day . . . once in a while it lets out a puff of warm engine fumes. Winter's back like it never left.

Got about seventy for myself. Figure I'll take one more ride, try for seventy-five. The only call on the radio's a Detroit Two which has been there over an hour.

"Eight-seventy-five for Detroit Two."

"Eight-seven-five?"

"Yeah."

"Eight-seven-five: the address is 1254 Spruce Court, an apartment."

"Twelve-Fifty-Four Spruce Court. Thanks."

"Thank *you*, Driver."

I drop below the Main Avenue Bridge, into the projects. There's no sign for Spruce Court: if you don't know where it is you're not supposed to be there. Either way you're not supposed to be there. The wind is filled with snow. I pick a building with a light on and pull over . . . keep the cab in drive with a foot on the brake. Hit the horn a couple times.

A curtain moves in a first-floor window. Through the wind it looks like someone's waving his arms. I decide to take off, and for some reason I don't.

And then someone's running through the snow. Looks like a woman.

She gets to the cab she can't get the door open. She's not wearing a coat. She yanks the door free and falls back on her ass in the snow. Gets up and scrambles into the cab and locks the door.

I'm not sure she's a woman after all. She looks like a frog with a wig. In a thin cotton dress and hard shoes. I decide she's a woman, or she's supposed to be a woman, or she's what's left of someone who's supposed to be a woman. And she's either black or white. Her eyes're staring as though she's blinked herself awake in a place of such ancient, untold, and unrelenting anguish that now all she feels is a little bewildered.

"Where to?"

Her voice comes in a high squonking howl, fading over a cliff: like bagpipes, or—like something shot down but never caught, left half alive to fester in the reeds. From another world than mine . . .

"YOU KNOW THAT BAR? YOU KNOW THAT BAR, CORNER TWENTY-EIGHT AND DETROIT?"

"Kilbane's?"

"THAT'S RIGHT! YOU TAKE ME ON UP THERE: I WAN GET ME A SIX-PACK!"

I hit the meter and consider this while turning the cab around.

At the top of the hill the meter hasn't clicked once. Kilbane's is dark. I pull to the curb and turn to her.

"They're closed."

"CLOSED! IT AIN'T *THAT* LATE—WHAT THEY CLOSED? I WAN GET ME SOME BEER!"

"Well, I can take you down Twenty-Fifth . . . Bim's might be open—"

"BIM'S! I AIN' GOIN IN NO BIM'S! *YOU* GO IN THERE!"

A knock at the window. It's a kid about my age, with a bandana round his head. I roll the window down.

"What's up?"

"Take me over to Fifty-Fifth and Broadway?"

"I got someone."

He glances at her, back there in the shadows.

"Hop in front," I tell him. "I'll take you after I drop her off."

He jumps in, slams the door and leans against it with a smile. I look back at her. "I'll drive you down Twenty-Fifth, okay?"

"I KNOW *SOMEBODY* MUS BE OPEN I CAN GET ME A SIX-PACK!" She looks nervous about this kid in the car.

"Where'd you pick her up?" he says.

"Down the hill."

He turns to her. "How you doing?" he says, with a smile.

"I'M OKAY! HOW *YOU* DOIN?" she retorts.

"Fine," he says. And then, casually: "So what's the deal? You a fag, or a transvestite or what?"

I jerk the cab to the curb. "Get the fuck outa the car."

He's going "Hey, it's cool, it's cool" and she's in back screeching and honking "WHAT YOU MEAN YOU CAN' TALK TO ME LIKE THAT I AIN'T NO FUCKIN FAG YOU BETTER SHUT THE FUCK UP—"

"I said get the fuck out of the cab!"

"Cool out, man, what's the—"

I throw the cab in park and grab the keys, get out and go around to his side and jerk open the door—he's gathering himself up saying "Look man" as I put one foot on the frame and grab him. His momentum combines with mine and then he's trying to find his feet on the ice with her leaning forward yelling "BETTER SHUT THE FUCK UP, TELLIN ME WHAT I AM!" I lock and slam the passenger door, go back around and get inside and pull away as he kicks the cab. Two blocks later I pull over again and turn to her.

"Look, I'm sorry about that, I uh . . . I'll find you some beer now."

". . . TALK TO ME LIKE THAT, I AIN NO DAMN FAG . . ."

Bim's is closed.

I swing the cab around and we ride the arc of the Detroit-Superior Bridge through the late-night sky. Ahead, downtown is a lonely celebration of light. Once there, the streets are empty, forsaken.

"I JUS WAN ME A SIX-PACK! HE TELLIN ME HE KNOW WHAT I AM, YOU TRYNA GET ME KILLED—*NOW* WHERE YOU TAKIN' ME? YOU SAY YOU TAKIN ME TO A BAR, I DON' SEE NO MOTHERFUCKIN BAR!"

I pull up to the London Grille.

"Here's your six-pack."

She sits a minute looking out at the bar, making sure it's safe to go inside. And then collects herself from the shadows around her and goes.

She comes back with a paper bag.

"YOU TAKE ME HOME NOW! AN' I DON' APPRE-CIATE YOU PICKIN UP THAT CRAZYMAN, RUNNIN ME ALL AROUN RUNNIN UP THE METER ON ME! SHIT, HE *MUS* BE CRAZY, THINK HE CAN TELL ME! I JUS WAN GET ME SOME BEER, DON' WANNA GET MIXED UP WITH NO GODDAMN FUCKED-UP CRA-ZYMAN LIKE THAT—"

It takes three minutes to get her home, re-tracing the arc and plunging below the bridge, and she's howling the whole way. The meter says five-something.

"*HOW* MUCH THAT SAY?!"

"Forget it. Just get out of the cab."

She struggles out and the wind takes her spinning away.

I walk into the office and Cleetus the nightman says "You got two calls. Some kid said you beat him up and ripped him off, and some—I guess it was a woman, said you tried to kid-nap her."

I pass him a five with my waybill and ask him to forgive me.

LOOKING BACK ON THE MOON . . .

"This music reminds me of the moon."

". . . ?"

"I had this place: an apartment on the top floor of this big old quiet building—only apartment building in the neighborhood . . . And I was way up high: I could look out over the whole Southside from this big empty apartment—"

"Were you alone there?"

"Yeah, I spent a lotta time on my own, there. And I had this room with nothing in it but a desk and a lamp. Bare wood floor . . . I mean—old painted wood, but nothing on it . . . and a radiator, by the window—one big window . . . And I used to sit for hours looking out this window . . . every night. January, this was. And every night was completely clear and cold . . . just as clear as can be . . . and from the window I could see out over the whole mill valley: the lights of the mills . . . and the white columns of smoke: white, white smoke rising in full slow plumes. Always rising, like slow motion, all night long . . . every night . . . And the moon'd come rising up between those plumes . . . and hang there . . . over the mills . . . And night after night the moon'd hang there so hard and bright . . . And there'd be no sound but the sounds I made and the hissing of the radiator . . ."

". . . ?"

". . . This was a period of particular silence . . . Yeah, January . . . And I'd sit by the window, looking out . . . and the glass

was cold, 'cause just the other side of the glass was January . . .
the universe . . . y'know?"

"Mm."

"And I just stared. This place wasn't like the one I got now.
Here I was way up high: basically alone, in silence—detached
. . . looking out over everything. And I just watched . . . y'know
. . . Everything they say about the moon is true . . . but there's
even more they don't say, too."

an escalator, invisible . . . the definite, imperceptible, buoyant
. . . careening, motionless, trembling . . . placement. out, over:
bright clear buoyancy . . . bouncing, reflected . . .

and the hissing
. . . of the radiator—

the cold of outer space: watching, waiting, watching:

wondering, and trying not to wonder, where she was, till
now . . . till now . . . till even now . . . (was she making her way
back here, right now?) . . . trembling, motionless, like the hissing of the radiator . . . waiting for, among other things, the
sound of her key in the lock (like a sound trying to conceal
itself), alone on the night . . . the white, white rising billows . . .
in clear carousel silence, night after night, watching:

and i never realized, until now, that i was like that moon.

Winter day with nothing much to do. At six o'clock I went to see Ed.

"What's up?"

"Nothing, I just walked in. I got twenty here, I'm gonna take a two-teamer with Feef."

"I'll walk over with you."

Feef was a bookie—a midget—who ran his operation from the storefront of a neat frame house on the hill. The window said *Candy Ice Cream Cigarettes,* which was true, but didn't explain the new blue Lincoln at the curb.

He was perched on a stool behind the counter, barely visible above the licorice and pretzel jars. Four guys were at the table; we stood behind them, waiting for the basketball lines.

San Diego Russ went to the counter to bet and a couple kids came in. Russ hung back, waiting. The kids began piling candy on the counter: Feef was bobbing on his stool, trying to keep up with them:

"Awright awright—Whattaya got? How much you got?"

One kid put two quarters on the counter.

"Okay: fifty cents. Five bubblegum, there's ten cents . . . lemon drops, box of cherry balls—thirty cents . . . two grape balls—thirty-four . . . You got sixteen cents left—come on, come on now . . ." One kid put a couple Atomic Fireballs on the counter; they rolled off, started bouncing—the other was reaching for the Tootsie Rolls—"Hey! Watch what you're doing! What's that? Whattaya got there? Hold on, hold on now—"

Russ was folding and unfolding his bet. Feef glared to keep him waiting. The first kid caught up with the fireballs over by the ice cream cooler, the second decided against Tootsie Rolls and put them back. Russ groaned. Feef was counting: "Awright, you got forty-three cents so far—seven left: what'll it be?" Now there were two guys waiting to bet. The first kid chose four pieces of apple gum and then put two back. Then both of them wandered to the cooler.

"Hey! Hey! You ain't got enough left for ice cream!"

Russ said "C'mon, Feef, lemme—"

"Stay right there and wait your turn!"

"Jesus Christ . . ."

Now there were three guys waiting to bet. The kids were oblivious; they got bored with the ice cream and spotted some wax lips left over from Halloween. They chose one set each and brought them to the counter.

"Those're a nickel each: you're three cents over—put three of these back."

They spent another minute figuring what to part with, and finally decided against one bubblegum and a grape ball.

"Can we have a bag, Feef?"

He gave them a bag and they left. He swivelled on Russ: "If you can't stand there with your mouth shut don't come back here!"

"Feef, I'm waiting to make a two-hundred-dollar bet here and you're worried about half a dollar's worth of candy!"

"You heard me: take your action somewhere else if you don't like it!"

Russ placed his bet and slammed out.

After thirty years of taking bets of all types and sizes—thirty years of sure things getting stuck in the gate and eight-to-five dogs winning in extra innings and the sorry songs of sorry men—the needs of the gamblers held no more importance for

Feef than those of any kid off the street. The kids made more sense.

Ed was going over the lines. "Cavs're only getting four. Sonofabitch, paper said six, I don't like any of these games. Fuck it: I'm gonna take the Cavs with L.A. . . . Naw, damnit— L.A.'s playing at home, game won't start till eleven. Denver game starts at ten . . ."

I said "Take the L.A. game if you like it."

"I ain't gonna stay up all night waiting for a score, I wanna know before I go to bed if I'm broke."

"Alright. I'll take whatever you take, for ten."

"You gonna take the same thing? I might have to change my bet: you're a jinx."

He scanned the lines again.

"Yeah. Cavs with Denver," he said.

The guy next to me was writing a bet. He changed his mind and crumpled the slip. Feef spotted him. "Hey! Don't waste paper!"

I was about to place my bet when three girls came screaming into the store and attacked the candy. I stood back. They were putting handfuls on the counter and reaching for more— one of them brushed past me to the pop cooler.

"Whoa—One at a time! Whattaya got?"

"Twenty-seven cents."

Ed said "Can you believe this?"

One-Leg Frank got into line ahead of me, muttering. When the girls were gone it took him a moment to get started on his crutches.

Feef said "What're you waiting for? Hurry up!"

"Jeez Christ, Feef—"

"I'm sick of your five-dollar parlays anyway! Go play the lottery!"

Rarely did a gambler give him any lip. Somehow he was more imposing as a midget. Plus he was the only bookie in the neighborhood.

"Go on: get out!"

Frank looked at him, shook his head, and hobbled out.

"Lousy cripple," Feef was saying.

For dinner, I fried porkchops and potatoes in olive oil and garlic and hot pepper and onions. I poured coffee while we waited for the first game to start. Around seven-thirty we went over to his place.

I tossed some laundry off a chair; Ed stretched out on the couch and dialed the game on a transistor radio. We watched a couple cop shows on TV and listened to the game.

By nine-thirty we'd hit the first half of the bet.

I walked out of Perry's with a coffee for each of us and slipped into Ed's car, sat on something hard. I pulled it from under me.

"Why you got this bottle of Scope in the car?"

"Case I pick up a hooker. I always douse myself with Scope to kill the germs, after I'm done."

"I see."

"Just a precaution."

We drove a few blocks and parked.

The avenue was long and quiet.

Outside the car, the night was damp, and cold. The sound of the radio, the light from the radio made it plain how small we were, in that night. Ed let the game's every development rile him up; I let it go in one ear and out the other.

After half an hour he started talking.

"When I was a kid, my old man used to come in the house every Saturday morning and say 'Who wants to go shopping?' Every-body—my mother, my brother and sisters all dive for cover. I was a fat little bald kid, I couldn't get away, he'd always nab me. 'C'mon Eddie—Let's go shopping.' He'd throw me in the car and drive to a bar on St. Clair, park outside and leave me there—out in the car. For like eight hours. With nothing to do: no lunch, no—nothing to look at—just stare at the side of a bar all afternoon. Once in a while he bring me out a pretzel or something. The sun is shining, I wanna go play ball with my with my friends, I'm locked in a car on St. Clair Avenue while my old man drank and start fights and fell asleep on the bar with the old-timers. Then around seven o'clock we'd go home. Without any groceries, whatever: nothing. Incredible. Next Saturday: same thing; he'd come in, ask if anyone wants to go shopping.

"He used to take my brother Stan inside the bar when Stan was just a little kid and stand him on the bar, make him fight these guys. That's why Stan's a maniac today, I blame my old man completely—for everything."

"What everything?"

"For making me what I am today. I coulda been a normal, All-American guy with a wife and a lunchpail and one of those winter hats with the flaps for the ears—"

"*[laughter]* "

"Coulda been sitting home right now, watching TV, eating a sandwich and getting ready to go to bed, insteada freezing my ass in a bust-out Pontiac, sweating a twenty-dollar basketball bet at eleven o'clock at night."

Up ahead, a car pulled to the curb and a girl got out. The car pulled off and the girl started walking slowly, glancing back.

"Hey, there's Wendy," he said.

"Who's that?"

"Girl I know. I picked her up a few times."

He started the engine. We rolled alongside her, came to a stop. I rolled down the window and he leaned over.

"Wendy. *Wendy.*"

She stopped and looked us over. She had long red hair that hung down straight—in her twenties . . . To say she was cute would be like saying you could live in a house of cards.

"Wendy: remember me? It's Jack: I picked you up last week."

She decided by the look of the car we weren't cops, and leaned in the window without recognition of the name Jack or of Ed's face.

"Hi . . . you guys looking for a date?"

"Wendy—It's Jack. I picked you up last week after you got beat up."

". . . Oh yeah . . . yeah . . . What's going on?"

"Nothing, we're just cruising around. How you doing?"

"Oh, not too good . . . I got picked up by the Vice the other night . . . I'm out on bail . . . I gotta be careful. You guys got any money?"

"Naw, we're broke too. I got a couple bucks: you want a coffee, or a sandwich or something?"

"No thanks . . . I gotta keep working . . . I need a hundred dollars tonight . . . I'm freezing my ass out here."

"We're gonna get some coffee; I'll bring you one. If you're still here, okay; if not, we'll save it for you."

"Okay . . . thanks . . . bye . . . Hey—with milk and sugar, okay? A lotta sugar . . ."

Halftime we were losing the game. We drove to the Hot Dog Inn. Another all-night joint, just a counter and stools . . . green walls . . . a three-hundred-pound waitress. I ordered three coffees to go, one with extra sugar. Taped to the side of the cash register was a handwritten list: one hot dog, eight-five cents; two, a dollar seventy. Ten were eight-fifty. Thirty hot dogs, 29.50; seventy hot dogs were 59.50—all the way to a hundred, for eighty-five bucks. They'd copied out the whole list, from one to a hundred.

The second half started. We cruised up Lorain, and then back to Detroit, to look for Wendy.

"She parks her car by the Big Egg."

"She drives to work?"

"Yeah, she got a little silver foreign car with a dent in the back."

The car was there but no Wendy. We parked and concentrated on the game. Denver was ahead by six. I put her coffee on the dash and sipped mine. I lit a cigarette, watched her coffee steam the windshield.

The car filled with smoke and drafts. Denver was down by two.

Denver was down by five.

Ed said "Ichabod called me today. He said he's out at one of those strip joints on Brookpark and this broad was giving him the eye—"

"One of the dancers?"

"Nah, just some woman that was in there drinking. He said she's giving him the eye—some broad about his age, sitting four stools down. Then she moves to another stool closer, and then another one—He says 'I hadda change stools to get away from her. I know these broads—I know how they are: they got one thing on their minds.' I said 'Whattaya mean, Ronny?' He says 'I know their marriage plans! They see you wearing a gold watch—I know how their minds work! I know their marriage plans!' Fucking guy. Broad probably wanted to ask him how come his sleeves're four inches too short."

Near the end of the fourth quarter there was still no sign of Wendy. Her coffee was cold. Denver was up by six with a minute to go. Ed started the engine and threw her cup out the window.

"Fucking whore. Anyway we might pull this game out— What'd you bet, ten?"

"Yeah, ten."

"Worth thirty-four, it comes in."

"Whattayou got, twenty?"

"Yeah, I usually come back out here and celebrate, give Wendy or Brenda fifteen, but I'm fucking beat. I gotta go down the hall tomorrow. That's how it works: I'da lost this bet, I'da been totally pissed off and discouraged, I'da been broke, and I wouldn't go the hall in the morning; but I hit, it gives me inspiration to go down there."

By the time we got back to the Southside the game was over: Denver had won by six. I went upstairs and got into bed. The apartment was warm. I decided to drive the cab in the morning.

It was snowing hard when I woke up. I got down to the garage at ten o'clock. Ten or fifteen drivers were waiting for Wooster to start handing out the cabs.

I sat there an hour, watching the drivers, listening to their endless maddening talk that all boiled down to I picked some-one up and went long, or I picked someone up and went short. They played pinball and read the paper. Most of them were black: sharp young guys who considered themselves players, and old men who'd been driving forty years and remembered wooden bridges and roads that weren't there anymore, and dark dangerous men who, in their utter final disgust with ev-erything and everyone, said nothing at all and wouldn't even sit down. There were a few white college boys, a few trackrats waiting for Thistledown to open, a few fat cynical family men with bellies like meal sacks who looked like they wouldn't fit behind the wheel of a cab . . . a couple lonesome ghosts who lived in rooms downtown . . . They ate candy bars and chips from the vending machines, drank coffee and pop . . . smoked cigarettes . . . Some carried briefcases with maps and city atlas-es, thermoses, notepads . . . One guy even carried phonebooks with him: white and yellow pages. A few came to work as neat and ready as soldiers, and some slouched in with only a handful of change money and a leaky pen to start out with. There were days when the place seemed to be all convexity, concavity— pervaded with every form of weakness and indulgence, idiocy and fatigue. After an hour with these guys I felt like I'd worked a twelve-hour shift.

First thing I did was drive back up the hill to pick up my thirty-four from Feef. Big snowflakes were falling in a day without wind . . . a pack of dogs loped across the road . . . I parked the cab and went inside. Feef's on his stool with a Dillinger haircut and black suspenders. The place was neat as a pin: candy, cases of pop . . . a framed charcoal portrait of his sister's poodle . . . snapshots of nieces and nephews on the big mirror behind him, along with souvenir decals from the Grand Canyon and Reno, places like that, sent to him from relatives. Feef himself never left town.

I said good morning to him and sat at the table while he figured what I had coming. Jimmy D was at the table, going over the out-of-town racetrack entries in the paper.

"How you doing, Jimmy?"

"Not bad, junior . . ."

He speaks in a slow whisper from the tomb. A little bow-legged guy—looks like an old jockey . . . wrapped in scarves and sweatshirts and sweaters, his coat over the back of the chair. Seventy-five years old—maybe eighty. Maybe *ninety*. Let me put it this way: Jimmy started out as a gambler on Bolivar Road betting fifteen-cent baseball parlays. His face when he takes off his shades is like a small full moon seen through passing cloud. He has the wide glazed look of a man who's been watching baseball bets go out the window since the days of Ty Cobb . . . of a man who *thought* he'd seen every way a horserace can be lost. He takes a kind of quiet bitter pride in having survived years of defeats that would've killed a more sensible man: his eyes look as though he's watching himself in disbelief. He didn't live on the Southside anymore, but he'd been betting with Feef for thirty years at least, and he never missed a day there. Twelve noon he'd be at the table, squinting over the entries and scrawling out slips: maddening combination bets no one but Feef could make sense of anymore: round robins, chain parlays, two-four reverses . . . They no longer spoke to one another.

"You betting any horses today Jimmy?"

"I bet the double at Aqueduct. I bet the numbers seven and four." He said this with the calm assurance of a man to whom winning is a very minor threat.

"You mean you're just picking numbers?"

"I do everything. I've done everything. The last time I hit a double was in 19 . . . 82. Seventeen eighty, it paid."

I noticed a big gold ring that said TRW. "You used to work at TRW?"

He looked down at the ring as though noticing it for the first time himself.

"Thirty years, I worked there."

"Really? Which one?"

"First at Sixty-Fifth and Clark, and then they transferred me to the plant in Euclid, Ohio."

"Yeah—on Euclid Avenue. My folks live out there."

"You know where the Beverly Hills Cafe is? That place still open?"

"Yeah."

". . . Drank a lotta whiskey in that joint." I could barely hear him now—I was leaning over the table. ". . . Fifth of whiskey a day, I was drinking in that joint . . ."

Feef said "Here you are, D."

I went up and got my money. Took it back to the table and counted it. Thirty-four-forty.

". . . Wonder if Mary's still tending bar out there," Jimmy was saying. "Lot of women out there . . ."

Jimmy was getting smaller by the minute.

The door opened and a lean old hillbilly came in, stomping snow off his shoes. He sat next to Jimmy and started writing what looked like a horse bet. He looked like he'd lived a hard forty-five years, in the dark, without saying much. He was wearing a red baseball cap . . . really a sad, luckless-looking guy . . .

"Yep," Jimmy said, "Lotta women out there . . ."

He took one look at the guy and confided in me. "I better not talk about women around this guy. It's a dead issue with him," he whispered. "Dead issue."

I laughed and told him I'd see him around. I bought a pack of cigarettes from Feef and went out to the cab.

For the first few hours I played the hospitals around University Circle: a big woman on swollen legs with a welfare voucher, speaking a deep dark language of suspicion and totems and wonder . . . an old couple from Mount Sinai who didn't know the way home: who looked like sad cooking and sounded like doom soup . . . and others, fading from sterile hospital light into the flickering neighborhoods where they lived . . .

At the Clinic Inn I picked up an Arab with leather bags and took him to the airport and then, after an hour's wait in the airport cab pool drinking coffee and avoiding conversation, brought a silent lawyer back to the Heights and then—like a three-team parlay: banging down Cedar Hill I caught a VA call: pulled into the turnaround and hit the lobby in time to see another driver walking out with my fare. I called out "Cab for Barstow!" and the fare looked my way and the driver shrugged and Barstow followed me out: a gaunt middle-aged man who looked like the war was only the start of his bad luck, with his son riding along . . . I took them all the way to the West Side, near Sixty-Fifth and Lorain, which put me over seventy-five bucks—enough to cover gas and lease and the fat part of the day still to come. I was playing the city like a piano.

When I pulled into the airport pool at seven o'clock all the night guys were out. A dammed-up river of yellow cabs and no rush coming. I left the keys in the ignition and went into the terminal to get a number. I put a dollar backup on 684, got a coffee and went back to the pool.

I got to the head of the pool just after eight, fed up with waiting. Doug, the starter, waved me down to the exit doors and I pulled up third out. I stepped out of the cab and wished Doug a good evening. The first cab left and I moved up. Doug had been a railroad dick, and he had the classic scarred look of the old cop. Nothing less than fives. I pulled to the head of the line. A guy in a suit got in and asked to go to Harley West.

"Harley West? They got a free shuttle—it's around here somewhere—"

"Look driver: you gonna take me or not?"

I had him there and was back in the pool in twenty minutes with exactly five thirty-five for it in my pocket.

Walking into the terminal I said hello again to Doug, to let him know I was back already.

I took my coffee to the pool.

Half an hour later Doug was flashing me down.

Sitting first out, I saw a weary couple amble out the doors toward my cab, as wobbly and precise as Destiny. Turquoise luggage. West-Siders; possibly Lakewood, but probably more like Parma, Berea—North Olmsted at best. Between six and nine bucks. I hopped out and threw their luggage in the trunk.

"Parma Heights!" the man announced, triumphantly.

Doug was watching me.

"See you in a few," I told him.

It was near eleven the next time he signaled me down. I had fifty-three for myself when he opened the door of my cab for a guy with an overnight bag and briefcase and said "Would you see this gentleman gets to Center One in Eastlake safely?"

"Absolutely. Thanks Doug."

Fifty bucks, flat rate, all freeway. Doug had been holding him for a "safe driver."

Half an hour later the guy gave me fifty, plus a five-dollar tip which I tucked into my wallet for Doug.

My twelve hours were almost up. Fifty for a last ride was good news . . . but after twelve hours even good news was just more news. And for some reason I couldn't go in yet. I headed back into town and slipped over to the West Side, to look for Wendy.

BREAKFAST

"Ed, you ever been to Mountaineer?"

"I been there twice. At the time it was called Waterford."

"I never been there. Are they running now?"

"Yeah, they run all the time. Fact I went there one time in the winter."

"Yeah?"

"Some *strange reason,* I decided to go down there. My old beat-up Falcon—the little stick-shift Falcons, y'know?"

"Yeah."

"Piece of shit: I decided to go to Waterford in it—why, I don't know . . . All I know is on the way home it started to snow: bad; real bad. I remember getting lost, taking like a hundred-mile detour. And this car was ratty as it was—Finally after driving like— It was only ninety miles to Waterford, right? I drove like a hundred, and I get to a sign, it says *Cleveland 80.* It's *snowing* and snowing I'm getting scared, I can't see a fucking thing on the freeway—Finally my red light—generator light starts coming on and I know it's gonna die, y'know? I can't see any lanes, I can't see the berm—I'm scared to pull over, there's nothing but mountains, y'know? I'm going slower and slower, finally the car conks out, I'm drifting over . . . Somehow I made it over to a berm, I get out: couldn't see a fucking thing, it was— I love snow, y'know, but not in West Virginia when I'm by myself broke, y'know. Musta been ten below zero, I'm out there about fifteen minutes—a jeep pulls up behind me, right? Fucking—

43

Man-Mountain Dean gets out: this is serious—at *least* six-five, and about *this* fucking wide. I mean big. Big hood on—y'know: *nnnng,* lumbering up to the car. 'What's the problem?' I go 'My car won't start, my hands're frozen,' I said, 'I live in Cleveland.' And this—creature said to me 'I'll drive you there.' I go 'It's only a hundred and seventy-five miles, *thanks,* y'know . . . Appreciate it.'"

"*[laughter]*"

"'Can I buy you a coffee or something?' y'know . . . I leave my car there, right? Knowing I'll never see it again . . . We get to a truckstop—and I found out it's a broad, y'know, ah . . . huge, huge—"

"*[laughter]*"

"*Huge* woman. Blonde-haired, short blonde hair—I mean just—grotesquely *big!* Fat! Pleasant face, y'know, but I mean— And everybody was staring at me, y'know, 'cause I go a good two-thirty, and she hadda go—quarter of a ton: she hadda go five."

"Man."

"What does the fattest person I've ever met order at a truck-stop? Large white milk and a piece of cake. Not a—classy discreet black coffee, or . . . y'know— It was a broad! I go *Holy*— Before that I's going *Fuck, motherfucker this,* y'know, I— *cocksucker!* Real nice to me, y'know: she says 'Well I'm going to Cleveland anyway.' This's when I lived on One-Fiftieth and Lorain. She drives me all the way to Cleveland in a fucking blizzard."

"What'd you talk about, the whole way there?"

"I don't rec—uh, just—trivia . . . I was—Wasn't sex, that's for sure . . . And we got there in front of the house, and I say *nonchalantly* 'Would you care to spend the night?' She goes 'Sure!' I go Aaww, *fuck me,* man— And I don't pass too much stuff up, y'know, but—"

"What—You just meant for her safety's sake—"

"I just thought y'know as a courtesy— I didn't give a fuck about her safety . . . What could hurt her? I just thought 'cause it was late, it was a blizzard out—The least I could do was say 'Stay overnight.' Anyway she gets in the house, and she layed in the fucking bed, and it was like a *mound*. Honest to God, Danny: it was a *big* hill of her stomach. Her tits were big, but they were just—by her stomach they just—they lost, they lost whatever they had. And—she had on these nylons, right? And her feet *really* smelled bad, I mean—I didn't say nothing but—they was terrible. She gets in bed and she layed there y'know and she's— 'Well, we gonna do it?' And I get on top of her . . . And I couldn't find her cunt. I couldn't *find* it, was—submerged by fat. I kept getting down there and poking around, I couldn't find no hole, 'cause it was—her thighs're—So I'm like—pushing her fat, with my hands, and holding it—y'know, trying to—dig into this—cavern of love, or whatever you wanna call it . . . And finally I got my finger in there, y'know?—and grab her ass, y'know? and she got real *cocky*, y'know? I remember it pissed me off, she goes 'That's my asshole, what's wrong with you?' And I'm making an attempt to *find* that little—fucking thing y'know and I just touched it a little bit, and she made me feel stupid, y'know?"

"Yeah . . . *[laughter]* "

"And I'm going Jesus fucking Christ, I—I didn't wanna say 'Lady, I can't find your cunt!' And then when I get on top of her I'm like halfway up to the ceiling, 'cause *I'm* fat—*she's* fat, we got—two big bellies laying on top of each other."

"*[laughter]* "

"So I says 'I can't—' I says— 'Somehow we can't do this,' she goes 'Well it's happened *before*.' Which, kinda took me off the hook a little bit . . . And we're laying there, now I feel like a total asshole, she's breathing on me, she smells . . . So she starts dozing off— Snored like a fucking horse—So—my buddy Tom Morton lived next door . . . So I tiptoed out the door, I said 'Tom! About half an hour, come pounding on my door—Say that you gotta get to work, or, y'know, your wife's dying—anything—and tell me I gotta come help you.' So half hour later he come pounding on the door: 'Ed Ed Ed!' And I hustled her up, I felt like a jerk, got her dressed, and—Then she looked kinda like a sad case, I said 'Yeah, we gotta go'— was still dark out; Got rid of her out the door and left. And I got into Tom's car, me and Tom went up to fucking Country Kitchen on a hundred and fiftieth and I told him the whole story."

"Man . . ."

"That day he took me back to West Virginia. I got my title, all my shit? Car was still waiting there—Snow was stopped now, right? Get in it: *vroom*, started right up. Incredible. He had chains in his car, he was gonna tow me someplace—Started right up, I went home . . . By the way the bed did break—The slats were actually splintered."

" *[laughter]* "

"That night, y'know, when we were—tryna make little rocking motions—I could hear like scraping sounds and the things were actually splintering. I weighed two something, she hadda go four. Maybe five. —Even six, possibly: it might even been six, it coulda went over the quarter-ton mark."

" *[laughter]* "

"We're talking eight hundred pounds in that fucking poor bed, man that thing was *rocking*—Like—like a fucking *vessel*; like a sea vessel *creaking* at the *moors* . . . We were up on the top floor! That fucker coulda went right through to the basement! And—Y'know that was real nice of her—Apparently she lived in Cleveland or something, but . . . And she had *no qualms* about staying overnight, not any qualms at all . . ."

Snow is falling on the streets of Cleveland like snow falling out at sea on the backs of whales that rise unseen and sink away, moving onward . . . Back home, the heater'll tick in the clustering yellow heat of those rooms./ A used-car lot, shining and abandoned to frozen light—festooned with glittering fringes and penants . . . / The cot, and my belongings, tangled in the lines and minutes of my existence there./ Any ride'll be a lucky ride, and it's past the point of cigarettes./ Fill the pot with new water and straighten up the table—but why? To set the stage for—fer what? For whom? For me, I guess it is . . . the way it is . . . / Riding through the whale streets . . . forks and bridges . . . past the point of choices . . . a kind of outcast again: too late for everything. Yeah; time to find my way home, for tonight . . .

My room was neat as a pin. A cot . . . a wooden stand with clock, telephone, and a few books . . . a stereo . . . records in whiskey boxes along one wall . . . an old brown space heater that cooked and clicked with a faulty thermostat . . . closet with clothes and a TV I pulled out for ballgames . . . one picture on the wall: a framed shot of some forgotten sepia Kentucky Derby, taken head-on from a low angle: two horses fighting for the wire—dirt flying—jockeys cheating, ahold of each other's silks—

I was on the floor against the cot in an empty Saturday afternoon, gazing across the distance that separated me from night. Couldn't think of a thing to do. It occurred to me I'd been born without imagination. What the hell did people do? I couldn't imagine. Ed was probably watching college basketball. That was one thing. I called my friend Al.

"Yeah."

"Yeah."

"What's up?" he said.

"Nothing. What're you doing?"

"Nothing, just making a few lists . . . learning some card tricks . . ."

When I hung up, the afternoon resumed its width. Al was killing time. Maybe it was kill or be killed. I suddenly remembered that I smoked. I reached the pack off the clock stand and brought the ashtray down. Then I went into the kitchen and brought back what was left of a bottle of Ancient Age. I was on a roll.

Twenty minutes later I decided I was hungry, I finished the whiskey and left the house.

The West Side Market was packed with late shoppers. I walked around in the meat building awhile . . . disconnected . . . distracted by roasts and chops and sausages. Finally I stopped and bought a couple T-bones. Then I went to the State store and bought a pint of J.T.S. Brown.

Ed was on the couch watching a basketball game with the radio pressed to his ear, tuned to a different game.

"I think I'm gonna hit this parlay. If I do I'll have twenty for you tomorrow."

"Good. You hungry?"

"Not really. Why, you cooking?"

"Yeah, I got a couple steaks."

"Oh; I thought you were gonna ask me to buy you dinner. Yeah, I'm hungry. You gonna cook 'em now?"

"Yeah."

"Bring 'em down here."

"Okay."

"You want anything to drink? I'll get a six-pack."

"No, I got whiskey."

"I'll get a six-pack."

An hour later he said "I hit that fucking two-teamer."

"Good."

"J.T.S. Brown, no water no ice."

"What?"

"Didn't you ever see *The Hustler?*"

"What about it?"

"Jackie Gleason and Paul Newman're playing their twelfth straight hour of pool, Jackie Gleason sends a kid to get him a shot of whiskey with water and ice. Paul Newman tells the kid to get him a pint of J.T.S. Brown: no water no ice. No glass."

"You want a shot?"

"I got some beer; you want one?"

"Yeah. Have a shot."

"I can't drink that stuff. Only thing I drink is Windsor, once in a while, and even that makes me cringe."

He opened a beer for each of us and I dished the food.

He said "One night when I's a kid my Uncle Walt come over, my mother lets him in, he goes straight to the kitchen table, sits down—he's already fucked up—starts pounding the table for a drink. Big guy, like six-five. So my old man brings out a fifth and pours Walt like three fingers in a waterglass. Walt drinks it down like a shot. Then he starts pounding the table again: '*Please* won't you pour me a drink?' My old man pours him another one—half the glass this time, straight whiskey—Walt gulps it down like water. Fucking slams the glass down, he's— clench his fists, y'know—*crying* 'Jesus! Why don't you pour me a drink?!' The old man's looking at him, y'know—pours him another one—I swear this's true—Walt downs it—shakes his head, he's—winces, y'know—getting pissed off now—fucking *pleading* 'My God Why Won't You Please Give Me A Drink?' My mother can't stand it, she goes out of the room—And my old man—starting to get *worried* now, 'cause they ain't got but this one bottle, Walt's shaking the table—*howling* like a fucking devil 'O MY GOD WHY WON'T YOU PLEASE GIVE ME A DRINK?' So he pours him one more—Walt starts flailing his arms around, pounding the table—'WHAT'S WRONG WITH YOU PLEASE WON'T YOU GIVE ME A DRINK?!' The old man runs upstairs, gets this—fifteen-foot bullwhip he got working on the docks, and—front of the whole family starts wrestling Walt to the floor. And—after like a solid half hour of brute struggle manages to get him tied up with the whip. Meanwhile my Ma's in tears on the phone—two guys in white show up and take Uncle Walt away—just like in the Three Stooges."

"Wow . . . How's the steak?"

50

I was pouring myself another shot, he said "This's getting to be kind of a Ken Hutniak situation here."

"Who's that?"

"Guy I met at the Coach House, this bar I used to hang out at. I was driving for 7-Up at the time, I was looking for a place. Met this Ken Hutniak one night, guy about my age, worked in the mills. He had a place in North Olmsted, said he's looking for a roommate, so I moved in with him. Hardly knew the guy."

"Yeah."

"Really a friendly guy. Next thing I know he's cooking me dinner. I come home from work, he baked a ham. He wasn't a fag or nothing, he was just a really friendly guy, he—lonely fucking guy, he wanted to be friends. Drove me crazy. We'd go to the Coach House, try to pick up some broads—Come home: I'm taking a bath he'd come put the lid down on the toilet and wanna talk! I'm tryna dry myself off, we're bumping into each other—he'd stand in the door—y'know, no big thing: just wanna talk . . ."

"*[laughter]* "

"He used to ask me if I thought he was handsome to women. Getting ready to go out, he's looking in the mirror—he'd say 'Ed. Hey Ed. D'you think I'm handsome to women?' What a-y'know— 'Am I handsome to women?' *'Yeah, Ken, you're fucking handsome to women!'* Weird fucking guy man . . . Absolutely not a fag, I know that for a fact; he was just a strange fucking friendly guy man, he—Like we were gonna be together forever! I couldn't stand it—I wanted to kill the guy!"

"*[laughter]* "

"Finally one night—It was my birthday, I went out straight from work, got drunk, came home real late, I get home—There was a banner over the door—hand-painted sign: *Happy Birthday Ed*, a chocolate cake on the table, kitchen light was on, he was in bed already . . . I called up this friend of mine to come get me. He pulled his car up, I moved out in the middle of the night, while Ken Hutniak was asleep. I was so desperate to get outa there—and I was terrified he's gonna wake up— Got all my stuff loaded into this guy's car and ran outa there full speed. This guy had a piece of that metal stripping on the side of his car was sticking out, I ran right into it: pierced right into my leg, blood spurting out . . . I remember I's wearing a pair of white pants, they were covered in blood, I said 'Just drive.' I left there in the middle of the night and I ain't seen him since. He's probably married now and got three kids. Although how any human being could take it I don't know."

I was laughing. "Why're you telling me this?"

"I'm just warning you."

"*[laughter]*"

"You keep cooking me steaks and spaghetti I'm gonna clear outa here some night you'll never see me again."

Three a.m., and night is settled like the foundation of an old house. The sky is lilac orange, complete, and the snow on the rooftops is beyond display, like patient waiting. Only stillness. I like the way it is between guys . . . the issue skirted . . . ready though quiet. I wonder where Ed's at. I wish he'd call me to come help him change a tire.

And into March I was driving and driving that cab: Wooster's face in shrouds of morning smoke and the railroad bridge at night; the wind brought snow and turned it to rain, the sky tried sunny went back to grey—the sky got soaked and froze again and came back sunny blue, and the world bared its muddy ass. I couldn't think of anything to do when I wasn't driving, so I drove the cab night after night and stayed out later and later and had plenty of cash and paid off some old debts and put some cash aside without knowing exactly why and kept driving the cab, prowling around loose and arbitrary, answering calls on the scent of a name. They'd say "Candy at the Diamond Lounge" and I'd be fumbling for the microphone yelling "I'll take that! Eight-seven-five for Candy!" and I'd get there and Candy'd be sixty years old in gogo boots, dead drunk and pissed off it was time to go home. Or it'd be "Lorain Two for Tina" and I'd stammer "I'll take it: 945 for Tina!" and Tina'd be eighty years old out front of the Pick 'n Pay with ten bags of groceries, and I'd take her two blocks, carry ten bags up four flights of stairs and then carry Tina up as well and she'd piss on my arm and give me a dime tip.

Nights were dark and dirty or clear by turns and I began keeping track of the hookers on Lorain, and stopped once at an after-hours place at Sixty-Ninth and Carnegie where they frisked me at the door, and I traded glances with a girl at the bar and got some looks from a couple guys who didn't remember having seen me before and I dropped all the money I'd made that night on dice and then got in my car and drove home, thinking I still hadn't found what I was looking for, or even what it was I was looking for.

The next morning Marie called and said she was broke and needed fifty bucks. I met her downtown at a place filled with college kids and bought her a cornbeef and gave her the money and felt like I should excuse myself for being there. Ed was winning one night and losing the next three and telling me he was still up on Feef.

And the weather was somewhere between warm and cool and it rained for days on end, and then for days it didn't rain but the sky hung heavy with the promise of it and I thought I could hear churchbells ringing across Lincoln Park, though none were ringing . . . And the neighborhood looked uncomfortable, all thawed out and exposed and waiting for spring. St. Patrick's Day was grey and cold but they roped off part of downtown for the parade, and I was out in the cab outside the boundaries before the parade started and picked up three big old ladies going up to Sixty-Fifth and Detroit to play bingo in a church hall, and as I pulled away with them I said "You just missed all that parade traffic" and the one in the middle set up a low moaning full of sorrowful wisdom like the lowing of a cow, saying "Ooh'n it's a good thing, too; I never did like no parade . . . all them people in one place, they could come along and drop a bomb and get everyone at once . . . that's how they do it. No I ain' goin' nowhere near no damn parade."

Back at the garage they kept putting cardboard down to soak up the muddy water we tracked in, but the cardboard just got soaked and churned up with the footsteps of a hundred drivers coming in and out and standing around talking and smoking, waiting for cabs. The track opened, and Ed and I went out for opening day and broke even, and then we went out for day two and lost, and the next day I drove the cab and Cleetus the nightman started giving me tips; and one night he asked if I was going out the next day: I told him I was, though I hadn't known it till that moment. He gave me a sawbuck and told me to bet a five-dollar reverse on Get Up Richard with Rainmaker in the fourth. Feef didn't take exactas, so I went out and placed the bet and threw ten on it for myself. Rainmaker got in there for second but Get Up Richard missed the board. And for some reason I felt sorry for Cleetus (this was a period in which I seemed to be prey to any random stray emotion drifting through): he was a hard-looking guy in his early sixties—maybe he reminded me of my old man—and I'd see him each night in the middle of nowhere behind that glass—It was only a few months later he died of cancer. I thought he was a mean sonofabitch at first: he didn't do much but grunt and shake his head, almost smiling to an invisible partner like he was permanently pissed off about a trifecta from ten years ago . . . And then one night my cab broke down and I had to get towed back in and he said just a couple words to me when I walked into the office—nothing special, but coming from a guy to whom every word was an expenditure I realized he'd noticed me—maybe because I was younger than most of the guys driving—and after that for some reason I wanted to talk to the guy: just a few words—and for him to like me, and I found myself trying to think of something to say to him as I parked under the railroad bridge every night and walked toward the office. And so when he gave me the money for this bet I was proud somehow of the responsibility, and I included in that responsibility that he should win: I was looking forward to walking in there and handing him his money and thanking him 'cause I'd bet the suckers too. When I walked in to tell him what'd happened he'd seen the result in the paper, and I told him I'd thrown a sawbuck on them myself and showed him the tickets to let him know I was on his side, and to assure him I'd actually placed the bet and hadn't booked it myself. It was no big thing. He was disgusted as usual, with that resigned disgust of old gamblers that said he'd either suspected the outcome all along or that we'd somehow been cheated, but either way it's part of the game. And it was no big thing to me either: I kept walking in every morning and pulling back at night under the railroad bridge which loomed as black and ancient as night itself, and even though Cleetus and some of the guys I looked up to were way past putting any money down on spring, I couldn't wait to see her come charging across the wire.

One night I decided to pick up one of the girls on Lorain and spent an hour and a half cruising back and forth and around and around the block with my radio off until finally I pulled over for a tough-looking chick with dark stringy hair shuffling from one foot to the other out front of Steve's Lunch. She thought it was funny being picked up in a cab and flicked her cigarette out the window as soon as we'd parked. I gave her fifteen, but although the search and chase had been exciting in a nervous tunnel-vision kind of way, the   act was somehow beside the point and extra, and amounted to almost nothing, and I managed to get it over with more by force of will than anything else. Afterward she asked my name and I told her, and she said hers was Kim, and asked me what I was doing out here paying for sex, so I asked her what she was doing out here selling it, and she said she had a Demerol or Dilaudid habit that took whatever she made in a night, and her boyfriend just got sent to Mansfield, so she had more of an answer than I did. I dropped her off and drove to the garage and pulled up to the fence under the bridge and walked the long walk to the office under that part of night that is eternal and continuous: I filled out my waybill and gave Cleetus a buck, and drove home and washed off my crotch and went to bed, thinking about Ed coming home with a big sticky wet spot from dousing himself with Scope . . .

The next morning I took my time under the shower at the gym and then drove out to my folks' place . . . I spent the afternoon with my old man and ate dinner with them when my ma got home, went and picked up Dave and we drove around careless of hours . . . ended up parked in front of a donut place at four in the morning, drinking coffee and listening to the rain hit the roof . . . watching it roll down the windshield.

The rain comes in veils; the sky hangs blank and waiting for the water to soak in, and then the rain comes in veils again. In a time not reckoned in days or weeks, the weather conceals mysteries: enter: jangling, ringing . . . echo and bounce: add, gently, to subtract as much . . . and fade . . . / Across a flat mile of rain: three figures . . . or two . . . / penny whistle?/ across plains of—planes of—distances of rain . . . the sound detached by distance and weather . . . enter: jangling . . . and fade . . .

Ed's (: big brown Pontiac . . . bare branches reflected in the windshield, in curving mentholated monochrome . . . bare muddy tree lawn, broken gate . . . damp ramshackle porch . . . green screendoor with no screen, red front door, torn-shaded . . . piled sink . . . a faint scent of Ben-Gay . . . kitchen table with newspaper and brown ceramic mug holding paperclips cut corners of twenty-dollar bills matches loose change a button . . . the squat brown Hotboy heater, fat pipe up into the wall . . . the fridge, rounded and old . . . garbage brown-bagged . . . a dresser by the door, table-clothed, arranged with telephone bill, envelopes for Master and Visa, notepad, pens, lists of debts and errands checkmarked and scribbled out . . . personal effects . . . On the white paneled wall, taped-up snapshots of John The Boss Rini in Vegas, Blue Sue's baby . . . headlines, newspaper clippings, a ten-dollar bill holding special significance, often torn down and spent and replaced with bills no longer original but symbolic. Linoleum floor. In the bathroom, rag towels and spent deodorants and stray colognes, a balled-up bandana wash-cloth . . . hamper and talc . . . the rug showing thirteen colonies. Bedroom off the kitchen, doorway-draped and dark inside . . . unmade bed . . . clockface luminous pink . . . a push-button phone without frontplate . . . nearly exhausted porno magazines . . . a dusty, possibly functional eight-track player with tapes . . . and on the brown paneled wall a picture, oil-on-velvet: a Spanish galleon deserted on high seas—electric cord

hanging down . . . In the frontroom a foldout couch, greygreen
. . . shades drawn, windows closed, another dresser . . . a small
black-and-white TV . . . a lounge chair in one corner matches
the couch, piled with laundry, a laundry basket beside the otto-
man, a transistor radio . . .) not home.

Shadow barge and manhole steam . . . dirty mist and the cling of a bare windbreaker, Monkey Island at the zoo: losing yer hanky, boy. Beer in a bag in the back of the bus—seven am, where you going now? Shorty's too small for the back of the cab, lives above the Seaport Inn . . . cleaves to the memory of broads who laughed at him. This joint used to be a place to go; now it's just the place I am. Under the bridges and among the gravel mounds . . . coffee and a chili dog at three a.m.: on display with a swollen bum and the sharp polyester spades: oasis X-ray light strips you to the bone . . . the bars don't open till five-thirty—it's workgloves and aspirin till then. I'll take another refill darling—"What'd you call me? Call me that again . . ."

The lights along the river are like compliments that've lost all meaning. The shades of night are like trains that've lost all romance. The only mercy in this night is that it don't blow out your match.

The light is yellow at the Jay Hotel, and one card is the same as the next.

*

So it's Saturday morning and it's raining. What's my name, at dawn?

"WHY YOU BE BUM?"

Ed says "I ever tell you that story about my mother winning the lottery?"

"Your mother? No."

"First lotto drawing they ever had, y'know the Pick Six? First week they ever had it—the pot was like a million dollars, and for five numbers out of six nobody knew what it paid: it depends how many other people get five outa six, if anyone gets all six—all these different factors, right? So my mother tells me to pick her up a ticket, she gives me the numbers . . . Ends up hitting five outa six. I watched the drawing on TV. I figured Holy shit: six outa six pays a million, five outa six gotta pay—I dunno—Who knows? Ten grand? Fifty grand? So I go back to Convenient where I got the ticket—You can't cash it till the next day, but they run it through the machine, tells you what it pays? Computer says five outa six pays thirty-nine hundred dollars. I's kinda disappointed, y'know? but still, I figured—my mother been working herself to the bone all these years while my old man's out drinking—This kinda thing don't happen to her; she's gonna be overwhelmed."

"Yeah, sure."

"I was so happy for her I decided to draw it out a little—build up the suspense, right? Call her up, she's overjoyed she hit the thing, she got no idea what it pays. I said 'Ma, I went to Convenient, I found out what the ticket pays. Now—Don't be disappointed: it pays seven hundred dollars.'

"Right away she's—'Oh God, Eddie: is that true? Seven hundred dollars? I can't believe it—' First thing she ever won in her life, I'm going 'Yeah, yeah . . . I hope you're not disappointed—' 'Oh no I'm not disappointed!' 'Okay, I'll talk to you tomorrow.'

"I hang up the phone I wait about ten minutes. Call her back. I said 'Ma? I lied. The ticket doesn't pay seven hundred dollars.' She's—'Aww, doesn't it?' I said 'No, Ma, I'm sorry. The ticket doesn't pay seven hundred dollars, it pays ONE *THOUSAND DOLLARS!*' 'O—Wha—C'mon Eddie, please—Did it really pay a thousand dollars?' I go 'Yep: one grand, even. Well, goodnight—I'll bring the ticket over tomorrow.' I hang up and wait about another—fifteen minutes, I call her back. 'Ma? I'm sorry, I'm—really—the ticket—doesn't pay a thousand dollars,' and she's 'Now Eddie cut it out! What does it pay? Just tell me, whatever it is!' I said 'Okay okay. You wanna know? This is it, now: five out of six pays FIFTEEN HUNDRED DOLLARS.'"

"*[laughter]*"

"By now she's—aw, man, she's completely elated, she don't know what to think, she can hardly talk sense, I said 'Okay Ma, I just wanted to set that straight before I go to bed here, I'm real happy for you—talk to you in the morning—goodnight.'

"Next time I called I told her twenty-one hundred. Aw. By now she was in tears. Crying on the phone: 'This is the nicest thing that ever happened to me!' This poor woman, y'know? Here I'm betting two grand a week on football giving it to these fucking bookies, I could just give it to her, it makes her that happy. Lousy two thousand bucks, makes her whole life worthwhile. She's asking if I need any money—This goes on all night. I keep calling her back as soon as I give her time for each new realization to sink in. All night I'm building this up—my mother's completely broken down, my sister's over there, both of 'em are breaking down—my mother's talking about now she can pay off all her bills—All night I'm calling her back saying 'Ma? I'm sorry, I made a mistake. Did I say twenty-eight hundred? I meant to say THIRTY-*TWO* HUNDRED!'—Finally I get her built-up to thirty-nine hundred—She's completely fucking shattered, just—frazzled—dazed—elated—She's worn out, so I assure her—I *swear* to her this the last call, thirty-nine hundred is the final amount—I love you—goodnight.

"Next day in the paper they print the amount for five outa six. Thirty-nine dollars. There's a little article about how the computer made a mistake."

"AWWWW!"

"Thirty-nine bucks. My mother called me right away tryna play it off, she's going 'Aw that's okay Eddie . . . at least I got something, it was fun for a night, there's always next week . . . ' I couldn't even talk to her."

"—Aww, fuck . . . *[laughter]* "

"After all the garbage she's been through with my old man, after all the disappointments me and Stan gave her, I gotta *torture* her into one more heartbreak. My grandmother was right when I went to see her in the nursing home, I told her I got a new job, I's feeling good . . . she looked me up and down and said 'Why you be bum?'"

The days had begun to warm. Or to lighten: as if there were more air to breathe, and a certain elusive buoyancy in reserve. I thought we might be in the clear.

And then one night it all went away and was gone, and I found myself shivering in the raw pure atmosphere of another winter morning laid bare to outer space, like the lid had been ripped off in the night and all warmth escaped upwards and out: scraping ice off the windshield while the car idled, sputtering; smelling the blue pure breath of gasoline in the car's labored exhaust . . .

Clouds began to roll in, and that afternoon we got hit with a motherfucker of a snowstorm, but there was none of the nervous communal excitement that builds around the coming of a big storm; by now it was just a pain in the ass and a weight on the heart. That night I sat at the kitchen table with the lights off and sipped whiskey and coffee and smoked a few cigarettes, watching the big flakes falling between my house and Ed's. The winds picked up and whistled for a while and then died away around one in the morning. I went out for a walk through the enclosed and muffled neighborhood, came back and went to bed with the snow still falling.

I woke up around eight: same story, with the winds back, raving and whistling and choked with falling snow and the snow they swept off the ground and into deep drifts against walls and fences and between cars and in the middle of where the street had been. A day like that was good for a hundred easy in the cab. I floated down to the garage. The drivers' room was buzzing, and Wooster was busy on the phone calling drivers at home, asking if they could work. He pulled my timecard and said he'd be sending us out around ten o'clock.

I churned the Buick up the hill home. I fried a couple eggs with hot pepper and drank my coffee with a shot of bourbon in it. Then I stopped to see Ed. He was at the table, listening to the news on a transistor radio, waiting for basketball results. The city was at a standstill.

I blew into Feef's with a gust of wind and snow. Feef lived upstairs, so it was no problem for him getting to work—but there, in the calm away from the storm, sits Jimmy D, squinting over the out-of-town entries.

I sat at the table, said "How's it going, Jimmy?"

"Hello junior."

He was holding the paper about three inches from his face.

I said "Jimmy maybe you should get some glasses."

"Why's that?" he said, lowering the paper.

"Didn't you see the weather? It's *rough* out there. Don't you ever miss a day with Feef?"

He looks at me with those big round eyes and that ball of tobacco in his cheek and says, calmly, "In January of 1937, Cleveland got hit with the worst blizzard in its history. Downtown was out of commission, all public transportation was down, roads were closed. There were fourteen fatalities. The National Guard was called in, the river froze, people went out of the house and didn't turn up until spring. I was here."

Then he goes back to the entries.

I smiled and got a pack of Luckies from Feef.

Before I left I said "Hey Jimmy. How'd you do, that day?"

"I hit the double at Fairgrounds. Twelve sixty, it paid."

*

I woke in the dark in the cold front seat of the cab. Sat up and looked around. I was parked in the middle of a snowblown wasteland . . . A parking lot. My radio was off. I switched it on and asked the dispatcher what time it was. "It's one-thirty a.m., Driver." I was going to ask her what the fuck I was doing out here, but I didn't figure she'd know.

I reached into my pocket and pulled out my money and counted it. Then I counted what I had hidden in a pocket inside my jacket. Then I reached under the dash to the place where I usually put my lease-and-gas money as soon as I had it. Found it there, wrapped in paper. It had apparently been a good night. After regular expenses and the extra charge for the three hours' overtime I was into, I had about a hundred seventy-five for myself.

I cracked the window, started the engine, and pulled out of the empty lot. I turned right, for the hell of it, and drove as through the slow unveiling of a very white dream until I figured out where I was.

I was about twenty miles out. I found the freeway—blown and deserted and drifting—and headed back to the garage.

/wow. the last part of this afternoon—that last round was a rough one. these windows . . .

i came home and it was cold in here, so i never did take off my jacket . . . and i sat down at this table, ready to get up again any minute, but there was nothing going on, so i never did get up.

and i was just another object under the windows here . . . just another shadow . . . and the light of day, silver grey, was so slow to turn that . . . time opened up . . . things come . . . flitting around the kitchen . . . slipping into other rooms . . . uh . . .

—yeah, so slow to turn, until—well, then sometimes things happen fast, and grey gathered purple, and sank into purple blue, and deeper . . .

And now night has come and I can zip my sleeves and sit up straight. The confrontation is over.

We're sitting on Ed's porch with a six of Schaefer's watching the world go by. It's the kind of neighborhood where there's always some baggy-pants motherfucker selling something out of a shopping cart, and if they're giving away government cheese on a Monday morning there's a guy in a baseball cap leaning on your fence by noon tryna get five bucks for it, although you can knock that down to a buck and a pint of cream sherry, and if you put a refrigerator door out with the trash on the tree lawn it's bound to get dragged away scraping up the middle of the street by a guy with a quart of Colt 45 jammed into his back pocket and a taped-up axe-handle tucked under his arm, and the little grocery'll give you cash for your food stamps at three-quarters the face value, and you never seem to see anyone in those stores buying anything but potato chips and popsicles and beer and sweets, and the favorite form of currency besides what the government prints is empty pop bottles and the favorite drugs besides what the government taxes are glue and tulio stolen from the paint factory down the hill, and people who don't know you by your name know you by your car, and most of the bathtubs have legs and most of the floors are covered with four layers of linoleum in floral patterns differing from room to room, and the gas station does a lot of business without selling much gas, and the payphone on the corner is always in use until it gets ripped out once a month, and the bus stop on the other corner gets the glass busted out of it at slightly less regular intervals, and there's always dogs and stray kids running back and forth, and the mailman is a friend or an enemy depending on what day of the month it is—

Pancho goes by . . . a hard little shambling Puerto Rican with diablo eyes in a pigskin face . . . always looks like he's ready for battle, just returning from it, or musing over battles past . . . He sees us and flashes the fist of power, sings out "YEEE-HAAA!"

Ed says "I worked for Budweiser today with the fucking Colonel. Don Davis. He's in the reserves, he's a colonel? Everything on the truck's gotta be straight. His uniform was—*pressed* to the hilt—shined shoes—"

"*[laughter]* "

"—His fucking Budweiser pin was shining. This guy's a total fucking lunatic. His shirt was starched—buttoned all the way up—He's got a bottle of Windex for the truck, everything. I lit a cigarette he almost went bananas . . . gave me a lecture about smoking, y'know? The koop de grace was—I'm throwing beer cases on the wheeler, haphazardly, just throw 'em on there . . . One's hanging this way one's hanging this way—but they're on the wheeler, basically, right?"

"Yeah."

"Fucking—Colonel: puts his hands on his hips and goes: 'Do you see what's wrong with this picture?' I mean I been on trucks for eighteen years already, y'know?"

"Aw god . . ."

"I go 'What, Don?' 'You don't see what's wrong?' Got his hands on his hips like I'm one of his privates or something, y'know? I go 'Well I don't see, Don,' he goes— *'That's not uniform!'*"

"*[laughter]* "

"I go 'What?' He goes 'Are you gonna fix it?' I go 'C'mon Don,' he goes— 'I always get guys like you on my truck!' So—I didn't pay no attention to him, I got the beer . . . No sooner do I walk five fucking feet the fucking beer dumps."

"*[laughter]*"

"*[laughter]*— '*I told you, you fucking guys*—' I hit a crack in the sidewalk—*[laughter]*—I says Motherfucker, man . . . It was so funny . . . He gave me a stern lecture, man . . ."

"Aw, that's great . . ."

"His fucking *dick* got hard, soon as I dumped that shit."

"*[laughter]*"

"He was in fucking heaven, man . . ."

From the gas station came the sound of a lugnut gun . . . and then banging . . . and then someone started an engine and revved it until a cloud of bluish exhaust came across the porch.

Three Puerto Rican girls walked by like accordion music under the trees, looking like they'd accept nothing less than perfection.

"You betting anything tonight?"

"I took a two-teamer for twenty; Chicago and Detroit."

A dog wandered into the yard . . . Ed went into the house and brought him out some baloney.

Evening pulled its hatbrim.

Pancho shuffled past with what looked like a shotgun wrapped in a blanket over his shoulder, a pint of Wild Irish Rose trailing from one hand . . . His *yeee-haa* came softer now. Apparently he lived on the streets. Midnight would find him camped in front of Professor Market under the light of the Pepsi sign. When they switched it off he'd move to a bus stop, everyone he knew gone home.

In like a lion, out like a lamb: crazy spring weather: slow sunlit exhalations, rain comes mixed with hail, and then empties out at one end of the street like a turned-off garden hose, while the sky breaks clear . . . A couple incisors in the air and golden fleece above. I throw the window wide and climb out on the ledge, Billy Lee Riley singing in the room:

Oh well I climbed up on the steeple and I—rang the bell
I want the whole world to know that I'm under your spell
I got your water boilin' baby: I'm gon' cook your goose!
Well I need your lovey-dovey, ain't gon' turn you loose!

Baseball season was starting.

Ed was on his porch, pretending not to hear the phone . . .

"That's that fucking Uncle John, he's been calling me for the last three days."

"Who's that?"

"My half uncle, I told you about him."

"What's he want?"

"He's a sick gambler, he wants to start betting baseball with Feef."

"Yeah?"

"It's a long story, I grew up with the guy on St. Clair, I ain't talked to him in years. He lives with his mother, never goes outa the house. They got three rooms over an auto part store, been there twenty-five years. He just stays in the house looking after his mother."

"She sick?"

"Naw, she just old, y'know. She's a tough old Polack broad, smoked two packs of Pall Malls and drank whiskey every day for sixty years, and now John decides she's too frail to take a walk to the store. He's got like a—like a mother complex, y'know? Constantly putting his arm around her, asking 'Are you alright Ma? You need anything?' *Every* fucking five minutes: kissing her—big wet smacks on her top of her head: you can hear him, over the phone: 'You want some ice tea Ma? (*smack!*)' And she's trapped in there with him 'cause John don't let her outa the house. And he don't go nowhere except to Convenient or the laundry, y'know, he—uses her as an excuse never to go out and face the world."

"Doesn't he work? What's he bet with?"

"He ain't been betting for a long time 'cause he ain't got a bookie. He owes one guy like three grand, so he's cut off till he pays it back. He's broke. Even when he's working he only made a hundred a week . . ."

"Where was that?"

"Delivering pamphlets. The absolute lowest form of spot labor. They send you out in a truck in the morning with thirty other derelicts, give you a neighborhood to cover—y'know, door-to-door, sticking fliers. He used to carry mace, in case of dogs. He thought of himself as a mailman."

"Of course."

"After eight years they let him ride up in the front of the truck with the driver."

"Yeah, right."

"Anyway, the office they report to's at Sixty-Fifth and Detroit, right across from his bookie, y'know. He said he could see the bookie eating breakfast every morning in the City Grill. So the guy knows where John works. After he cut him off John was paying him ten dollars a week, or some ridiculous fucking thing—towards the three thousand."

"Well what's he supposed to do?"

"Bookie don't even know John's right name, John gave him the name Tom Collins or something. But he quits the job, to take care of his mother, he says."

"What's he live on?"

"His brother comes over, he's got a sister; they give him haircut money, and John manages to scrape up a few pennies here and there, his mother gets a social security check . . . Anyway now baseball's starting he figures this his chance to make a big hit. He called me a few days ago—I dunno how he got my number, my mother musta give it to him—and I mentioned I been betting with Feef, so now he's been calling to see if I can get him in with Feef."

"Yeah. You know how Feef is . . ."

"Aw, no way—I ain't even gonna bring it up. Fucking guy blows up if you say goodmorning to him. Besides, John's a perpetual loser."

"Yeah?"

"So I'll take his fucking tens and twenties and tell him I put 'em in with Feef under my name. I'll tell him Feef ain't taking any new action till football."

"*[laughter]* "

"Danny, the guy's a perpetual loser. He bets mostly parlays, which any gambler will tell you are impossible. I know because I bet 'em myself. And even when he hits he'll wanna bet it all on another parlay. He's got some kind of—grandeur illusions he's gonna make a hit and keep building it into the thousands. He wants to make enough to pay this bookie back and wipe him out too. I know because he keeps asking me how much action Feef'll take. 'Will he take a thousand-dollar bet? Will he take a thousand-dollar two-teamer? What about ten big ones? Could he handle that? Who is this guy? I can't be dealing with no small-time bookie . . . '"

"What's he got to start with?"

"Get this: he cashed a two-hundred-fifty-dollar life insurance policy for the opening of baseball, and he donated his body to Science for fifty bucks. He's really hyped up about—"

"He what?"

"Donated his body to science. He found out about a place you can go and pledge your body to science: they put like a—some kinda tattoo on your foot and when you die they take your body. Fifty bucks."

Saturday. Opened my eyes after a forty-dollar night in the cab, the window open wide. A warm breeze.

I stood on Ed's porch, watching the business of the street. People look dazed on a Saturday morning: emerging from a week of work, unsure what to do with a day off. They're moving back and forth, pulling themselves together . . . a little stunned . . . intimidated by all the options a sunny Saturday seems to offer . . . sorting through them . . . before shuffling into gear and becoming inevitably involved in the same concerns they were involved in the Saturday before. There's that brief moment of guilt when you realize you're alive and don't know how to live, and you look at the sky and sun and feel like you should be doing something spontaneous or fulfilling . . . until you find one of the convenient excuses that're always waiting for you to do nothing but go shopping or do the laundry or whatever . . .

I heard the door open and turned to see Ed emerging from his chambers—barefoot, in checkered pants and a T-shirt, squinting resentfully at the sun.

"Whattayou want boy?"

"I'm gonna get some breakfast. You coming?"

". . . Uh—Yeah, gimme a minute to get my brain together here . . . You going to the Spot?"

"Yeah."

"Do me a favor, get me a paper and a pack of Newports. Here, waitaminute, lemme find some cash—"

"I got it."

"No, no, I got it. Whattayou think I'm a fucking bum?"

He leaned inside and ruffled through papers and loose change . . .

"Here: here's a buck."

I come back from Abdul's, he's leaning on the porch rail.

Walking to the Spot there's a big slouchy guy coming toward us.

"Aah shit. I didn't wanna wear these check pants, but if the Mayor's wearing 'em I guess it's okay."

"Huh?"

Guy's got a cigarette with two inches of ash and a challenging look in his eyes . . .

"The Mayor. Mayor of the Southside."

I turn to look as he passes. *Racing Form,* back pocket.

"Who's that?"

"Don't you know your mayor when you see him? He's on his way to a meeting with the Sewer Commission."

"What're you talking about?"

"That fucking guy—I stop at the Spot for an egg sandwich on my way to the hall: he's in there. Nine-thirty he's on the corner by the drugstore with a couple of his aldermen. In the afternoon I see him patrolling the streets. Look out the window at midnight he's walking past. Come home from a card game last night, he's wandering around under the bridge, y'know, making—estimations on projected street repairs. I see him on Fourteenth, he's down by the projects, discussing racial issues—In Abdul's, chatting with local merchants— At least twice a day he's in Feef's, talking with his constituents—"

"Yeah, yeah . . ."

"I see him buying numbers, supporting the school system—"

"*[laughter]* "

"The guy never sleeps. He's the mayor."

"I thought Pancho was the mayor."

"Fuck no, Pancho's a Mex. Mayor's got Pancho in charge of neighborhood security."

At the Golden Spot we sat down, Ed opened the paper to the sports and folded it over. A girl came and filled our cups and we ordered.

"What're you doing today?" I asked him.

"I dunno, I got sixty bucks. I'm gonna fill out a couple lotto tickets, and then I's thinking of possibly hitting the track for a few races—get back in time to put in a bet with Feef, and then shoot out to Vegas Nite at St. Mary's from five to seven, then there's a possible game at TJ's."

"That all? We could pitch some pennies while we're waiting here . . ."

"Many possibilities."

"Shoot a little craps between races . . . ask around about a cockfight for after TJ's . . ."

". . . many possibilities . . . the Indians're playing—"

"The Indians're in town?"

"Opening day."

"Who they playing?"

"Boston."

"Fuck, let's go down there."

"Yeah, it's a possibility, I—Naw, no, I couldn't do that—"

"Why not? Let's go down there, sit in the bleachers."

"No really Danny, I couldn't do that, uh—"

"Why not?"

"It's fucking opening day, all the families'll be down there with their plastic coolers and their Indians hats—waving flags . . . Y'know the typical—All-American—dildo guys with their programs and headphones and souvenir bats yelling YAY! GO INDIANS! and all their kids'll be jumping around, climbing over the seats, yelling HIT A HOMERUN! YAY BRETT BUTLER—I LOVE YOU! I LOVE YOU MY FATHER'S

AN ASSHOLE! You know what it'll be like down there."

"Yeah I guess."

"I wish you'd meet a broad, get me off the hook. If I had your looks and my personality I'd have broads knocking on my door. What're you—twenty-two? twenty-three?"

"Twenty-three."

"When I was your age I was out every night! I don't do it now because I'm a fat, bald, broken-down slob: my back is broke from lifting cases for twenty years, I'm tired all the time I don't have the energy to go out meeting people, so I gotta rely on these whores I pick up, and various other—tactics I've mastered—But you're a young guy, you got youth on your side!"

The girl came with our plates.

"Jolene," he said, "This guy's always knocking on my door, hanging around . . . I don't really mind too much 'cause he's good for a fin once in a while—I don't wanna cut him off completely, but basically he's a—lonely guy, he needs a girl-friend."

I sighed, embarrassed.

"Ain't you got any friends you could fix him up with? What about you?"

"Sorry . . . I'm engaged."

"Well you must have some friends—"

"Jolene—"

"I realize he ain't got my personality, but he's basically— good-looking guy, he's got a car—"

"I'll ask around," she said.

"Yeah—Let me know," he told her. "And let me know if you decide to dump your fiance. I got a car too. And I could use another shot of coffee when you get a chance."

I shook my head.

He said "It's no joke. You'll turn into an Uncle John before you know it."

"You heard from him?"

"Called me nine o'clock this morning. He wants a three-teamer for fifty. He's starting out with a bang."

"*Fifty?* Where'd he get that?"

"I told you he donated his body to Science."

There was a crash from the kitchen.

"What if he hits it?"

"He hits I'll be on the first Greyhound as far as fifty bucks'll take me."

"He's gotta catch on to this . . ."

"Hey, I ain't tryna rip him off: he hits, I'll pay him, one way or another. Besides, John ain't the most worldly guy. He spent the last forty years in his room."

"Yeah, what's the deal with him?"

"His parents gave him Coca-Cola out of a baby bottle. He spent the next eight years under his bed, naked, with the old shoes. Kept to himself during school, stayed in the house at night . . . Graduated from high school and spent another five years in his room. By then the family's starting to get a little concerned—start pressuring him to maybe go out and get a job of some kind, y'know . . . He got a job in a pie factory. Lasted one day. They put him at the end of a chute, and as each Mrs. Smith's pie came sliding down the chute he's supposed to wrap it in plastic. The pies start coming faster and John panicked: he's wrapping one pie another one gets by him, he—reach for it—stick his thumb in the crust—another one coming down he get the cellophane tangled up . . . Pies sailing down the chute, dropping on the floor—people were yelling at him . . . So he retreated to the bathroom, started crying. Come back out, they gave him another chance. Same thing: pies flying all over the place, John's in cellophane . . . The experience was so revolting it put him back in his room for another seven years."

"*[laughter]* "

"Seven years. Think about it. That's another seven years of his life John was MIA, holed up in his room. Then he started with the pamphlets."

"What about women?"

"Well . . . Sixteen years after he graduated, when he was thirty-four, John started to blossom out a little, socially. He met a woman in some hillbilly bar—a complete horse—350-pound hillbilly woman with a pushed-in face, about forty-five years old—"

"Yeah."

"Really: good, solid three hundred pounds. She's divorced, got one kid in reform school and another at Brushy Mountain State Pen in Tennessee—she's completely in love with John. He don't see her no more. She lives way the fuck on the West Side, he'd take like three buses to get there, then three buses home. Simple date, nine o'clock movie, he gets home three in the morning. She don't know his phone number, his address, or his right name. She been seeing him two years, thinks his name is Tom Collins. Totally in love with him. Whenever they have a fight she puts an ad in the classifieds: 'Tom: please come see me. Love, Barb.'"

He paid my laughter no mind, eating his eggs and glancing through the paper. Then he said "You feel like taking a ride out there for a few races?"

"I think I'm gonna stick around here . . . think things over."

Stepping outside he said "C'mon, I wanna play a few lottos."

Across the street the Mayor was talking to a couple of old-timers.

Ed said "See? There he is, discussing the issues of the day."

We crossed to the drugstore.

"Post time's one-thirty," the Mayor was saying. "I ain't taking the goddamn bus! Ain't nobody going out?"

I looked him over. His head was too small, and he was wearing a huge pair of workshoes worn through at the heels to his socks. The ash on his cigarette was impossibly long. He looked like a clown from a circus in Hell.

*

All afternoon I tried to get something up for the night. I called Al, Jack, and Dave, but each of them was out. Around six-thirty I got a number from the girl Ed claimed was in love with me. I decided to believe him if 721 came in.

I walked to the Greeks and Mihale made me dinner.

The other room was hung with smoke and the slapping of cards. At a table by the window Tony sat like an old orangutan, chewing an ancient cigar, gazing alternately past his reflection to a place in the night above the Greek Orthodox church and across the table with a patient smile for Nick Stavros, who was going through the paper.

Nick was saying "There can only be one boss. Just like there's only one boss in the sky. Once in a while America's gotta step in and show everyone who's boss, and then everything's fine again."

Tony smiled and shook his head.

Nick said "Ain't that right Danny? Tony here don't believe that—"

"Well, I dunno Nick, uh—"

"—these here—"

Tony said "Now let's hear what the *boy* has to say."

"I dunno," I said. "I don't like anyone telling me who's boss."

"That's right, you tell him, my boy. When I see you come in, look just like you daddy when he was a young man. How's you daddy?"

"He's okay. How you doing, Tony?"

"You see you daddy?"

"Yeah, sure."

"When you see him tell him Tony says hello."

"Okay. How come you ain't playing cards?"

"There's no one good enough for him," Nick said from behind the paper.

"These men," Tony said, "They pass the time. A waste of time."

"Your father used to play Tony. He was the only one who could beat him once in a while."

"That's right: you daddy—he was a concentrate, was a good with cards. He teach you cards?"

"Naw, I don't play cards."

Tony said "That's okay. You daddy good at cards, you maybe good at something else. You a young man, have plenty time . . ."

At seven-thirty all attention was turned to the television. Saturday nights there was a drawing for the lotto, in addition to the three-digit drawing. I looked around at the men checking their tickets against the numbers on the screen; Lea was ringside. Somehow even if any of these guys hit the thing, I couldn't see it making much of a difference in his life. Lea would be walking back and forth to the drugstore with eight million dollars in his pocket, sitting in front of the TV at seven-thirty with that many more tickets.

A few months back there'd been a picture in the paper: some bust-out guy from the West Side had hit the damn thing for like five mil and they'd picked him up a few months later for shoplifting. The money from his first installment check was gone and he was deep in debt. The picture showed him slumped in a sleeveless undershirt in a kitchen chair, stunned, with a sea of recent losing lottery tickets at his feet. He was described as an alcoholic and inveterate horseplayer. I'd cut the picture out and given it to Ed, and he'd taped it to the wall.

. . . The number came 712. So I had forty coming on the box price. But I was still confused about the girl behind the window. Nick insisted on paying for my dinner. I said goodbye to them.

"Remember now," Tony said, "When you see you daddy,

tell him Tony says hello. *Whenever* you see him, always tell him Tony says hello."

And there I was, walking through the immediate early dark of the April street: trying to catch one clear promise out of the jittery confused language of promise the night was whispering. The breeze was spiked with purples, golds, and silvers indiscernible to the eye, with rustlings beyond the ear's perception. I stopped on the porch and looked around, and then stepped into the close blackness of my stairway. Hit the lights in my room. I found myself alive and unfocused: I wanted to punch a hole in the wall, dive into the air, kick the door off its hinges. I wanted someone to talk to. I did some pushups and then some sit-ups—threw the window open and sent out a yell—I put a record on and grabbed a beer from the fridge, cracked it and took four or five gulps and called Alex and called Dave and neither was home so I sat on the edge of the bed with something from inside me dancing in front of me and smoked a cigarette, feeling in the air that Saturday night was starting to happen.

I washed up.

. . . The avenue widens under streetlights—floating alongside and trailing behind me like a filmed background, tilting as though the camera's hand-held: a big Puerto Rican dance joint up ahead, the B&E: guys on the sidewalk . . . I slow down, checking it out . . . spot a parking space—And the front door blows open, the boys jump back and a wall of flame carries across the pavement, engulfs a parked car—people run out screaming, I think Not tonight and keep going . . .

The warm weather's brought out a whole new crop of hookers: a tall blonde out front of the Dairy Mart . . . two brunettes in the light of a phonebooth . . . a shimmering Spanish girl steps out of a doorway . . . Suddenly it's overt, exciting—like some two-bit Vegas: headlights, taillights—jockeying, double-parking—It pulls me in like a revolving door: I'm cruising with the flow: stopping, starting—diving for the curb to just miss and beating down dark sidestreets, around and back. I spend half an hour up and down Lorain and Detroit: I spot Wendy's car . . . two guys pounding something in a doorway . . . a fat hopeless broad sitting angry on a wall in a Sea World T-shirt . . . three kids with big sticks around a pinball machine in a pizza joint . . . And then I make a wrong turn and the revolving door spits me out, and I realize I don't necessarily want a hooker: I just want contact with tonight.

Couldn't lay a glove on the West Side so I picked up the shoreway and shot east. The lights went out and I was into the dark territory of Route 2 . . . figured I could catch Al at the Cosmopolitan. I looped into the parking lot and circled a few times, looking for his car. No dice, so I stopped at Burger King for some fries and hit the Taco Bell drive-thru for an enchilada before saluting the enormous flag over Gastown and heading to McDonald's and then filling the tank at Sohio and Shell. I picked up a dozen assorted at Mr. Donut, caught half a double feature at the Euclid Avenue Drive-In and then stocked up on windshield fluid at Sunoco so I'd have a clear view of everything to come . . . bowled a quick game at Palisades and hung out with the gang outside Martin's and picked up a couple majorettes at the Kentucky Fried Chicken and took them to Euclid Creek and had to fight for a spot on Lover's Lane . . . dropped them at a late-night sub shop and bought a motorcycle and an anchovy pizza down the street and . . .

 . . . The film ran steadily past, and finally I parked in the Heights. I knew a girl named Sadie and I thought she might be working.

The place was crowded, music was playing. Sadie was mixing a drink behind the bar. She served it and rang it up and gave the guy his change and laughed at something he said. She saw me and came over smiling.

"Hey baby! What're you doing here?"

She leaned over the bar and kissed me on the lips.

She said "I thought you only drank at home alone."

"Yeah, I decided to take the show on the road tonight."

She laughed. "What're you drinking baby?" Everyone was Sadie's baby.

"I'll have a shot of bar bourbon."

She poured me a big Wild Turkey, the eight-year-old, and then slipped away before I could pay for it.

When she came back I thanked her and wished her health and swallowed half the shot, expecting trouble and finding only warm assent as things began to feel like they were working inside and around me and Saturday night was here.

That's when the manager came out and said "Last call."

Sadie moved along the bar taking care of the final push. When she came back she had another Turkey for me and a shot of B&B for herself.

"My first one tonight."

"How you been?"

She rolled her eyes and exhaled. I waited.

A guy about my size came up beside me in a torn T-shirt. He smiled at her, sweetly, and asked if he could get another rum-and-Coke. She smiled back, not so sweetly, and introduced him to me as Willy.

I said "Hi Willy." We shook hands and his smile increased.

She went to fix his drink; he said "You a friend of Sadie's?"

"Hardly know her." I pulled out a cigarette.

He glanced down the bar at her and then, turning to me as though curious for my opinion, he said "Some chick, huh?"

I looked at him for a second and said "Well, she pours a good drink. Good luck." I took a sip and lit the cigarette.

Sadie brought his drink, they exchanged bitter smiles, and he took it back to his table of friends.

She said "That's the guy I've been living with for two years. And that girl in the leather jacket at his table is some chick he's been sleeping with."

"Mm."

She was waiting for something more.

"Why's he bring her here?"

"He thinks I don't know. Or he doesn't care. I've been looking for a place. Willy isn't working, so I'll never get him out of my place. So I'm just gonna move out at the end of the month. Let his floozy support him."

I nodded. She downed her B&B.

Willy's table got up to go and he came to the bar. He told her he'd see her at home, later. She didn't bother to return his smile this time, so he turned and gave what was left of it to me, and I smiled back, and he left.

Twenty minutes later I decided to get out of there myself, so I thanked her for the whiskey and told her to give me a call, and she gave me another kiss.

I hit the car pretending to feel sorry for Sadie and pretending to feel sorry for myself, until the silence of driving enclosed me and I realized I didn't feel sorry, just bored and a little frustrated, and then not even that; the world running behind glass, and the whiskey working . . .

Ed's car was gone.

I sat in the dark on the bed . . . waiting to merge with the night—to be absorbed by it . . . trying to hear a place of silence inside me, and hearing only the buzzing in my head . . .

The world fell away and spread below me. Sunday morning on the railroad bridge. The sunlit blackness of old iron, over the river, above the sun-spread land . . . I'd picked up the tracks on the bank and, thinking twice, had ventured onto them . . .

as the hill fell away in a steep tangle of green and gold and the river bared its shimmering width . . .

I stepped from tie to suspended tie in the smell of oil-black wood. As long as a train didn't come I'd be fine.

From the stripes of shadows I scanned the day. Ahead, the tracks broke into light and stretched in a trestled curve across the valley and along the other side to a tunnel. Behind me was the neighborhood along the ridge: the spires and domes of churches . . . below was the winding river . . . I had a moment of foresight—of detachment—of joy—

Two sunlit blades of grass growing from a crack in the oil-black wood, stirred by a light breeze.

SITTING IN THE CAB POOL WITH THE DUKE . . .

I said "How many cigarettes you smoke today?"

"A billion; I got a billion under my belt so far."

"Yeah; yeah."

"You?"

"I hit a billion around seven o'clock—a billion, billion and two, something like that. Anyway I just bought another pack. I'm off to a trillion now."

"Yeah, no use stopping now. A billion's a nice round number, but now that you broke it—"

"Oh yeah," I said. "Obviously. It's like breaking a twenty-dollar bill, y'know. Once you break a twenty it's gone; you can write it off."

"Yeah, right . . ."

". . . Looks like they're moving down, here. I'm gonna go back to my cab."

"Okay man. I'll see you at the trillion-mark."

DISTANT HILLS

On the porch, a weekday after work. He's brought out a photo album, black-and-white snapshots. Ed was stationed in Korea during the Vietnam War.

"Here's Ernie Kovacik: killed while changing a tire. He was putting one of them big truck tires on a rim: he's pumping it up and the fucking rim blew outa there, hit him square in the face. Killed him instantly.

"I actually enlisted. One day I get a letter to report for my physical. So I went downtown . . . I get done, they tell me to sit outside in the office and wait . . . And then the guy comes out, tells me just be patient, they'll be sending me to Georgia in a few hours! I didn't even have time to—y'know: go home, say goodbye, get changed—pack a lunch—Nothing! I made one phonecall, I said 'Ma I'm going to Georgia in two hours!' She burst into tears on the phone . . .

"I was a village rat, in Korea. I hadda be out, at all times. Some guys were married, stayed at the barracks, read a book . . . I needed action, I'd go out, fuck six different broads and then get a courtesy blowjob on the way home. That's how much—*stamina* I had in those days . . .

"On the way back to the base was a guy sold egg sandwiches; a little alley there, and this guy had a table, like a lemonade stand. He had a bunch of—just—black, syphilitic chickens, lying around in the dirt—half dead—and somehow he torture 'em into pushing out one last black or brown or green egg, about the size of a golfball—and he'd fry it in his dirty black frying pan—in the earth—and then, with his dirty, shit-eaten hands he'd press it onto a piece of black, moldy bread, totally burnt—You get these egg sandwiches: they were *black*. Cost like a penny, I'd eat ten of 'em on the way home. Never got sick."

"Who's that?" I asked, pointing.

"That's Miss Kwan, my long-lost Korean sweetheart. I lived with her in a little hootch for like six months. One time before I met her: I'm coming back to base in a topcoat, it's late, I hear the bells for midnight. 'Cause midnight they lock the gates, right? I got my hat pulled over my eyes, going past all the little hootches . . . Y'know, you could pay a broad five bucks a month and stay with her in the hootch, she wash your clothes, give you a massage, whatever—like a *wife*: five bucks! And a lotta them broads got rich doing that, by Korean standards. They lived—just—in little huts, with a dirt floor, mats on the floor— And they'd have TV's in there, record players, whatever . . . So it's Friday night, I just drank fifteen of them OB beers, I get the idea—start kicking open these hootches—guys're jumping outa bed: 'What's going on?' I'm going 'Get up, This the lieutenant—Get your fucking pants on, start marching!' —Down the whole street: I'm kicking doors open, guys're stumbling out . . . And it was *freezing* outside man, I—Whole street was frozen, it was late—I rounded up all these guys, I got 'em marching down the middle of this alley—in the moonlight—They all thought they're getting arrested! And they were *scared*, man: some of 'em just got to Korea just young kids—They were worried maybe they're gonna get sent to Vietnam to the fucking jungle— And some of 'em—turn around to ask me who I am, ask for some ID, I'm going 'Never mind that you piece of shit, I'm your commanding officer! Keep marching!' I had like twenty-five guys, all in a herd, just—marching toward the base in the middle of the night!"

"*[laughter]*"

"And then I seen the MPs at the gate—in the distance—I

94

said Holy fuck! I'm going to jail for this! Impersonating an officer? *Why* I did it I don't know, I was just—drunk—what ever possessed me to do that, I had two dozen guys all marching in line ahead of me, man I ducked into a hootch—That's how I met Miss Kwan: she was watching TV. She start chattering at me tryna throw me out, I give her a twenty and *begged* her to keep quiet . . . And I looked out the door of her hut there, they all marched right to the MPs and turned themselves in, the MPs don't know what the fuck's going on—all these guys confessing their sins: 'I stole a loaf of bread,' 'I snuck out without a pass'—I seen 'em milling around in the moonlight, the MPs tryna figure it out, all these guys—turning around looking for this—ghost lieutenant . . . And I was terrified! I figure They're gonna fucking court-martial me! I stayed holed up with Miss Kwan, it was like the red light district, right near the base there . . . And the next day I burned that fucking topcoat.

"For the next month I heard guys talking about that. To this day I dunno what came over me, why I did that . . ."

He turns a page. Four snapshots of a sunny afternoon. In a wide field before distant hills are two small figures, bent over a cylinder. Beside them on the grass is a spread of darkness which, taking shape in the second picture, has become a huge balloon by the fourth, bellying above and casting them in shadow.

"What's this?"

"That's me in the service of my country."

"?"

"I was a ballistic meteor crewman; that was my title."

"Yeah?"

"I blew up balloons."

"*[laughter]* "

"It was very specialized and high-polished—"

"For what?"

"There was a little instrument box that hung down from

the rope—it recorded the air temperature at different altitudes. They used to shoot off these little Honest John rockets: they had circles of luminous paint on the hillsides, for targets? And somehow they needed these air temperatures to gauge 'em, y'know. They never once hit the circle in the two years I was there."

"*[laughter]* "

"I didn't shoot off the rockets, I was strictly—y'know—blew up the balloons. Ballistic meteor crewman. It was kinda technical 'cause you hadda know how much air to put in there, y'know. When the canister shut off it was done, y'know."

"*[laughter]* "

"The job was equivalent to being a weatherman in civilian life."

"Right. Who's the other guy?"

"That was Kim, my assistant. There were all these little Korean helpers all named Kim."

"And what'd he do?"

"Well he held the rope, while I was blowing up the balloon."

"Uh-huh."

"But these guys only weighed about eighty pounds, tops. Sometimes they'd forget to let go of the rope—"

"*[laughter]* "

"Y'know, you take your eye off him for a minute—Next thing you know he's in the air! 'What?' All you can do is wave goodbye!"

"*[laughter]* "

"I know of at least two that got carried away and were never heard from again . . ."

I was heading out for the garage, locking the door when the phone rang. I fumbled back into the room and caught it.

"Hello?" I said, betraying a slight desperation I hadn't been aware of . . .

"Hello Danny? It's Sadie. What's wrong? You sound all out of breath—"

"Nothing I just ran up the stairs. What's up? How you doing?"

"Oh . . . I'm okay, I guess . . . I broke up with Willy."

"Oh yeah?" Boom-boom, boom-boom.

"His girlfriend's been calling here . . . I told him I was moving out. He started crying."

"Mm."

"Anyway he's going to his parents' house for a few days. What're you doing tonight?"

Oh y'know. Just—shooting off some Roman candles, y'know, setting the woods on fire—

I said "Nothing. Why?"

"Well I don't have to work tonight, I thought you might want to go for a ride or something."

"Sure. What time?"

"Oh, I dunno . . . I could come over around eight."

"Yeah, or I could pick you up . . ."

"No. I'd rather come over your house. I'll call you around seven-thirty."

"Okay. You wanna eat dinner here? I'll have it ready when you come—"

"I'm supposed to eat dinner with my friend Dee Dee. But I'll call you around seven-thirty."

"Okay, good. I'll see you then."

Suddenly a whole day stood between me and seven-thirty. I went to the gym, I straightened the house, I ran around filling up time . . . I was eager for Ed to get home so I could talk about it, about anything. I cooked a tomato sauce for us.

When I saw his car I gave him half an hour and then went over. He was at the table waiting for the phone to stop. Apparently the world was still old for him.

"That's fucking John . . ."

"So?"

"I already talked to him once: he calls me right when I step in the door. I did thirty stops today, one of the worst routes in the city—I wanna soak in the tub and try to get my brain together I gotta be aggravated with John's insanity. He had Detroit for twenty last night—they're eight to five: they win by a cunt hair, as it turned out . . . All night he's calling, telling me they're the best team in baseball. Musta called here twenty fucking times. 'Yep! Detroit: the best team in baseball, the best team in All of Baseball!' I'm lying here, not only tryna sweat out *my* bet but jinx his bet too. As it turned out I end up hitting my bet—no thanks to John calling here breaking my concentration—Then, like eleven-thirty, the games're over, I'm in bed here, cooling off—Phone rings again. Sonofabitch—I pick it up, figure maybe it's you, or some broad. 'Well? What I tell ya? Detroit is the best team in ALL OF BASEBALL!' Here it's John. Basking in the glow of his winnings of twelve-fifty. Anyway he wants a three-teamer tonight, I gotta go get the lines and put something in for myself . . ."

Over dinner I said, "I got a date tonight, man. Remember that girl I told you about Sadie?"

"Sexy Sadie?"

"Yeah. She called me this morning, she's coming over."

"Don't bring her over here, okay? the place a mess, I ain't in the mood to be cracking jokes—"

"Okay."

"I got a couple swallows of vodka on top of the fridge—"

"That's okay."

"Got that bottle of Scope in the car if you want it."

My idle ran faster as the time got close. I wanted more talk, more distraction. The phone rang; Ed stayed put.

"You grew up with John, right?"

"Yeah, well, we had a house there off St. Clair, we used to play together after school. John was fucked up even then. He used to say to me one hundred times a day: 'Would you rather be six foot tall with a one-inch head, or one inch tall with a six-foot head?' He asked me that constantly: 'Six foot tall with a one-inch head, one inch tall with a six-foot head.'—Demanding! He nearly made me retarded! I couldn't—I didn't know *what* to say: I didn't *know!* I didn't wanna be neither, but he insisted. Relentlessly—pressuring me with that question: the one-inch body with the six-inch head, I mean—the six-foot body with the six-foot head—Sonofabitch! Used to scare the shit outa me! I still don't know the answer!"

He kept me laughing till twenty past seven, and then I went to wait for the call.

But she never called. At ten o'clock I went next door, to relax in Ed's bitterness. His phone was ringing when I walked in.

The long open span of the Lorain-Carnegie Bridge was empty as I nursed a rattling Checker over the river toward the garage. From above the lights, the stone guardians of the bridge were frowning down: the Muses of Transportation—each holding its little carriage, or Model A, or truck . . . I was just another bit of movement in the night . . .

I'd started off at the Huntington stand on a clear afternoon. A blind man got in the cab. He was carefully dressed in a camel hair coat and matching cap and big wrap-around shades. He folded his white cane as I pulled out. He was going out toward the track, southeast of the city—Lee Road, Warrensville—an area I was unsure of. He said I should follow his directions. I put myself in his hands and hit 77 to 480. There was no smalltalk, only his clear commands from the backseat. It was kind of exciting. I took the prescribed exit, turned right at the intersection . . . I followed his instructions for half an hour . . . under the freeway, past the gas station . . . wending our way . . . he described it all precisely. We wound up in a field. The road went right into a field of mud and came to an end. It was the site of a future housing development, no houses . . . just weeds and mud. There was a line of forest at the far end of the field. A dragonfly landed on the windshield. I described our surroundings. We sat there in the sunlight . . .

I turned left at Ontario and left again at Eagle and let successive broken ramps lead me down to the dusty floor of night

. . . the cab garage, directly below the bridge . . . all potholes and gravel . . . I pulled up to the pump and watched its numbers roll while the tank filled, smelling gasoline . . .

I'd finished up with a call from Metro, the emergency room. It'd been on the radio for hours. "Scranton Three . . . Scranton Three . . ." If a call isn't picked up right away it sits there . . . stinking of poverty . . . no one wants it. I drive up, it's late—well after midnight. I leave the cab and go through the glass doors. The waiting area is bright. She spots me right away and starts pulling her man up out of his seat. They get in the cab—a girl about my age and an older guy, he's all beat up. She hops in front, he crumples into a corner of the backseat. She's cheerful, tells me where to go, it's right nearby . . . a little street off Fulton. She makes conversation, she's giddy. I'm quiet, she flirts with me . . . I keep an eye on him in the mirror, he's fumbling with something . . . rustling, moaning . . . There's an alley, a light goes off. I pull the cab into a little dirt court . . . they live behind another house. The meter says 3.85. She hops out, gets him out of the back, he's groaning. He doesn't know where he is. She leans him against the cab and gets money from his pocket . . . four singles—it's all he has—she hands them to me. She steadies him against the cab and then stands in the open cardoor—"Here's a tip," and she lifts up her T-shirt. Her tits are small. She holds the shirt up for me to see, I look long enough to be polite. Her chest and ribcage dim in the shadows. She drops the shirt and closes the door and guides him toward the house.

I parked the cab between two others. I gathered my waybill envelope, pens, vouchers . . . trash . . . In the backseat I found a plastic baggie and held it up to streetlight. There were trickles and clots of blood . . . a gob of glue at the bottom . . .

I walked toward the garage and tossed the baggie away.

The squids of night have moved in across all that clear tangerine blue . . . as the crack closes again and promise turns to postponement. Good Friday. It didn't rain today like Grandma said it always would, but still she was right, in her way. There's a candlelight procession through the streets of the Southside: the Greeks are proceeding, according to procedure . . . protected at each barren intersection by signal-flashing police.

My ears're ringing. Above the far-off sound of passing mystery trains and the wavering all-night sound of the mill valley, they are ringing. I close my eyes and can almost see the red blinking lights of radio towers, and also the slow candlelit procession, below and against the packed and collected squids of night.

HOLIDAY

It was a day without shadows . . . y'know . . . just a few . . .
halfhearted ones . . . A day like how, uh . . . like the way holidays find themselves to be . . . y'know, like: "This's the holiday?
Oh, so here we are . . ." Like someone started a rumor about
a holiday and people gather like shadows to see it through . . .
The word gets around . . . but more a vibration than a word
. . . a low pitch . . . a tone . . . And the day itself is just a blank
plateau . . . a vague table of . . . y'know . . . shadows . . . like us
. . . just a few . . .

*

Later, a slant of sunlight across old wallpaper reminds me of
my grandmother . . .

AT THE MARS, OVER STEAK AND EGGS . . .

"John called this morning; somehow he come up with another ten—"

"What happened yesterday? Obviously he lost that two-teamer . . ."

"Yeah, and get this: his first bet come in, right? The Bluejays? He wins that one easy, and then he had Detroit at night, right? That was his pick of the day: Mike gave him that one, and he loves Detroit anyway. I liked 'em myself yesterday: I was gonna bet 'em with Feef and then John calls and says he wants 'em, I said Sonofabitch—Now I can't bet 'em, y'know? So I told him to call me back I'll get the lines from Feef, y'know? Detroit's favored. Not much: they were like six to five—John calls back I tell him they're *eight* to five, right? 'Cause I figure he'll change his bet and take New York, which he does. He didn't wanna, but supposedly it's his last twenty and the Bluejays're three to two so no way he's gonna take two locks for twenty won't pay shit. He was pissed, too: he's going 'What the fuck kinda bookie is that?'—all this shit, 'cause the paper said six to five. But he takes New York, Detroit wins, John loses. And that was his pick of the day because Mike give it to him, and now Mike's fucking pissed at John—Mike ain't even talking to John—"

"What Mike? Who's Mike?"

"Mike. Little Mike."

"Who's that?"

"I didn't tell you about Mike?"

"No."

He looks at me, goes back to his eggs, takes a swallow of coffee.

Says "About two three years ago John starts talking about this Mike. It's Christmas, John needs money to get something for little Mike, it's—Mike's birthday coming up, John's going out to get a little pair of pants for Mike: Mike this, Mike that . . . nobody knew what the fuck he's talking about: his mother, his sister, brother—*my* family—Everyone's wondering Who's this Mike? This went on for like a year. And John's—pretty secretive anyhow, he don't say too much about it, but over the course of a year, people—starting to wonder, y'know?"

"Yeah."

"Remember I told you about that three-hundred-pound hillbilly woman John was seeing on the West Side? Big Barb? People start to think Maybe John had a kid by this Big Barb. Maybe John actually got her pregnant and he's got a little boy over there named Mike! Right? Be the logical thing to think—"

"Uh-huh."

"Turns out—I don't remember what happened, John musta finally come out with it—Turns out Mike is a six-inch-high plastic hippopotamus."

". . . *[laughter]* "

"—Grey little plastic hippo with one ear kinda singed off—"

" *[laughter]* "

"John rescued him from the incinerator and adopted him, brought him home to his room, cleaned him up—"

"Waitaminute, I—He's serious about this?"

"Absolutely. Absolutely serious."

"What's the rest of the family think?"

"Well obviously they musta thought John was completely fucking *whacko* at first, but he talks so serious about this—like as if Mike is a little kid—Somehow they all got sucked into this too! Now Ruth—John's sister Ruth comes over, she knit a little tossle hat for Mike for the winter, to keep Mike's fuzzy plastic head warm in the winter—with a little M on it . . ."

"No way."

"Danny, I swear to you this is true. John's brother Don, who's a Councilman in Wickliffe—bought Mike a little helicopter for Christmas so Mike can sit inside it and watch TV—"

"*[laughter]* "

"By the way: John put out the word Mike wants one of them little plastic batting helmets you get in the gumball machines? If you can come up with one—in blue—John'll be eternally grateful."

"I'll keep my eyes open."

"Mike likes to sit on the arm of the chair and watch the games. That's why I said: Mike ain't speaking to John at the moment 'cause that Detroit game was Mike's pick of the day. John said he got up in the morning and the paper was on the table open to the sports, Detroit circled in red, and Mike just standing there. So John needs this batting helmet to appease little Mike. Blue."

I got the cab at the curb, I'm heading out of the house—

"Hey boy."

Ed's leaning on his porch rail, sizing up the evening like a familiar foe.

"What's up?"

"Got the cab, huh?"

"Yeah."

". . . yep, yep . . ."

"You need some money?"

"Naw, naw."

"I got it—"

"Naw I worked for Stroh's today . . . Plus John's supposed to drop off a ten . . ."

"John's coming here?"

"Yeah, stick around, you got a few minutes."

"How's he getting here?"

"Bus. He's taking two buses over here at rush hour to drop off a ten. I think he's getting suspicious, he wants to see for himself this bookie really exists."

"You're not gonna take him in there—"

"No, fuck no. I already told him Feef ain't taking any new customers. He just wants to see the place; we'll take a walk and John can wait outside."

The 81 bus goes past, having left a man in its wake. He's crossing the street from half a block down . . .

Looks like anyone else, in the evening sunlight.

He approaches without any particular friendliness. He un-latches the gate and comes into the yard pulling from his back pocket an envelope. Skinny build, greasy hair parted on the side, a black plastic jacket over a half-buttoned flannel shirt. He's unshaven and suspicious . . .

Ed tells him "This Danny, lives next door."

John makes a noise, says "You the cab driver?"

"Yeah."

John opens the envelope and removes a folded paper and hands it to Ed. I glance over. It's a list, written in ink in a delib-erate hand as though John's relished the tracing of each letter, each numeral. As though care and deliberation in writing the list would insure a successful outcome for the bet. He wants a three-teamer for ten dollars. He's written the name of both teams for each game, plus projected odds, with a projected total in the bottom corner. Beside each of his winning teams is a scrawled picture: a little tiger, a little bluejay, and what looks like a little white sock.

John stands, hands in back pockets, watching Ed read the list, waiting for Ed to recognize the beauty of the equation.

Ed looks up and says "Alright, you got the ten?"

John smirks as though Ed's hopeless and steps up to walk him through the list. Only when he has carefully explained the obvious logic behind each pick, taking into account pitcher, team record, injuries, and home field advantage, does he pro-duce from the envelope the two precious fives which are his ticket for tonight's glory: his payment for a chance to hear the universe admit Yes John, you were right.

Ed pockets them, keeping the list, and says "Let's walk over there and I'll get the final lines and put this in."

We leave the yard. Ed walks as though retaining enough dignity not to break into a sprint. John slouches along like the games are being played for the gamblers and can wait. Ed points out Feef's, tells John we'll be right out.

We go inside, Ed copies the lines for John. The Indians game's a pick so I bet it myself. Ed puts John's ten with twenty of his own on a two-teamer.

Back outside, John's at the corner, drinking an orange pop.

Ed gives him back the list, tells him the odds are like the paper said. John's lips are orange.

Walking to the house, John seems oblivious to his surroundings. He walks in a tunnel of gambling that extends from his room to wherever he goes. I offer to take him home in the cab.

"Ed, you wanna take a ride? I'll bring you back here and by then it'll be time I can shoot out to the airport for the seven-thirty rush."

So Ed gets in back, John gets in front.

John doesn't say a word the whole way. I drop him at an auto part store on St. Clair. He disappears into an alley without looking back. Ed gets in front, I pull away from the curb.

Ed says "That—what you just saw—is his whole life."

"What is?"

"Scraping up ten, fifteen bucks for a bet . . . Now he'll make himself a sandwich and a pitcher of ice tea and lie on his bed, listen to the games. His whole life—that bet."

"So what's his life if he loses?"

"Don't matter. Either way he's right. He hits, he's right about the bet. He loses, he's right about *everything*—the whole universe."

"Huh . . ."

"That's the thing about a real—sick gambler like John: you almost *wanna* lose, just so you can relax, like—Hey, I tried, I got fucked again—Life's as fucked up as I thought it was in the first place. Y'know, it's—In a strange way it's comforting."

". . . Yeah, I could see that. Like It's out of my hands now. I ain't responsible."

"He once told me, he said, 'The only thing better than gambling and winning is gambling and losing.' That's one of John's immortal fucking quotes."

I dropped Ed home and took one of his radios so I could listen to the game in the cab.

Around ten-thirty I called him from the airport.

He let it ring seven times: I was about to put it down when he picked it up. He waited, not speaking.

"Ed?"

"Danny?"

"Yeah."

"Fuck, I thought you was John. Fucker called me fifteen times already: 'Did you see that? See that double play? See him strike that nigger out?' *'Yeah John, I got the game on in front of me!'* Lousy ten bucks I gotta listen to his shit all night."

"How's he doing?"

"He hit the first game he's getting blown out in the second. Last time he called he said he's going to bed. Thank God, man . . ."

"How 'bout you?"

"I bet the Indians game. Who'd you bet? The Indians?"

"Yeah."

"For twenty?"

"Yeah, man: looks like we got it."

"Yeah. By the way, John says you're a fag."

"What?"

"That's what he said, man, don't get pissed—John knows these things—"

"Where'd he get that from?"

"Says he can tell. He says he can see it in your eyes, you're definitely a fag."

"—fucking guy."

"You can't fool John."

"I gotta go see if the cab line moved."

"Okay, uh . . . I'm gonna finish the game and hit the sack

here."

I sat in the pool and listened to the rest of the game. The Indians won it, nine to five. Felt good to me: better than losing.

At the head of the line I was thinking about John, wondering if he was awake. A guy got in the cab and wanted to go downtown. I hit the meter and forgot about John.

Chutes and ladders, round the curve and over the hump! Loop the loop and burn down straight: yellowlight and yup, just made it: yellowlight and yup, just made it: yellowlight and— yup! Just made it! Run that red for the hell of it, clear green ahead—Bang! There we go. Give some brakes and get some fishtail, spin her back into slot and bang! it's all yours . . . Side-street it through shadows and out again, to streetlit widths: wait a heartbeat and make your move—Punch it: *pow!* Here I am and there I go: fast and precise and holding tight, up high in the saddle: rise and fall and holding tight: jiggle and bump and holding steady as the signals unfold red to green and red to green to green to green: gas and springs and a little bounce: green and green and here's the street: lasso the sign and pull us round and here we go and here we are, because Mr. Lockwood at 7102 Lawnview has been waiting to go for a ride, and the airport's about to break . . .

It's a warm night in early May. There's a breeze of sweet possibility blowing round the Southside. A streetlight shines through young leaves. I go next door Ed is sitting on the steps of the porch with a five-dollar radio trying to pick up a White Sox game he's got fifty bucks on. He's down six to four in the seventh, and now the radio gives only static. Trees nod and rustle, there's an occasional yelp from a dog down the block . . . It's the kind of a night lovers look back on. Ed, red with sweat, wiping his forehead, is turning the radio every which way: he stands up, maneuvering the aerial toward each of the four winds; he climbs up on the porch rail for better altitude . . . He sits back down, pointing the aerial up, down, and around, with no luck. He points it toward me: "Here—stick this in your mouth a minute . . ."

The phone rings inside.

"Goddamn it these assholes been calling me all night, tryna get a game going. I can't talk to 'em again . . ."

He lets it ring a couple times more.

Then he says "C'mon: c'mon inside! Pick up the other phone."

I follow him into the house and pick up the extra phone and keep quiet. Ed, master of a thousand voices, answers in the voice of a woman who sees to it she's never alone for long.

"Hello?" he breathes . . .

"Uh—Hi, is Eddie there?"

"No he's not, sugar—Who's this?"

"Uh—This is Ronny—a buddy of Eddie's."

"Hello Ronny. This is Crystal. Ed's mentioned you."

"Ed mentioned me? No kidding. What he say?"

"Well, he says you're a *very* good card player . . ."

"Oh-ho, well, now that you uh—I guess I *am* practically a professional, uh . . . pretty cool under pressure . . ."

"And well-dressed—"

"Hey, did Eddie say that? Well, I own a few suits, and I like to wear a few rings—gold rings—when I go—"

"And nice-looking . . ."

"Ahh—heh-heh . . . I am taller than the average man, and I—Say, uh, Crystal: how long have you known Eddie?"

"Oh, not so long . . ."

"No? No, I don't recall him saying—uh—Well, Crystal, we'll have to get together sometime for a drink: you and me, and Eddie . . ."

"Sure hon'. I'll tell him you called."

Ed hangs up and comes into the room.

"Aw man—I hadda bite my fucking tongue to keep from laughing! Did you hear that? My own buddy tried to stab me in the back! These guys're so stupid Danny—They would never in a million years believe that was me. I wanted so bad to say This is *me* Ronny, you stupid fuck. 'I never crack under the strain.' This guy sits there all night with his red face—hand shakes so bad he can barely hold his drink: you've seen him yourself. 'Gold rings—'"

I picture Ronny with his grey funeral suit in the storage closet of the Finn Cafe . . . We're still laughing when the phone rings again.

Ed says "Sh! Quiet—pick it up!"

He answers this time in the voice of a girl in a trance.

"Yeh?"

"Hello? Is Eddie there?"

"No."

"Who's this?"

Silence.

"Hello?"

"This is Darla."

"Darla? Hi Darla. This TJ."

Silence.

"Eddie's not home?"

"Nope."

"What're you doing?"

"I'm not doing anything."

"No? Well, you wanna go for a ride on my motorcycle?"

Silence.

"Darla? I got a motorcycle—we could—"

"Don't like motorcycles. I had a crash."

"Oh, well, uh . . ."

"Ed's at Roy's. Are you Roy?"

"*No*—I'm TJ."

"TJ . . . Ed's mentioned you before . . ."

"Oh yeah? What he say?"

". . . He said you're . . . sick gambler . . ."

"Sick? I'm not sick! He's the one that's sick! At least I got food in the refrigerator! What's he got in the refrigerator?"

"Two beers . . ."

"Yeah, well who's sick? Him or me? I've got steaks in my refrigerator. You wanna come over and have a steak Darla?"

"I'm a vegetarian."

"A vegetarian? Ah come on—you must like steak. You wanna come over and—"

"Well, bye." [*click*]

Ha! The Pony Express: here he comes, with the word! Johnny Appleseed sowed the land with seed that sprang up into telegraph poles like pickets across the face of the map, and blossomed into telephone poles while his back was turned/ a guy in a tophat sinks the golden spike as the East Coast begins to reverse itself past the windows of the Iron Horse and the West Coast waits with poised confetti and tonight is silver and goodnight is purple and dawn turns to gas as soon as you've said it, and clouds form and threaten rain rolling into dissipation and the streams run to rivers and the rivers run to sea and the sun and moon're clicking time like pickets across the face of the map—Jesus! look at the map on that guy, tripping along the electric wires: ranging . . . careening, wyoming— balancing from radio towers—It's a hellofa dizzy death-defying thing, ain't it: the whole place rolling forward and picking up speed and leaving every single person who was ever here spoked, and stranded, and planted along the tracks like pickets across the face of the map.

Springtime was a sustained breath of encouragement. I felt dizzy and unworthy of it. Already the new green of spring was maturing into the fixed green of summer. Beating it through the streets, or blown along the concrete limbs of the outer city, I could feel the precious minutes of a potent season running through the meter of the cab. Idling at the corner of a hundred and fifth and Olivet, my hands dirty on the wheel of a Checker, I watched one branch with a white blossom on a blue sky. Crashing down Buckeye, one elbow in the window breeze, I caught a scent that threatened to disperse me in particles of hope . . .

The people who got into my cab didn't seem to notice. They were going about their lives. Maybe there was no way to talk about it. Maybe springtime was a secret we concealed from one another, more frightening than love.

The pocket of my leather was cool as I reached for my Camels. I smoked cigarettes to cut my excess energy and attain these moments. In the motherly shine of morning and the turning light of afternoon and the dead railroad dew of late night the new leaves hung true and I lit cigarettes behind a hand cupped as though to contain a moment. Still the season escaped me.

I consolidated my hopes into Sadie.

I left the Buick at the curb and hit the bar with two to my favor.

She saw me coming. No one else looked up, denizens of the fathomless deep that they were. Let 'em sleep. Sadie had shiny hair of a brown that warms this side of black. She met me down the end of the bar.

"Hey," I said, secretively.

"Hey baby. Wanna drink?"

"Sure."

"Shot of Wild Turkey?"

"Sure."

She went to get it. I didn't look around, just waited, looking at my clasped hands on the bar, glad to be there.

She set a full rockglass down. I got a kiss on the cheek with it.

"Now look, Sadie, I been thinking about the road."

"Oh yeah?" she said, leaning closer.

"Yeah, y'know. Cheap motel rooms, gumbo, trumpets, wild-flowers . . ."

"Go on," she said.

"Okay." I took a sip of the bourbon. "Weird radio, deserts, ghost towns, diesel moons . . ."

"Okay."

Someone called for a drink. She went to get it.

She came back with a drink of her own. "Where were we?"

"Uhh—Red plush carpets in Vegas, palm trees, boulevards . . . How'm I doing?"

"Great. Then what?"

"Well we ran into an ocean."

"Oh."

"The only way is up."

She put a hand on my wrist and shot some sparkle into my eyes. I drank some more bourbon and she remembered something.

"There's one problem, baby."

"What's that?"

Someone called for a drink. She went away and came back.

"So?" I said.

"Willy moved back in."

I laughed, felt foolish. Drank some more whiskey.

"His parents threw him out. But it's just for a little while."

"Okay," I said. I looked at her, and I must've looked funny because she laughed.

I didn't stick around. I hit the street and the stars were bright.

Ed and I are out on the night, riding in the open windows of the Pontiac up Lorain . . .

He says "I was gonna stop over Angie's place."

"Who's Angie? That girl you picked up the other day?"

"Yeah she lives on Forty-Seventh; I want you to meet her."

"Why?"

"I dunno; so you see I get a—halfway normal broad once in a while. She's cute: you'll like her."

"What'd you see her again or something?"

"Yeah she called me. She actually found this matchbook I gave her with my number, said she wanted to make a few bucks, I went over and gave her fifteen for some head."

"Well what'm I gonna stand around there while you get a blowjob?"

"She'll give you one too: I got an extra—"

"Ed . . ."

He turns a corner onto Forty-Seventh, a street like a mouthful of broken teeth.

"This a bad fucking street," he's saying . . .

"Ed: what're you doing?"

"We're going to see Angie!" he says, getting impatient with me.

"For what?"

"I dunno, she—I kinda like her. She seems kinda goofy, but she's actually—y'know, kinda—constructive chick . . ."

We're walking across a vacant lot.

"Whattaya mean 'constructive'?"

"She seems like she's tryna get herself together. She got a guitar up there, says she practices every day, she got a little barbell, she's got books . . . I just want you to meet her: you'll be proud of me."

The backyard's dark and muddy; the moon glows behind a high thin beach of cloud. A dog starts barking in the next yard.

Bottom door's open. We step into a blackness that pulls itself in after us and I follow his cigarette up.

". . . Fucking neighborhood . . . dunno if somebody's waiting with a ball bat . . ."

At the top of the stairs he starts rapping on a door, hard.

We wait. No sound comes.

"She's kinda hard of hearing, got cotton stuffed in her ears . . ."

He bangs on the door.

"Ed maybe she ain't—"

"*Angie! —Angie! It's Ed!*"

Still not a sound from inside. The dark thickens—it's on my face—I panic.

"Angie!"

He gives the door a kick—

"Ed, what the fuck you doing? Maybe she ain't here!"

"Aah she just don't hear too good—" BOOMBOOM-BOOM, pounding on the door to break it down: "*ANGIE! IT'S ED! ANGIE!*"

"I'm getting outa here. They can probably hear this across the street." I start down the stairs, he's waiting.

"Sonofabitch . . ."

He starts down after me and from the top of that blackness comes a muffled sound. The door opens and a slant of light falls across the landing.

We turn back up and there she is, holding the door open and staring out like she's going to find someone there at eye level—which in her case is about four foot ten. If we've come to the right place it's definitely the wrong place.

"Angie."

She looks up—it's a coincidence—she opened the door and someone was there.

Ed says "Can we come in?"

She steps back and we shuffle into the bare light of her kitchen.

She stands fearless and riveted, staring up at Ed without surprise as the fulfillment of a prophecy. We meet at last. She's a small woman with a round head and high cheekbones, full mouth . . . and big pink shades like the eye sockets of a skull. Someone told me once that any woman under five feet tall and under a hundred pounds is crazy.

Ed says "This my friend Danny."

She's staring at him. He starts to say something else, but the first signal hits her and she turns and shouts "Hi!" and goes back to Ed . . .

Maybe it's the nakedness of the light, or maybe it's my presence, but even Ed's a little uncomfortable. He tells her we're going to pick up something to eat, and does she want us to—

"What?" she shouts.

"We're gonna get a coffee and a sandwich. You want us to bring you something back?"

"What?"

"Do you want something to eat?!"

"No."

"You want some—"

"I'm making dinner now!"

I glance around for any sign of dinner being underway. Nothing on the stove . . . There's no sign of the place having been organized into any kind of living-pattern. It looks like she moved in yesterday.

"You're—"

"I'm cooking spaghetti!"

I have the feeling Angie's reciting the wrong script. And

then I notice: on the floor, in the dust beside the fridge, an electric frying pan with an inch of dusty water, and ten or twelve strands of pasta lying stiff and stuck-together in the bottom. No steam, nor any clue as to how long Angie's been waiting for dinner to be ready.

"Ed, let's go get something to eat and come back."

"Yeah. *You sure you don't want a sandwich or something?*"

No response.

"Alright we'll be back in a—"

"*Oooo: could you get some beer?*"

"Yeah we'll—no problem. What kinda beer you want?"

She's moving backward as though with the force of thought. She backs to the sink, reaching into memory . . .

"*There was one kind of beer . . .*"

Ed's going "Miller? Michelob? Stroh's? Molson?"

"Milwaukee," she whispers.

"Milwaukee's Best?"

"*No, no—*"

"Old Milwaukee?" I ask.

"THAT'S IT!"

I'm shaking my head, Ed's going "Okay, we'll bring you some Old Milwaukee. Listen for the door—we'll be right back . . ."

We leave her rigid against the sink, staring at the doorway.

Waiting in a drive-thru line, a brown bag of Old Milwaukee on the seat between us . . .

"Whattaya think?" he says.

"Kinda cute. Kinda short, too. Better find out what she weighs."

"What she weighs?"

"Forget it. I'll tell you one thing though: be a good idea to find out how old she is."

"Told me she's twenty-two."

"Yeah, she told you she's cooking spaghetti for dinner, too."

"Hey I ain't tryna fuck her over or nothing, I just like her; she's—tough little kid . . ."

We pull up to the window.

"Sugar with your coffee Sir?"

"Sugar's poison," he tells her. "Chicago Joe told me that."

In the black of the stairway Ed's pounding:

"ANGIE! ANGIE IT'S US! OPEN UP, IT'S ED!"

He tries the door it's unlocked, it opens: and there's Angie, still at the sink, exactly as we left her.

He says "Jesus Christ. Didn't you hear us out there?"

No response.

"Angie, what're you doing?"

"WHAT?"

"Here: we brought you the beer, and a cheeseburger in case you get hungry later."

"I'm cooking spaghetti."

Ed opens the fridge and the light doesn't go on. He sticks his hand inside.

"It's warm in here. This fucking thing work or what?"

No response. I ask him if it's plugged in.

"Sonofabitch . . ."

"THE MAN IS COMING TO TURN THE REFRIGER-ATOR ON."

He plugs it in; the refrigerator ticks and hums into process.

"It's alright it's working now," he sighs.

Standing around the kitchen, nothing's being said. I crack a beer, light a cigarette.

Ed says "So what were you uh—"

"I was studying. I have to keep studying."

She heads for the other room. I look at Ed, raise my eyebrows. He follows her and I follow him.

Angie's on a mattress on the floor, in a nest of clothes and books and papers: a patchwork of clashing colors and objects in a maelstrom of purpose. A small TV is on without sound and Angie's going through a book, turning pages and taking notes and staring at the TV . . .

Ed sits behind her on the mattress.

"So uh . . . I dunno, you need anything here?"

No response. I'm in the doorway.

In one corner is a barbell, tangled in scarves . . . weights on one end, the other end resting on the floor.

"My car!" she says. "Can you take me to look for my car?"

"What car?"

"They stole my car: I had a car! Can you help me find it?"

"Yeah. Okay."

"Good, I saw them driving it today." She's still staring at TV.

"Angie," I ask. "You got a driver's license?"

"I have a driver's license!"

"Oh yeah? Can I see the picture?"

She's taking notes and staring at TV—and then she dives into a pile of clownrags—

"I had it here somewhere—"

I spot an Ohio license on top of an unplugged clock. Twenty-two years old.

Ed says "Angie: play the guitar for Danny; he likes music. Whyn't you play him a song?"

There's an electric guitar on the floor. It's got two strings, both hanging loose . . . unwound . . .

"Aah that's alright, maybe some other—"

"I don't have time now! I have to keep studying!"

Ed says "What the hell're you studying?"

He picks up the book from which she's taking notes.

"Aah jeez."

He shows it to me.

Fundamentals of Arc Welding.

"Let's go, Ed."

He replaces the book beside her notes.

"Alright, uh . . . We're gonna take off, here . . ."

She's staring at TV.

"Angie?"

"Yes?"

"We're gonna go. You need anything? You got any money?"

"No," she says, without a hint of asking for any.

He puts a ten on top of the television; I'm on my way to the door.

"Bye!" she yells, as he closes the door behind us.

sadie i know yer hiding in the clustered shine of the streetlight through leaves—i hear you in the crickets and i brush against you scooping into the lake-bottom shadows of this room. come out from behind the tune of the icecream trucks: make yourself known, so i can—/ i suspect yer waiting just beneath the skin of the phone/ —make myself known to me and you both.

i like the way a cactus looks.

"Aah, hell." I say, reaching to dial the phone.

This must be the night . . .

At the airport people are funneling in. Downtown, they're streaming into the Flats, headlights, taillights, groups of them trickling through dammed-up traffic, flooding into the bars, spilling out on the sidewalk, floating along beside the river's black indifferent shine. They flow west and east and south—Detroit Avenue—St. Clair! Superior!—Carnegie up to Cedar! They collect around the bars—jam up—get whirled around, carried away . . . Something's in the air. I'm all over the place, I can see it—I'm the gondolier!

Something in the air is calling the whole town upward—It's above the lights—behind the clouds—This must be the night when I remember how to fly, when the breeze can take my weight at last. I'm zooming round a freeway bend—The moon is up—a sickle of moon with a sidekick star: two parts of a symbol whose meaning is lost—buried—My exit!—though the effect is undeniable. I'm at a redlight, the Checker's hot and idling high. I gotta lose this cab. Driving a cab on a Saturday night—Where is everyone? I got my lease and thirty for myself—It's early yet! And Saturday nights can go from early to late in the blink of an eye . . .

Stuffing cash into my waybill I'm racing ahead of myself—a leaky pen, try it again—trying to shape a night out of tonight. The clock on the wall says eight-thirty-five. I slip Cleetus a deuce and split.

I'm out, I'm free. Down here, the night air is purple. What do I *do* with it all? Driving back up the hill home I decide to check in with Ed, as a stall . . .

He's pacing in the green light of his kitchen.

"What're you doing tonight man?"

"I got John's fifteen here, I was gonna take a ride later on, see who's out. I'm gonna wait till eleven, after the games. John's got a three-teamer going, he's losing already."

"Good, good . . ." Now *I'm* pacing around, this kitchen's too small for us.

Then he says, as though giving warning—"John told me today: Little Mike—turned into a killer!"

"What?"

"He got his first taste of blood! Mike caught a mosquito—"

"*[laughter]* "

"Caught a mosquito—killed it—and then he started kicking it all around the room, stomping on it!"

"Really?"

"John says after one mosquito he's a completely different personality."

"Son of a *bitch*."

"And John hates violence: he says he knows Mike doesn't get it from him. John's scared—He says he don't know what's next!"

"*[laughter]* "

"Can you believe that lunatic?"

"Man." Already I can feel the movement of time. We seem very strange, talking about this in this dark kitchen.

"Alright, I'll leave you to your green light here; I'm going out."

"Yeah alright, uh . . . What's up? Where you going? You gonna meet Al somewhere?"

"Yeah I—maybe . . . I'll probably give him a call, see what he's doing . . ."

"Yeah alright. Stop back later, you see the light on here . . ."

"Okay man. Good luck."

My stairway smelled like the dust of years. Like the smell of my grandmother's staircase, just up the street, when we came to the Southside to visit.

I ran a bath and called Al.

"Yeah."

"Yeah."

"Where you, at home?"

"Yeah I was driving the cab but I took it back to garage. What're you doing tonight?"

"I dunno, I's—probably go downtown, stop at the Jack of Hearts . . ."

"Maybe I'll meet you there."

"Alright good, I'm gonna take a shower, get ready . . . probably be there around ten."

"I'll see you there."

The grey linoleum bears a wet footprint, a rough rag of towel thrown aside. Open and close the cabinet mirror and run the tap in the sink. I get shined up and greased back: dark and sharpened. A night like this, the illusion of purpose is what you need. Electricity's crazy until directed. The club's only an ignition-thrust away, up over the mills and into town; plenty of time. A red bottle of wine on the table, still corked. I must've been waiting for this. Gathering silence in the dark . . .

I sit at the table, having a sip and a smoke in the window. Almost hate to go.

And then I leave rooms and stairways behind—The street hangs out its lanterns—the moon is high and sharp, poised with a sidekick star. Roll down the window and breathe in purple. Royal night. Royal night and fairy lights—one glass of red and velvet ravens—deepest blue into clearest black: the march has begun: the march upward into heaven tonight.

But:

It takes a while to park downtown, the warehouse windows loom, I'm walking, and then I'm waiting in line to pay my way in. Already something's changing, in the night. Even outside the music's too loud and the air's filled with attitude. I get my hand stamped at the entrance and walk on through . . .

So this's what we do with electricity; well alright.

Strobe lights! I spot Al—he's here, setting casual traps; he comes up to me, he's shouting in my ear I'm shouting in his ear you just get here? Just walked in, See that chick over that's the one I was telling you wanna beer? No, whiskey. This my friend Tommy, Hi Tommy in the ripped-up leather? That's my future wife. Fucking packed in here. Yeah, double Wild Turkey—straight, yeah, Huh? What? I'll get this one, No I got it man. Lookit this guy: how can he stand himself? They're crowding into the gas chamber to dance—bass-and-drum machine and the song never ends. Aw, man, look who's here, Yeah they threw him out last week, I threw him out myself last night, What? You want another beer? Watch out, man: Sara at six o'clock, I know, I seen her, This girl's been looking at you, Aah I see her every week, she's a cumbucket—

I stand around talking to Al and Tommy reels by and then I'm alone, I mill around, I assume various positions, I talk to Al. I talk to what's-his-name, I hide from what's-her-name . . . I'm watching—waiting, without wondering . . . and I feel the night going from early to late, and nothing's happening. I gotta get outa here, I need some air.

I let the empty streets of downtown lead me to the freeway ramp.

And I left downtown behind me, pushing out into a bigger night—the real night: . . . losing size for silence, visibility for vision, and the few first intimations of something to come . . .

Running along the dark and patient lake, night seemed to come from there. Buildings and walls of trees and houses took shape and disappeared from there. And the lake vanished, leaving only night.

I made my way to the suburb where I'd grown up, the free-way let me go, and only in shifting down into the stillness of a neighborhood caught unawares did the sound of my engine reach me. Suddenly self-conscious, and cautious of disturbing the neighborhood's sleep, I pulled as quietly as possible into the driveway of the house where Dave lived with his mother . . . quietly, into the deep shadow between houses, and cut the engine.

There was light from the basement windows; Dave's room. I tapped.

"Dave?"

". . . Danny?"

"Yeah."

"Hold on, man."

In the dim light of the basement room, Dave was pulling on shirt and shoes. I shook out the day's first cigarette and tossed him one as well. He didn't smoke, really. When I was around, he smoked. He was showing me things . . . this and that . . . things newly acquired—stolen, or come-upon: a brief show-and-tell, putting us up to date. I leaned over and drew flame from a candle near his bed as he pulled a jacket from a chair. There was a hushed sense of this developing gracefully, as though planned . . .

Deep in shadow we slipped into the car.

I turned the key, trying by gentle force of will to hush the ignition; let the car roll back down the driveway, leaving the headlights off, so as not to disturb that shadow.

Rolling up the street I pulled the headlights on and we pushed out to take part in the night.

The half bottle of wine lay on the seat between us . . . but Dave didn't drink, so I let the bottle fall, upright, into the back. Before we took the freeway ramp I stopped to buy a bottle of water.

And again the night widened: . . . spreading overhead and out in all directions. We didn't talk, it got quiet, and the presence now of stars triggered the few first intimations of the reality of night: that night is what is continuous and forever present. We'd started out with half a tank of gas, and now by the dashboard light we were down to a quarter tank.

It's hard to say just what happened from there on out (night was happening. The night unfolded and we unfolded with it . . . gathering peripheral mysteries and carrying them ahead with us . . . the black roadbanks erupting and falling, recombinant . . . At one point we ran alongside a train awhile, then it fell away . . .

We wound up where we'd never been:

Parked the car and walked away from it . . . stood off the road a ways, staring—(and I was wondering and I guess he was too why it was that we didn't come here all the time: this seemed like the only place there was . . .)—up at the stars:

becoming, first, slowly reacquainted with the existence of stars:

up there:

steady . . .

seemingly brittle—as brittle as our perception of them . . . and then, time still passing, standing out in a field, trying to find the point at which the stars quiver to piercing stillness:

intimations of wonder:

watching:

looking around, now and then, but always back to the stars.

And then: having glanced around yet again, I looked up and saw the stars in color: saw through my conception of them as points of white light and saw them, suddenly, calmly, in simple, obvious, and undeniable breakdowns of red and blue and yellow.

I cocked my head and took a few steps back, in order that this new perception of them should return to my old one, but the colors remained:

clear, distinct, and irrevocable.

That's when time stood still.

. . . Parallel tracks of twenty-three or so years had led us here,

to be caught in the moonlight. The hour had been late: now the hour was in abeyance—gone:

in exchange for a moment:

suspended: heightened: still:

bathed in a clarity of which our untrained senses could detect only the bluish, rudimentary lower limits . . .).

*

Back in the shadowed front seat of the car . . . closer now, hav-

ing experienced aloneness together . . . we drank some of the
water. I shook two cigarettes out of the pack . . . the second
cigarettes of the day. Struck a match and lit his, gazing into
the matchglow . . . lit mine, shook out the match and started
the engine. We headed back home below empty, taking home
a moment.

Sunday broke on a big scale, a real beaut, a sure thing. The breeze was up, hope was high, the world was snapping like laundry all around. I went next door to be sure Ed shared my sentiments. He was up and around already, wearing one of his better shirts and a clean pair of pants. He had the paper stripped to the sports.

He said "I's thinking of taking a ride to the Big T."

"Right."

"Alright, we'll leave early, John's got ten. 'S gonna run over there, pick it up on the way. He lost that three-teamer, called me already this morning, says this's his absolute last desperation bet. This don't hit, it's his final bet for the year. Him and Mike're holding a betting conference, Mike's wearing his lucky helmet."

"Oh, he got a helmet, huh?"

"John's brother Don picked one up. He hadda spend four dollars in quarters to get a blue one, but—"

"Where the fuck's John coming up with these tens and twenties every night?"

"This is it, man—his last ten bucks. Must be still left over from that life insurance policy. He cashed in his life and his carcass—Ain't nothing left."

"So this a big day for him . . ."

"Yeah—and get this: what does John want for his absolute last-ditch desperation bet? A four-teamer. Feef don't even take four-teamers: no bookie does. John's—'Will he take it? Can he handle it?' I'm going 'Well I dunno, he might take it . . . ' Y'know. The guy's so pitiful you gotta feel sorry for him. So I figure I'll slip him this one, give him something to do today. He ain't gonna hit it anyway, and then maybe that'll be the end of this for a while, 'cause it just ain't fucking worth it, getting involved with this lunatic, all these phonecalls."

And then the phone rings.

I'm sitting in the Pontiac at Feef's curb toying with the radio while the engine gutters and stinks. Ed comes out and slams into the car.

"You get the lines for John?"

"Yeah I got 'em," he says, pulling away. "Fucker bets a five-teamer! A four-teamer was bad enough, and then he turns around bets a five-teamer!"

Crossing the river, he's indignant:

"Now you think—if John had any shred of sanity left: he's got ten: you think he'd pick a two-teamer—two heavy favorites even—he'd get back twenty-five, thirty bucks—and have something for tomorrow, y'know? *Vegas* don't take five-teamers. Next time he'll pick a nine-teamer. Then both leagues: every game. He wants to build a fucking empire on a ten-dollar bill!"

In front of the autopart store he hits the horn. I stick my head out the window. John appears on the roof in the sunlight, framed against a cloud-running sky. Ed hands me the list and I get out.

John lets something drop and I catch it—a paperbag balled up and wrapped in rubberbands.

"You get the lines?" he calls down.

"Yeah, you ready?"

He's got pen and paper up there with him.

"Alright here it is. Detroit's a three-to-two dog . . . Chicago's favored six to five . . . Seattle's a six-to-five dog . . . Philly's an eight-to-five dog, and the Dodgers are a pick."

". . . Good," he says.

I slide back in and Ed pulls away without a word. I get the bag open—"The hell's this?" Along with the ten and the careful list of his picks, there's a ham sandwich. I open it up— Ed glances over— Two slices of spiced ham on white bread, with mayonnaise. "Fucking lunatic," Ed says, "Throw it out the window." I look at him. He takes it off the seat and rolls the window down, tosses the sandwich out and rolls the window shut.

"Cheer up," I tell him, "we're going to the track."

We park at the mall across the street and traverse the glaring parking lot through a sea of cars to the track. In the cool concrete dimness of the interior, Ed buys a *Form* and moves to get a program.

"Don't bother, I'll get it from Daniels."

"Who's Daniels?"

"Y'know the guy upstairs, the cashier . . ."

"You mean that lunatic by the fifty-dollar window?"

"Yeah."

"How'd you get involved with that guy?"

"I ain't *involved* with him, he just gives me the program once in a while."

The downstairs tote says nineteen minutes to post. Heading for the stairs Ed's looking around over his shoulder . . .

"Let me know if you see a guy in a wheelchair looks like Howdy Doody. He's a bookie: I owe him three grand for two years now."

"I doubt if he'll be on the second floor."

"You never know. He's crafty."

"You want a hotdog or something?"

"We just walked in the door!"

"Yeah, so I'm hungry; I'm gonna get a—"

"No. First rule of parimutuel betting is you don't buy nothing to eat until you hit a race. That's two bucks you could make another bet with."

We come off the stairs and bingo: Daniels—"HERE'S MY SWEETHEART!"—fifty paces—Ed goes "Holy fuck" and veers in another direction. Everyone's looking—the cashiers, all down the line . . . Daniels is beckoning, beaming at his window. I close the distance before he can say more, shake his hand, ask him how he's doing . . .

He's looking especially festive today—a man of about fifty—in a big sloppy balloon of a shirt—pink and white stripes . . . wide paisley tie . . . I ask if he's got an extra program handy, pretending not to notice the wild uncontainable grin; he says "Certainly son," and slides me one. I open it, glance over the first race while Daniels floats behind the counter, rubbing his hands.

"Hear anything about the first race?"

He reaches over, taps a finger on the five horse.

"Oh yeah?"

"He ran a good workout yesterday, and Rivera switched his mount to him."

"Great. Thanks."

"Can I get you something to eat? Want a coffee?"

"Sure."

He slips off his stool, I glance back at the program. The five. Fool's Progress. I look to the board. At the moment, he's twenty to one. Daniels is calling me—"Sugar?"

Heads turn.

"*No*—no sugar, just milk." They're all looking at me again.

"Mustard on the sandwich?"

"Yeah, yeah—fine."

"How about some potato salad?"

"Yeah—whatever!"

He's busily fixing all this—"Apple danish?"

"Yeah, fine: great!"

He comes back with a sagging paper plate and a fork. I turn

away, laden, and make my way to find Ed.

"I ever tell you about John going to Waterford on the bus?"

"No."

"I'll tell you after the race."

We decide to split a couple doubles, five bucks each. I don't mention the five, but at the window I hook him up with our picks for the second race: Tagalong and Crazy Legs. Fool's Progress is sixteen to one.

We go out to the grandstand to watch. From the walkway between the grandstand and the box seats we have a clear view of everything. The race goes off, they break in a tangle. Our two key picks—frontrunners—are fighting for the rail. One of them gets there and the other's right behind, four lengths ahead of the field. Into the turn we've got a horse ahead on the rail and another making a move. Coming out of the turn they're debating, and the rest of the field is catching up. Someone's coming fat on the outside—I check the screen—It's the five! He's moving up, they rumble past us—the five's out front—I check the board, sixteen to one, and there it is: Fool's Progress, showing the way . . .

"Motherfucker—Who was that? We got both our horses out front and get beat by a sixteen-to-one-shot?"

"That's right," I tell him. I try to play it cool but I can't help it, I start laughing. I hand him the tickets.

"Holy fuck," he says. "Why the—What— How did you have that horse?"

"Daniels. Now all we need's the second half."

Ed leads the way up into the grandstand seats and we settle in with the *Form* and program. Ranged among the empty seats are other people, mostly alone, checking a program, lifting a coffee cup from the floor, watching the infield toteboard or gazing out at the bright empty arena of afternoon . . .

"Oh, I was gonna tell you about John."

"Well wait. I don't wanna hear no bad luck stories yet."

We decide to stick with Tagalong and Crazy Legs at seven to two and five to two and I go down to bet. I bet each of them five to win and then together in a quinella. The desultory stir of people is resolving itself into congregations, ranked at the cashier windows . . . Like a mind forming a thought. The view from the grandstand is what that mind sees: the wide placid spread of the track, the infield . . . a distant wall of trees, and small houses . . . white clouds piled along the horizon . . . The only thing happening is far away, at the bottom of the back-stretch . . . some slight activity near the gate . . . so minor you barely notice. It's hard to believe that momentarily all the attention of this enormous mind will be focused there . . .

The bell rings and people are shouting. As the horses come clattering past us we're out of our seats and we're shouting too . . .

Tagalong wins easy, Crazy Legs runs out. Minutes later the prices appear on the infield tote. We get 22.80 for Tagalong and the double pays 182.60. After two races we're ahead a hundred each. I try to remember the last time I was a hundred ahead and can't.

Daniels is talking to a guy in a windbreaker. The guy steps aside to wait and then says "I'll talk to you later, Gene." Daniels waves him off. I hand him the tickets.

"See that guy?" he says.

"Yeah."

"He's a judge in Parma Heights—very nice man."

"I hope so, if he's a judge."

He runs the tickets through the machine and slides me the money. I give him back twenty.

"Thanks a lot."

"Thank you, son."

"I gave Daniels a sawbuck for each of us."

"Fine," Ed says.

"Can I buy you a coffee now?"

"Cigars," he says, and we head to a concession stand.

He gets us each a cigar. We unwrap them and light up, taking a moment to bask in the glow of the first two races before plunging into the third. Ed's cigar looks natural; mine feels unwieldy.

"Alright. Tell me about John."

"There used to be a special, degenerate gambler bus—from Cleveland to Waterford, took like two and a half hours. Makes a hundred stops, picking up Johns along the way—You leave at like five in the afternoon to get there for seven-thirty post. Right? So John, who considers himself an excellent horse-player by the way, takes his twenty-four dollars he got from delivering fliers all day, and gets a brainstorm he wants to go to Waterford at night, and the bus—I don't recall what it cost, it musta been ten twelve bucks . . . Cost you a couple bucks to get in the track: I remember he said he didn't even get a *Form*, just a program— He had ten bucks left, to bet with. Which, in the first place, you'd have to be a complete dildo to sit through a two-hour bus ride, at night, to go bet ten dollars on horses at a little shit track in West Virginia, right? Let alone: what's he do with the ten bucks? Bets it all on two five-dollar doubles— Loses 'em both in the first race, and then has to sit—through the next eleven races—"

"*[laughter]*"

"Without even half a buck for coffee. He said he didn't even wander around, just sat on a bench, through the next— eleven—marathon races."

"Christ."

"Can you imagine that? You'd think, with ten bucks in your pocket you'd spread it out a little, bet two bucks a race until you hit something. Not—bet it all in the first race on fucking hunch bets—and doubles yet besides! Bus pulls outa there after midnight, stops at fifty hillbilly stops on the way home—"

Then he says "Speaking of John, I gotta check these games."

He pulls out a radio and clicks it on, composing a look of wary concentration—presses it to his ear, thumbing the dial and getting mostly static. "Can't get nothing in here." He pulls out the aerial and points it around . . .

"Can't hear a fucking thing," he says. "I'm going over by the patio, see if I can pick it up over there; plus I gotta check the basketball score on the TV . . ."

By the fifth race we'd gotten rid of our cigars, but we were still up about eighty-five each. Ed pointed out a Detroit horse called Bold Entreaty: a closer in a distance race, mile and seventy.

I said "How you wanna do this? Win and place?"

"He's a closer. He'll either win it or run out. Get me ten to win."

I put him in with Daniels, ten win for each of us. He was five to one.

We went to watch him from the fence. They went twice around the track. Bold Entreaty ran as though keeping our secret. He won by three lengths. We shook hands and hit the stairs. Ed went to check the games.

Daniels was talking to a tall guy in a suit. He introduced me.

"Son, this is Paul Cameron, the bishop at St. Michael's."

"How you doing?" I said.

"Holding my own. And a little of theirs."

The bell rang and it was official. I collected our one-twenty and wished the bishop luck and bought myself a hotdog.

Ed walked by on his way to check the reception in the grandstand. He said "I'm losing that fucking basketball bet."

I gave him sixty, said "So what? That's twenty bucks."

"Yeah, well I'd still like to hit the fucker. I bet it with the late game: that's worth seventy, it comes in. That's a ninety-dollar swing."

I shook my head and applied mustard.

I found him again by the rail with ten minutes to post.

"I been waiting for baseball scores, here." He switched the radio off. "John's losing two games and winning one."

"Here's the *Form*."

"I dunno, I kinda like the eight."

He stood glancing from the *Form* to the board. We couldn't agree on a horse. I took a longshot called Don't Blink, he took a horse called All Too True. Neither of them did a thing.

Ed was buying a coffee. I said "See anything this race?"

"Naw they're all pigs. I got no idea at all."

"I'll talk to Daniels, maybe he heard something."

He hands me a ten. "I got no heart for this race at all."

I go inside, hang around and watch the board. With a minute left I get into Daniels' line. The folks ahead of me are crowding . . . slapping programs and craning their necks to speed things up . . . Daniels is going at his own pace. He's more oblivious and out of control as the day wears on. Tie loose, shirt untucked, hair on end . . . A bettor steps aside to examine his tickets and Daniels leans over to confer with the cashier behind the fifty-buck partition. The next bettor's at the window rapping his knuckles on the counter, guys're bitching . . .

I step up with a second to spare—Daniels smiles—he's beatific—rocking back and forth on his stool—I'm going "Gene! Gene!" trying to bring him back—"You got anything in this race?" He shows me four fingers I say "Twenty to win." He punches the ticket and the bell goes off . . . the line behind me disperses, grudgingly, and Daniels says "His trainer just put five hundred on him."

The four is nine to two. I find Ed near the reserved seats, toying with his aerial.

"Four horse," I tell him.

A five-and-a-half-furlong sprint, below a cloud-running sky. The four was running a race of his own. He took it all the way.

Ed was floored. "I guess that guy ain't a maniac after all."

We were sailing. I gave Daniels another ten. I wanted to start calling people: I wanted to call my old man—I wanted to call Sadie . . . Money won is sweeter than money earned. My mind raced with hopeful constructive thoughts of what to do with it.

I gave Ed his half and counted my roll. One seventy plus.

"Ed—Let's get outa here."

"What're you, kidding? What's the problem?"

"I dunno, I never been here till the eighth race—I'm nervous."

"Don't worry. Just lock up part of what you got and keep the rest to play with."

I put one-fifty in a separate pocket and kept twenty, felt better immediately.

Ed said "We'll leave after the next race if you want."

"Two more."

He pulled out the radio and tried to dial into—Static.

"Sonofabitch. This piece of shit—I gotta go out on the patio for one game, another comes in from the grandstand, I get another one from the rail . . ."

"What about the basketball?"

"Yeah, thanks for reminding me: I'll be right back. Here's the *Form*."

In the next twenty minutes I caught glimpses of him: aiming the aerial out the patio door . . . coming out of the men's room . . . lighting a cigarette under a TV screen . . . heading toward the ecorche . . . At one point he hustled past me toward a support pillar with the radio pressed to his ear saying "I'm gonna shimmy up this pole for better reception—"

With two minutes to post he found me on a bench.

"I lost that fucking basketball bet. John's winning on the patio, he's tied-up near the ice cream stand and he's down two runs in the paddock. Who you like here? I didn't even look at this race . . ."

"I like the one."

"The chalk?" he said, taking the *Form* . . .

145

In a minute he said "Fuck it," and glanced at the board. "Gimme ten and ten on the twelve; he's four to one."

"You like that horse, huh?"

"I'm just taking a shot. What's his name?"

"Tricky Nicky."

"Aah Jeez. Put ten and ten on whatever you bet."

I put our money on Shining Example.

Tricky Nicky won it easy, Shining Example ran third.

"Fuck Ed, I'm sorry."

"Yeah, yeah . . ."

"God damnit," I said, when the price appeared. "Almost seventy-five bucks . . ."

"We're not talking numbers here buddy: that's six blowjobs . . ."

He stayed put for the ninth. We took our time and studied the *Form*. The later it got, the more races gone by, the harder it was to stay focused. We were sitting on a bench on the second floor. An old woman in a red dress suit floated toward us, searching her purse. She had a silk scarf tied over her hair and lots of makeup.

"The Lady in Red," Ed muttered.

"You seen her before?"

"Oh yeah, she's a fixture out here. Only bets to show: hundred-dollar show tickets."

Ed scanned the *Form* as she stopped to apply more lipstick. She looked as though she'd only seen herself in a compact mirror for many years. She snapped her purse shut and moved on . . .

We narrowed the race down to My Purse, the one, and Mr. Bonaparte, the five.

He said "You wanna take an exacta here?"

"Yeah."

"Get us a one/five for five bucks."

"We gotta box it."

"Yeah, alright: here's ten."

Daniels was shaking hands with a guy in a jogging suit. The guy turned and walked off.

Daniels said "See that man?"

"Yeah. Who is he, the mayor?"

"He's a pickpocket."

"I'll stay clear of him then."

"Oh, no need, son, he's gone straight. But he used to be one of the best in the city."

He looked at me gravely. I always got the impression he was imparting some larger body of information . . .

Then I remembered why I'd come. "Hey, uh—Gimme a one/five reverse for twenty."

He punched the ticket.

"Like another coffee?"

"No thanks, I'm nervous enough."

He grinned demonically—"Good, son—Good for you!"

We found a place on the fence near the finish line and held it. The sun was warm. We watched the distant slow procedure of horses being led to the gate and coaxed inside. From the infield pond a flurry of geese took flight.

And they're off: everyone wakes up as the chaos of the break settles into a kind of order by the first call. My Purse is running third when we lose them behind the toteboard. When they reappear I can't make out who's who. As they're heading into the far turn I get a fix on My Purse, third on the rail, and the announcer puts Mr. Bonaparte fifth. We need them to run first and second. I lose their numbers again as they fatten and set down for the stretch, and then My Purse is making a move: jumping into second and launching an assault on first as Mr. Bonaparte slips into third and My Purse jumps out front of the four horse by a nose a neck and a length and Bonaparte decides to capitalize on the four's discouragement, but the four isn't giving up—"C'MON WITH THAT FIVE!"

"FIVE HORSE!"

"EAT HIM UP, BABY—C'MON WITH THAT FIVE!"

as the five halves and then quarters the four with My Purse
way out front now and running for the pure pleasure of it as
the five eclipses the four as Ed hits me in the shoulder and the
moment dissolves into laughter . . .

We went straight to a downstairs window and waited for
the bell. I slid the guy our ticket and we watched the digital
read-out: $304.40.

Ed counted me $152 and I said "Now let's get the fuck outa
here before they lock us in," and we walked out into the bright
indifferent continuum of the world outside.

*

Ed clicks on the car radio . . . dialing . . . tuning . . .

Before hitting the freeway we stop for gas. While he fills the
tank, probably for the first time in years, I have a sensation of
money seeping down into our lives like water into dry earth. I
catch the baseball scores. When he gets back in the car I break
the news.

"Fuck John," he says. "Three games is a fucking miracle.
You mean to tell me he's gonna hit two more today? No way.
Absolutely no way."

The ride back was a breeze. Construction barrels flying by,
I counted my money. Minus expenses, call it three hundred.
My rent was one-twenty, so I had enough for rent, bills, and
groceries for a month. I'd won a month.

Ed was saying "Northfield's open tonight . . . Take this three
hundred out to the trotters and . . ."

". . ."

He looked at me.

"Fuck you," I said. "You gotta be kidding."

"Well I *was* kidding as a matter of fact, but if you'da said yes
I'da gone."

"I'm all wired, I could use a drink."

"I'll take a ride with you, you wanna get a shot. I gotta stop

148

home first, get my brain together. I'm sure John's called fifty times already."

THAT NIGHT . . .

I went for a walk.

The night was whispering all around me, like it does . . . turn around—no one there.

Green light behind the shades, Pontiac at the curb. *Semper Fi* says the bumper sticker. Ed keeps a yellow hard hat on the back dash, in case a cop pulls him over or finds him with a whore. It worked once, parked among the ivy, by the river. She couldn't have been more than sixteen. The flashlight caught the hat . . . "Aah, let him go, he's a working guy . . ."

A day becomes just any night.

I went upstairs and called Al.

"Yeah."

"Yeah. What's up?"

"I'm doing a couple loads of laundry . . . reading this book about how to make bombs out of household objects . . ."

"How 'bout later?"

"Aah there's a couple bands at the Underground, I might go check 'em out . . . probably starts around nine-thirty."

"Okay."

"You gonna go?"

"Yeah mayb—I dunno. Maybe I'll see you there."

I called Sadie. No answer.

I sat on the edge of my bed and counted the money again, but that only took a minute.

Nine-thirty I got into the car.

I walked into the Underground, Alex wasn't there yet. I got a shot and a beer, feeling bored not only with what was happening but with anything that possibly could happen.

The place was painted black and washed with beer. A girl dancing caught my eye; automatically I reached for a cigarette. It was Marie. Some goofy-looking guy, she was dancing with. I moved closer but stayed within the darkness.

Her eyes were alight with laughter. The light of the stars. I looked the guy over. Actually, he looked okay. Marie was dancing as though attempting to shake off past and future. For a few moments, she achieved the present . . .

And she wasn't Marie anymore, the Marie I'd made her. She was the Marie I'd found. She was a girl, alight.

I decided to leave her there in the present. Drank the shot and left a smile. I'd had my day, and certain nights are just someone else's.

Around midnight I got back. I parked and saw the green light go off.

I knocked. He came to the door.

"Yeah?"

"Whatsa matter?"

"Y'know that five-teamer John bet?"

"He hit."

"Yeah."

"How much?"

"About four-fifty."

I was watching him.

"So that's about it from here," he said. "He wants two-fifty tomorrow, I just talked to him. Good thing we went to the track today."

"Mm."

Then I laughed and shook my head and said goodnight.

Monday morning I went to the gym.

Carl descried me in the steam room.

"IS THAT YOU, PAT?"

"How's it going, Carl?"

"Taking it EASY, hah Pat?"

"Yeah, w—"

"No work today? (OH it's too hot in here.) TOO HOT, Pat!"

"I quit work, Carl. It was interfering with my career."

"QUIT WORK? You quit w—"

"I had a big day at the TRACK yesterday, Benny!"

"Benny?"

"I hit a TRIFECTA!"

"You—"

"My working days are OVER, Sam! Seven BIG ONES!"

"(Seven hundred dol—)"

"Seven THOUSAND, Carl! I'm through with Lincoln and Jackson: I've got NEW friends now."

"Wh— H—"

"It's Mr. Grant and Mr. Franklin from now on," I said, and left him moaning in the steam.

I worked out and then went to the roof, lay in the sun for an hour.

Ed was at the table, not answering the phone.

"Where you been, boy? You leave me stranded at a time like this? Phone rang eleven times already."

"What're you gonna do?"

"Yeah, sure: 'What're *you* gonna do?' Thanks, buddy."

"Alright: what're *we* gonna do? He's *your* uncle. He's your flesh and blood."

"He's my *half* uncle. Which from now on I disown him. Anyway, I already called him, told him I'm working, calling from a payphone—I told him I don't get off till six, tryna buy myself some time. He already sounded suspicious. He said Feef better not've had a heart attack overnight."

"You owe him four-fifty?"

"—Yeah, a basic four-fifty. He wants two-fifty today, says he wants me to hold the rest and bet with it."

"I dunno what you're so worried about; the guy's basically harmless, plus he's desperate, so he's got no choice but to—"

"Aah you don't understand, he's capable of calling my old lady, getting her all upset, he's capable of coming over here try to burn the place down, going into Feef's and fucking things up for me there . . ."

At six o'clock Ed called John and said he'd loaned me his car for an hour. He said he had the money from Feef, no problem, and he'd bring it when I got back with the car.

John, reassured, felt comfortable enough to grumble a bit before betting two hundred of the imaginary four-fifty on a two-teamer: Detroit and New York, both heavy favorites.

The games started at seven-thiry.

At eight o'clock the phonecalls started. Ed told him I wasn't back and then dragged my name around in the mud while I listened on the other line.

John was saying "Did you see that? Niggers can't hit. See that double play? We got Feef sweating now. See that grab? Three up, three down. Niggers're natural athletes. (You okay Ma? You want another blanket? Want some ice tea? No? —*smooch!*) Ice tea's the world's greatest drink. Hah? You see the news tonight? They let that hillbilly kid off. He's back on the streets already! There should be no judges, just vigilante law. (You want me to turn on the vaporizer Ma? No? —*smooch!*) Mike caught an ant in here today—Devoured it! Waitaminute, here's the scores— New York's up by two! This is easy! (You okay Ma? . . . Ma, that's no way to talk . . .)"

We sat in the gathering dimness of the room, fixed grimly on the television as though watching a game that had already been played.

In the sixth inning Ed told him I'd called up drunk from the East Side, on the way to my folks' place to sleep it off an hour or two. John was so carried away with impending victory that he barely noticed.

We took a seventh-inning stretch up to Perry's for a meal, ate in the car. Detroit Avenue looked like a runway to doom, a few stragglers idling along the way. Vice cars prowled.

By ten-forty-five, John had picked up another two-fifty. We heard it on the Pontiac radio. Bad news finds you where you are. Ed didn't say a word. For a full thirty seconds.

We got back to the house the phone was ringing.

"Baseball's the easiest thing in all the world! Fish in a barrel—just like shooting fish in a barrel. From now on I'm a professional gambler. I pick better than ninety percent of all professional gamblers. Make sure you're at Feef's bright and early tomorrow—"

"I'll make sure John. I'm going to bed now. Goodnight."

SEVEN BILLS

I was frying eggs and thinking that life itself is really the only worthwhile entertainment. I slid Ed his toast. The best trick is to see your own life that way.

Ed always ate like it was something to be gotten out of the way of the next cigarette, the next game plan. He was putting away the last of his breakfast when I sat down to mine . . .

He lit a Newport and opened to the sports. We heard his phone ring, next door. He shook his head without looking up from today's schedule, exhaling pointedly . . .

"Driving the cab today?"

"I dunno."

"Fucking Tuesday, track's closed . . ."

"What's the score?"

"He's up to seven hundred."

"Whattaya got left from Sunday?"

"I got about one-sixty."

Two in the afternoon. The day was beautiful, like a heartbreaking girl waiting for someone to approach her, getting impatient, ready to turn her attention elsewhere. I was spending it with Ed. We were on our way to Westlake.

"So I talked to John, told him I's calling from a payphone."

"Yeah?"

"Told him I got to Feef's too early to get his money but I'll get it after work. I asked if he wanted something on one of the afternoon games."

"Did he bite?"

"Took the Reds at three o'clock for a hundred."

We parked in front of a beverage store owned by a man named Phil The Biter.

Phil glared when we walked in. He told the kid working for him to watch the register. Phil headed for a back room and we followed.

From a file cabinet he produced a deck of cards, and atop a stack of Cotton Club cases he dealt himself and Ed into a game of gin rummy.

There was a crash from the front of the store. Phil winced and sank teeth into hand before lurching out of the room. Ed and I glanced at each other before Ed glanced at Phil's cards.

I was on my way out as Phil came back. I got a beer, left some change with the kid and went back to the game.

Before I could crack the beer Phil was on me—

"You PAY for that?"

"Yeah Phil; ninety cents."

And so we spent the afternoon. When Phil lost points or succumbed to other irritations he bit his hand to contain his anger. After three rounds, the fleshy part of his left hand, between thumb and forefinger, was riddled with purpling toothmarks. He lost again and started on his wrist, growling like an animal. He lost the fifth and leaped at Ed, snarling—we jumped back—

"Calm down, Phil!"

"Jesus," I said, setting bottles aright . . .

Fortunately Phil won the sixth hand.

He kept winning till five o'clock. Ed lost fifty bucks, and stole a carton of Newports on the way out.

We were home in time to call John at six.

The Reds had lost and now he was agitated.

"He wants his two-fifty from yesterday and he wants two

bills on Detroit. Fucker's on the ropes now. He's got the sha-bobes," Ed said, stepping onto the porch.

"He's got what?"

"Shaboby fever. He'll keep betting till it's gone, just to get it over with."

"Like a death wish."

"Yeah, he can't help himself."

He went to Feef's and put his last hundred in the world on San Diego, a three-to-two dog. I went next door and called Sadie, to no avail.

Around eight o'clock I took a walk through the bath of twilight. A yard dog barked and a stray stood watching for my next move as I floated, preoccupied with horizons, past sidewalk talk that sounded small beneath the sky . . . I bought a number and went back to Ed's.

When the San Diego score had made its way through the airwaves he switched the radio off and said "Well, that's worth like two-fifty tomorrow."

The Detroit game finished soon after.

John had lost, in the ninth.

The phone rang and rang. Twenty-four times, it rang: we counted. He was down to four hundred.

"What're you gonna do?" I asked Ed.

"I'm gonna take him his fucking two-fifty tomorrow, that's what I'm gonna do. I'm sure he'll tell me to keep the rest, and I'll just let him bet that fucking one-fifty down to nothing. And then I'm gonna cut the fucker off; that's it."

I hung around a few minutes more and then got up. The phone started ringing for one last shot, almost feebly . . . five little times, and then died, for the night. Ed didn't move.

I picked up a *Form* to pass the time in the drivers' room. Wooster pulled my card and I spent the next hour and a half in a corner, trying to shut out the crushingly repetitive talk of the drivers. I picked out a quinella at River Downs and a hunch in the feature race at Thistledown. When I got the cab I drove to Feef's.

He and Jimmy were talking about an old friend whose son was at an out-of-state college.

Feef was saying "The kid's been down there three years. He's got a year to go, and then he's coming up here for another four years."

Jimmy said "Another four years? What the hell's he going to school for?"

"Studying to be a lawyer."

"A lawyer? Christ, we got more lawyers in this country than hamburgers."

*

With light still wide in the sky I pulled up to the ABC Bar.

I had to ring a buzzer. This was a quiet oasis in a rough part of town. I stepped into the darkness of thirty years ago and said "Cab for Cartwright?" The bartender put a finger to his lips, came close and pointed to an old man slumped on the bar.

An old woman sat the other side of him, watching my approach with a kind of polite repressed terror. I sat down and ordered a shot. Peripherally, I felt her eyes widen and then collapse into what she hoped was a smile. The bartender poured the shot and I turned to the woman, said "Here's to your health." Her eyes widened with horrific disapproval before glassing into frightened conciliation . . .

"Taxi driver?" she ventured.

"Yes ma'am."

A shudder overtook her but she came back hopeful:

"For—*him?*" Nodding toward Cartwright and then darkening. She was a picture of white propriety gone mad with itself and coming apart at the seams . . .

"Uh-huh."

She brightened, and darkened again.

I said "Don't worry."

She inhaled a gasp, as though caught in the act, and said "Drinking?" and shook her head to banish the thought.

I said "I'll see he gets home okay."

She started nodding with sickening kindliness, as though to allay any offense taken, and then glowered and then smiled and then shuddered, looked around.

I slapped Cartwright on the back: "C'mon, Sir."

He began to rouse himself and then sagged.

I slapped him again, a little harder. "C'mon Mr. Cartwright, they're waiting."

He pulled all there was of himself together, slid off the stool and stood, swaying. He was a tall guy. I took him under the arm. His companion registered a fluid series of smiles, apologies, and doomy forecasts as I led him to the door . . .

We emerged. I glanced to the right and saw three kids with sticks coming up the street. We took a few shuffling steps toward the cab, the kids got closer. Cartwright let out a disgusted moan and stopped in his tracks. The kids were laughing, pointing—

Cartwright's pants were around his ankles. Pale green boxer shorts. Someone hit a car horn as I stooped beside his naked white legs . . .

I got him into the cab, got an address out of him and got him back to his family. They were waiting on the porch.

The night got dark, and I forgot why I was out there. My life was like that old woman's face in the bar: a fluid series of contrasting emotions. I had a hundred for myself and the twelve-hour mark in sight. After a point the money didn't matter. I didn't need a hundred dollars; I needed a million.

For the moment a shot would do, so I stopped at a bar and drank a few whiskies and smoked a few cigarettes, and then I got back in the cab and rolled the window down and started to drive.

Whenever I got lit I wanted to get everyone into a room: my folks and some old girlfriends and some who could've been except for circumstance, and Ed and Al and Jimmy D and Dave, and maybe hold a seance and get the ghosts of the important dead on hand too—my grandmother Carrie and my Uncle Mike, Abraham Lincoln . . . Charley Patton, St. Augustine—and maybe all together we could shed or pool the personal darknesses enclosing each of us which're our only real possessions and hash things out into one moment of recognition and understanding and celebration and maybe come up with an answer and a roadmap for the days and years to come . . .

I hit the freeway.

I was hungry for the face of God or the Devil—either would do—and I was left alone with myself on just any old road . . .

DOWN BROADWAY AFTER MIDNIGHT

"God, look at this rain . . ."
     " . . ."
     [swish . . .]
"You want something?"
"Nah; nah."
     [slam.]

[click: slam.]
     "Okay."
     [shudder . . . swish . . .]
     "Goddamnit . . . she forgot the . . . fucking—"

[Lower Broadway rolls behind the rain . . . to the left, the world caves into blackness, tiny lights, and rising smoke . . . wish of tires on street, flashing construction barrels . . .]
     "What's up, man?"
     "Aah?"
     "Whatsa matter?"
     [Reaches Newports off the dash, gets one out, lights it— forearm on the wheel, squinting ahead through the rain, preoccupied . . .]
     "God damnit."
     "?"
     "—spilled coffee on my—fucking—"
     [Rustle of napkins from a paper bag . . . *wish* . . .]

"You want some coffee?"

"No."

"What's going on, man?"

"Aah, this fucking guy . . ."

". . ."

"This fucking custodian, out where my mother lives. This guy Artie, right? My old lady's—taking a shower the other day, right? Here this guy Artie's up on a ladder, right? Looking in the window. She screams, my old man goes out there . . . Guy says 'You don't like it move.' And—my old man ain't that sick, he coulda kicked the guy's ass, but he's—totally worried and nervous now about everything, and—You just can't do it, y'know? Ain't like when my old man was the terror of St. Clair—Now the guy *sue* ya, y'know?"

"Yeah."

"Anyway my mother works hard, she's in constant fear of being even one day late with the bills, y'know . . . She don't need this kinda aggravation, y'know . . ."

"Yeah"

". . ."

". . ."

"But this guy's been—y'know, making her feel uncomfortable about being there . . . He parks his fucking trailer, blocks my old man's car, he don't come to fix nothing; it's been going on a long time. Maybe he's tryna get 'em outa there, I don't know. I was over there one time I was gonna kick his ass—My mother: 'No don't go out there, cause any trouble,' y'know . . ."

"Yeah."

"So I guess I'll be forced to take care of the guy by other means, y'know."

"Like what?"

"Well I don't really wanna—get into that right now, uh . . . We'll see."

[*wish* . . . the black, the lights, the smoke rising . . . toward home . . .]

Half a bottle of velvet red and the rain hits the puddles like the sound spring creepers make. The Buick reels and swerves of its own accord and someone hits my flank with what sounds like a brick around Eighty-Ninth and Chester. Still, you gotta hand it to the guy, waiting out in the rain like that . . . A note in pen on a chunk of brown paper waiting under my door to tell me Sadie dropped by. Strange, how you can will a thing into happening and then not be there to witness the event. The day was absence itself. The sky got dark with cloud and then dark with night and the streets bristled with moisture as I watched from the high clear window of a friend, and then drove home. And now I'm back in the room.

WINDOWS DOWN

"When did you start with the trucks?"

"Nineteen seventy."

"How old were you?"

"Twenty. I just got out of the Army . . . just fought in Korea for two years—"

"*[laughter]—fought!*"

"There was a DMZ there, every—once in a while they'd throw a little shell across to let us know they were there, but— It was dangerous. My mother wrote me every day saying 'Get outa there before the fighting starts!'"

"*[laughter]*—What were you gonna do, run?"

"Yeah, she said 'Make a run for it! Head for Sweden or something.'"

"*Sweden?*"

"Yeah. But when I got out, after protecting your asses for two years— It was rough, y'know; I had post-Korean syndrome—I was spent!"

"*[laughter]*"

"I was totally—sexually spent. So I seen this ad in the paper: wrapping coins in the basement of the Federal Reserve Bank. Looked like a perfect low-key job for me, y'know: simple, no pressure . . . So they gave me an aptitude test, I told 'em I'm a veteran, I got the job. Told Dad, y'know; 'Great: job at the bank . . . ' They stick me in the basement with a pile of coin-wrappers and this change machine, where the coins pop out—I'm down there three days: I loved it! Then the third day the boss comes down, he says 'We have the results of your test: we're moving you up to the fiscal department!' Says I gotta start wearing a suit to work . . . I had a whole passel of leisure suits, and—"

"You had a what?"

"A *passel* of leisure suits, so—y'know: dress-wise I was ready to go, man . . ."

"*[laughter]* "

"No: leisure suits were good back then: I had like five of 'em, man: brown—dark brown, light brown . . . And I had a buncha flowered shirts that went perfectly with the things. Anyway he puts me at a desk with a phone—The fiscal department: sixth floor, I'll never forget. Here, it's the agency where they take care of all the money matters for the bank: big-time stuff! And this asshole that's supposed to be teaching me— he's leaving like in a week? he don't give a fuck if I learn or not, y'know? so he basically ignored me . . . And I'm supposed to be watching him; he's making out checks—ledgers, invoices . . . And all these people're *staring* at this—new guy in the office, you feel like a jerk anyway . . . and this guy quit— I had no idea what the fuck I was supposed to do: absolutely no idea. I got a rubber stamp and a big checkbook, the phone's ringing—I'm approving—y'know—six million dollars for the Sohio Corporation, uh—"

"What *were* you supposed to be doing?"

"I just—signed checks! I signed a bunch of 'em, I don't know . . . I'm sure there's some rich people in Cleveland walking around now 'cause of me. Fucking lunchtime—twenty years old: *bam*—right across the street to Moriarty's Bar. Didn't even drink then, right? I'm drinking triples for lunch, just so I could feel—more like a man, or—get up enough courage to face the afternoon . . ."

"Yeah."

"And I tried a couple times to ask the boss—y'know—what

the fuck I— It was insane. The boss kept coming down, telling me what a good job I'm doing, I'm approving this, refusing that: millions of dollars, coming across my desk every day! I was terrified they're gonna find out about me and throw me in the fucking pen! I go home at night I'm thinking—I'm gonna put Cleveland out of business! All I wanted was a simple job wrapping pennies in the basement, make my four dollars an hour and be—happy; no pressure—Not be up in the fucking *steaming*—y'know, *smelting*-pot upstairs!"

"*[laughter]*"

"Finally—I was there about two weeks; if I'da stayed another week I'da bankrupted the place. I went to the boss and told him I was quitting. He couldn't believe it. I said 'My mother's real sick, I got personal problems at home, but I appreciate the fact you gave me this job in the fiscal department . . . insteada wrapping nickels with the blacks which I wanted to do in the first place, you dumb fuck—thanks for ruining my career . . .' And I never went back."

"Then what happened?"

"Then I made the biggest error of my life: I went to Coca-Cola. They hired me right on the spot."

"And that got you into the Union?"

"Yeah. But I lost that job. I was so naive at the time—This how stupid I was: there was a safe in the truck, but the top was broke—and I went to fill a Coke machine, I had like four hundred dollars in change . . . and I didn't lock the door of the truck. Come out, somebody took the money. I told my old man, and to this day he thinks I took it. They fired me. I come in there, I go 'I got robbed.' Y'know, and everybody does that—Least once a year you rob yourself. I was too stupid to rob myself!"

"Yeah."

"Then I went to Suncrest. Maury Bloom. Always gives you a piece of fruit when you walk in his office. He handed me a pear, says 'How long you been in the Union?', I says 'Couple years.' He handed me a list—I swear to God, Danny: three hundred ten, plus forty-two, plus thirty-five—'Add this.' I added it, he says 'Alright, you're hired.' That was how I got the job! Delivering sixteen-ouncers on Harvard and Union. The fuckers all put their shit in the basement. You gotta go down these trap doors—It was a bitch. But you could steal the empties."

"How?"

"You take out twelve cases of empties, give him credit for ten on his bill. And that's only small-time: that's only two cases."

"So then you go to Pick 'n Pay—"

"Yeah, then you get twenty, *thirty*: you're talking sixty dollars! These guys ripped off the supermarkets for months—years! They got boats, they got homes! In the twenty years I been in the Union I know six guys that got caught, stealing. And they all got fired and they all got better jobs. As rewards. Within two weeks they had a better job at another company. It's a good reference to steal when you're a Teamster: it shows that you're a *Teamster*."

"Pull over here man; let's get a sandwich."

Springboard! *(one, two—one, two, three, four:) Bang!*

Spun like sparks and spunk like joy: extend and flourish—readysetgo and the blocks're flashing past/ holding tight and riding high: dip and rise and bounce and jiggle holding steady the electric wire won't let you go: deeper and faster as the layers unfold and you're muttering a steady monologue to let you know you're still there . . . I was riding that taxi hard on the night through the tender corridors of May with the windows down and the lilac blowing in: I saw some girls walking in the easy final grace of spring and threw an astral lasso around 'em . . .

I don't know about god or guardian angels, but maybe we've each of us got a saxophone blowing in the night, if only we can hear it . . .

Wooster called my name and handed me a brand-new Chevy. I gassed her up and banged up the ramp into town.

Took a Detroit Two call: Twenty-Fifth and Bridge—a Mr. Grant, at Grant's Bar-B-Q.

I pulled up and hit the horn. The place was a doorway with a hand-painted sign.

Mr. Grant came out on crutches. He was an old guy in a shake-and-bake suit. I got out and held the door for him. I held his crutches while he grabbed hold of the roof and, with a kind of swing, dropped himself inside, apologizing for time and what it does . . .

He said "I surprised you come so quick! Last time I call a cab I waited more'n two hour and that cab still ain't come."

"Well I was right nearby."

"Yeah! But lotta these drivers don't come around here! All they want is that airport money! What's your name, Driver?"

"My name's Danny."

"My name Frank."

"Okay," I said, waiting in the mirror.

"I surprised to see you Dan! This trip be worth your while. We ain't going to no grocery store!"

I laughed, the cab still idling.

"Some of these drivers think people can't afford to pay no money! This a special day, be worth it."

"Where we going?"

"We going up on One-Sixteen and Buckeye. And back. You know how to get to One-Sixteen and Buckeye, Dan?"

I scammed a U-turn, broke through market traffic, beat a couple lights and floated the bridge—He was saying "I could tell I'm in good hands! Lotta these drivers try to run you around—Hey Dan: you better hit that meter!"

I did so.

"How long you been driving a cab, Dan?"

"'Bout a year."

"You like it?"

"Yeah, I like it."

"Good. Got to be careful though—These people crazy out here. You carry a gun?"

"Naw."

"Naw . . . you a youngblood! Take carea youself. I bet you ready to duke it out, though."

"I ain't had any trouble."

"Naw, but you might though. Watch out!"

I laughed.

He said "I bet the girls is crazy for you. Bet you gotta keep 'em away with a stick!"

If this guy had a tattoo it must've said YES. He seemed to be saying Yes, Yes, and YES!

"What're we looking for, Mr. Grant?"

"Nephew told me it's a white house up there sell arthritis medicine—Up on One-Sixteen. One of my customers told me too. I ain't even tell my doctor about it. He just tell me not to go, want that money himself."

"What kinda medicine?"

"I don't even know. Might be a cream, I think. Or a powder. Customer told me he take it with a bath, take away the pain. He got arthritis in his shoulders, say he feel like he could fly. Say it make me walk again. I done tried everything else—that epsom salts and copper and Chinese massage girls and all these here pills the doctor give me and don't none of it do me no good.

171

All the doctor do is take my money—Man tell me I get this medicine and follow every instruction I'm gon' walk again, I got no choice but to give it a try . . . This my last hope!"

A Hundred Sixteenth and Buckeye was a place full of life that had nothing to do with me or mine. We found a white house and I pulled into the drive. I walked up to knock at the side door.

A women answered. Pretty. Suspicious, but unafraid.

I said "I'm driving a cab. I got a guy wants to buy some arthritis medicine."

She glanced through the screendoor down the drive and then pushed her way out, past me. She carried confidence to the window Mr. Grant was rolling down. I leaned on the hood, overhearing.

She asked of his symptoms, and, trusting her, he gave her personal information. Fifty dollars was mentioned. I felt him fumbling ahead of himself and ahead of any wariness the years had given him: handing money out the window—anticipated and separated in full. I glanced and saw her folding the bills up small, walking up the drive . . .

She returned with a brown bag—instructing him carefully on the use of its contents: a hot bath, and no dinner—maybe a glass of wine, or two—but no more than two—and a candle might help . . . Mr. Grant was nodding, repeating her phrases—quickly, afraid to take up too much of her time . . .

She walked by again, nodding once to let me know I could take him back to his world and return to mine. I slipped back into the cab and let it roll down the drive . . .

I said "That a sharkskin suit?"

"Sharkskin, that's right. Only one I got left. Don't make 'em no more. One time I had three of these suits: one in grey, this here one in green, and one in black. Never wear through—last forever. Lost the other two in a flood. Lost all my clothes. Lost everything. All I had left was this suit: so happen I was wearing it at the time. You treat 'em right they keep on goin'. That's why they stop making 'em."

Cutting across Fifty-Fifth, I stopped to pick him up five gallons of kerosene. And then sped him back to Twenty-Fifth Street, stopping again at the market to run in and pick him out a few pounds of chicken.

The trip had taken just over an hour.

He handed me the twenty-five-dollar fare plus ten.

"Twenty-five's plenty," I said, turning to hand him back the ten.

"Aw no," he was saying, gathering himself up. "This my day. I got what I need . . ."

I got out and walked around to open the door for him.

I wanted to say good luck, but didn't.

"Stop by and see me," he said.

"I'll do that."

AGAIN, IN THE POOL . . .

Duke's putting out a cigarette—resolutely disgusted—indignant with the final poison coils of unnecessary smoke it gives off . . . He coughs—shakes his head . . . I offer him a fresh one.

"FUCK *YOU*," he says. "I SWEAR ON MY *LIFE* I AIN'T GONNA SMOKE ANOTHER CIGARETTE FOR TEN MINUTES AT *LEAST*. Even if it takes me a lifetime."

"Oh c'mon, it's only ten-thirty, you can't quit now. Endeavor to persevere."

"I dunno."

"Empty your ashtray first. Start fresh."

He sits a second. Then pulls the tray out, opens the door, empties the ashtray on the ground. Replaces it in the dashboard.

He sits another second . . . exhales, preparing for the trillionth round . . .

"Wow," he says. "That's better than jogging. Got a cigarette?"

"That's the spirit."

He takes one from me, and I light us up.

REALITY IS A SLIPPERY BUSINESS

I stepped outa the bar and the night squealed and roared like a truck. Or waitaminute—maybe it *was* a truck, squeezing to a stop . . . or maybe the circus went past/ the light went through a series of quick subtle variations, shedding itself like snakeskin. Nobody noticed but me. The street came alive with the sounds of night wherever I turned my head, with the fires of life wherever I cast my glance: the pavement arched itself into rolling hills with great possibilities beyond each rise; I decided I was enjoying myself already. This lifetime was good for about a night, I figured . . . Jupiter came out brighter than the rest, and I beat it, down to—

Three o'clock in the afternoon Ed calls.

"—I'm on West Forty-Seventh, I came over to see Angie, she ain't home. I can't get this fucking car started—all these fucking hillbillies staring at me. They got nothing better to do than sit on their fucking porches all day, I'm out here like an asshole, fucking around under the hood—"

"Where are you?"

"I'm surrounded by killers and drug addicts—Time I get back to the car there'll be nothing left of the fucker. I just got the fucking thing back from Roy, I gave him a hundred bucks he said he fixed the fucking thing. I been calling you all afternoon, I called everyone, no one's home—"

"Whoa, whoa. Where you at, right now?"

"I'm at some hillbilly bar, I almost got in three fights already, I been drinking triples all afternoon. I been here since twelve o'clock; where the fuck *you* been?"

"What bar you at?"

"—I dunno, the fucking—Some fucking bar on Lorain. Everybody's staring at me, I'm gonna kill one of these motherfuckers in about a minute—"

"What's the name of the bar? You're around Forty-Seventh and Lorain, right?"

"*(—Yeah fuck you: I'm on the fucking phone here, you got something to say?)* . . . cocksucker . . . Yeah. Where you at home?"

"Yeah, you just called me here. Wake up, man. Where you,

176

at the Wheel?"

"I'm at the—fucking—John's Bar or something . . . On the right, as you're coming up Lorain."

"I'll find it. Just hang on. Don't start no shit with nobody."

I found Fat John's a couple blocks past the Hot Dog Inn. Ed was giving the barmaid a hard time. Only one other guy in the place.

"About fucking time," he said. He was on a roll.

I got us a couple shots of Windsor and we drank them.

I put a five-dollar tip on the bar and said "Let's go see the car."

"Yeah let's get outa this shithole . . ."

I pull nose-to-nose with the Pontiac, we get the hoods up . . . no sign of life from Angie's. A few people on porches down the street, but the scene is incidental and random, nothing like how Ed sees it, and as we're jerking cables and jarring the battery and reaching down into the tangled heart of the old Pontiac, I realize that his anger and embarrassment are all to do with Angie. We coax a flutter from the starter and give the Pontiac a jump; she resigns herself to life again . . .

Then we're taking the cables off and slamming hoods, and here comes Angie from behind the house with a polka-dot babushka and bright orange pants tucked into spray-painted gold platform boots . . . a big carpetbag slung from her shoulder, and deeply involved in some rippling philosophical or ontological or mathematical but probably closer to pathological discussion with herself . . . or maybe she's just listening to the sound of her blood— Walks right past us adjusting the bag until Ed says "Angie!" and she stops to face us—

"Hi," she says on cue. "Can you give me a ride?"

We took the Pontiac; now it was running we didn't want to shut it off. Angie's original destination was forgotten. Heading up Lorain, she spots a red Malibu carrying six Puerto Ricans and says "That's my car!"

"Angie—"

"That's my car! They stole my car! Chase them!"

"You sure?"

"That's it! That's my car—It was red!"

Ed skillfully manages to let them get away from us and I'm going "Aah, shit, they're gone . . . We'll get 'em later."

Ed says "Angie, you hungry?"

Half an hour later we're parked on Walton Avenue, having finished a few hamburgers and coffees, and Angie's in the middle with hers untouched, submerged in tranquil currents of her own . . . Ed makes a few attempts at conversation, gets no response.

And then she bobs to the surface, saying "YESTERDAY I WAS HITCHHIKING AND THIS MAN PICKED ME UP AND SAID HE'D GIVE ME FIFTY DOLLARS FOR A BLOWJOB—SO I GAVE HIM A BLOWJOB AND HE TOLD ME TO GET OUT OF THE CAR AND WAIT FOR HIM WHILE HE WENT TO GET THE FIFTY DOLLARS. I WAITED FOR TWO HOURS. I HOPE I SEE HIM TO-DAY BECAUSE I NEED THE MONEY . . ."

I didn't bother looking at Ed, just lit a cigarette, and he carefully put the car in drive and pulled away from the curb, drove back to Angie's place . . .

In front of her house, I looked over in an inevitable way as he reached his money out of his pocket and separated two dollars from his last ten and asked Angie if she needed a few bucks, and in response to her utter lack of response handed her the eight, which she took without a word, glancing at it as an afterthought, stuffing it into her bag as I opened the door . . .

"BYE!" she said.

IN ED'S KITCHEN . . .

It's dark outside. Ed's pacing the kitchen . . . organizing personal effects . . .

"You going down the hall tomorrow?"

"No, I'm busy tomorrow."

He's got his back to me.

"Oh yeah?"

Beyond the screendoor, stars chirp.

"What're you doing?"

"Tomorrow's May thirty-first," he says. "I'll be drunk tomorrow."

". . . Why's that?"

"Thirty-first of May every year, I get drunk."

". . ."

"That's the day Mitty died, thirty-first of May."

". . ."

"I think about her that one day and then I try to forget about her the rest of the year."

In his kitchen, next afternoon . . . a fifth of Windsor on the sink . . . half the whiskey gone. Open shoebox on the table. The box contains papers and old snapshots.

He flips me a photo of a soldier in summer dress, saluting from an empty lot. Below the cap's peak, he's anonymous as any soldier. Clean-shaven, though around the mouth can be seen the ghost of who Ed is now . . .

"How old're you?"

"Eighteen years old."

"Handsome."

"The nation slept peacefully."

He hands me another of himself, in white T-shirt . . . trousers tucked into combat boots—he's mopping a hall, watching himself in the camera . . .

"I got into a fight with a hillbilly. I hit him in the head and broke my hand. Went to the doctor and told him I slipped on the stairs. I don't think he believed me, but I ended up getting twenty-eight dollars a month for it—"

"For what?"

"Disability. I got twenty-eight dollars a month for like five years after that—even when I was home, and then they cut it off. So my old man tells me to go down the Federal Building and appeal the fucking thing—He says 'Look at Deacon Joe. Twisted his knee in an army softball game—in Missouri: he's been getting forty bucks a month since World War Two!' So I said Fuck it, if Deacon Joe can get it— Go down the Federal Building, I got my story all together in my head—You get an interview with an appeals officer, whatever—He was a captain. And I go in the room, he's behind the desk, tape recorder on the desk . . . So he's—y'know, 'What's the problem?' I told him they cut my disability, and—y'know, I'm tryna keep my story straight and build this up like it's a major thing—I'm going 'You don't know what it's like! My hand swells up whenever it rains, I can tell *time* with the bones clicking in place, y'know—It hurts!' He says 'Can you open and close it?' I said 'Yeah, but it hurts all the time—It hurts right now!' I told him I do heavy work, I said 'I lift cases of pop, and all day long the thing's—y'know, I can hardly work, I can hardly jack off—You don't know what it's like!' And he's sitting there, he's listening . . . Waits for me to finish and then he puts his arms on the desk, he's got a hook on each arm."

"Aww, wow . . ."

"I said 'Well, thanks for your time' and got the fuck outa there. And I'm sure the whole thing was a setup, but even still . . . I felt like a total jackass. The whole thing's my old man's idea in the first place, him and his fucking Deacon Joe . . . But what a fucking shock. I was taken aback for weeks, after that . . ."

He unfolds some yellow papers . . . glances over them. "Fucking receipts from the funeral home . . ." Folds them and flips them back into the box.

"Who paid for the funeral?"

"I paid for most of—Vince gave me five hundred I think, I paid for the rest. I paid 'em in installments . . . I think I gave 'em five hundred down which I hadda borrow . . . she didn't have no insurance . . . Flowers cost like two hundred, the whole thing cost like two thousand. And I: y'know, I didn't know noth—I— Where do you begin? Lucky this Old Man Vince helped me with all that shit, 'cause . . . Y'know, I called the funeral home, Komorowski's? 'cause he suggested it, in the neighborhood . . . Vince kinda helped me there, with the arrangements . . . But the people were real nice, whole thing went off without a hitch, I mean . . . Her family didn't like me at all . . . y'know . . . There were no major arguments . . ."

"Where's she at?"

"She down in uh . . . Highland View Cemetery, by Thistledown—I used to go out there on holidays and put flowers on her grave; now—as years go by I kinda . . . don't go out there too much. Every once in a while I go, just—y'know, clean off the stone . . . bullshit with her for a few minutes . . ."

"You wanna go for a ride?"

"Yeah, uh . . . Yeah alright."

"Yeah, let's go get a few drinks."

Out on the sidewalk. There was a moment of unspoken decision . . . his car or mine . . . he'd already been drinking. He'd never looked more solid to me.

He drives a car like a man used to driving a truck: in full command, and lights a Newport, just another ornament. Rolling over the tracks:

"How'd you meet Mitty?"

"I met her in a bar."

"Where? On Broadway, or—"

"Yeah; yeah . . . She had a lotta friends there, and she thought I was the biggest asshole in the world. And then one day we just went home together and—She stayed with me for five years after—Just come home with me—We didn't particularly—care for one another that much, y'know, really—"

"Yeah. Where was her family?"

"Her family lived in PA: Washington, Pennsylvania. That's all she talked about all the time: Washington, Pennsylvania."

The market's open today . . . cars parked and double-parked . . . people taking care of their needs, and the needs of their families. We float past.

He says "Whattaya wanna, go up to Myron's or something?"

"Sure."

"Alright, let's—take a ride up Lorain first, I wanna check on my precincts here."

"I gave her a hard time; I—She gave me a hard time, I gave her a hard time. From the beginning!"

"Why, because she was drinking?"

"She was drinking I was gambling—She drank a *real* real lot, I mean a *real* lot."

"Was she different when she drank?"

"Aw, she just—Jekyll and Hyde, I mean there—She's nicest person in the world when she was sober, y'know, she'd cook dinner, house be nice, everything—y'know, we go the show—But once she had a couple drinks in her, she just keep going, and then she was mean, nasty—"

"Why'd she drink so much?"

"I dun—She drank long before I knew her . . . When I went to Vegas one time by myself—First night I called her . . . She's going 'Please Ed—please come home, I'm sick, I feel real bad I miss you—I—*Please* come,' y'know. Killed my whole vacation, I was there four days, worried about her . . . Then, soon as I got home we got in a big violent fight, she left anyway, it—It was—Hundreds of stories like that . . . "

In Myron's Bar, a few people there, but not really . . . just like we're not, for them. Everybody's got the place to himself. Ed's got a double Windsor in a waterglass; I do too.

He says "I told you about Big Ted though, right?"

"I dunno . . . "

"Alright, I figured if she got a job—doing something, it would keep her busy, she wouldn't drink so much. So what do I do, I find her a job in a fucking bar."

"*[laughter]* "

183

"Right? But it was a neighborhood Polack bar—"

"Where?"

"It was around the Fleet area. But I shoulda known, y'know with the booze there and—guys were gonna flirt with her, and—There's no way she could resist that . . . "

"Yeah."

"And then every now and then I'd call there she'd be drunk behind the bar, I'd go '*Why* you doing this?' Course now I realize What the fuck? I know she's gonna do it, it was stupid. Like I was some saint or something. And she'd go 'Well, I'm having a good time,' or whatever and—"

"She was older than you, right?"

"Yeah, she's about—eight years older. Not that she'd go home with anybody, but if somebody offered her some drinks, she'd—go over their house, that's for sure . . ."

"She'd go where the bottle was."

"Yeah. I called there one time, to go pick her up, and—she was drunk, right? Now I'm no fucking toughguy, by any means, but I was *really* jealous of her, y'know . . . and I'm saying 'I'll pick you up in half an hour,' and she goes 'Waal . . . I'm going home with Ted.' And I hear this guy in the background say 'Tell the asshole to hang up the phone.' I said 'Who was that?' She goes 'That was Ted.' I said 'Is he talking about me?' She goes 'Ah I dunno, I guess so—' I said 'Put him on the phone.' She goes 'Naw no no no . . . ' He's—'Aah, hang up on the asshole!' Y'know, it's like two in the morning she's drunk, I'm supposed to pick her up, I go What is this? I was *fuming*, man. I said That's it, I'm gonna fucking kill somebody; this is enough of this. So I go down there, and it's her and these two other guys and Ted's in there. As he's known as *Big* Ted, right?"

"*[laughter]* "

"This fucking guy—No exaggeration Danny, was a *good* six-five, and a good three hundred, maybe three-fifty. This guy was a monster: I mean a *monster*. He was big. But I was drunk and pissed off, and I walk in there—I go 'Who the fuck's talking

to me on the phone telling me I'm a fucking asshole?' He goes
'I did.' I go 'Mitty, is this the guy that's fucking with—wants
you to go home with him?' She goes 'Waal I—I dunno—' I
go 'That's my girlfriend.' He goes 'Oh.' I says 'You motherfucker—You come outside, I'm gonna fucking kill you.' I said
'I don't care what it takes—I'm gonna kill you, one way or the
other.'

"This guy coulda killed me in a fucking split second, y'know?
I really gave it to him, and the guy backed down, y'know? I was
pushing him hard. Finally she was closing up—he walked outside, I said 'I'll be out there in a minute you motherfucker—' I
got outside the guy was gone.

"The next day we go out . . . We go to this fucking restaurant we stop in all the time. So I'm sitting there having a coffee, she's sitting across from me . . . Here comes some fucking
guy walks in. Sits next to me. This guy's got arms like this: big
tattoo, y'know . . . I go to Mitty, I go '(Mitty—*look* at this *big*
mother*fucker* sitting *next* to me here.)' She goes 'Y'know who
that is?' I go 'Who?' 'That's Big Ted.' I go 'Big Ted? I—You
gotta be shitting me!' I looked at him, he just kinda nodded,
didn't say nothing to me I didn't say nothing to him . . . I go
Holy fuck . . .''

"*[laughter]*"
We decide we need another shot, after a close call like that.

"Another time this old guy—kind of an old toughguy, broken nose, looked like a little miniature Joe Palooka—Liked
Mitty a real lot. He never fucked her, never wanted to go with
her, just—like to be with her 'cause he was a lonely old man.
But he'd get her drunk all the fucking time; he'd see her in a bar
and he'd buy her all the booze she wanted. His name was Jim.
And I hated the sonofabi—I'd call every bar on Fleet, looking
for her—Here she'd be at the bar, I go 'Who you with?', she go
'Well Jim's here . . . ' 'That motherfucker! Put him on the phone!'
And she'd put him on, and he didn't know who I was, y'know?
Say 'Jim this is Ed. I'm gonna kill you motherfucker!'—he'd

hang up the phone on me. Man I'd get in that fucking car I'd run down there he'd be gone.

"One day at this Village Cafe I caught him. I searched every bar on the East Side: every bar, I'm walking in the snow . . . Finally I found her with Jim. I go 'Jim you sonofabitch,' I says, 'I told you about giving her fucking booze . . . when you get outside I'm gonna break your head open.' *I'm seventy years old I got a bad heart! You better stay away from me, I'll call the fucking police!'* I said 'I don't give a fuck, Jim; I had enough of you.'

"So I go outside, wait in the car—And she wouldn't come out either, she *wouldn't* come out. I tell her 'Come with me,' she's with Jim. That old man come sneaking outa the bar . . . I'm across the street in the car. Took the fucking car and floored it across the street, went right up on the sidewalk and *pinned* him against the fucking wall—"

"What?"

"I stopped like inches short and he was *frozen*—I got him pinned against the building, I said 'Jim you motherfucker . . . You had it, man.' *'Please please—I'm getting a heart attack!'* A few people start coming outa the bar . . . Finally I let him go."

"Another round, here."

"One time we was living on Union, there's this guy just got outa the pen that liked Mitty. Real fucking—bastard, real weasel. He used to hang around the bar, and I'd be working, he'd try to pick her up alla time. And I said 'Stay the fuck *away* from her,' y'know? And he starts coming over the house, right?—when I'm not home, knocking on the door wants to go out with her. So she told me about this. So one day I stayed home from work and the fucker—bigger than shit, knocking on the door, y'know? She answered the door, he said 'Hey, let's go have a drink.' Man I whipped that door open I said '*You* motherfucker I *told* you don't ever come over—' So I grabbed him by his shirt, y'know? But I turned my back, say something to Mitty—And here there was a baseball bat in the hallway, right?

186

I *just* fucking ducked, for some reason—He swung that bat—
right at my fucking head. Hits the *wall,* y'know, put a big fucking
hole in the wall—"

"Woulda killed ya."

"Woulda killed me. I knocked him down the steps—he
rolled all the way to the bottom . . . He got up and I chased
that fucker for five blocks . . . finally I gave up, I couldn't catch
him."

"Can I have a water?"

It was darker in the Avenue Bar.

"Did she die in the hospital?"

"She died in the hospital, yeah . . . I was with her every day
after work, y'know; she was really in bad shape then . . . her
liver was gone . . . She couldn't talk to me, she was in a coma
for like a month . . . so I just go there and y'know—talk to her
. . . And then one day I'm running late on my route—I get tied
up in traffic . . . Time I check in and get outa there it's seven
o'clock . . . Get to the hospital—Here the nurse is making up
her bed, taking flowers outa there . . . I said 'Nurse? Where's
Mitty?' 'Oh, she passed away.'"

" . . ."

"So this Old Man Vince, that liked her a real lot, old man
lived next door— He'd take her to the store, watch out for her
in the bars . . . He was in love with her; he really was in love
with her, y'know? He was at the hospital every day too. And I
said 'Vince,' y'know, 'She can't be dead—' Even though I knew
she was dead. Y'know and Vince closed her eyes and—"

" . . ."

"And—boy, I left there with a bad attitude, I said You heart-
less *bastards,* y'know? And then Vince told me, he says 'Hey,
they see—hundred people die a week, here.'"

"Yeah."

"And . . . two days later we went to the funeral, with the
procession? I was in the car by myself, I think— And, com-

ing the other way was these kids: they were graduating, it was the end of May . . . And they had all these pom poms on their cars, and blowing the horn, y'know . . . And we sat at this light, I remember sitting at this light . . . And these kids are blowing their horns, about twenty cars—yelling out the windows— y'know— 'Seniors!' y'know: 'Seventy—' whatever the year was . . . And I'm thinking to my—I said Here's—Isn't it funny how life is, here Mitty's dead, y'know we're going to bury her now and here's these kids, their life's just beginning, y'know? And we're here and they're there, on the other side of the street. And they're cheering 'Heeeyy,' y'know: 'Look at me! I'm— Senior!' And—that's— Kinda touched me, y'know? I said Jesus Christ—Life is so fucked up, y'know?"

Another bar . . . Clark Avenue now, and that much deeper into the day. We shoot a game of pool; he beats me easy. I drop some quarters into the juke.

"Was there a time before she went in that you knew how sick she was?"

"We used to have violent arguments, I'd say 'If you don't get some help you're gonna die.' I said 'You're sick.' Her eyes were getting yellow, I know she had jaundice, because her liver was shutting down. She's been to the hospital twenty times, I said 'You gotta go back, you gotta quit. You're gonna die.' And finally—She realized that she was in bad shape, y'know; she didn't wanna go to the hospital 'cause she knew—that was it. It was like forty-five days before she died and she was—First time I ever seen her scared . . .

"Y'know—but, funny part was she went there—And I didn't realize it was that bad until she went into a coma, and— Her last couple days that she was awake we're *arguing*—in the hospital room! Right? She's dying—I'm arguing with her!"

"About what?"

"Just about anything, just arguing. And then the next day she goes into a coma, I can't even say—'Hey I'm sorry, I'm sorry we argued—' Nothing. There's thirty days of silence then."

OY, JESUS . . . BACK IN THE POOL . . .

Duke slips into the back of the cab, I ask him how it's going.

"Good, man. I set a new record for smokes tonight. One trillion."

"Good work. Care for another?"

"Yeah; I just got a breath of fresh air. I didn't like it, didn't agree with me."

I light it for him.

"Thanks. Wow . . . I'd be afraid to even go *near* a doctor's office . . ."

"Why?"

He laughs.

"Listen," I tell him. "Someone told me just the other day—this chick told me her friend's aunt—a smoker for years: a *heavy* smoker—She went for a chest X-ray, doctor said her lungs're still pink."

". . . *Who* was this?"

"Oh I dunno. Somebody's best friend's aunt. But we can coast on that for a while. I'm sure by then there'll be new evidence."

"What're you, working for R.J. Reynolds or what? How long you been smoking, Danny?"

"I didn't start till I was twenty-one. Never touched a cigarette till I was twenty-one. And this after standing up to heavy pressure to *start* smoking all through school, from peers—my parents—"

"Teachers—"

"Yeah: my guidance counselor told me I'd be a smoker—"

"In the yearbook, voted Most Likely to Smoke—"

"Yeah—all that shit. But I was waiting to make my own decision. And then—this just a couple years ago—I'm sitting in a restaurant eating breakfast with a friend and his girlfriend—I remember it was a Tuesday. And uh . . . She offered me a cigarette, I said 'No thanks, I don't smoke.' She said 'Really? You *look* like a smoker.' I said 'I do? Hold on a minute.' Went to the machine, bought a pack of Luckies and I been smoking ever since."

"Good thing you caught that in time."

"Yeah! Yeah . . ."

" . . . "

" . . . "

He said "It's like you'd always known there was something missing, but you couldn't put your finger on it."

"That's right; exactly."

"Yeah," he said. "But everything's better now, right?"

"Aw, absolutely."

My last ride took me way out past the airport, and I headed back in driving eighty miles an hour feeling every curve and sway in the road. The moon rode the whole way with me—a bright late moon like a secret promise—with a tape of Elvis singing about a blue moon and a mystery train, Scotty Moore sitting on a fence and lazily roping wild things, and then the live-wire wide-open sound of Gene Vincent—Cliff Gallup's million-tripping guitar spun out of the momentum of night, and I felt my heart stretching at the mast, so I rolled down the window and let the night wind tear through the car and howled along to the mean spare sound of the Burnettes going *whack! whack! whack!* coming untucked and apart at the seams . . . The night was wild and wide and it lay open before me: the only thing missing was a girl. I took her home.

It was a windy day, and so bright the wind had a shine to it. I heard later there'd been tornados and flooding in the southern part of the state, but for me it was just getting on toward evening on a hell of a windy day: I was downtown in the cab after the offices had closed, a few people straying out and clinging to lampposts—hats and skirts and hair flying . . .

That afternoon I'd been wondering how to take better advantage of this job: the cash and free time inbetween—I was thinking I should take a trip, or try to do some writing. It was a rare thing to have gained a moment's perspective, and I was savoring a kind of buoyant bird's-eye view of the options the cab job afforded me. I picked up an old woman at the Bond Court Hotel. She worked in the kitchen there, and she was going home.

I pulled onto Lakeside, into that blank white classical part of downtown where judgments are made. The front passenger window was open. The wind blew in and stirred up some vouchers on the seat: I looked over and grabbed for them and *WHUMP!*

I'd run into the car ahead of me.

The guy got out—he'd been waiting at a light: a shiny brown Park Avenue, his father's car, he said. I'd busted one of his taillights. He wasn't angry because he knew it was my fault and it was Yellow Cab and it'd all be straightened out with change left over . . . Pretty soon the woman in back wised up and started saying she'd bumped her head on the headrest of the front seat and maybe we better call an ambulance to get it checked out, just in case.

I made the proper calls and waited in the cab in the bright wind until Mr. Cohen from the claims department showed up in the company's black Impala.

He was clear and serious and polite . . . he took care of whatever diplomacy was needed there, and then drove me down to the garage and they towed the cab back in, for some reason . . . insurance purposes, I guess . . .

No one was there but Cleetus, the sun getting a little lower toward evening—just like the end of the story. Which it was; that was the end of that job.

I drove up the hill as the wind was dying down. Ed wasn't home.

Around seven-thirty I walked to Lincoln Park. Some kids had a softball game going. I sat on a bench near their third-base line and watched. The grass of the park was striped by the long shadows of trees . . . Technicolor.

I'd been sitting there quite a while before I noticed I wasn't watching the game at all.

I was fully awake in bed before I remembered that the world was wide again . . .

This town was just a town, in a landscape that spread away in all directions—big slabs of surface miles in the morning sun . . . I decided to go to the Greeks, to consider my position.

Walking up Fairfield, I felt different in the world. I recalled my old man telling me he'd been classed as a malingerer in the service. The word had an exciting ring for me. Like a new profession. And I remembered a picture in a photo album: an album my grandmother had kept. In the white borders of the photos she'd written the subjects' names . . . to keep them from slipping into the shadows of the black-and-white past. There was a shot of my father as a young man—out of focus, as though the camera had been jarred—with an arm around a buddy . . . a sunlit morning in the steel mills . . . The inadvertent joke of her caption read *Ray, when working.*

I drew a certain feeling of strength from this . . . of precedence. Of others, whose respect for the work ethic was tempered by a more sensible conception of time, and reserved for people who took work more seriously than they did. For those who were working, in other words.

The Greeks was almost empty; I took a window seat.

George Poulous was in the corner, cheating at solitaire.

"How you doing, George?"

"I've had a headache for three years," he said.

Mihale set coffee and ice water. I lit my first official cigarette as a bum. I gazed out the window . . . no particular place to go . . .

While I was with Marie I was always thinking in future memories of San Antonio and Lake Pontchartrain . . . endless telephone poles and Colorado mountain-town rooming houses . . . witchy women and desert moons . . . the flash of Reno and scrapes in Mexico border towns and East St. Louis and who knows what the hell else. I kept her living under a nervous dawn while I dreamed cozily of freedom and the strange scars it would bring—I wanted to live like they do in songs, and since I'd been free of her I'd done nothing but listen to songs—other people's songs . . . I guess having a dream for three years is better than having a headache for three years, but the end result's the same: you're at a table in the morning cheating at solitaire.

I decided I needed some sympathy after my recent trauma—a little indignation. I finished the coffee and went to see Ed.

He's in an up mood.

Lights a cigarette: "Angelface called me just now."

"Angelface?"

"Angie. She still got that matchbook with my number."

"I lost the cab job, man."

"I've lost fifty jobs. Anyway I's gonna take a ride over there: you wanna go?"

I laughed. "Okay."

He drove. I watched the market roll past . . . the near West Side . . . I felt like a tourist.

We managed to pry Angie like a barnacle away from the rock of whatever multifaceted moment she was involved in, got some food and parked by the river. Sunlight fell with democratic evenness. Bags rustled.

I got out of the car and walked to the edge, threw a stick into the brown water and watched it bob to the surface, float . . . I looked up and down the river . . .

Back in the car, Angie was rattling off the details of last night, staring straight ahead as though she wasn't used to reading from cue cards:

"I was practicing guitar and I heard pounding and then two men I've never seen before were in my apartment shouting at me, and I told them to get out of my apartment! And they started chasing me and trying to grab me but I got away—And I didn't have any clothes on, but I climbed out the window and they kept trying to pull me back, but I started screaming and I got onto the porch and the woman next door saw me and she started yelling at the men. She told them she was gonna call the police. I stayed on the porch, and when I went inside they were gone—but they broke the lock on my door, and now I have to fix it. Do you have a drill?"

Meanwhile Ed and I are going "What?" "What was that?" "You mean they—" "This was last night?" "Are you sure?" "*What?*"

When she'd finished and gone back to her milkshake there was a stupefied moment, and then I said "So last night a couple guys kicked your door open and tried to rape you?"

But the moment was gone; she was swimming somewhere else.

Ed said "Angie you can't stay in that place: you're gonna get fucking killed. We'll go get your stuff and you can stay with me."

"NO, I already paid the landlord! If I leave then no one will know where I am! And pretty soon I'm going to buy a house! As soon as I get my car back I'm gonna look for a house! All I need is a new lock—Do y ou have a drill?"

We dropped her back on West Forty-Seventh. "GOODBYE!" she said, gathering her bag across the frontier of her yard . . .

I could tell it hurt Ed to leave her there.

"You must be nuts, asking her to move in," I told him.

The sun continued to fall with democratic evenness.

"Hello? Wild Magnolia . . ."

"Sadie?"

"Yeah."

"It's Danny."

"Hi hon; what's up?"

"Whyncha gimme a number for tonight."

"My number?"

"Lottery number. Three digits."

". . . Eight, two, six."

"Thanks."

"You gonna come see me?"

"Yeah, I might be up there."

"You better."

"See you later."

I spent a couple days going through the closet, trying on different shirts. They were few, and old, but each represented a different aspect of my personality. To me. No one else would've noticed. In a gathering dusk I'd stand at the open closet, a favorite sleeve draped through two fingers. At times it seemed I was wasted in my current role.

I'd choose a shirt, take it off the hanger.

In the bathroom, at the small cowboy sink, I'd run a comb under the cold tap. The medicine cabinet mirror was old and imperfect, blurred in places. The only thing in the cabinet was a can of Royal Crown pomade. I'd comb some grease into my hair, watching for a true glimpse of myself in the tricky old mirror.

Impeccably prepared, I'd lock the door and go down the dirty stairs. I'd get in my car, turn the ignition, and pull away from the curb, trying to figure out where the hell to go.

One day I was driving down Fourteenth and saw Marie waiting at a bus stop. I pulled over, she got in. She could tell right off I had someone on my mind, maybe it was the shirt. I dropped her off downtown.

That night she called. I was just lying around looking at the clock . . .

A couple nights later she called again. I was on my way out but I stuck around and talked with her, lying on the cot as dusk thickened in the room.

When she called next she said she was feeling restless and wanted to go for a ride. It made me nervous but there was no reasonable way to say no. I pulled up to where she was staying and she came skipping out like she was on a date. She looked almost new to me, sliding into the front seat, as though she'd prepared herself in some indefinable way. Her boyfriend Eric was away for the summer, she hadn't heard from him. We drove up Franklin to Sixty-Fifth for ice cream. We sat on the warm hood of the Buick while the cooling engine ticked in the summer evening.

"How's Ed?" she'd say, making conversation.

"He's alive."

"How're you?" she'd say.

"I'm good."

I started going to the gym every day. I took my time working out and then lay in the sun on the roof, and took my time in the shower. I took more every day.

"No work today Pat?"

"No work today Carl."

"Well, thanks for the ride, and the ice cream . . ."

Marie's eyes were that rumor of battle which the sky reflects. She wanted us back together, it was obvious. I didn't want any part of it, but I couldn't help thinking of her as being all alone in the world. The phone would ring with me already reaching for it—certain signals travel faster than wires can carry them . . .

"Well, thanks for the ride, and the ice cream."

*

The bar where Sadie worked was not the kind of place I'd hang out if not for her. It seemed to have a theme of some kind, which I could never narrow down to anything more specific than Life Is Good or You Are Safe or Let the Good Times Roll. The drinks were expensive and people went there in gangs to have fun. It wasn't my kind of place, and I stuck out. I'd get there early and we'd chat while she rinsed glasses and filled the juice containers . . . She was part of this bar life and she took it in stride, loosely and preoccupied and professional. Her night was beginning, my night was this. I'd play a few songs on the jukebox and we'd have a smoke while I sipped a big bourbon as though I was just passing through, trying to just be there with her before the first wave of revelers rolled in to wash me down to some lonely pensive margin at the end of the room . . .

The sun's rays had lowered, lighting a row of ashtrays along the bar. Sadie came around and sat on the stool next to mine. She stirred a drink, put the straw aside and took a sip.

She let a breath out, dreamingly. She was gazing at a place where the wall met the ceiling. Then she turned my way and slipped an arm behind me. The heat of her hand on the small of my back sent a shiver up my spine.

"So if I move to New York are you gonna come see me?"
"Okay."

"Really?"

"Why not?"

She picked up the straw and toyed with the ice in her drink. I sat there wondering whether we were dreaming one another.

After dark everything changed. The place was crowded and she was too busy to talk. Outside, leafy shadows rustled. The Buick under amber streetlight sat waiting. I unlocked it, got in. Sadie—

Just when I'd wake up to let the air out of myself she'd fill me up again, with a word . . . or a glance . . . with contrived proximity . . . With hot air, basically; hot breath.

"Where you been tonight?" Ed said.

"Ohh, out and about, y'know . . . Glad to be back."

The shadows of the Southside were dead still.

I had enough for the rent, and I was nickel-and-diming Feef.

SUMMER JOURNALS

I

The bed stays unmade, and things're piling up around it: popsicle sticks and lottery tickets, record covers and maps to a hundred places and scraps of paper that read "$2 double: Chief Red Bird w/ Wacky Patty," and "$2 place parlay: Susie Queen w/ FollowMeHome." Chicago the cat is curled up dead beneath a car and the flies're building, Ed's still got a half bottle of Scope on his front seat, and the telephone's buried so deep it don't hardly ring. Marie suspects, and Sadie's got her mind on other things and ain't nobody but me sweated into this bed in a long time. Senator Foghorn Leghorn of cab 486: the boss asked him how come he always wears those shades, even at night, and Foghorn says real slow "So motherfuckers can't see my *eyes*," and Foghorn was always giving me cigars I wasn't man or maniac enough to smoke and it's always other people's songs ringing around this room and—y'know, I'm getting enough sleep, but my dreams're getting stranger and more realistic all the time. I been carrying this billyclub to fight off the vampires with, but that ain't really the right way to deal with vampires—and last night I went for a ride in the empty part of town to watch the sun set and I saw mosquitoes coming in clouds. So now I got mosquitoes *plus* the vampires, and, uh— something's driving me crazy: I feel like I'm a marked man, y'know? And you've gotta leave the house *sometime* . . . Might be time to leave town for a while, 'cause my numbers ain't hitting and these horses're finding the damndest ways to lose, and what with the cat and all, things're starting to stink.

HIPPO YEARS

"John called up this morning . . ."

"What's up?"

"Mike's birthday today."

"Oh yeah?"

"Five years old."

"Should we take him over a cupcake with five candles?"

". . . Well I assume John's got something planned . . ."

"What's that in hippo years? Are hippo years like dog years?"

"I think hippo years are like people years, 'cause John says Mike'll be starting school in the fall. John's in a dilemma because Wilson Elementary is all black now. He's checking up on private schools."

"*[laughter]* "

"A man who's never had to deal with black people—ever. Except when he was in high school, with the Water Fountain Confrontation."

"What was that?"

"When a black kid pushed him by the water fountain . . . John chipped his tooth or something, turned around and knocked the black kid down the steps. His big moment of *glory*, at East Tech . . . in 1967 or something, knocks this—colored kid down the steps . . . And he still talks about it to this day: 'Remember when I threw that nigger down the steps?' That was his Vietnam."

"What're they doing to celebrate Mike's birthday?"

He looked up from the paper.

"They're betting a three-teamer for ten bucks. Mike got ten for his birthday from Uncle Ron. You feel like taking a ride?"

We hit John's and hit the horn. He came out of the alley and leaned in my window, clean-shaven, a few bits of paper on the left shoulder of his flannel shirt. He saw me glance at them and brushed them off irritably, muttering "Aah, fucking confetti . . ."

We left him there and swung out to the track.

0-200 AT THE 2300

Duke and I are perched at the 2300 Club, two am. I figured he'd be there after work, so I waited.

Place always feels like last call, no matter when you come.

"Last call." The bartender's voice comes straight out of something that's been going on a long, long time.

The Duke says "I'll have another Rolling Rock and another shot of Echo."

I'm gazing at the ancient savage dent in the guy's forehead . . .

"Rolling Rock and a Heaven Hill . . . thanks."

He sets the beers and pours the shots—takes money from what we've got on the bar. Looks like he got hit with an axe. Whatever it was, it looks like the blow pretty much decided things forever.

Something on the TV about elephants . . .

Duke says "I like being part of this circus of life."

"Yeah?"

"Yeah . . . But they keep putting the elephants on ahead of me, and then they stick the trapeze guys in there, and then the chimps and the dancing bear—They keep pushing my act further back towards the end. I'm getting ready to go on and the seals come out— Y'know. I'm starting to feel like I'm never gonna get to go on. The Flory-Dory girls'll be out before I get a chance . . . "

He says "Whattayou been doing?"

"Nothing. Y'know."

He lifts his whiskey. "Good luck."

"Salut'."

He takes a cigarette. I light mine but he keeps his fresh . . . toying with it . . . musing . . .

He turns with a smile. "Can you get this one started for me? I can't inhale deep enough anymore, but if you can just get it started I'll manage the rest on my own . . ."

"Smoke a lot today?"

"Couplea zillion."

"What would you do if I wasn't here?"

"Well usually I carry a turkey baster to get 'em going: I stick 'em in the end and pump 'em up till they're burning good. After that they practically smoke themselves . . ."

"I'll have to get one of those."

"You can have mine; I'm gonna quit."

"Me too."

"No really: I gotta quit. They're killing me."

"Definitely. I'm quitting too," I tell him.

"Of course," I add, "Even if I quit completely I'd have to have a couple packs a day—"

"That goes without saying. If you can cut back to forty a day you've basically quit."

"Right. But it'd just be—ostentatious, to go without 'em at certain moments. Like right before bed: I *gotta* smoke ten or twelve right before bed—"

"Or in the shower— Yeah, naturally. But apart from that—"

"Sure."

"Okay then, this is it," he says. "Starting tomorrow."

"Definitely."

"Here's to it:"

"Salut'."

I remember going into Mickey's, the three of us . . . Ed was wearing a black dress shirt, untucked but neat, I was wearing shades, Angie— Who knows what the hell Angie was wearing: you could look right at her and not know what she was wearing. We must've looked like a prize crew, walking in there out of the sunlight, a—like a Tuesday afternoon, nobody in the joint . . . We talked to the manager and Angie went into the bathroom to change. Ed paid for a couple shots and spent the next few minutes bitching about the price. Ed wasn't cheap, but he was vigilant about anyone trying to beat him . . .

Mickey's was a go-go bar on Clark. Angie'd seen an ad for dancers in the paper and started stitching together an outfit: we were waiting in the Pontiac and she came out of her house, finally, clanging in the wide hot sun—She was the most dissonant collection of horns and gongs and feedback and spoons . . . And she's walking past the car hitching up that big carpetbag filled with her whole world: makeup and books and an iron and ringing telephones—I said "Hey *Angie!*" and she stopped in her tracks, ready to confront her fate, whatever it might be, but it was only us, and she said "Oh," and I got out to let her into the middle and she slipped inside pulling the bag, searching for scraps of paper and brushing up on geometry . . . She said she'd created an outfit to dance in, yanked it all tangled out of the bag: some cockeyed stringy leopardskin bikini she'd fashioned with a pair of garden shears and a curtain and black

213

thread . . . I turned my attention out the window as we rode.

While she was in the bathroom we watched the girl onstage: a black woman—a real centerfold type in heels and a purple lace corset, six foot tall—climbing the firepole and spinning down, kicking and shaking and writhing away . . . The jukebox is pounding, and the girl snakes back and wraps herself around the pole—snaps her head back in ecstasy over the two ultimate studs in front of her: the fat balding guy in the black shirt and the little itchy scumbag in the leather jacket and shades— Grinds against the ten-foot pole like it still ain't big enough . . . Bland and seamless and professional, as the song fades out and she picks herself up and looks around . . . The manager calls her off.

The place is quiet. Angie's down back, by the jukebox. Apparently she's gotta play her own songs.

I walk over and give her a couple quarters and she's like five full minutes taking her time, scanning the selections, bathed in the glow of the machine . . . asking the manager how number 146 goes—the guy can't believe it . . . we're starting to sweat . . . Finally she drops the quarters in and the music starts as she's clambering onto the stage, dragging her bag . . . She sets the bag beside the pole and straightens herself, gazing fiercely at the hot red light . . .

Angie's dancing to a different song, it seems. There she is in her red metal-flake platform heels from 1974 and heavily su- tured zebra bikini . . . stopping . . . listening . . . milling around . . . Like a three-year-old girl dancing at the insistence of family friends. She does a few bumps and stops again to check the song in her head, clutching a leftover quarter in one hand . . . She sings half a verse aloud . . . still with the big pink shades on . . . drops the quarter . . . follows it as it rolls and steps on it, looks up, gazing at the horizon and just—lost; hopelessly lost and forgotten . . .

Ed and I turned for our drinks at the same time . . . I put my cigarette out . . .

Back in the sunlight, Angie's relating how the manager told her she needs a little more experience. We walked across the street to a corner store—Ed needed oil for his car and I got a coffee.

Ed said "Angie, you want anything?"

She stopped and thought about it hard, and in earnest—looked around and said "Do they have jellybeans? I'd like some jellybeans . . . "

SUMMER JOURNALS

II

Feels like November. Summer dark surrounds the light of another cracking kitchen . . . the whiskey's ebbing off.

The real story surrounds the light of another cracking fancy. Sadie's got her own thing.

Is this June or July?

That's Fast Eddie on the wall: solid black amid a Vegas whirl—he's saying Whatsa matter with you, boy?

Jimmy D'll be squinting over the entries tomorrow: ain't had a winning day in thirty years. Feef'll be parked on Detroit after dark, waiting in his modified Lincoln to pay too much for something priceless.

I was trying to recall the last time I went out and won myself something, and y'know—damned if I can remember the last time I took off these shades, and uh—Huh? No I really can't recollect the last time I broke an honest sweat. I need a fire to break a sweat. But I'm definitely gonna hitchhike to Spain—soon as I find the right jacket to wear.

It's nighttime in June: the leaves're heavy and the streetlights are shining down. The old man's awake in the dark, listening to the trains go. Ed's asleep in the fading tension of another ninth-inning defeat, and I'm at the plate—swinging at wild pitches and watching strikes go by.

Is this June or November?

THE ORIGINAL SUE

He says "You need a ten?"

"If you got it."

"I can give you fifteen."

"Ten's fine."

The sun slants through the yard fence.

"Thanks." I feel like a new man.

"You eat yet?" he says.

". . . Naw, I—didn't even think about it."

"Sure, everything's easy when you're a bum. No need to keep your strength up, or keep track of time . . . Just let one day roll into another . . . "

"Yeah, it's okay."

China joint, amid the clatter of plates and the passing of waiters:

He says "Broad over there looks just like the Original Sue."

I glance. "Who's that?"

"Broad I was seeing for a while. You want some of this?"

"No, I got plenty. Why'd you call her the Original Sue?"

"Well I've been involved with more than one Sue. She was the first."

"Mm. When was that?"

"Couple years ago. I met her over the phone, as Lisa. I—"

"What?"

"I called her up as a woman, I told her my name's Lisa."

"*Why?*"

"Something I do once in a while, it's a good ploy."

"I don't get it. You disguise your voice?"

"Yeah, it's just a way in. I dial a number at random, a woman answers I pretend I got the wrong number, you end up bullshitting with 'em . . . People are so bored and lonely they'll talk to anyone. 'Specially if it's another woman—it's over the phone, y'know, they feel safe . . . "

"Yeah—?"

"Tell their innermost fantasies to a total stranger they've known for five minutes. Shit they'd never *dream* of telling their husbands or their closest friends. Y'know, uh—their husband don't fuck 'em no more, they got a dildo in the closet, uh . . . they have fantasies about the little boy across the street, they like to watch their daughter take a bath—Anything. And—After you do this for a while you realize how fucked up the world is: not just you. I've met—three or four broads already—over the phone—that I actually ended up going out with and seeing for like two three months."

"Really?"

"At *least* three or four. I don't always talk to 'em as a woman, but it has its advantages, 'cause they'll say shit to a woman they won't say to a man. Like Sue: I knew from talking to her as Lisa that she was interested in getting together with another broad, maybe having a guy there to watch or whatever—I knew she didn't like to fuck, but she liked to play with herself and have a guy watch: she was totally into herself, her own body—All this shit that I was interested in from a broad."

"Yeah."

"Now they got all these phone sex, party lines: I been doing the same thing on my own for years. Sometimes after Lisa talks to a broad for a while she'll set her up with her friend Jack. Me. Then when I meet her face to face, I got an edge, 'cause I know what she's into. And I *need* that edge because obviously I can't rely on my looks or my money: I gotta rely on my wits. 'Cause

I'm too old—I can't be going to bars, tryna stand next to some broad, catch her eye, try to start up a conversation—and then if I do manage to pick her up, she might be into something totally different than me—I can't do that kinda shit anymore."

"Uh-huh."

"Anyway, this Original Sue: we talked about every—sordid thing you could think of, right? And she wanted to meet me—"

"She was married?"

"Yeah, she was married . . . "

"What was her complaint, about that?"

"Her complaint was—Just a typical, 'nother All-American story: bored housewife who likes to get into a little bit of crazy shit, her husband who just likes to work, fix the house, be a normal man, y'know . . . "

"Yeah."

". . . screw in the missionary position once a week, that's it. Anyway, I talk to her for three weeks as a woman, and finally gets to the point—How'm I gonna meet her? So I'm out in North Olmsted . . . snowing like a sonofabitch, I'm drinking wine in the truck. I called her from a payphone, I go 'Uh . . . Are you a friend of Lisa?' she goes 'Yeah?' I go 'Well . . . I dunno how to tell you this, I hope you don't get pissed, but—I'm Lisa.' 'Fuck you,' she goes. I said 'No, it was me, I hadda tell you, I didn't wanna leave you hanging: you been so nice, I didn't wanna just never call you again . . . So I figure I might as well end it, tell you there's no Lisa.' I go 'Whattayou think about that?' I figured *wham*: phone's going down, it's all over with, right? She goes 'I'm *glad* you're a guy: it makes it even better!' Y'know? 'Cause we were talking about—y'know—kidnapping women, and—y'know: put 'em in the back of a van and—hanging them, and then throw 'em in the park and stepping on their head—"

"Uh-huh."

"All kinda— She liked brutality. We never got into that, but

219

in the right circumstances, she's very capable of doing something like that, y'know? Let's go pick up some girl and run her legs over and leave her in the park to freeze to death—"

"..."

"And then stick my tit in her mouth before we leave. It was really heavy stuff, y'know? And she said 'Wow, that makes it even better that you're a man! Now we can meet—'"

"Now we can really *do* this!"

"Yeah, y'know. And so we agreed to meet, I met her in a bar ... and right away we started talking just like on the phone— had a couple drinks—And for a whole year after that I seen her at least two or three times a week. Husband never caught on— He's on his way to work, I'm coming over—Couple times we'd stop at the same light, I'd look at him, he'd look at me, kinda like—nod to me, I'd nod to him, like—y'know, another day at work, here we go, how you doing ... just two guys, acknowledging the fact we're both screwed and going to work ... I'm thinking Well, I'll be fucking your wife in about five minutes ... have a good day at the post office ... "

"*[laughter]* "

"After like six months he worked the night shift, so she— 'Whyn't you spend the night here?' I said 'I don't really wanna do that, that's dangerous!' We're laying in bed one night, I roll over: see this big thing on the floor, y'know? Pick it up, here it's a shoe. That sonofabitch musta been a size fourteen, I go Holy ... "

"Fuck."

"I think she actually wanted him to catch us; it woulda been a turn-on for her. One time I's over there during the day, she says 'I'm gonna take a shower: sit on the edge of the toilet and watch me.' I go 'I'd rather not be in this tiny little room with the water running I can't hear nothing,' she says 'Don't worry about a thing, my husband's at work.' I says 'Sue, he could get sick, or—he get pissed off at work ... y'know—maybe he's calling, you don't answer he comes home ... ' Her husband walks in that bathroom door: what do I do?"

"Yeah. Not like you're the refrigerator repairman."

"Yeah! Come to read the meter—anything! I hadda dry her off . . . I *loved* it, y'know, but . . . She didn't give a fuck, she took ten twelve Valiums a day . . . "

"Uh huh."

"One time he went hunting, and Sue's mother lived in Maryland. As it turned out her mother was gay. Seventy-five years old and gay."

"Really?"

"Lived with another woman for like thirty years. I'm sure they didn't do anything, but . . . Anyway, Sue wanted to visit her mother. Took her husband's *brand-new car*— We drove down there, we go to her mother's house, and Sue says 'Mom knows I'm married . . . You gotta pretend you're gay.' I couldn't act gay, but . . . I hadda answer a few questions the right way, y'know. We're sitting on the couch, her mother goes 'What's your name?' I go 'Jack,' or—I think I changed it to uh . . . less masculine name than Jack—"

"Yeah."

"—think I changed it to Bruce, or . . . Terry; something like that . . . She goes 'You like animals?' And Sue goes 'Yeah he's got some angelfish at home and a little pug.' I go 'Awww . . .' Her mother goes 'You living with somebody?' I go 'Yeah I'm living with this guy for a long time, y'know . . . Chuck . . . we get along . . .'"

"What'd you do down there?"

"Well we went to a couple dyke bars, Sue try to pick up a girl, I waited in the car . . . She ends up coming out with two *good-looking* chicks. She says 'I'm going back to the motel with them, we're gonna stop someplace first—Take the car, I'll meet you back there.' Brand-new car! Here I'm in Washington DC, I don't know one street from the next . . . I didn't even know the name of the motel! I drove around for like three hours just getting lost—I went to Virginia, Baltimore—"

"*[laughter]*"

"In five minutes I hit four states! I was gonna get stickers for the car. Finally I found the place at five in the morning and she wouldn't let me in, she had the two broads with her, she says 'Go get breakfast.' I was already pissed, I said Sonofabitch, the whole point of me coming here was to watch her eat pussy! I think I went to get coffee . . . Come back, the broads were gone."

"Mm."

"Next morning we go to this restaurant, Sunday morning, eating breakfast . . . She says 'I'll be back in fifteen minutes.' Be a sonofabitch if she don't go: I'm in the restaurant a good *hour*. Right? and people're coming in, waiting for tables . . . So I went out—It was a hundred degrees outside. I'm waiting by the restaurant, wait another hour—Now I'm really getting pissed. There ain't a bar in sight—And if there *is* a bar I'm afraid to go there 'cause what if she pulls up I'm not around? I have—very little money on me, don't know where the motel is—Finally I sit on the curb, reading the paper—I was out there—*six hours*."

"*[groan]*"

"Finally she comes, right? I get in the car I'm *fuming*, right? She goes 'Yeah, I went to my mom's for a while, this and that,' starts driving . . . Like nothing happened. I go 'I been out there six fucking *hours*.' 'Well I had things to do, I got tied up.' I go '*Sue* you *stupid* mother*fucker*: don't you realize I was there six hours sitting on the curb?' She—totally made nothing of it!"

"How's her husband put up with her?"

"I don't know, he musta give up on her by now. He took so much—*garbage* from her . . . And she hated the fucking guy anyway. So she said. She used to buy bags of Oreo cookies—hide it in the closet—She sit in the bathroom with the door locked eating cookies. So he wouldn't ask her for none. Just to show you what kinda person she is. She burned down the house once, totalled the car *repeatedly*, uh . . . come home alla time fucked up, bleeding . . . The guy must be a fucking saint."

"That's one way to look at it."

"One night she come over the house totally stoned and drunk. This was after like two weeks of not talking to her. She come pounding on the door, she's going '*Open up you mother-fucker!*' I don't let her in, she puts her fist through the window. And she cut her hand pretty good, she's bleeding, y'know—It was freezing outside, she come in: '*You're a sonofabitch: I decided to tell my husband!*' I said 'Sue, what for? You're the one's gonna have to put up with it. What's he gonna do to me? Beat me up?' I wrapped her hand up a little bit—finally I push her outa the house. She's barefooted, her hand bleeding, totally stoned in the middle of wintertime: runs in the middle of the street— '*Someone help me, Someone please help me!*'"

"Aw, wow . . ."

"'*Someone call the police! This man rapes little girls!*'"

"*[laughter]* "

"I tried to grab her she just tore away from me—'*Fuck you!*' Like a lunatic: I couldn't do nothing with her! So I ran back in the house—Here's this guy walking, across the street—She runs up to him, grabs his arm: '*Mister! This man rapes little girls!*'— pointing at the house!—'*He's raping a little baby right now!*' I'm going Holy fuck, now I'm gonna have the cops down here— Lucky the guy thought she was crazy. She's out there a good thirty minutes—Next door in the gas station there's a bum beating on an oildrum with a big stick: *boom-boom-boom-boom*: some—prophecy of doom, like an old Indian or something— She's screaming . . . Finally she gets in her car and takes off. Spins around on the ice—Takes off—sixty miles an hour up the street . . . She called me two days later tryna apologize. I said 'You just proved that I could never ever trust you. That just killed the relationship.' And it really did, 'cause that was about the last time I ever talked to her . . ."

—Wake to the sound of intrusion from the stairs.

Girls: laughing, maybe drunk. One am. Roll out of bed, pulling on pants and boots . . . they're coming up, they're at the door—

"Danny?"

"Wake up, Danny!"

"C'mon baby: outa bed before we jump in there with you!"

Sadie. And sounds like Anna from up the street: Sadie and Anna.

Flip the bolt and they come jostling in the dark—"Where's the light?" The light comes on. A bottle of wine between them and I'm there with my hair on end and some kind of look on my face. I get a kiss from each of them.

"What's up?"

"We've been drinking wine at Anna's."

"Yeah. So you came to drink it here."

Anna says "Did we wake you up?" as Sadie's moving around the place . . .

"Yeah, well, y'know . . ."

Sadie says "D'you always sleep with your boots on?"

"Never know when you're gonna have to make a run for it."

"Oh yeah? Do you always have girls coming over and waking you up?"

"Sure. Didn't you bump into the last two?"

"You must be worn out. Here: have some wine."

224

She's got the bedroom light on now, poking into my life.

Anna says "We're going to the Harbor Inn."

"We came to kidnap you."

Funny feeling. I'm looking around through a visitor's eyes . . .

"D'you—"

Aah, there she is, and there's my riled-up bed. I feel all exposed . . . Wonder if she can pick up the scent of her image.

I grab a jacket, cut the lights and we're crashing down the stairs, I'm putting a comb through my hair . . . And we're piled into the front seat of Sadie's Toyota, the bottle floating around, and I'm laughing to myself about the way things develop in the dark and then explode into the light . . . They're way ahead of me; at the moment I'm running third.

The place is crowded, the juke's up loud, people're dancing as Anna stops to talk with someone and Sadie and I are heading toward the bar. Glad I hit Ed for ten before bed. Sadie orders a vodka tonic, top shelf; I get a fix on an attitude and ask for a double shot of Ten High, which isn't even on a shelf but down below the bar where it belongs. Sadie's fussing through an alligator pocketbook—

"I got it, Sadie."

"No, I wanted to get this round: lookit all the money I made at the bar last night!"

"That's alright, I hit a bet. What's Anna want?"

"Get her a kamikaze."

Anna comes with a smile.

"Here you go," I tell her.

"Thanks. What is it?"

"Drink up."

Sadie says "Here's to dreams come true."

We touch glasses, they laugh. I drink the shot and it feels like rain on my grave . . . the beginning of perfect . . .

From then on the lights glowed not with enmity but with amity and the music was all encouragment and I was in danger of Sadie's eyes.

Anna made her way into the crowd and left us there together. Sadie, from the way she was looking at me, was on the verge of something. I couldn't let her get away with it.

"Where's your boy tonight?"

"He's at home. Probably sleeping."

"I bet he ain't sleeping."

"Yes he is. He doesn't care what I do."

"Mm."

"Why?"

"Just curious."

"He got fired from the record store and he quit the band. Now he doesn't do anything but sit around listening to records and taking drugs."

"So you're out letting off some steam, huh?"

"Yep."

"How've things been?"

"Terrible. He's flat broke and—"

"No, I don't mean—"

"I've been supporting him . . . He hardly even wants to have *sex* with me anymore!"

"Hey. Sadie."

"Well you asked how he was doing!"

"I asked how *you* were doing. Forget it."

"Besides, we're buddies," she said, slipping an arm through mine.

"'Nother vodka?"

"I'll pay for these. What do you want?"

I looked around for Anna, as though only she could get us back on track. She was dreaming over the jukebox. It hit me that I wasn't running third. We were on three separate tracks.

Sadie and I touched glasses again, and there was the magnetism of proximity. Just as I was turning to surrender, she said:

"I saw Marie the other day."

I sighed. "Yeah?"

"I was at the Phantasy with Lulu, and Marie was there with some new guy: Peter."

"Yeah, I run into her once in a while; she seems okay . . ."

"We asked them if they wanted to go to breakfast, but she said they had other things to do. She was really wasted."

"Uh-huh."

"Do you miss Marie?"

"Why? Where'd she go?"

"You know what I mean."

"Umm . . . I think about her . . . y'know . . . Whattaya mean? Do I miss living with her?"

"Yeah."

"No."

Anna came back. She seemed solid and strong and sensible. We took part in her until she left again.

Back on the Southside, we watched her go through the gate, and waited till she was in the house.

I asked Sadie if she was okay to drive.

She said "Yeah, I'll be okay. How do I get back through downtown?"

"Here," I said. "Drive around the corner and I'll show you."

She drove to Literary and partway down the hill: I told her to pull over and gave her directions. And just when I thought the night was over she turned and we kissed, awhile.

Then she said she had to get home.

SUMMER JOURNALS

III

Why do these things put me out of orbit? On a smoky hill her mouth opens up: like the lay of the land widening open at the top of a rise. And just like that, there's nothing else to do in the world. I'll spend the next few days listening to the beat of my heart. People ask me questions I can barely hear them above the beating of my heart.

What's it to her? Nothing much, probably. A drunken moment overlooking the valley: take it or leave it.

Nick Stavros is on the corner in a boiled white shirt and a straw dress hat. In the light of Sunday morning he goes to visit his sister.

. . . Sitting drunk at Thistledown—Ed and I killed the pint. Hit the second race, got nipped in the third. No payphones at the track—my heart's gonna burst. I'm restless as a horse come awash in the gate.

The bottle broke and things turned ugly. We were escorted out by the head of security.

"Man I wish I hear from Angelface: I got a few bucks in my pocket, I can't do nothing with it. Can you believe they suspended us from the track because that nigger hit me in the mouth? They didn't do a fucking thing to *him*—"

"He's a trainer. You got anything to drink?"

He says "I got a half pint of vodka on the shelf; have a slug of that."

"Naa, I don't mean—It's nine o'clock in the morning; you got any juice?"

"No juice; I got ice water in the fridge."

I pour some into an orange plastic cup, swallow a gulp and wince.

"—What is this?"

"Springwater, tastes funny."

"How come it tastes so funny?"

"That's 'cause you're used to drinking that shit water from the faucet, that's why."

"This don't taste right."

"That's artesian springwater," he explains, patiently, "bought from Fazio's."

"This must be a spring on the Southside."

"You're just not used to— Where'd you get that cup?"

"In the dishrack here—"

"Aw, y'know what? I used that cup I had Pine-Sol in that cup, I was tryna clean the sink. I must not a rinsed it out all the way—"

"Goddamnit, what's the matter with you?" I sat down with the Pine-Sol glowing in my throat. "Now I *need* a fucking shot of vodka to chase that with."

I got up and took a swig from the bottle and sat back down, annoyed with him. I lit a cigarette.

Then I said "What was that you said you seen that guy before?"

"What guy?"

"Knox: the head of security at Thistledown."

"Aw. I went out there—This like five years ago, I would never do this now—And I had a pocket fulla them—Not cherry bombs, but—"

"M-80s?"

"Yeah."

"Aw man."

"I used to sit up on the steps leading to the grandstand—Y'know there's that series of stairways, all in a line. But some of 'em were closed at the top, with like metal garage doors, right? So, you could sit up there, nobody'd fuck with you. So I's sitting up there reading the *Form*—And I had these M-80s in my pocket. So I tore the filter off my cigarette and stuck the wick of one of these firecrackers in the unlit end—right? And walked down the steps, y'know . . . with my *Form* and my program . . . and my hat and my pipe and my glasses and slippers and just sat on a bench like an old man reading the *Form*—"

"*[laughter]* "

"'Bout ten minutes later: BOOOOOOM! Fucking people scattered, man—'*What* the fuck?' y'know. These things were—equivalent to a jumbo firecracker, but inside a big *monumental* fucking concrete thing man it sounds like a fucking *grenade,* y'know . . . And everybody's kinda looking, y'know . . . No big deal, I said That's fucking great, man . . . So there was like six of these stairways—I go to the next one, go way up to the top there, read the *Form,* look around like John Dillinger . . .

put another wick on there, light it . . . Walk down, I'm just relaxing—BOOOM! People: '*What the fuck, another one?*' Some of the old-timers're getting pissed off, y'know—People get *mad*—disturbed, y'know. When you get scared you get mad; I know that myself. I thought Man, this is great! Nobody in the world—know I did that, man I—I could see how people get away with crime, y'know?"

"*[laughter]*"

"So I went to the next one, right? Totally in the clear, people kinda milling around . . . I put another one on there, go down— Same thing: *booom!* and everybody runs over there— Now the security guards are out, 'What the fuck's going on here?'—They got radios, Knox is there—sportjacket—I walk over—fold my *Form* under my arm—'What's wrong, Officer?' 'Some kids are throwing firecrackers from up there; we'll get 'em!' 'Aw, yeah? That's dangerous! Where they, from them cracks up there?' 'Yeah we think they're dropping 'em.' So while they're investigating I backtrack and put another one up there—BOOOM! They go running up there—

"Six of them fuckers I lit off, right? The whole security force was out— Then I got scared, I go Man—This is big time! This is like inciting a riot, or—Causing Mayhem, y'know—They got a crime, like—It's called Mayhem or something. The whole track was shook up: even the jockeys were wondering what's going on, y'know—'Somebody shooting us?'"

"*[laughter]*"

"I got one left. Here's Max the Mailman, who lost three homes—his wife—his business—Everything he ever owned. He's totally in another world: nine thousand keys on his ring and nine thousand pens in his pocket, he just walks around in a daze. Max the Mailman. Lost his mailman job for thirty years—he had a side business— Total—racetrack degenerate.

"They got this big rubber plant there with all these wood-chips. I got one left. So I bury it in these woodchips, put the cigarette there. I walk away, I'm waiting, I'm waiting . . . Here comes Max, reading his *Form*—stands right next to the fucking thing, I go *Holy* fuck— BOOOOOOOM! fucking—chips flew up—'*WHAT* the fuck?!' He jumped so far—He's looking around, patting his hands all over his—y'know, make sure he's all there . . . Woodchips flew all over the place. The grand finale."

"*[laughter]*"

"Nobody could figure it out! The security guards are dildos, as you know, but even so . . . —*Why* I did that; but I walked outa there going Here I just fucked up this whole racetrack! If you were there, you'd have to think What—There some fucking rioteers, or—y'know: somebody losing their head shooting?"

"Yeah, right."

"And—I did it so nonchalantly, and—discreetly walked back down and sat on the bench, and then five minutes later—*boom*; walk to the next one: *boom*; y'know: *boom* . . . I did it with no regard for my safety or nothing—"

"*[laughter]*"

"I went back the next day, and—honest to God: the next day and the next day after that they had extra security people out—patrolling around . . . like, for a *week* they were shook up there. I cost 'em a lotta man-hours . . ."

Early that afternoon Sadie called.

"Hi Danny."

"Hey, Sadie."

"How're you doing?"

"I'm okay. Been thinking about you a lot."

"Really? I've been thinking about you too. What're you do-ing today?"

"I'm uh—Nothing. Why, you free?"

"Well, I might have to work tonight, but I thought maybe we could go for a ride this afternoon. I wanna get out of here for a while."

"Okay." I sounded surprisingly calm, to myself.

"The only thing is, Willy's got my car. Would you mind pick-ing me up?"

"No, that's fine. I'll see you in a while."

She lived in the Heights. I parked across from her building and stepped into the bright squint of mid-afternoon. Her street was listless and leafy. I crossed it, and saw myself coming in the glass door, and wondered if this were an embarcation. In the cool of the buzzer room I waited for her answer.

She came in a hurry, slinging a camera over her shoulder, and I followed her quick smile into the heat. No fateful kiss. I unlocked my door and leaned to unlock hers. She dropped into my front seat and we pulled into the glaring road. Turning onto the boulevard I caught her looking at me and said "So where we going?"

"I don't care," she said. "I've got my camera; whyn't you show me around where you live?"

I headed west and she turned her head to the moving world, allowing me the same adventure, in furtive glances, as I'd afforded her.

At a stoplight she looked across the distance between us and smiled. "How you doing, Danny?"

There were a lot of things in that smile. It was as though she were granting us that moment of assessment. I wanted to confess everything.

Maybe I did when I said "Well . . . y'know, uh . . . I uh . . ."

"I feel good," I decided. "I'm glad you called."

"Me too," she said.

I took her to secret spots on the near West Side where she could take pictures of black soaring drawbridges, ivied viaducts, and hills of gravel and salt. We slunk along the river for a shot of a freighter as big as the world. Stepping away from the bank she slipped an arm around my waist and then looked around, surveying the scene. I put an arm around her shoulders and we walked like that through the weeds, separating at the car. The afternoon was poised, like a flower on a vine suddenly singled out by the sun, catching and holding all it can sustain of the light in the thin membrane of its petals, until the sun moves on.

At rush hour we hit the freeway heading east. Sadie was talking about records and bands, about people at the bar where she worked, and I was listening as though to hear the bright language behind a code . . .

I pulled in at a suburban park and cut the engine in the visitors' lot. We walked, oblique to one another, through the shadows on the grass, as squirrels made play of living. On the cliff overlooking Lake Erie were three kids, boasting around a beatbox. They laughed louder as we approached, and talked bolder. I lit a cigarette and one of them said "Yo baby: take our picture!" Sadie'd snapped it already, and he protested for another chance. She joked with him and forwarded the film and the others crowded into the picture, jumping around until what had started as a joke became essential, the kids peering to identify themselves in her lens, as Sadie took shot after shot of them.

She curled up on the seat as I swung the car backward and pulled out. She had to go to work.

She said "Thanks, Danny. I don't know what's going on. I don't know what to say. All I know is that I want to see you."

I pulled into traffic and looked her in the eyes, hoping she'd see that both our eyes were open.

It took twenty minutes to get her home, and those twenty minutes were like a change of subject. We pulled across from her building near the end of daylight.

She said "I'll call you on my next day off," and then she was gone. I drove west, wondering what, on that film of hers, she had any investment in.

WEEKDAY DRIVING AROUND

He's saying "If I's a cop I'd—You're driving at night, four
o'clock in the morning looking for a whore, right? There's
a fucking guy—driving a bicycle— I would just like to stop
my car—say 'What the fuck are you— *Why* are you out here?
Where are you *going?* Or—Here's a guy—walking up Carnegie—no one else in sight, nothing but empty buildings— 'Why
are you here at nine-thirty in the morning?'"

"Exactly."

"'Why are you outside—at quarter to six on a Monday
morning drinking a Pabst—on the corner of Thirteenth and
Chester?' I'd just like to pull the truck over, roll down the window: 'Awright, where were you born, Where you been—How
did you get to peeling a banana at twenty after eight on East
Ninth and Euclid? I mean—What brought you to this *point?*"

"Hey whatever happened with—"
"Looka this: Butch's . . ."
"Looks rough."
"Last time I's there—I's in a bad mood 'cause of Mitty,
whatever—And I'm—As usual when I'm drinking I'm acting
like an asshole, I start making cracks about West Virginia . . . I's
just looking for trouble. And—these two guys said something
to me, start a fight with me so I beat 'em up . . . Just to be a bigshot, y'know . . . And I beat 'em up pretty bad, I's kicking 'em,
think I hit one of 'em with a chair . . . And—I stayed in the bar

and drank . . . On the way home a *caravan* of cars followed me, I was totally *drunk*. Three carloads of guys followed me all the way to Twenty-Fifth and Denison, Forestdale Apartments . . . At least ten twelve guys got out with bats—chains— I just *ran*, man—I ran into a building ran out the back into my building and up to my apartment, looked out the window—couldn't see nothing— Went out the next day, all my windows're broken all my tires're flat, they slashed up the seats . . . But that coulda been my head. I just let 'em have the car, like a sacrificial lamb."

Back downtown, we're prowling through a backwater north of St. Clair: quiet streets of beverage warehouses . . . the police stables, the firemen's training academy . . . loading docks . . . Ed takes it slow—he points out a small brick building—The Gotcha Inn—beside a tunnel set under the tracks . . .

"See that place? I got called there for a meeting one time with a couple bookies, set up a rendezvous there . . ."

"Yeah?"

"Yeah, remember that place. Guy named Val Munger. If they ever find me floating in the river, that's the guy who did it. Hangs out at the Gotcha Inn. Him and his buddies."

"What was it about?"

"I owed 'em like five grand. Five—four grand, something like that, not much."

"For how long?"

"Like a month, y'know. And I didn't pay 'em, finally they arranged to make the meeting with me. So I met 'em at the Gotcha Inn, and they—played the role with me, this is a while back now . . . I says 'Hey, I ain't got any money.' I hadda get half drunk to go down there . . . I ain't like John, I can't tell 'em I lost it in a card game like John did to his bookies."

"What?"

"He told his bookies he lost it in a card game with a buncha hillbillies. 'And if I find out they ever cheated me, I'll kill 'em all!' Honest John. He wasn't so honest that day . . ."

"Alright, so what happened with this—"

"Anyway, they say 'You owe us five grand—How you gonna pay us?' I says 'I'm broke.' They go 'We know you're broke, we checked on everything, we—bank accounts—We checked on you.' I says 'Well I—pay you so much a week or something.' They go 'How much?' Now we're talking about that right? so before we got to that—they slide me a picture, upside-down picture across the table right? 'Here's a picture of a guy,' right? They go 'You wanna get even with us? You see this guy here? He hangs around Coventry. He's supposed to be in California but we know he sneaks around 'cause his mother lives in town. You find the guy for us. You sit in this bar every night till you find him. When he comes in there, you give us a call.' So, as it turned out I didn't do it, I came back the next week I told 'em I couldn't find the guy or something like that—"

"Why?"

"I didn't even attempt to do it,"—he's indignant: "I'm not gonna nail another fucking poor slob like myself, I'm gonna go fink on somebody? fuck them. So we made an arrangement, they says 'Alright, you gonna pay us so much a week. How much you gonna pay us a week?' I go— 'How's twenty bucks sound?'"

"*[laughter]* "

"I owe 'em five grand, right? Take me forty years to pay 'em."

"*[laughter]* "

"They go 'Twenty a week? We're talking two hundred a week.' I says 'I ain't working, man. Twenty bucks.' So three weeks in a row I dropped it off to the bar—fucking barmaid there, I gave her twenty bucks in the envelope. I'm on the list—five thousand, now I owe 'em forty-nine-eighty, y'know? I did it about three weeks, I says Fuck this, This is ridiculous, I never went back there again. Guy called me a couple times after that—They called my mother once which pissed me off

. . . Called my mother and says: 'He can run but he can't hide.' And that was the last I ever heard of 'em."

"Were they mob guys, or—?"

"They were half-assed mob guys," he says derisively. "Just—All bookies know some kinda bigshots in the mob, or little guys—They all—half-assed mob guys . . ."

"They were big enough that they were looking for somebody else and they had bothered to check up on you—"

"Yeah, as it turned out, as I look back on it now, I'da laughed at 'em today, back then I was mildly afraid . . ."

Back to the West Side, coasting . . . Johnny's on Fulton goes by . . .

"How's John?"

"He found a bird, on the porch. A baby bird, and he was raising it in a shoebox. And Mike does not like animals. He's jealous of other animals. And—John come into the room and Mike be standing by the box, looking into it, y'know? Watching this bird that's—taking John's affections away from him. And yesterday John got up the bird was dead: all the feathers were like ruffled over the box? And Mike was standing there with a little smile on his face looking at the bird. And John *knows* Mike killed the bird."

"Wow."

"That gave me fucking goosebumps, man: honest to God."

"How come you're not working today?" I ask him.

"Well they been sending me regular to this Burdette Wine, off Ninety-Third, but Burdette's closed today for inventory or something. Pretty good place: they call down the hall and ask for me by name."

"Yeah?"

"The receptionist out there, this Jenny? Nice broad. *Super* personality; always got a smile on her face, always laughing . . ."

"What's so funny?"

"Me, I guess. I always stop and bullshit with her a little bit . . . She told me the other day she said she always looks forward to seeing me."

"Really? She nice-looking?"

"Aw. Couldn't find a better-looking broad. Probably got guys calling her every night."

"Hm."

"Sweet Jenny."

. . . Detroit Avenue, inevitably.

He says "You want me to buy you a blowjob, cheer you up?"

"What?"

"You're obviously a little depressed, you're bored—"

"Ed . . ."

"I got an extra fifteen here, I'll just pull over and get a coffee—you can take the car—"

"Forget it."

"See this broad? Up ahead?"

"Who? Yeah. In the blue T-shirt?"

"Yeah. See this guy walking behind her?"

A lone Puerto Rican man, limping three steps behind her with a can of beer in a brown bag.

"Yeah."

"This fucking guy— That's her pimp! You'd think he'd—"

"She must be the only one out here with a pimp."

"Yeah. You'd think he'd—stand discreetly off to one side, let her do her business. Or wait on a corner, y'know? I've tried to pull over and talk to her three or four times already, he's always right there behind her—Staring at you! Lookit that fucker . . ."

They go by.

Ed swings a U-turn, drives back, rolling down the window . . .

Across from them he slows the car.

"Hey!"

They stop: a dumpy puzzled hooker and her pimp, a small, nervous guy—suddenly alert—

"*You* are the worst pimp in the city!"

She turns to look at her man and he stands there, nailed and bewildered.

"The *absolute worst* pimp in the entire city."

The man looks deflated. We drive off.

i feel everything and nothing for you, sadie. any case i'm here again and groaning over what i've made you—my sleeves're gorillaskin, the lights have their say and i'm hooded underneath. (shiver) someone walking on my grave . . . no shine on the bedroom walls in the dark, the running slipping reflections along the hood of the buick, the red of the oil light comes on . . . the clothes in the closet, i dunno what they're up to . . . / give us a scream, esquerita—no, not like that; like this: *yyyyyyyyyiiiiieeeeAI!*/ the night roofs of cars're shined like piano—/ johnny?/ . . . shuffle on the stairs . . . d'you really exist or have i created all this? —sick of this pregnant telephone/ today was a day—/ the walls're chalk, and this warehouse yearning/ —like no other/ the softball team's favorite girl/ —like any other . . .

I was trying to milk momentum out of a sterile jukebox—you were busy at the other end of the bar. I didn't bother to dangle the keys anymore, just sat in place like a plant. How did I used to do this? When did I pawn my point of view?

LAUGHTER

The afternoon's rolling down Detroit Avenue cellblock in a '74 Pontiac Dumpster: *Racing Form* floormats, fastfood bags and sportpage seats . . . Scope, transistor batteries and menthol cigarettes—the usual equipment . . . Ed's got the windows tinted just right with a year of basketball baseball and football smoke and I got my very dark shades to heighten contrast and cut the blinding overcast grey of lost weekday afternoons. There goes Wendy, parked in her Toyota . . . shooting coke into a purple scar in her throat . . . another lonely form of entertainment . . . A voice in the Avenue Bar says "Here comes the Terminator," as we mount our rocking-horses and Ed bets twenty quarters on the same song . . . "Only thing I like better'n a shot is *you*," says a voice to a barmaid who ages as we watch, and another says "Anything he like better'n a shot he ain't had in ten years." Ten years. "Make it a double," and it seems like there should be a—What day is this? I had something important to tell someone. Pass me that bottle. We should have rain . . . we might as well. Man, this's gotta end somewhere, but Ed's got it on cruise control. And I'm as cold and useful as a parking meter in the rolling empty stretch of Detroit Avenue on a lost weekday afternoon.

I picked up a cheeseburger from the G-Spot for dinner, ate it from the styrofoam tray in the dimming kitchen, trying to think of something to do.

Called Al.

"Yeah."

"Yeah."

"What's up?" he said.

"Nothing. What're you doing?"

"Just sitting around . . . listening to Frank Sinatra . . . reading *Mein Kampf* . . ."

I sat on the steps of the porch.

The girl from the drugstore walked by, pushing a stroller. Across the street, an immense Puerto Rican kid stopped to look around. I gauged him at five hundred pounds. He lobbed a contemptuous glance my way and rolled on.

Time passed. A rooster crowed, and crowed again. He'd be fighting in someone's basement tonight.

A red Cougar slid by: the guy had transformed his tires into whitewalls with paint. His radio was so loud the whole street was one clear thumping stereo—

Baby I can't stand to see you happy . . . More than that, I hate to see you sad . . .

Music stood in the air after he'd turned the corner . . .

The phone was ringing upstairs. I crashed into the apartment and grabbed it—"Hello?"

"Hi," she said.

". . . Hey, Marie. How you doing?"

"Oh, okay. What're you up to?"

"Just uh . . . watching the world go by. What's up?"

"Well, I'm going out tonight with some friends? And I'm just completely broke because the copy shop isn't paying us until Friday this week . . ."

"I ain't got much . . . I can give you twenty—"

". . . Are you sure?"

"Yeah, sure. You gonna pick it up?"

"Well they're coming to pick me up any minute—"

"Yeah. Well just stop by here on your way, I'll be here."

"Is that okay?"

"Sure, why not?"

"Okay . . ."

"Okay."

". . . Thanks," she said, trying to say more.

I took a fifth and a beer to the porch, lit a cigarette on the steps.

They rolled up in a big green Plymouth, about five or six of them, laughing and talking ahead of one another. Marie got out, trying for the moment to disengage herself from them. She came through the gate and I got off the steps, kissing her on the cheek and slipping a folded twenty into her hand . . .

"Thanks," she said.

"No problem."

She asked if I wanted to come along and I thanked her no, told her to enjoy herself, wherever they were going—dancing or rock climbing or skinny-dipping . . . She waved and they pulled off, and I went back to the steps.

It was too wide out there. I went upstairs.

I picked up a book and read a few pages but felt dishonest, so I let it go.

After dark I went back down. Ed's car was there.

"I been running around all day tryna scare up enough for a two-teamer, managed to get twenty-five—I got Oakland and the Reds. Got a call from Angelface. She wants to go out on Detroit, try to make a few bucks, so I'm gonna take her over there, park the car and listen to the games, keep an eye out for her. Maybe get a blowjob out of it."

"Uh-huh."

"Talked to John today. He put out the word he's looking for a sombrero for little Mike—"

"A sombrero?"

"His sister went to Mexico with her fiance and come back empty-handed. Mike's been pulling a face, so if anyone can come up with a little straw sombrero for Mike, John'll be off the hook."

I was sitting by the window when he pulled away: freshly talced, a transistor on the seat beside him. The Ricans were break-dancing on flattened boxes on the corner . . .

I ran out of money.

I'd seen it coming, but I couldn't pull myself together. I was still adjusting to leisure. Hanging around Ed didn't help. He was just winging it. I had this feeling that if I kept myself open to possibilities and free to choose, everything would arrange itself to suit my new-found priorities. In short, I didn't want to work.

I was digging through my desk one morning when I came upon a Visa card.

Blank. A new beginning.

I'd gotten it in the mail by one of those accidents of random selection. Somebody up there thought I was a good citizen.

In the light of a new morning it was obvious this was no accident: this was fate: the big knowing smile of fortuity. I took it straight to the bank.

"You have a five-hundred-dollar limit, Sir."

"Yeah, I'd like a hundred-dollar cash advance, please."

I headed east, to spend the day with my father.

On the way I stopped at a big discount store to pick up some things I needed: razorblades and talc and Royal Crown . . . Making my way up and down the aisles, I spotted a display of suntan lotion. It was a stand of shelves under a big sign: two silhouettes, male and female, relaxing on a beach at sundown. The shelves were stocked with brown bottles, each with a little straw sombrero atop its cap.

Glancing around, I palmed a bottle and strayed into an al-cove and started struggling with the sombrero. It was glued on tight and the cap unscrewed and the aisle started smelling like coconuts. The straw began to rip and under my T-shirt sweat trickled down my side . . .

A man in a white shirt walked by and I cooled it, bending over to examine the tampons.

When he disappeared I pressed on, thinking What the fuck am I doing? Here I'm risking embarrassment as a shoplifter tryna steal a straw hat for a plastic hippo . . . That fucking John's got *me* sucked into it now!

I got the sombrero loose, pushed it into a pocket and went to the checkout with my heart pounding.

It was still light when I got back to the Southside, but a whole day was gone: another day.

Ed was home.

I took a Pabst from his fridge and he said "It's been two days now, I still ain't heard from Angie."

"What happened the other night, when you took her out on Detroit?"

"I took her over there, gave her a beer, she was kinda danc-ing around on the curb . . . Couple guys picked her up, she made a few bucks . . . And then she went in the City Grill—I was waiting, waiting . . . I waited another hour, listened to the rest of the game, she never come out. I came home."

Ed and I are at the fence, assessing the morning . . . taking stock . . . listing the options, weighing the pros and cons and drawing up an agenda when Jimmy D comes by, shuffling his way to Feef's.

"Hey, Jimmy."

"How's it going there, kid?" he whispers.

"How you doing?"

He stops. He says "I haven't hit a baseball bet in sixty-three days. Yesterday was sixty-three days. Today will be sixty-four."

"Wow. What about the horses?"

He hands me a slip of paper listing yesterday's horse bets—names underlined and scribbled out . . . full of loops and arrows . . . I can't make head or tail of it.

"What's this thirty-seven minus twelve?"

"I bet thirty-seven dollars on horses yesterday and I won back twelve."

". . . Yeah. Well, with any luck today you'll lose it all. Still, I don't see how you could lose sixty-three consecutive baseball bets."

"It's them fucking three-teamers. I'm betting five-dollar three-teamers. Two games come in, I lose the third."

"Why not bet two-teamers?"

"I can't afford it."

Pancho comes by, with that alky buzz: "Hey amigos . . . Okay, bueno, coños . . . Be very careful, eh? Bueno—goodbye—see you . . ."

Ed says "I meant to tell you, Danny: yesterday there's a big fight out here, up by the bar. Middle of the street, about twelve guys: chains, bats—one guy's chasing a girl, they're all screaming . . . This Pancho walks up—walks to the middle of the street—Takes off his shirt *and his pants*—"

"Oh come on—"

"Takes off his shirt and his pants, and sits down, in the middle of the street—In his shorts, with his legs crossed—"

"You mean like Gandhi?"

"Yeah; like an Indian or something—Sits in the street, the sun's beating down—Cat Lady told me he's dying, so now he goes into the street and defies cars to hit him: he's not afraid of anything. Thing is: you're coming this way with the sun blaring in your windshield—You're lucky if you see the fucking guy! Cars're swerving around him, hitting the horn— And then he gets up—everybody's looking at him—Pulls his pants on— Goes up to the guys're fighting and puts his arm around one of 'em, starts muttering some Puerto Rican incantations or something—And breaks up the fight!"

"Just like Gandhi!"

Jimmy turns to watch Pancho making his way.

"Yeah," he says, "I see him around here with that big stick, he looks like he lost his flock. I asked him where's his sheep, but he don't understand nothing . . ."

The breath coming in the window is cool, tonight. Cool breath from a purple sensibility . . .

I feel like an ape—an ape in a cage with changeable bars: as big and beautiful as any other ape out in the brush, in the trees—but stuck in this stinking jail, waiting to be set free—/

. . . the corner of a glass ashtray holds light, in the dark . . . the shoulder of a bottle . . .

"I like any song with a train in it," she said the other day.

. . . a particularly cool breath tonight, from the purple core of the world at large . . . I feel like a skeleton.

/ Or waiting to set myself free:

The next evening I stepped into Ed's kitchen and was surprised and a little spooked to see a blond boy bound to a kitchen chair. Suspending judgment, I looked around, and Ed came out of the frontroom. I glanced again at the chair. It was Angie, sitting bolt upright.

Ed said "Get this. Five days I don't hear from her, right? Calls me this morning—By some complete miracle she still got that fucking matchbook—Calls me twelve o'clock says she's at the Justice Center. She been eating baloney sandwiches for five days—says she's calling 'cause she's getting tired of baloney."

Angie, as a presence, is fiercely alert, but somewhere else.

"She got arrested for Solicitation at the City Grill, bail's like a hundred bucks—Luckily I *had* a hundred here I hit Feef last night, otherwise she'da been fucked! Jump in the car, go down there—I'm walking around the halls tryna find out where they got her— See this fucking bus parked outside—There's Angie, in the line! I go Holy fuck— Warrensville House of Correction on the side of the bus. No trial, no hearing—nothing. One phonecall. Run to the desk, tell the broad I come to bail out a friend of mine—She says I gotta get a bondsman. Where the fuck am I gonna find a bail bondsman? So I'm running down the hall—Here's this old guy leaning against a column—hat pulled over his eyes—Looked like he's asleep, y'know? I said 'Where can I find a bondsman?' Moves the hat—hands me a card—Carl Green: Mr. Freedom. He was a fucking bondsman!"

"*[laughter]* "

"So anyway I paid the hundred—In the nick of time: she'da been out by Thistledown, breaking rocks. Got her outa there, they set a court date for three weeks, I gotta keep an eye on her, otherwise I'm responsible for the other nine hundred . . ."

Angie was scrawling, avidly, on a sheet of notebook paper, oblivious. Ed was lighting a Newport.

"So what happened, that night you took her out?"

"Took her out on Detroit, I's waiting for her—She goes into the City Grill . . . And she's hanging around there, guy comes up to her, says 'Hey, my friend over here's looking to meet a girl. He'll give you sixty bucks for some head. But he's afraid to ask, he's kinda shy . . . All you gotta do is walk up and say "I'll give you a blowjob for sixty bucks."' Vice cops. Obviously, right?"

"Yeah."

"Those BASTARDS!" Angie said.

We looked at her. She was scribbling.

"So, being the innocent, trusting waif that she is, she goes up to this other guy, says 'Uhh, Hi, I'll give you a blowjob for sixty dollars—' *Bam*: flips out a badge, they close the place down, throw her in the car, place been closed ever since. And that's *totally* against the law, according to everything I know about prostitution. A total setup, she just walked right into it. And—vice cops are the absolute lowest scum of the Earth, as you know, but even I was surprised, y'know—"

Angie let out a triumphant laugh and sat straight up.

"Angie you want something? You want a beer, some lemonade?"

She was staring at something invisible to us, right above the door . . .

"So that's the story," he said, putting out the cigarette. "She gotta go to court in three weeks, I told her she can stay here till then. We went to her place, picked up her stuff . . . —We're walking outa the fucking Justice Center, y'know? I said 'Hey

Angie—I got a surprise for you. We'll go to my place—I *know* you must be hungry, so I got a nice, big *baloney* sandwich waiting for you.' She goes 'Ohh . . . Okay . . . '"

Angie said "Will you take me to look for a house tomorrow? I have to buy a house. And I have to go to the library."

Headed for the day's first mirror the sight of the kitchen table registers in my mind, apparently for the first time in weeks. It's as good a mirror as the one in the bathroom. Standing there in the morning kitchen and then sitting at that table shining in the sunlight, I'm struck by the motions I go through unawares— by their cumulative result—By all the *objects*, piled and littered across this damn table—many of them beyond explanation: coupons, an amusement park cup . . . a baseball schedule, a rhinestone bracelet, a candy necklace, various pills . . . packets of soy sauce, firecrackers, notes on napkins . . . a homemade brass knuckles, a butter smear and a broken cigarette dispenser . . . candle wax, two betting slips, a plastic roulette wheel, an old phonebill, a cigar, a postcard . . . couple of nails and screws—a doorknob, a suitcase key— *Who lives here?*

Sitting at the morning table with my hands in my lap and a trace of a smile on my face. My life is like the emperor's new clothes.

I'm ready to start the clean-up when Ed sits down and un- folds the sports over the whole mess, waiting for breakfast, making topical observations as the sunlight fills with curling smoke . . . I get to work on breakfast, making coffee and hash- browns and frying eggs with pepperoni and a couple chili pep- pers. The state of the table is only a symptom, so I leave it like it is, clearing enough space for our two plates and disturbing Ed's diatribe . . .

Ed's eating faster and faster, following one thing with another—eggs to pepperoni to potatoes to bread, trying to kill or at least keep pace with the sting of the peppers.

"—Wow," he says. "Jesus."

"Have some coffee."

He grabs a swallow—winces—exhales—"That makes it fucking worse!"

"Sorry."

"You don't belong in this neighborhood," he says. "You should be up on Coventry or something."

"Whattaya mean?" I ask, offended.

"Danny: face it. You're a gourmet kinda guy. You eat fucking romaine lettuce, you take pleasure in eating, you—"

"You're crazy."

"—Last night I came up here, you're eating fucking pasta, and salad with all kinda greens only a gourmet like yourself would know about . . . There's a fucking—some kinda symphony music playing, candlelight—"

"That's 'cause the fucking bulb burned out."

"Danny: I know about people, and I can tell you're just a different—Someday you'll be a millionaire, you'll have a broad on each arm, you'll go to the opera, driving a big fucking car—"

"I'm driving a big car now."

"—You won't even come to the Southside anymore. I'll see you at the fifty-dollar window at the track, I'll be in the two-dollar line, tryna get your attention—"

"I want you to know I feel the same about you."

"Thanks," he said. "In the meantime, you got an extra ten?"

"I's just gonna ask you."

I slipped our plates into the sink, ran some water and sat back down . . . lit a cigarette . . .

"You hear from Angie?"

"Aww man," he said. "Why'd you have to bring that up?

Why'd you have to bring up the tragic subject of Angelface?"

". . ."

"Ain't heard a peep! I come back from the hall there was no sign of her. No guitar, no geometry books, no note—Nothing! Drove to Forty-Seventh—No sign of her there—She just vanished! The fucking court date's in like two weeks, I pray to God she surfaces by then, otherwise I'm responsible for that nine hundred, which obviously I ain't got . . . That's the payment I get for helping her out. Not that she'd intentionally skip, but you know how addle-brained she is . . . I'm sure she completely forgot about it already."

I got up to wash the dishes. "Heard from John?"

"Yeah. Get this. John's brother *Don's* got a daughter name Cathy—"

"John's niece."

"Yeah. Cathy was bringing her fiance over to Don's house, to meet the family. Okay? John and his mother were invited, so they went . . . and John brought little Mike with him. And Mike don't like animals, like I told you. John had Mike in his pocket. Anway . . . Cathy's fiance is there in the livingroom, they're having coffee, right? And the cat comes in the room. John says Mike seen the cat, man—I dunno if he got pissed off or whatever but he—somehow he got out of John's pocket and he went after the cat: underneath the coffee table. And they were *fighting* under the table, with everybody sitting there and this normal *guy*, tryna go out with Don's daughter, and this *loon* sitting across from him there . . . And Mike and the cat are fighting, right? John dives under the table—to separate 'em? He's under the table, he gets up the fucking table turns over—coffee all over the place . . . This fiance's looking around at everybody, John's like rolling around on the floor . . ."

"*[laughter]* "

"Anyway, everybody was tense, after that . . . cups all over the place . . ."

UNDER THE CROUCH OF EVENING

I said "So you think they're gonna hire you at Burdette?"
   "They gave me the papers to sign, I didn't sign 'em yet . . ."
   "Why not?"
   "Well it's a big decision, uh . . . big decision. They asked for my uniform size, uh . . ."
   "?"
   "That's it. I'm gonna get a uniform and a hat—one of them hats with the flaps for the ears, go to K-Mart and get a black lunchpail, a pair of thick black workshoes and maybe some thick glasses—"
   " [laughter] "
   "I'll just cash in my chips."
   "Attaboy."
   "I might as well, 'cause I got so many marks against me by now, from working outa the hall . . ."
   "Like what?"
   "Like that—time I turned the truck over, y'know . . ."
   "When was that?"
   "Couple years ago, coming back from Sandusky. It's a long fucking run, y'know? and I get to East Ninth Street: the exit there, where the freeway loops around—I felt myself dozing off man, I made that turn: scariest moment of my life, I felt the truck tipping over— Ain't like you can do anything about it, I'm—whoooaa— Just flipped on its side, rolled down that little embankment—fucking top of the truck peels off like a

can of tuna—All the wine spilled—hundreds of cases of wine all over the place. I woke up I was upside down with a lit cigarette in my mouth—gasoline dripping on my face— Within seconds: at least ten cars stopped and people ran to help me— pulled me outa the cab. Which you would do anybody would do. People—No matter how much hatred there is in this world, when someone's hurt like that people *stop*. Fucking TV3 News come down there—The truck was upside down! Wine was all *over* the place. Not that much broke, because it was five hundred cases of pints, and they're hard to break anyway. Maybe fifty cases broke. That's still a mess: you're talking six hundred pints of wine man, the whole freeway was high. And this the God's truth: there musta been forty winos down there. 'Cause the truck was there like four five hours . . . Every color tennis shoe, every color tie . . . every different hat . . . This's Night Train Express wine, cheapest rotgut— Every fucking leisure suit you ever wanted to see in your life. It was a hell of a selection: I was looking at 'em myself."

"Uh-huh."

"Pink shoelaces, blue sunglasses—"

"*[laughter]* "

"Cops come down— They asked for some wine! Can you believe this? So I put like ten pints—He says 'Put it over there, not by the car.' Never got a ticket, never got fired—Nothing!"

"*[laughter]* . . . that's great . . ."

"Then about a week later, the boss's on my case about the baloney slicer—"

"What was that?"

"There used to be a place off Twenty-Fifth called the Market Street Exchange, they had a fucking meat slicer weighed two ton. I made a delivery there, right? Through the back kitchen door, same as I do every week . . . About an hour later I call the company: 'Vinnie wants to talk to you.' Vinnie Toomb: his name was Toomb: T-O-O-M-B. He looks like a sloth: his back's curved, he drinks Tyrolia wine. Pull in: there's

Vinnie, two supervisors, and another bigshot with their arms crossed—I go Holy fuck, man—What'd I do now? They go 'Open the back of the truck.' I go The fuck, man? They think I got a broad back there, or—? I open up there's nothing back there—Vinnie says 'I wanna see you in the office.' Sits down, he says 'Market Street Exchange called, they said you got their meat slicer.' I kinda smiled, I said 'What, Vinnie?' 'After you made your delivery the meat slicer was gone.' And I remember, 'cause I bump into this thing every week: it's in the kitchen, you can barely get by it with the wheeler. Fucker's *wrought iron*, must weigh four ton; I remember I always scrape my arm on it. I go 'Vinnie, you mean that slicer they got in the back room?' 'Yeah. They accuse you of taking it.' I says 'Vinnie that thing weighs four ton,' I said '*Snow* Brothers with their *crane* couldn't take that motherfucker! You think I picked it up put it on my shoulder and threw it in the back of the truck?' I laughed out loud in his face! After a while he calm down, he realized how stupid that sounded. But they were waiting for me! They were gonna try and trap me! I said 'Vinnie, that thing couldn't be moved by *God*.'"

"*[laughter]* "

"But even if you're in the right, this shit builds up against you. And this Vinnie Toomb knows me anyway from way back, he used to be general manager at Sun Valley when I was working there. So he knows all about me. I had a card game in the back of the truck, one time during a blizzard. Me and Franco, I lost all the company money, drank all this wine . . . didn't do half my route . . ."

"Whattaya mean, you ran into Franco on the route?"

"Ran into Franco, we got six guys together we set up a bunch of wineboxes—"

"Outa the blue? You just—"

"I used to see him alla time, he lived in Westlake."

"But I mean you ran into *six other guys?*"

"He knew guys out there, within ten minutes we had six

guys playing poker in the back of the truck. Started like one in the afternoon, y'know, and there's wine bottles rolling around . . . I barely got in on time, lost all the money—"

"Well what'd you say?"

"I don't remember, I got away with it though . . ."

"Well no: *how* did you get away with it?"

"I didn't lose all the money, I lost like three hundred of it. When I checked in, I wrote up a couplea charges that weren't charges, like—Joe's Grocery paid me two hundred dollars cash—I told Vinnie 'Joe wasn't there, so I said I'd pick up the money tomorrow and they signed for it.' And maybe the next day Vinnie wasn't there, the secretaries don't know what's going on, so bit by bit I covered it. Eventually he caught on to me; I remember when he fired me he said 'Ed, you're a hell of a driver, but you should never have a job handling company funds.'"

"*[laughter]* "

"I never forgot that. We were always at each other's throats. One time he took me in the office, said 'This company's a big *wheel.* And—this is a spoke, and this is a spoke'—y'know, he went around the whole wheel—'All spokes. And—See this one wobbly spoke? This is you. You're the wobbly spoke in our wheel.' Then he told me to get out of his office. Every day I come in there, he'd say 'When you gonna quit?' I go 'Fuck you, whyn't you fire me?'"

"This the same guy who's in charge of the hall now?"

"Yeah. We're starting to get fed up with each other again, they wanna hire me at Burdette, so I guess I got no other options."

Off the porch, in the sky, a plane was lighting its way through clouds . . .

Rain was at the windows.

We were sitting at the 2300 Club, Sadie and I. She'd been partying in the Flats and I responded to her call, got in the Buick and drove downtown and parked on the desolate shine of Payne Avenue.

I had a five left in my pocket and ordered two more shots.

Rain lashed the windows and I turned, while Sadie chatted with someone down the bar. The lights outside were like old explosions, hanging in the mist.

She looked me in the eyes and said "Will you come home with me tonight?"

"Sure," I said. "Listen Sadie—"

"Another drink?" she said, hauling her purse up.

We left the bar in a suppressed eagerness, out into a wide complete rain, soft and swirling and almost silent. I followed her taillights through shining streets. I was shivering at the wheel. I clenched my jaw to contain it, and then the rest of my body, and turned on the heat . . . And within that heat and through a corridor of rain I went on shivering. Must've been nervous.

We disturbed the dark of her apartment only once: a kitchen light went on, then off. She pulled a bottle from a cupboard and drew me toward the bedroom.

There was a fumbling of buttons and fabrics before we

tumbled into bed. Laughing, she reached the bottle off the nightstand and handed it to me.

I remember the pearly expanse of her, the night outside the windows as I went down.

She was far away, I was alone. I rose up, the heavy purple cover slipping off my shoulders, and our mouths closed. She lifted her legs around me and came, quick, as though to leave room . . . I came and crashed away from her, pulled her close and lay listening to rain ticking at the window.

I woke up hungover but not confused.

Eventually we got up, and she made us some eggs and toast.

PHONECALL

That night I called her at work.

"Wild Magnolia—"

"Hey Sadie."

"Hi Danny."

"How's it going?"

"I'm okay, how're you? What're you doing?"

"Uh I just been—looking out the window."

"Baby can I call you back? we're really busy here—"

"Sure."

"Are you at home?"

"Yeah."

"Okay I'll call you back in about an hour."

"Okay."

The thing about sex is—

It changes everything.

I sat up on the cot as though afloat, while the apartment tried to reclaim me. In the kitchen, the faucet dripped. Shadow seeped across the carpet. The light changed, the room got dim.

The phone rang.

"Hi. God, we're so busy tonight. There were all these assholes in here . . ."

"Yeah?"

"I'm so tired, I was so hungover today . . ."

"How you feel now?"

"I feel okay now; Misty gave me a hit of speed."

"Uh-huh."

"Willy came in tonight."

"Oh yeah?"

". . . He's here now."

"Mm."

"Danny? Are you okay?"

"Yeah."

". . . He needs a place to stay for a few days, so I told him he could stay at my place, but he's gotta be out by next week."

"Uh-huh."

"Danny? I've been thinking about you . . ."

"Yeah, me too. I'll let you get back to work, uh . . . Gimme a call."

Walking back from the Greeks, the sky's an inscrutable impenetrable blank, and the air's full of water. Looks like it's shaping up to an all-night rain.

And so it has, so it is . . . Camel streaming, cold coffee, and a neglected shot of whiskey; the night outside dripping and motionless, misted and pollen-sodden, back-lit, puddled, and full of sounds: a motorcycle, two bottlerockets . . . a radio through the backyards. My roof must be leaking.

EVENING

Strike a match against a lighted Ferris wheel turning a block away . . .

Behind the wheel of the Hungry Buick;

exhale, the light goes green . . .

In the near distance: green leaves in profusion, against a wide and yearning summer sky . . .

Deuce-and-a-quarter, Olds 88—all the big cars're great.

Trees rustle within themselves.

Headlights along the flankside.

. . . Riding in cars, protective of a coffee between your legs . . .

There's a whistle up my stairs, and Ed comes up with a bottle of Lambrusco and a six of Pabst.

"Here, I got you a bottle of wine from the truck."

"I can't drink that stuff."

"Why, what's the problem? This ain't up to your gourmet standards?"

"It's too sweet. You're better off freezing it and making popsicles."

"Just put it on the shelf in case you bring a broad back here. They like this kinda wine."

We take the beer to the porch.

"Get this," he says. "Second day as an official employee of Burdette Wine, I got my uniform, my hat—I'm on Great Northern Boulevard, this broad comes flying out of a driveway, cuts me off—Almost killed us both, right? I gave her the finger, says 'You fucking whore . . . ' I go round the block— Here comes this fucking car chasing me, right? I pull in front of the beverage store—on the street—This fucking guy gets outa the car musta weighed four hundred pounds. Fat guy, big fat guy . . . Come running up to the truck—'You motherfucker you give my wife the finger you sonofabitch—' He's *slobbering* over himself, right? his face is beet red—Jumping up and down like a fucking *lunatic!*

"So—I'm real calm, right? and this guy's—'Get outa that fucking truck I'll beat your fucking head in!' I says 'Well your wife cut me off,' he goes 'You called her a fucking whore, you sonofabitch!' I says 'Well, Sir, she *is* a fucking whore,' y'know? I's real calm, 'cause if he hit me, I was gonna *fly* outa the truck and lay on the ground—"

"*[laughter]* "

"—Flat on my back in the middle of the street till the paramedics got there: I'da *sued* the motherfucker. I *wanted* him to hit me. First of all he couldna got a good blow in 'cause he hadda reach inside the window, he mighta got me one good shot. And—He wanted to grab me but he *knew* not to do that. He's going up and down, 'Get outa that fucking truck! I'll *take* you outa there!' I said—real polite, I says 'Pull me outa the truck then, go 'head . . . you motherfucker you . . .'"

"*[laughter]* "

"So he's scream—This about ten minutes, cars're pulling over—My buddy's in the beverage store across the street—He don't know what's going on, he sees this big gorilla jumping up and down . . . I thought this guy was gonna get a heart attack. I go 'Your wife—don't know how to drive a fucking *car*, man, I––She tryna kill me?' He goes 'You son—I—I'll kill you!' I says 'Waitaminute: *I* know what you're tryna do you're tryna *rob* me, aren't you?'"

"*[doubled laughter]* "

"'You know I have three thousand dollars in cash here— POLICE!—OFFICER! OFFICE—I'm *tryna* make a living delivering wine, I'm—Don't hurt me—I *have* money here, okay I *have money*—' Oh, then he went crazy. I'm going 'SOMEBODY HELP ME!' I said 'This a busy time of year, you *know* I have money here—*Why else would you be tryna hurt me?*'"

"*[laughter]* "

"Oh, he's going '*You rotten motherfucker*—' Finally he went away . . . but I had him so shook up . . ."

The story trailed off in circular repetitions and I regained my breath.

Then I said "How's Jenny?"

"Who?"

"Jenny. The receptionist."

"How you know about her?"

"You told me about her."

"Oh. She's great, man. Nicest broad in the world. Every day she's—'When we gonna go out? When you gonna take me out?'"

"Whyn't you take her out?"

"Aah, this broad's a thoroughbred, man. I can't ask her out."

"You never know . . ."

COURT DATE

Ed had been fretting and bitching and speculating about Angie since the day she disappeared. The yellow bond receipt he'd taped to the wall said eleven am. He folded it into a shirtpocket and we drove downtown with about twenty bucks between us. There wasn't a chance she'd be there.

The lobby of the Justice Center was much bigger than it had to be: cool granite and high open space . . . a few modern sculptures placed here and there, as though to display their insignificance . . . a stylish oak Information Desk in the distance . . .

The elevator sealed us in with lawyers, cops, and the relatives of defendants. Only the lawyers spoke, in low tones that sounded like gossip.

We stepped into a long roomy waiting area, the massive wooden courtroom doors on both sides . . . big bay windows at either end . . . up in the mist . . . high above the streets . . .

People were dressed up. There were alert Latinos, listening for familiar words, commands . . . and poor whites, grim and darkly awaiting the worst . . . and tired skinny black women, worried about which verdict would be best for their men, or boys, or daughters . . . for themselves. There were fathers who'd said their last word and mothers full of helpless guilt, their sons in new suits watching even now for escape routes . . .

And in the midst of this held breath of hopeful respectability we spotted her: Angie: framed against the far bay window, pausing to dig for cigarettes—a polka dot scarf, paisley halter, lemonyellow miniskirt and homemade black felt boots . . . big pink shades, lots of lipstick. How could a judge mistake her for a prostitute? Whatever this was for Ed, it was only an appointment for her.

He said "Angie."

She looked up and said "Oh, hi," and went back to digging for cigarettes. If he was planning to say something else, Angie'd stopped him cold.

A guy in a blue Teamsters jacket walked by, looking at us.

Angie found a cigarette. "Have you got a light?"

Ed came up with a lighter. The Teamster circled around . . . floated closer—paunchy, furtive . . . haunted.

Angie said "This's Henry."

Ed and Henry shook hands with a shock of recognition. Two fat, lonely, wary slobs watching out for Angie . . .

Henry drifted away, came back. Eventually we all went in through the heavy wooden doors.

There were lots of cases to be called and nowhere to sit. We squeezed against the wall. Henry stood on the other side of the room, glancing over at us . . . wondering about our involvement with Angie . . . filling unexplained pockets of time with our faces . . . imagining us nude . . .

Ed appeared hardened toward any development.

The bailiff called her up: Angela Catherine Beam.

She was busy collecting her swirling possessions She hauled her carpetbag out of the wings and up in front of the judge—

*

She got off with a suspended sentence and a fine.

The fine was exactly equal to what Ed had posted for bail, and nothing more was said of it.

Angie was applying more lipstick and talking about getting

272

her car back as Henry took her arm and nodded to us and hurried her out of there.

There was a ticket on the Pontiac. We left its pieces at the curb. The sky was grey and without meaning.

Ed didn't feel much better after the trial than he had before—she was gone again—but we went down St. Clair to a strip joint to celebrate his not having to come up with another nine bills . . . Thirty bucks later the sky had cleared.

On a sunny afternoon we pull up in front of John's to pick up a ten. I step out to wait.

He comes out on the roof without a shirt. Looks different.

"John—You losing weight?"

"Yeah," he calls down, "I'm on my new weight-loss program. I'm down to one sixty-five; I've lost fourteen pounds already."

"Yeah, I can tell. What're you doing?"

He drops me the balled-up paper bag.

"I've been running the stairs. Every day I run up and down the stairs a hundred times. Forty-eight stairs: twenty-four up, twenty-four down—forty-eight hundred per day. This'll be my tenth day: I've done 48,000 steps. Got fifty flights under my belt already today."

"That's—"

"Twenty-four hundred steps."

"Yeah, that's great. It ain't even noon."

"Yeah: I got rid of my gut. You oughta get Ed up here, do a few flights."

"Good idea. Keep up the good work."

Back in the car I opened the bag, handed Ed the ten and took out the sandwich.

Ed looked over. "Ham?"

"Salami, this time."

He rolled down the window.

Racetrack traffic was backed-up on the freeway.

Ed said "I gotta go on a diet myself. Gotta get in shape for Jenny. Sweet Jenny Smolinski."

"Yep."

"She called me this morning, can you believe that? Wanted to go to the beach."

"Really?"

"Yeah she's like that, y'know . . . sun-and-surf kind of a broad, which you know I could never uh . . ."

"Yeah; yeah."

"Lying there with my—shrunken head and my big gut, like some monster washed up from prehistoric times—"

"*[laughter]*"

"Kill the whole relationship right there. I rather keep my clothes on for a while here. She got a—tan slim body, I got a big white one, but she's such a dildo she's willing to let it ride . . ."

"But that's great she called you."

"Yeah, I dunno what she's after . . ."

"Well . . . Maybe she wants someone to make her laugh."

"Exactly: she wantsa laugh at me."

"Naw, that's not what I—Y'know, she just lonely or something. She wants some company."

"The hell she calling *me* for? She must have thirty guys wanna take her to the beach."

"That's what you think. That's what the other thirty guys think too. Meanwhile she's stuck in the middle till someone makes a move."

"Well she'll have her chance tomorrow night; the office having some kinda party at the Holiday Inn on Rockside."

"You gonna go?"

"She made me promise I'd be there, but I—I can't do that. That's not my kinda scene, a fucking disco . . . I'd be totally out of place there. I might stop in for one drink."

"Yeah, good."

"Maybe she'll meet some guy her own age and I'll have her off my back."

"Off your mind, you mean."

"Yeah, whatever."

First thing at the track, I got fifty in cash off my Visa at the Customer Relations office.

Luckily I hit the first two races, so I had money to lose the next five or six.

On our way out I handed the remains of my *Form* to a guy at the foot of the stairs. Another guy asked Ed for a light, and then said "Hey—How you doing?"

"I can't remember where I seen your face before . . ."

"Poker game!"

"Yeah, yeah," Ed said, extending a light. "You sent me home a few times."

The guy showed a moment of pride and then asked for Ed's program.

I rode back with five bucks in my pocket, Sunday evening on the way, nothing to do.

Later I went next door; Ed was on the phone with Sweet Jenny.

The hometeam's playing ball for a change tonight. Stretched out in the hard narrow seats of general admission among a handful of strangers, a fat half moon hanging up between the overheads—the night above domed and roofed out by the glare of those lights . . . and below, spread out, the grass of the outfield is greener than green, the uniforms of the fielders whiter than clean . . .

The pitcher into motion, the ball vanishes and then appears with a *crack*, rising white and straight and high—diminishing to show its speed: high and back: goes foul.

The field looks like America herself: the long white lines of the road, surrounded by darkness . . . the players bright, like outposts along that road, surrounded by night . . .

Bottom of the fifth: maybe they'll win this one. If they do it's a double saw from Feef tomorrow. If they don't, it's still a night out.

The waiting, all spread out . . . the pitcher into motion—ball disappears and *crack*, is soaring back, diminishing to show its speed toward the stands—Colors there rise and mingle, converging near the souvenir ball . . .

Way in the upper deck, all alone, is John Adams, with his drum; I've seen his picture in the paper. He takes three buses across town with a kettledrum, hauls it into that high corner and drums resoundingly at key moments for team support. One man on, and the team's only homerun hitter comes to bat: *BOOM*-BOOM, *BOOM*-BOOM, *BOOM*-BOOM, *BOOM*-BOOM . . .

Stretched out in general admission, jacket draped over the seat beside me, I reach for cigarettes . . . light one. The spread-out waiting, pitcher into motion . . .

The hometeam's a losing team, but they've got to win sometimes in spite of themselves. Top of the ninth and they're ahead by four. I grab my jacket and head for the stairs . . . down the ramp and into the outer arena, resounding with ballpark echoes: concrete and girders and ramps . . . hit the men's room for a piss in the big old stadium, and then out into the parking lot, into the night—a night glared and tainted with echoes and the image of something left behind: the green of the outfield, of mythology . . .

Ed picks up the cereal box, looks over the ingredients and gives it a shake. "Man, I'm starving. I can't wait to eat some of this at seven o'clock. Two days on my diet, I been doing real well. It's making me sick and it's killing me, but I'm doing it."

". . . So all you're eating is Rice Krispies?"

"No, naw, I'm having normal food, I had—I stopped last night I had a salad and a glass of ice water . . ."

"Huh . . . Good for you. If John can do it you can do it."

"He just called. Said he's still running the stairs. He said he's going for a million."

"They must love it at the autopart store."

"They got a sign above the desk: *Caution: Lunatic Above.*"

"Right."

"He said he's in a bar today on St. Clair—one of them Croatian joints with the buzzer on the door?"

"Yeah."

"No one but him and the barmaid, she's doing crossword puzzles, he's staring at her . . . He says he looked her straight in the eye—'Like a snake with a rabbit,' he says. He thinks of himself as a Casanova, y'know . . . Says her eyes going back and forth from the paper to John—she can't concentrate, 'cause John's got her under his spell."

"Right."

"And he's sitting there, he starts rubbing his thighs, y'know? Suggestively rubbing his thighs: his *powerful* thighs, he says, he's—'I've always had strong thighs—'"

"*[laughter]* . . . Christ . . ."

"So the barmaid's getting more and more nervous, John's rubbing his thighs faster and faster, and she's—y'know, *(gulp)*— Only the two of 'em in the place, and she start pacing back and forth, John's hypnotizing her with his eyes—And she grabs a bottle, pours herself a shot—"

"*[laughter]* . . . So what happened?"

"I dunno, he left it at that, to keep me hanging. Just to show me what a ladies' man he is. I could tell he wanted me to ask, but I wouldn't give him the satisfaction. Broad was probably terrified! Figured she had some kind of a nut on her hands, staring at her and rubbing his legs like a big cricket there—"

"*[laughter]* "

"But I told him about some of these broads I pick up like Wendy, Brenda—just to give him something else to think about besides baseball—And he goes 'You mean you *pay* for it?' I said 'Yeah, y'know, once in a while I got an extra twenty I take a ride.' He says 'You're sick! *I'd* never pay for it—I *never* had to pay for it!' I's—I was so pissed off I was speechless. Here's this total *dud*—"

"*[laughter]* "

"Total mullet never goes out of his room—Every night I gotta listen to his fucking lunatic remarks— I was so pissed off Danny I was practically strangling the phone . . ."

"Well anyway, how'd it go last night with Jenny?"

"Aah, I went out there, the fucking music's playing . . . And she was there, she's all dressed up, got her high heels on, y'know . . . We had a couple drinks, about fifty guys asked her to dance, but she insisted on sitting with me—I felt like a total jackass there with the lights, y'know, the music . . . Finally I told her I hadda go, she gimme a kiss goodbye . . . I got in the car and come home."

ON A BORROWED TEN

It was getting late.

In the men's room I rinsed my face and caught myself in the mirror: I looked familiar.

"What're *you* doing here?" I said aloud.

The night air is warmer and cooler than expected. A higher, more spacious, more fragrant night's been going on the whole time—right outside the bar.

Grab the jacket from the seat . . . roll down the window, slip inside . . .

It's a good idea to keep testing the door to your cell. Once in a while you find it open.

The old mailtrain song chugs into motion and lights're flashing by along the sides and up the hood, and all kinds of green secrets are rustling in the dark and the limbs of dogwood and crabapple shag and sigh past your face and down your spine and it's all happening here for a change . . .

Down at the lake, Gordon Park, it's only blacks hanging out. A guy to my left, singing like smoke, and a big Regency to the right, packed with fat women spilling laughter like the flash of gold teeth, while the men lean against the fenders and the kids play in the grass before the rocks . . .

Like happening into a secret club here. Cars pull in and cars pull out . . . you hardly ever see a fishing rod, but something's going on and you wish it were you.

I hit the shoreway.

In the home stretch I stumbled onto the mills again:

There it all was! Every time I hit that bridge I felt serious—exultant—committed!—like I wouldn't leave Cleveland till I could grasp that view—*possess* it—articulate how it hit me: the lights—below and abreast and abroad—the smoke in columns—in billows and plumes and trails and trains and that lone leap of fire: a crown a lick a tower a crest an arm a spire of—*god*damnit; missed again . . .

Stepped out of the bar the streets were awash with the sting of sodium lights, raining. Everywhere the ruins and remnants of orange. I looked up to the high operatic falling of rain, caught in streetlights . . .

The street was wet and wide. The ride back took forever.

The clink of the gate sounded like it was attended by other ears than mine. Rain was falling into trees, into the yard.

On instinct, I approached Ed's porch.

They were casual in the shadows. Ed on the porch rail and, I knew, Jenny, on the porch floor against the wall, just away from the rain, a bottle of wine in the cradle of her crossed legs. I felt they'd been awaiting me, but then I was drunk.

"Where you been, boy?"

"I dunno. All over."

"Jenny this Danny, Danny this Jenny . . ."

Her smile was one you'd abdicate for, though it plainly offered you the option of keeping your crown. She was more than Ed realized, or more than he'd expressed. Around my age.

I said "Can I hit that wine?"

She extended it gladly, as to a new partner; said "Ed's been telling me about you."

I took a slug and handed it back.

"Ed's been telling me about you too."

I fished for a cigarette, found one, lit it, and exhaled off the porch into the rain. Realized Ed wasn't drinking. Keeping his wits about him. Good luck.

I felt Jenny regarding me as yet another interesting facet of Ed's world.

Ed was a good host, in the dark. He got us laughing, wondering toward the source of him.

In a while I said goodnight to them.

I got tired of the game and started switching through the channels. I landed on a nature show.

Two scorpions were attempting to mate.

They approached one another with stingers raised: arched for the kill. In order to consummate the act, they had to maneuver themselves into a situation in which neither could kill the other, all the while trying to kill one another. They managed to get locked into a stalemate, the male dropped a sperm packet on the ground and dragged the female over it . . .

The phone rang.

Marie. No—Sadie.

"Hey baby," she said.

"Hey."

"What're you doing?"

"Nothing, just watching the game here . . . getting ready to go out . . ."

"Oh yeah? Where you going?"

"Ah I got some stuff to take care of, gonna take a ride. Why, what's up?"

"I thought you might want to meet me for a drink. Willy went to New York for a few days."

"Yeah . . . I can't really put this off."

"Okay . . ."

"Okay, uh—Yeah, okay. Thanks though."

"Sure Danny."

"Yeah. See ya Sadie."

I put the ballgame back on and watched another few minutes.

Then I went to bed so I could quit reaching for the phone.

*

Telephone!

"*Hello?*"

"Hey."

"Duke?"

"Yeah."

Two-thirty.

"What's up?"

"I need a lift."

"Where you at?"

"Hundred Seventeenth and Clifton. My car's fucked. Starter went."

"Whyncha call a cab?"

"I did. Isn't this Dan's Gypsy Cab?"

"I forgot. Wait'll I get my babushka, I'll be right there."

"Fronta the Shell station."

His grey '75 Malibu was parked on a sidestreet. We tried to jump it but it wouldn't take.

Back in the Buick he said "So how's your smoking going?"

"Aah, same pack a day. Only thing new is I can't afford it."

"See Everett Koop's out?"

"Who?"

"C. Everett Koop. He's outa there."

"Who's that?"

"Surgeon general. He's retiring."

"You know his name?"

"Hey, the guy's on every pack. He's been quoted worldwide."

"Uh-huh."

"Y'know. He don't just smoke and drink—He's got a *job*."

Duke lived on a quiet street. I'd never been there.

He was renting the bottom half of a sturdy frame house . . . nice big porch, big tree out front, a settled calm inside.

The place was furnished in the orderly yet casual fashion of a guy a year or two out of the service, which Duke was. I admired the place, envied him his life there immediately.

"You want coffee?"

"Yeah, sure."

I went into the bathroom to piss.

Flushed the toilet and turned with a start to find a uh— an iguana. Perched atop the shower rod. Three foot long, of thorny green—mosaic, alive, quickly pulsing at the throat, indifferent to me.

"Hey Duke."

"Yeah."

"There's a dinosaur in your bathroom."

"Yeah, that's Gary."

"Yeah," I said, walking into the kitchen. "What's uh—"

"He likes it in there."

I opened his refrigerator.

"What's he eat?"

"He likes lettuce; he eats a lotta lettuce, carrots . . ."

"Yeah."

I let the door close and peered out his kitchen window at darkness.

"I gave him a Bavarian creme donut the other day, he loved that. He's fresh outa the jungle, he never seen no vegetable like that before."

"What's he do?"

"'Bout the same as me. Hangs out, watches *Bonanza* with me in the mornings . . ."

"He smoke?"

"I been tryna get him to start, but he can't seem to figure it out. He forgets to take the cigarette out of his mouth. Just leaves it hanging there, like Vic Morrow. You want sugar?"

I rinsed out my cup, put it back in the rack.

"You can crash here if you want," he said. "That couch folds out."

"Nah I gotta get back. I might get another call. Oh—my car's on empty: gimme a buck for gas."

"That's why you came out here, ain't it? Anything for a buck."

FRANCO

Ed comes back from the trucks looking ten years older. He lets the gate swing shut and leans against it.

"Where you been?" I ask him.

"Played cards all night at Joe's, went straight to work. I can't do this much longer, I'm getting too old."

"Do what? Play cards all night?"

"No: *work*. Really man, I— I come home at night so beat up I feel like *crying*. I don't see no way out, but I can't lift these cases too much longer. Only thing got me through the day is I knew Miss Appleblossom be waiting there."

"How's she?"

"Says I need a woman to put my life in order. Which reminds me I still ain't heard from Angelface."

"Oh yeah: Angie. Perfect woman to put your life in order. How'd you do at the game?"

"I won a basic forty. Played with this guy Franco man, he—The guy's dying. He's literally dying of gambling. This guy chain-smokes ten packs of Pall Malls a night so nervous y'know . . . Last night he comes with about three four hundred bucks . . . Loses it as usual, right? And he's begging. Everybody goes 'Fuck you Frank—you owe me two hundred from the last game!' 'I-a pay you tomorrow. Please, I—' 'No, Frank.' And Joe would always break down and give him something, right? This time Joe says 'Fuck *you* Frank'—Threw him outa the house! *Physically*: grabbed him by the sh—'*Get out!*' Right?

"'Bout three hours later Frank comes back. This is like four in the morning he comes back—with five rolls of quarters."

"Aww—"

"We go 'Frank, *where* in the fuck did you get five rolls of quarters at four o'clock in the morning?' He loses it like in a half hour, right? Now he's broke again.

"He goes 'Joe, maybe you gimme some money.' Joe goes 'I'm gonna *kill* you Frank.' Finally—Frank keeps begging, Joe goes '*Fuck* you'—takes the fucking cards, throws 'em against the wall—'I'm getting the fuck outa here, I'm going running. I can't stand this motherfucker. You guys play your fucking cards.' Joe puts on his sweatsuit—Frank goes 'Joe, maybe you gimme—' '*Fuck you!* So Joe—runs outa the house starts jogging. Joe jogs like five miles a day, right? Hits the street—He looks back— Here comes Frank, outa the house—Chases him down the drive!"

"*[laughter]*"

"Here Frank's got his tight Italian suit on, his tight Italian shoes running after Joe—"

"Yeah: hard shoes—"

"Hard shoes—fucking *tie* on . . . He's smoking a cigarette—Joe says the cigarette's dangling out of his mouth—"

"*[laughter]*"

"Joe's jogging like a deer—he says 'Fuck *him:* I'm *losing* this motherfucker.' He's running a good two miles through the park—Here's Frank, ten steps behind him. Two miles! Right? —Outa shape—little pot belly on him—nerves're shot—chain-smoking as he's running yet— Joe says 'I swear to God, man, I ran about four five miles—through the woods—up the parkway—Here's Frank, ten steps behind me!' He couldn't fucking believe it."

"*[laughter]*"

"He got back to the house—Sat down—We said 'Where's Frank?' he says 'That motherfucker's right behind me!' Two seconds later Franco comes in the door—First thing he says—

'Joe, maybe you gimme some money?'"

"*[laughter]*"

"These guys—laughed so fucking hard— That's the *power* of a sick gambler! Frank's wife come down to the Finn one time. A baby on each arm—and a fucking pistol, like Ma Barker—"

"Not with a pistol . . ."

"She had a twenty-five automatic. *'I'll kill you motherfuckers you bastards ruined my life*—' She goes '*You motherfucking Fast Eddie, you cocksucker*—' And his wife was a nice, gentle—y'know, she don't say cocksucker—I said 'Hey, don't blame me, I lose too—I don't got your husband's money,' she grabbed me by the hair, shook my head around— She chased Frank outa the bar, it was a scary fucking scene! Y'know, she just totally lost her mind!"

"Yeah."

"Aw it's heartbreaking, man, it—They divorced now! He had a beautiful home out in Westlake—two cars—he worked at the mills he made a thousand dollars a week— Cute wife, two good-looking kids—Blew it all! He's *remarried* now to a really good-looking woman. Who's got a house."

"Yeah."

"'Cause he's a good-looking Italian guy."

"Maybe he ain't gambling as much. Besides last night."

"He plays *poker* up on the fucking *crane*."

"*[laughter]*"

"It's like fifty foot high: way up there. They got air-conditioning in 'em. And he owes the black guys down there *tons* of fucking money from—He bets seventy bucks a day in numbers! With the bookie, y'know? And then payday comes: 'Hey: you owe me five hundred for the numbers.'"

"Yeah."

"He's hanging by a fucking thread . . ."

The gas station next door had half the neighborhood on edge. Every day a crowd of hillboys congregated, revving exhaust into the yard, barking in the sun and smashing bottles, hauling carburetors and wheeldrums to and from the junkyard down the hill, jacking trucks all over the sidewalk, stealing batteries and sniffing glue . . . A couple blacks would wander by and all of a sudden there'd be chains flying. Throughout the afternoons they were making test runs: roaring out in clouds of poison gas and sailing off the curb, bouncing into wide fishtails round the corner and around the block eighty miles an hour scattering kids and dogs . . . Much of this was absorbed in the general commotion of daylight, but then they fixed the big Arco sign, brought some girls in and started playing night games. By mid-July they'd transformed the street into a twenty-four-hour pit stop.

The owner of the joint spent his time at a station he owned in a cleaner, quieter neighborhood.

Under the full burden of midsummer any sleep came hard won. Then they started holding motorcycle races. I lay awake one night till three while they were ripping up and down Fairfield—I heard someone say "This'll wake 'em up," and the air burst into firecrackers . . .

In the morning I went over Ed's.

"You hear them fuckers last night?"

"Yeah," he said. "Pick up the other phone."

I went into the frontroom and listened while he dialed.

"Neil's Arco; Neil speaking."

"I'd like to speak to the proprietor please."

"The what?"

"The owner, please."

"Yeah that's me: Neil."

"And are you also the owner of the Neil's Arco station at Fairfield and West Tenth, Sir?"

"Yeah, that's me: what can I do for ya?"

"I'm speaking with Mr. Neil—?"

"Stanley. Neil Stanley. Who's this?"

"Mr. Stanley, my name is Mr. Brooks, I'm an attorney in Maple Heights, and I have here a petition of complaint against your operation on Fairfield, Sir—"

"(sonofa—) *What?*"

"I have five hundred signatures from residents and home-owners in the Tremont area, demanding that the Neil's Arco station at Fairfield and West Tenth be closed down—"

"Are you kidding?"

"This is no joke, Mr. Stanley. I have signed complaints regarding drunkenness among your employees—"

"(*Je*-sus Christ . . .)"

"—Apparently they've been throwing parties at the station after hours—I have the signed complaint of a teenage girl who was propositioned by one of your men—"

"Look, you people can't bully me—"

"It's your employees who're bullying you . . . uh . . . 'Oil and gasoline spills'—the place is a fire hazard—"

"*How long has this been going on?*"

"I have complaints here dating back to June the third. Apparently the station has been turned into some sort of clubhouse for—"

"Meet me down there in fifteen minutes!"

"I'm a busy man, Mr. Stanley, I don't make housecalls. I'm calling as a favor to you to see if this matter can't be resolved out of court. Otherwise I'll be obliged to put this petition into the hands of a prosecutor at City Hall—"

There was a click. Mr. Stanley had hung up.

We went out on the porch.

Ten minutes later a big Olds came wheeling into the station.

There was a lot of yelling, mostly from Mr. Stanley. It didn't last long. We went back in the house.

The station was closed for three days. On the fourth it opened with a whole new crew headed by a guy from West Virginia named Lige who cleaned it up, turned out to be the best and most honest mechanic we'd known, and went home to his family every night.

Saturday night, Vegas Nite at the church—Hundred-and-Second and Lorain, swamped inside the yellow light . . . We've parked the car a few blocks away and strolled toward St. Ignatius to see the Big Man, toward the lights and tents. Summer night in full bloom every Saturday ("I've worked all week so fire me out a cannon Saturday night: here it came and there it goes . . . Sorry baby, my heart came unbuttoned and I lost all my cream on the Tilt-a-Whirl somehow . . .").

We find Fast Eddie inside a tent at one of the tables, deeply entrenched, without spare concentration for surprise at seeing us. We mill around, Al and Dave wander off . . . I watch a few hands and slip him a twenty and slide back out. Pierogis and some kind of jaked-up roulette wheel: bet a couple bucks in quarters and lose them in winnings of thirty-five and forty cents . . .

Music is blowing across the grounds. It filters among the slow jostling crowd, it mingles with passing talk . . . hangs in the air with the food smells and flashing colored lights . . . I'm heading toward its source . . . good song . . . the film I'm supposed to be living out . . . toward a clearing . . . it's loud—the music and its meaning doubling up and beginning to ring . . .

There's an area set aside for dancing—plywood down—moored like a raft in a pool of yellow bug lights . . . presided-over by a crackling sound system . . . the speakers up on posts—roaring, buzzing . . . The whole scene's been wired up by some hillbilly to keep the kids happy. Maybe—hup! behind that speaker—a guy in a baseball cap . . .

People are dancing, but something's off. I stand at the edge watching, takes a moment why. It's the bug-lit faces—one, another, a few more . . .

They're mentally challenged . . . most of them. Downs kids. Or not kids—they're adults like kids, dancing . . . maybe a dozen of them . . . They're moving around . . . they're on the beat, they stray off . . . get involved in little eddies of private thoughts: a chopping motion, a repetitive gesture . . . they're having fun, dancing to music that doesn't take them into account . . .

The speakers rattle up on their posts. The guy singing is singing about himself—he's young and tight—driving a car, he's riding the crest of night—taking control . . . The dancers are a thrift store come to life—asexual—Silence dumps them back together . . . They're moving around in the silence between songs—they seem confused . . . A new song begins and they bump back into motion as four or five people, finding themselves a minority, trickle away, disturbed . . .

Now they've got the floor to themselves. A woman in sweatclothes bows back and forth like calisthenics, another in a knit cap shakes her head. A man in a *Born in the USA* T-shirt removes his strapped-on glasses and cleans them on his shirt, holds them up to the lights . . .

At the end of a song the DJ does something to the turntable—the red cap ducks down, disappears . . . the dancers convene, bewildered. The same song begins again and they haltingly regain their enthusiasm . . .

Two couples come laughing up beside me. They hesitate—it's intuitive . . . they look it over, figure it out . . . decide not . . .

The song ends and leaves the dancers stranded, and then begins again. The DJ's nowhere in sight, he's cut them adrift—afloat their own private party. I was watching them stumble and dance to that same song and then I turned away . . .

One of the men at Ed's table was a big olive-skinned guy with a massive head and kinky hair, wearing the usual gold chains gold rings and a loosened noose of a tie . . . He was obviously simmering, about to come to a boil.

He lost three close hands and started muttering to himself while the game went on around him. Ed shot me a glance and cocked his head toward the guy. Must be Gus the Greek.

I wandered off and got a beer in a plastic cup. I carried it away from the tents and drank most of it by the snow-fence, gazing at the bright Sohio station across Lorain and the empty sky above . . . Left the rest standing in the summer grass.

I went back to Ed's table and hovered behind him. He slipped me a ten. I folded it into a shirtpocket, meaning it wasn't official yet. A sad old winehead employed by the church came by to cut the pot, expertly extracting three bills and dropping them into a basket . . . moving on with a rag hanging out of a backpocket. Gus barked an expletive—everyone jumped—He brought a hanky to his mouth, disguising it as a cough . . . I looked around for Al and Dave, didn't see them . . .

I sat down to watch the game. Ed raked in another pot. Gus the Greek was apparently having a bad night. He moved his ass around on the folding chair and rolled his shoulders. Ed jerked his head and raised his eyebrows while Gus cut . . .

And this time Gus was certain. He called and raised and raised again—he was pushing hard, with a winning hand. I watched over his arm and thought I heard the steam of victory whistling from his ears—

Only to see him lose, as a stranger across the table shyly dropped a superior hand.

Gus the Greek dropped his head and sat still. Glances were exchanged. Then he smacked his palms on the table, raising them into fists and slowly shaking them at the sky, rolling his eyes upward, his voice trembling with faith—"God, you bearded motherfucker," he began. "You fucked me again! *Jesus Christ, you fucked me right up the ass this time: once again!*"

We all flinched. Gus threw a few punches at the sky, rising from his chair, building toward an aria—

"YOU GOT WHAT YOU DESERVED! YOU'LL GET IT AGAIN—I'LL BE FIRST IN LINE WITH THE HAMMER AND NAILS! I'LL NAIL YOU TO THE CROSS UPSIDE DOWN BY YOUR *BALLS,* YOU BEARDED FAGGOT MOTHERFUCKER!"

He gathered the cards into a slippery pile—ripping them in half, cards falling out of his hands—quarters, eighths—tossing them in the air . . .

Ed and the other players—two of them were women—were cowering just below the table, expecting the skies to open up . . .

A momentary awe had passed through the tent. And then the games resumed and someone called for a new deck.

Gus crashed back into his chair and caught his breath.

I slipped out of the tent and away from the corrupting yellow lights and found my friends. We left. Heading out, I saw the dancers waiting for that song to start again.

NICKEL-AND-DIME

Yeah I wanna get a cash advance for a hundred dollars please. Some ID? Just take a look. O it's been a long hard road ma'am: from the leafy eastern suburbs through the fiery cauldron of first love gone cruel and then blown like a spent balloon along the empty reaches of the city. And just now someone had a hold of my heart but she dropped it. Now it's back to business as usual: fives and tens, nickel-and-dime. I can't honestly say the impulse to look for work has gotten any stronger. Hey Ed, uh— What I want is to live like Ed. —Some ID? The gentleman against a sunburst on the back of I.W. Harper says *Always a pleasure* . . . I've always felt it a duty to knock some of the shine off myself. Never knew where to start. Things happen fast. If you wait long enough. Balconies posted on the sky.

CROSSROADS

"I can't believe you're still thinking about Angie."

"Angelface?"

"Yeah."

I was over there watching a ballgame, a Sunday afternoon.

He says "Every day I been doing sit-ups, and I say her name after each one: Angelface, Angelface, tryna send her a message."

"But you got this Jenny in the palm of your hand. She's crazy about you."

"Miss Appleblossom?"

"Yeah."

"Waitaminute; score check—"

He clicks a transistor, holds it to his ear.

"How many fucking games you listening to?"

"Yesterday I had four radios lined up here—I's listening to four different games: brown, beige, purple, pink. And every time my one team would bat the other would go out, y'know? It was perfect: like a nice little chain of events. For three innings: okay brown, they're out, beige coming up to bat—lined up like a little train: double play, out, fly ball, strikeout. Home run, base hit, single, double. It was incredible! The odds against that must be a million to one, it was going so smooth: for three innings—Then *this* fucker hits into a double play—Now the brown's batting, the pink's still up, then it was Hup! line drive, Whup, fly ball, single—Threw the whole thing outa whack, I said You motherfuckers! I shut two of 'em off and threw

303

another one against the wall."

"*[laughter]* "

"This my fourteenth radio this year. Pisses me off: they cost like four bucks and I throw 'em against the wall. This one I can't, this a eight-dollar radio man, gonna take a grand slam for me to break this motherfucker."

The phone rang.

He said "This is it. This call will turn out to be the answer to my prayers or a total pain in the ass. Angelface or John."

He let it ring three times more and then grabbed it.

And then he was covering the mouthpiece—"It's her." I shook my head. He slipped into his bored, hurry-it-up phone manner: as though he'd heard it all before and was impatient to check a game score. "Yeah . . . yeah. Yeah. Yeah." The answer to his prayers: a total pain in the ass.

He put the phone back and fixed his eyes on the TV. "What I tell you? She's calling from Henry's, wants to know if she can stay here for a while."

I groaned.

"I told her I'll meet her in the parking lot at Denny's, 91 and Euclid, Henry's gonna drop her off. Get this: Henry's—While she's talking to me I can hear Henry's in the background—'Is he gonna be there? He's coming, right? Tell him to hurry—'"

"He's throwing her out, huh?"

"Aah I dunno what the situation is, uh, probably said she could stay there a while, maybe it ran into complications. She says he's too high-strung. Said she thinks he needs some medicine to calm down or he's gonna get a heart attack—something like that. Anyway you feel like taking a ride? I got no gas in my car, we'll take your car, I'll drop you off at the folks', pick you up on the way back."

I had just finished dinner with my folks when I heard the horn outside. I kissed them each goodbye.

Ed stepped out of the car and met me coming round the

trunk. "Waitaminute," he said, "I wanna show you something."

He opened the trunk. It was bulging with trashbags, the two-string guitar laid across the top, a glimpse of books and colored fabric, a big stuffed bear jammed into a corner . . . He shut the trunk and handed me the keys.

Angie was up front, in the middle. I got behind the wheel and moved the seat forward, her carpetbag wedged between us. I said "Angie, you wanna throw that bag in back?"

"No," she said.

Driving to the freeway nothing was said. Ed tuned the radio to a music station, something I'd never known him to do. We were heading up the ramp into the sun and Angie started singing along: "*It's all too beaUtiful! It's all too beaUtiful . . .*" She sang one chorus and then floated to a level above words . . . I looked at her; Ed was lighting a Newport, preoccupied, squinting ahead . . .

Ed and I were hauling her stuff into the house and Angie was back and forth between us, making sure we didn't lose or break anything. There were pots and pictures, notebooks and rags, tools and shoes. Buried beneath it all were the barbell and some loose weights.

Angie was trumpeting ahead of us: "I tried to tell them! They're looking for me *right now*, but I DON'T WANNA BE THE BABY IN THE BAND! Tomorrow I have to find my car! And that Henry's a very sick man! He'd better watch out! There's no time to waste!"

I closed the trunk and carried the last bag into Ed's kitchen, dropped it on the floor. Then I went up to my place and left them to set up house.

At ten the next morning Ed's car was still out front.

He was at the table with his forehead resting on hands clasped as though for prayer.

He said "I called Burdette, told 'em I won't be in today."

"Talk to Jenny?"

"Yeah, I told her I got Angie staying here for a few days."

"She pissed?"

"No, naw . . . y'know . . ."

"Where's Angie?"

He reached for a cigarette. The bathroom door was closed.

"She been in there—two—solid—hours."

"What's she doing? Maybe she got lost."

"Every once in a while I bang on the door, I hear her rustling around in there . . . I'm gonna bust the fucker down in a minute, I gotta use the bathroom."

"Go use mine. Door's open."

Annoyed, he went to my place. I sat at the table.

In a minute Angie came out, in a long T-shirt and nothing else, her hair smeared back with Vaseline. She stared blankly at me, momentarily confused at the shifting quality of the stage she inhabited.

"Hi," I said. "Ed's next door."

She decided I was an illusion and went into the frontroom.

Ed came back and Angie came out in a short purple dress, went straight for the newspaper on the table. She found the classifieds and started scanning . . .

"I have to buy a house," she said.

"An—"

"I have fifty thousand dollars in the bank."

Ed was watching her. And then he remembered who he was dealing with.

"Here's a house for $28,000. West Thirty-Second Street. Will you take me to look at it?"

"Angie . . ."

"And on the way back I want to find my car. And I have to go to the library. Is there a library nearby?"

"Angie—"

"We have to hurry!"

He said "You feel like taking a ride?"

"No thanks, man. I'm gonna do some writing today."

"Don't say nothing about me being fat. Or bald."

"How 'bout stupid?"

"That's okay."

*

That night I again went to my folks' place for dinner.

We had a shot and a beer. There was roundsteak fried in olive oil with garlic and onions. Greenbeans with oil, oregano and lemon. Rye bread. A salad of escarole and dandelion greens. Coffee. Cantaloupe. As though anything not expressed in the simplicity of that meal was better left unsaid.

A kitchen, three rooms and a bathroom. Three people. I peeked into my former bedroom. Felt that nothing lingered there, from before. Felt nothing at all, for that small apartment of rooms I'd grown up in. Just a space. I saw that it had always been temporary. It had never felt any more permanent for me than it had for the two of them. I wanted something to lean back on.

I opened a drawer and turned through a book of snapshots.

The couch of the past—there and gone . . . Nodding frond-shadows on a street-lit wall where men have parked their work and gone home. The couch of the past . . . the warmth and winterlight of old photographs . . . like a chair pulled out from under you.

My mother slipped me a twenty. I said goodbye and felt I was abandoning them to silence.

*

Eight o'clock I parked behind the Pontiac, went to Ed's.

Angie was in the kitchen, writing in a notebook with a stack of library books beside her. Ed was in the frontroom watching a game.

"You get the house?" I said.

He looked up at me.

"Who you got?" I said.

"KC, John's got Pittsburgh. He wanted Houston at six to five but I told him Feef had the line at eight to five, so he took Pitt instead. They're losing four to nothing. I just talked to him. He says ants are taking over the world."

"What?"

"Ants. He says the ants are taking over the world."

Ed was steering a tricky course.

On my way through the kitchen I stopped to check what Angie was working on.

She had three books. *Advanced Trigonometry . . . Secondary Engineering . . . and How to Increase Your Profits Through Corporate Investment.* She was scribbling furiously.

FROM A RED NOTEBOOK

We took Angie to the movies the other night, some Vietnam War picture. Two hours of explosions, insects, bamboo cages, blood and rats. Ed got her a big box of jellybeans on the way in. She sat bolt upright the whole show: like a test-monkey strapped to a chair. After the credits we told her it was time to go.

She took the change from jungle warfare to Lorain Avenue without batting an eye, ate the jellybeans on the ride home, without a word.

————————————

Angie throwing I Ching on the frontroom floor . . .

————————————

At forty mph, Angie spots a clock in a yard sale and demands that we turn the car around. We double back and park the car, follow her up the drive—she takes her bag with her. She examines the clock for ten minutes while the woman who's running the sale nods encouragement. Angie decides the clock isn't the particular clock she's dreamed of, or had a premonition about, or had stolen from her, or owned in a previous life, so she puts it down and turns abruptly toward the car. Ed buys it for her anyway, along with a green transistor radio and a necklace with a crescent moon pendant.

I was feeling great.

Cool bath, clean shirt, fresh grease, my legs up on the porch rail, nice breeze . . .

As the summer unrolled without my existence taking aim, I felt increasingly wary and undeserving of such moods—as though they were on a tab somewhere. It was true enough: Al had stopped over with a twenty . . . Nevertheless I was feeling great.

I took sip of whiskey and lit a cigarette.

A blue Caprice pulled up and parked with care.

Jenny got out. Inside me a rooster crowed.

She looked around for Ed's car and saw me on the porch. She brought a smile to the fence.

"Hi hon'."

"Hi," I said. "C'mon in."

She unlatched the gate and glanced again for the Pontiac.

She came to sit on the steps.

"Ed ain't around . . . Don't know where he's at," I said, as though wondering myself.

"Oh, I was just in the neighborhood . . ."

I laughed.

She dropped her head and smiled at herself.

I said "You want a beer?"

She tossed her hair back and said "I'd love one."

I went upstairs and came back with two beers and an empty

glass.

"You just get off work?"

"About an hour ago," she said. "I stopped home. How about you?"

"I'm still working," I said, lifting the pint. "You want some of this?"

"No thanks. So what do you do, during the day?"

"Uh . . . I dunno, the days just seem to go by before I can figure what to make of 'em . . . y'know."

She was looking as though trying to figure what to make of me.

"But how do you—"

"Go 'head and say it, Jenny. I can take it."

"Say—"

"You think I'm a bum."

She laughed.

"It's okay, Jenny."

She sipped her beer and looked off the porch.

"Has Eddie still got this girl staying with him?"

"Yeah. Far as I know. I ain't seen him today."

"Hm."

"It's a temporary thing. Kinda like a bridge loan. With high interest."

"Maybe I will have a taste of that. What is it?"

"Bourbon. Wait, I'll get a glass—"

"That's alright."

"Nah, hold on. What'll the neighbors think?"

I went upstairs and washed out a glass and brought it to her. She reached for the pint and poured a confident couple fingers.

She tossed the shot down like medicine, waited for worse, and then smiled—first to herself and then to me. I took a hit.

She said "I don't get it! I can't understand him."

"Is that why you like him?"

"I can't figure him out . . ."

I lit a cigarette. "You're too good for him."

"No I'm *not*," she said, as though she'd been hearing that all her life—or at least from Ed.

I hadn't meant it that way. I'd meant that Ed had come to be stuck with certain particular tastes.

I said "Well maybe Ed thinks you're better than he deserves."

She laughed; tossed her hair again. She was really beautiful. "You hungry?"

"No thanks," she said. "I'm gonna drive home."

She got in her car and I sat there and watched where she'd been.

MORE FROM A RED NOTEBOOK

Ed takes Angie to a Vegas Nite at St. Leo's. He gives her a roll of quarters to keep her occupied at the roulette wheel and takes a seat at one of the poker tables.

At the end of the night she's got seventy-five bucks and he's got three. He borrows five dollars for gas and she gives him back his other five, too, so he stops at a White Castle on the way home and gets her a hamburger, which she leaves cold on the front seat.

He takes her to his folks' place for Sunday dinner. Figures if he can't get any joy or satisfaction out of her, he can at least use her as a prop to impress his mother with ability to find a girlfriend.

Toward the end of the ride, Angie slouches down in the seat, expressing serious fears about the approach to Willoughby, which she regards as the stronghold of her enemies.

When they get there, she insists on staying in the car, saying "I can't let them see me. I don't wanna be the baby in the band."

Half an hour later Ed comes back and persuades her to come up to the apartment, where she refuses to speak, takes one bite of a turkey leg, and then finds her way into the bathroom, where she remains for the rest of the visit. Ed's mother

is unimpressed and worried. His father tells him he'll end up as
a bum in the park.

———————

Ed stops over. "Where were you last night?" he says. "I stopped
over to see if you wanted to go to the game, I put a hundred
on New York."

"I's out driving around with Dave. New York won, didn't
they?"

"Yeah; yeah, they won."

". . ."

"Aah jeez," he says.

"That's alright, forget it."

"I got ten; you want ten?"

"No, just gimme a deuce; I wanna get cigarettes."

With a show of disgust he flips a fin on the nightstand. He
says "How you think it feels to have the kinda friends who ask
to borrow two bucks?"

"How you think it feels to *ask* someone for two bucks?"

"Where's this put us now?"

"*[laughter]* Anyway, you went to the stadium—?"

"Yeah. There's this guy—You shoulda seen: big fat guy—
he's selling cotton candy—"

"Seems like you're always telling me a story about a big fat
guy."

"That's 'cause I'm fat. Anyway this—fat cotton candy vendor's running up and down—running the whole time, I said
'You move pretty good for a big guy,' he says 'Hey: I'm the
number one cotton candy vendor at the stadium.' He was really
proud of it! He goes 'I bring the Indians *luck* when I run! It's
true! You remember last season when they were down ten to
nothing against Milwaukee? I started running—I was all over
the place! I made sixty bucks that night! They came back and
won the game!' I said 'Yeah I remember. You cost me three

hundred bucks, ya fat fuck.'"

"*[laughter]*"

"Inbetween innings y'know they play the organ music? Angie gets out there—she's in the aisle, dancing to the organ music—just—completely in her own world . . . Looked really cute, there . . .

"Middle of the eighth inning she says 'I used to be six inches taller! Then I started taking the drug *nye!* My friends told me it was good! I took it for a year and lost six inches in height!'"

"Wow."

"Weird fucking chick, man."

Angie:

red seeps out from inside the white. stare for more than two beats and everything begins, as though relieved, to breathe again. look away, before it all becomes too much of itself/ the world re-confirms itself with every instant—the procession of archetypes/ every face conceals a skull and every image bears a grin/ too high above the politics of a given moment to com- ment or reply/ the past is a series of signals and clues point- ing forward to right now when i remember and recognize and incorporate them/ what do I look like? what did I look like a moment ago? how do they see me? can they tell?/ moments unfolding to unfold again: i must learn to avoid tangents/ WHAT'S MINE!/ that tack on the wall and its shadow, the brown ceramic mug on this table—within stillness, everything trembles with significance/ A CONSPIRACY!/ i know who they are. Jeffrey said—/ here's that man again—/ i have no time for lies: i have only time to be . . .

"Look what Angie give me this morning."

He hands me a scrap torn from a newspaper ad: "BALD-
ING? THINNING? RECEDING? NEW SCIENTIFIC
CURE FOR BALDNESS."

"*[laughter]* "

"Can you believe that shit?"

tenoclock is gone. lake wind fans a cigarette ember brighter:
lift and carry, to withdraw . . . to brighten—more: to carry
off two orange points—one . . . another: two arcs blown into
blackness. before the black night of the lake: . . . whatever has
opened to the night breeze will close again . . . or, later, sleep
will do the job.

lake wind holds the ember's glow—wavering, into more,
and less, and more again . . .

i'd rather not go home yet.

CHINA JOINT

We sit in the silence of Chan's. A silence so serene, so polite, it's never been profaned. On the walls, tall scrolls reveal snow-capped mountains and cherry blossoms in deft black lines. There is the whiteness of clean tablecloths, table after empty table, beneath fragile hanging lamps, unlit as yet in late afternoon. At a corner table, the only other couple in the room is sharing a meal in a kind of humble deference to the surroundings, handling forks with the delicacy of chopsticks, lifting weightless teacups . . . The one waiter moves on tiptoe, nodding, smiling, careful not to intrude . . . Ed, with both hands under the table, looks around and then *click*:

"*—Henderson smacks a line drive to center field—*"

"Turn that down—"

He dials it down, raising the radio to his ear and narrowing his eyes. The waiter approaches, disturbed . . .

"So what were you saying?"

"This fucking Angie, man—There ain't another guy in the city woulda done what I did for her—Today alone! I buy her breakfast, I take her to the thrift store, take her to the library, buy her lunch—Take her to the track and give her money to play around with—I musta spent seventy-five bucks, easy. It ain't the money, it's just—She completely—No sign of appreciation—Nothing! Don't even register! At the track she says she wants a rootbeer float and a hotdog— She pours half the rootbeer on the ground, eats one bite of the hotdog and throws it on the ground—And you know that's one thing I can't fucking stand, wasting food. And—I take her around all day, give her whatever she wants, and the end of the day I gotta practically *beg* her for a little head! A total whore in the first place! She'll fuck a total stranger—suck his dick and let him fuck her for a five-dollar bill and a Miller's—a total stranger who just as soon cut her throat and dump her in the alley—But for a friend! And I'm the only friend she's got, believe me."

"I think you're beating your head against a wall."

Stepping onto Ed's porch I can hear a transistorized afternoon game through the screen. His inner door's open so I step inside.

He's at the table with a radio in one hand and a lit candle in the other. He looks at me and then resumes his focus . . .

"What the hell you doing?"

"Sh, sh. Key moment here."

"*And we'll take a break here at Cleveland Municipal Stadium—*"

He sighs and sets the candle down.

"Where's Angie?"

"In the other room."

"What's uh . . . What's with the candle?"

"This my last resort, John's candle trick."

"*[laughter]* "

"It's me against John here! I got Boston he's got Cleveland. I'm ahead three two in the bottom of the ninth, but he's got his last ups. I got a hundred on this game, so does he—"

"*—One down, a man on second—Here's the pitch: —swing and a miss.*"

"C'mon, strike the fucker out!"

"Ed—"

" . . . "

"*Strike two!*"

He brings the candle slowly closer to the radio—"I gotta see if I can blind this batter here—"

"*[laughter]* "

"*O and two the count, here's the pitch: —struck him out.*"

"Yeah!" he growls, blowing out the candle. "Holy shit—You got a match?"

I fish a book out of my pocket and toss it.

He's fumbling to get it lit: "This no joke, man: John's probably got his candle too. He's tryna blind the pitcher I'm tryna blind the batter—It's his candle against mine! I ain't even sure this *works* over the radio: at least with TV you can see who you're blinding!"

"*. . .*"

"*Ball one.*"

"Sonofabitch." He narrows his eyes and aims the candle from a different angle.

"I wish I had a camera," I tell him.

"*Ball two.*"

"Fucking Cleveland's a six-to-five dog: he hits this bet it's like a three-hundred-dollar swing."

"Just concentrate."

"*—Butler hits a pop to center field . . . Evans makes the grab, and the game's over—[click.]*"

"Whew," he says.

"Close call."

"Well you're only supposed to use the candle in crucial situations," he says, wiping carbon off the radio.

It was a Sunday afternoon, we were going to just make post time. I jumped up on the porch and leaned in the door:

"You ready man?"

"Yeah, Angie's just getting herself together here. How you set for cash?"

"I got like twenty bucks. Hey: one of the Greeks gave me a tip for the double. But we gotta get outa here, it's almost one."

Angie came out of the frontroom and brushed past me with a guitar and an armload of books. She set it all down at the edge of the porch. I looked at Ed.

He said "Angie, what're you doing?"

She went back to the frontroom.

"Angie—"

Came back with a bag of clothes and the yard sale clock.

"Can you open the trunk of your car please?"

"What's going on?"

"I have to take these things with me. It's not safe to leave them here."

"Angie who the fuck—"

"Ed, open the trunk for her and let's get outa here."

The front seat was broiling already. Ed lit a Newport and tossed the pack on the dash. I rolled my window down while Angie went into the house for something else. I let go a sigh of annoyance.

And we're on our way, chugging along 77 with maybe time to still catch the double, when Angie says "We have to go back."

Ed doesn't flinch, just keeps driving, forearm over the wheel.

"Can you please turn around? I forgot to—"

"Angie, what the hell's the *problem?*"

"We forgot to nail the windows closed."

I kept my eyes on the road ahead. As though by keeping very still this would blow over.

"What the f—"

"Do you have any nails at home? I have a hammer in my bag—"

"Angie it's ninety fucking degrees out here! What the fuck you wanna nail the windows for?"

"In case they try to get inside!"

"Who?"

"They're trying to get to me!"

"*Who?* Who the fuck you talking about? Who the fuck's gonna try and— You're with *me!* What the fuck're you worried ab—"

"*PLEASE* TAKE ME BACK!" she roared. "YOU'RE TOO STUPID TO UNDERSTAND! WE HAVE TO GET BACK!"

Something cracked open in the front seat of the car. Ed stuttered and then blew up:

"SONOFABITCH—"

He swung a mean slice across two lanes and up an exit ramp.

"Awright! You wanna go back? I'm gonna take you back to the house and you can fucking sit there with the windows nailed shut waiting for someone to break in and steal your rags! You got absolutely no consideration or appreciation for—"

"*NOOOOOO!*" she howled, "*I don't want to stay there alone! I*

323

want to nail the windows so they can't get in! PLEASE don't leave me there alone!"

She burst into tears.

"*WHO?*" he yelled. "WHO THE FUCK IS COMING? WHO THE FUCK IS COMING INTO *MY HOUSE*—"

"AAAIIEEEEYOU DON'T UNDERSTAND! THEY CALL ME ON THE TELEPHONE!"

We sailed off the entrance ramp, toward home—

"*WHO?* WHO CALLS YOU?"

"THE *DEMONS!*"

I turned my head to the window. Ed was driving like a blowtorch in the sun with Angie screaming between us:

"WHY WON'T YOU UNDERSTAND? THEY CALL ME ON THE PHONE AND THEY KNOCK ON THE DOOR—WHY WON'T YOU HELP ME? I THOUGHT YOU WERE MY FRIEND. WHY ARE YOU TRYING TO HURT ME?"

"NO ONE'S TRYNA FUCKING HURT YOU! ALL I'M TRYNA DO IS WATCH OUT FOR YOU AND YOU FUCKING—"

"*I DON'T WANNA BE THE BABY IN THE BAND! I TOLD THEM I DON'T WANT TO GO AND THEY'RE TRYING TO TAKE ME BACK TO BE THE SINGER! THEY'RE THE ONES WHO STOLE MY CAR AND THEY'RE TRYING TO STEAL THE MONEY I HAVE IN THE BANK! WHY WON'T YOU BE MY FRIEND IN-STEAD OF THEIRS? AS SOON AS I GET MY MONEY I'LL GIVE YOU SOME!*"

She growled and pleaded and flew in all directions, and Ed kept driving. She'd lost her mind, but Ed didn't seem to see it. He took it personally. I counted the minutes to home.

"YOU'RE JEALOUS! YOU'RE JEALOUS OF ME BE-CAUSE I'M RICH! BECAUSE YOU KNOW I HAVE FIF-TY THOUSAND DOLLARS AND YOU DON'T HAVE ANYTHING!"

Ed was driving hard.

"YOU DON'T EVEN HAVE A HOUSE AND YOU DON'T HAVE ANY MONEY AND YOU HAVE TO GAMBLE AND YOU'LL NEVER HAVE *ANYTHING* BECAUSE YOU'RE TOO *STUPID* AND *FAT* AND *UGLY!* YOU'RE JEALOUS BECAUSE I'M *SMARTER* THAN YOU! *[laughter]* YOU'RE JEALOUS BECAUSE YOU'RE *UGLY* AND *STUPID* AND I'M *BEAUTIFUL* AND *SMART* AND *RICH!*"

We pulled up in front of the house.

"Angie, get out of the car."

"No."

". . ."

"You'll *never* get rid of me because *I'm* in charge now and there's nothing you can do."

She was on a roll.

I got out but she stayed put.

The porch crowd across the street was watching. What if she got out and appealed to mob sentiment? *This man's trying to hurt me!* What if she suddenly lapsed into coherence and called the police? *This man kidnapped me and he's forcing me to have SEX with him and trying to steal my money!*

I leaned into the car, said "Angie, there's a phonecall for you. It's the bank manager."

She leaped out and Ed followed her toward the house, unlocked the door . . .

The only person she called was Henry. We could hear her from the kitchen:

"Hello Henry? Can you come and pick me up here? This man is crazy: I think he's going to have a breakdown. He's got high blood pressure; I think he's taking speed: he's very nervous all the time. I think he's going to have a heart attack . . ."

Ed had withdrawn into himself. I went next door.

325

I sat by the window and lit a cigarette.

Pretty soon I heard the bang of a screendoor, and saw her bags fly over the fence onto the sidewalk: one . . . two . . . three . . . four.

Ed's across the table without a shirt rubbing Ben-Gay into his shoulder. "Quit staring at my fat gut," he says, and then winces. "This fucking work is crippling me."

"You oughta see a masseuse."

"Yeah I was thinking of going to that Korean joint on Twenty-Fifth."

"Aw yeah. Perfect."

". . . Fucking Angelface . . ."

"Aah. Now you can concentrate on Jenny."

"Fuck Jenny, I'm sick of talking about her. I happened to mention Angie's gone, she asked if I wanna go out tonight. She don't know what the fuck she wants."

"You're the one don't know what he wants. I don't see why you gotta make it so complicated. So you take her to a movie: what's the big deal?"

"'Cause I know for a fact it won't work. It's too much pressure: this whole thing started as a joke, and she's too stupid to leave it that way. I don't mind her calling me—I *like* the fact she calls me every night. I'd like to just be her friend, but she's pushing it too far. She got no business being with me, and I don't wanna be some kinda—charity case project, like she's gonna straighten out my life for me or something. She just a little lonely and confused at the moment."

"Confused about what?"

"Aah she just broke up with some guy she been seeing for a

couple years, she's looking for a place, she wants to move out of her mother's place . . ."

"She lives with her mother?"

"She lives downstairs her mother lives upstairs. Her mother owns the house."

"Huh."

"So y'know, it's a . . ."

"Your folks still looking for a place?"

"Hah?"

"Weren't your folks looking for a different place?"

"Aah? Oh yeah that was uh . . ."

"Remember a few months ago we were driving in the rain one night, you said the custodian out there was fucking with 'em?"

I can sense his surprise. He doesn't remember telling me.

"Yeah that kinda blew over, uh . . . That custodian's gone now, he's working somewhere else."

"What happened?"

"I—basically saw to it he was uncomfortable at that address."

"Uh-huh."

". . ."

"Whattaya mean? How?"

"Just—little things at first, I happened to get hold of some of his mail—Artie was his name . . . and I happened to pick up Artie's Master and Visa bills, y'know, got his account numbers . . ."

"Yeah. So then what?"

"Well I ordered him a lotta books, and records I thought he might not have . . . I carried his account numbers around with me, in case I saw something he might like."

"What, through the mail?"

"Yeah I ordered him a few things from magazines that I thought he wanted for the winter . . . because he worked outside a lot, I figured he needed hip boots, 'cause there was a lotta plowing . . ."

"*[laughter]* "

"I called this Alaskan gear company, ordered him a couplea Nanook Boots of the North for like seventy-five dollars a boot . . . *I* figured, to make amends to him because I figured he *needed* this kinda stuff. Six Mountie fur caps with the flaps—"

"*[laughter]* "

"—from Montana . . . specially made for his head . . . y'know . . . a *canoe* I got him for the summer . . ."

"No way."

"Lotta pairs of size triple-E workshoes outa these magazines . . . I ordered him a bow and arrow—crossbow . . . Good one, too; and I got him a few magazine subscriptions . . . really perverted stuff I figured Artie might appreciate as long as his wife didn't get the mail . . . a Big John inflatable sex doll . . ."

"*[laughter]* "

"And then there were about a dozen tenants that I made it a point to find out their names. And I would call and say 'This is *Artie*.' Y'know? 'Mr. Wilson this is Artie. And uh . . . I was gonna shovel the snow in front of the driveway this week?' 'Uh, yes Custodian . . . ' 'But—your wife's a fucking—cunt *whore*, I ain't gonna shovel *your* fucking snow. Tell her I'll stick my dick in her ass next time I see her. Bye, this is *Artie*.'"

"*[laughter]* "

"'Mrs. Greenbaum?' 'Yeah.' 'I bumped into your car with the lawnmower, put a little nick in it, this's *Artie*; bye.' They got twenty-five people looking for him, the guy can't figure it out! Y'know, first he gets a pair of snowshoes in the mail, then everybody's giving him dirty looks— I had his car towed a couple times, called the towing company and said I was the landlord, I thought it was abandoned . . . Just another, little, mini aggravation for Artie."

"Right."

"Then I started threatening his life, said 'This's Joe Smith from down the bar, you been fucking with my wife I'm gonna kick your fucking ass.' And his wife got on the phone tryna protect him I called her a fucking whore . . . This was like the Stage Two of this. And then I found out this police woman's phone number. Friend of a friend of a friend who had a young daughter."

"Right."

"And—I just— I thought Artie might be into photography, I wasn't sure . . ."

"*[laughter]*"

"Artie was interested in child pornography, y'know, pictures and stuff—"

"As it turned out."

"Yeah; a rotten thing for a man to be into, but he was into it . . ."

"Uh-huh."

"Somehow he called this police woman's young daughter a few times and he was saying he wanted to take pictures of her. Said he would pay her, but not to tell her mother. But Artie's not so sharp, see? so he called there one time and the mother answered, and he said 'Is little Melissa there?' 'She's sleeping right now, what do *you* want?' So Artie, stupid fuck that he is, said 'Who's this, the babysitter?' So she caught on right away— She goes 'Yeah, this's the baby-sitter, who's this?' 'Well she was supposed to take her blouse off and I was supposed to take some pictures of her standing on her head with no blouse on. But I don't want to her mother to know.' '*You don't want her mother to know?*' —*Seething,* y'know? So Artie goes 'I'll give you fifty bucks a session if you just call me ahead of time and tell me when her mother's not there.' Man I could *feel* the steam coming outa the phone . . ."

"*[laughter]*—You asshole . . ."

"I go 'Okay my name is Artie So-and-so, I wanna take some pictures of little Melissa but *don't tell her mother.* 'Cause that Melissa's a sexy little bitch.'"

"*[laughter]*"

"She goes 'What's your number?' I go 'I'll give you my number but *don't tell her mother!* '*Okay: please!*' I gave her the number, said 'Make sure you call Artie now, 'cause I want her daughter bad. Have a nice day, bye.'"

"*[laughter]*"

"Now how do you explain this, the police come to your house—'I didn't *do* this'? Obviously they can't pin it on him, but it hadda be a major aggravation for Artie.

"Finally—under strain the guy cracked. I call there, he'd say '*Who are you? Whyn't you show your face, you coward? you been harass-ing me for three months I got fishing rods piled up here the police come to my door, my wife don't talk to me—Show your face you sonofabitch I'll fight you to the death!*'

"So then the end of it—the final koop de grace was: this whole time I was fucking with Artie—and it's tiring, you can only fuck with a guy for so long . . . And—This whole time I had a similar thing going, parallel to this, with this guy Bim, from Bim's Bar on Twenty-Fifth Street."

"Yeah, like the roughest bar on the West Side."

"Yeah; so I had both these assholes in a frenzy, asking me 'Who are you? Name a place and a time and I'll be there!' So I called Bim and said my name was Artie, called Artie and said my name was Bim . . ."

"*[laughter]* What'd you have against Bim?"

"Bim threw me out of his bar one time for tryna give him a Canadian quarter. And—Bim had a mother complex. I knew this from delivering to the bar: his mother was always there, he was always doting on her . . . And, as it turned out, Artie kinda liked Bim's mother a little bit, y'know?"

"Fuck . . ."

"And Artie, stupid as he is he'd call up Bim and say he wanted to take Bim's mother out, y'know? And Bim didn't like that."

"*[laughter]*"

"And then Artie started getting out of hand, said 'I wanna get your mother in the alley, fuck her in the ass,' y'know. And

331

Bim just went crazy. Finally Artie revealed his number to Bim and vice versa—I arranged for them to meet on a certain corner, Wednesday, twelve o'clock—I's gonna get a coffee and a sandwich, park across the street . . .'"

"*[laughter]* "

"As it turned out I didn't get a chance to witness this— meeting of titans, something else came up, but far as I know, Artie is no longer manager of the Crestview Apartments. And Bim ain't been seen behind the bar in a while. So, y'know. Don't ever fuck with me."

"Got it."

"Anyway that's enough stories here, I gotta concentrate on these games. Fucking John hit me last night for forty, told me to put the whole thing on a three-teamer."

"You didn't bet nothing?"

"Well I think that's enough of a bet, don't you? He hits this sonofabitch it's worth like three hundred."

In a while I went home.

The phone woke me at midnight.

"Chalk up three bills for John," he said.

DOWN SOUTH IN NEW ORLEANS

I

Tuesday was a frontrunner: couldn't ask for a better morning, and then she quit, going into the turn. The sky was grey and the air got cool. I drove to Twenty-Fifth and got a pint of Heaven Hill. Broke my last five on a pack of smokes from Abdul and went upstairs.

I rinsed my favorite shotglass, the fleur-de-lis. When I set it on the windowsill the sidewalk was damp.

I set some old New Orleans music happening and grabbed a kitchen chair, opened the frontroom window wide and sat down, crossed my legs and cracked the pint . . . lit up . . .

Drank one quick to get the introductions over with and sat back, watching the smoke being seduced out the screen and over the neighborhood . . .

Tipitina, Tipitina!

OH LET'S SEE, there must be about a hundred fifty ways to look at the world . . . hundred and fifty-two—hundred fifty-*five*, to be exact. The idea is—Well alright then, *ten thousand*—Twenty million, to be exact—and the idea is to choose the right one for the right time . . .

Somewhere this music existed in time, but the drummer's rolling shuffle insisted it was neverending. Jostled at the bar, up high on a stool, blurred in a moment of laughter and motioning for more, exchanging places with those beside you and dreaming upward, no distinction. You're here to live.

Me Big Chief me got'm squaw
Me gon' buy me a great big car—
I filled the room with smoke and ass and brass and rolling
leapfrog piano and let the afternoon extend . . .

II
My ship's at anchor, my suitcase packed
I got a one-way ticket ain't coming back
Life's a pleasure, love's a dream
Down south in New Orleans . . .

This fiddle-and-accordion—slipsliding, sidewinding—as though
(which it is) sideways is just as important and maybe more fun.
Once in a while you see through "time" . . .

NO THANKS

I kicked his door open, said "You wanna beer? Christ, it's hot in here . . ."

Found him on the couch, phone in hand.

I sank into the lounge chair.

"Jenny, you'll be divorced someday . . . Huh? You'll marry some guy with money, you'll end up one of these lonely house-wives drinking at home . . . Hah? No; just listen. Someday, I'll see you again, after you're divorced, we'll be together again. Listen. Reap your wild oats, your dancing, your discoing, your—high society stuff . . . I'll catch you on the rebound, after all that's outa your system, when you're a little more beat up . . . Someday I'll see you around."

I got out of the lounge chair, stepped into the yard, flicked my cigarette at a needy dog and went upstairs.

I was dreaming of Memphis at dusk when the phone rang.

I picked it up, looking back at my window seat as though at the source of that image.

"Hey boy. What're you doing?"

"I'm sitting here wondering would a matchbox hold my clothes."

"Hah?"

"You think I could make it to Tennessee on two bucks?"

"Yeah, put two bucks of gas in the car and meet me at Myron's. Fifty-Eighth and Detroit. It's just like Tennessee in here."

"You there now?"

"Yeah."

"See you soon."

Suddenly, the night was young. I was glad for a destination, even if it was only five minutes away.

Ed bought me a double shot of Echo and a Bud. I reflected that even when I didn't have money to pay for it, even when I wasn't necessarily looking for it, alcohol was beginning to find me with a sort of opportune precision. I drank the shot and saw the flipside of the coin. It said Of course!

I said "Are we celebrating something here?"

"Yeah," he said. "That's one way of looking at it. Get this. I'm out on the truck today—This a really busy season, y'know?

The fucking wine is so high on the truck it's just unbelievable. I get there in the morning, it's just so much work you don't even wanna start, y'know? And by ten in the morning it's ninety degrees already— *Ran* all morning; I mean—Did a super job. And I know I'm a jack-off and I know I'm a jerk, but when I get on the trucks I know what I'm doing."

"Yeah."

"And I was in a fucking hurry, this's like one o'clock: every stop taking ten, fifteen, twenty cases. I get to this Open Pantry in Berea . . . One case of wine, they want. One case. So when you get an order like that you say Okay, that's a two-minute stop: in and outa there, right? I come in the store with a case of wine . . . fucking teenage broad working there . . . Put the case down, she's talking to some girl, nobody else in the store, right? no other customers. I'm waiting a good five minutes. Bill's like fifteen dollars. So I said real politely: 'Fifteen-fifty.' Totally ignored me . . . I says 'Uh, Miss: here's the bill . . . ' She pushes it away, she goes 'I'm *talking.*' I go—I think I whispered 'Jesus Christ' under my breath, y'know? She goes 'I DON'T HAVE TO PUT UP WITH THIS!'—Runs into the back room! Here comes this—huge fat pig of a lady, some big hippo musta weighed three hundred pounds—'You don't talk to my help like this! I don't want you in my store no more.' I said 'What *is* this? I want my money for the wine, whattayou starting all this trouble with me for?' 'I'm calling your company!' Over nothing! She says 'You cussed out my employee in front of the customers.' I said 'Lady I didn't say *anything!*' 'You fucking guys are all alike!' I took the case of wine, went outside the store; I said This is— I was in there for like twenty minutes . . . Now I got a headache . . . You gotta save your aggravation for the big stops."

"Yeah."

"I got in the truck . . . called Burdette a half hour later, Jenny answered the phone, right? She goes 'Bernie's pissed at you: Open Pantry called.' I said '*What?*' 'Bernie wantsa talk to you when you get in.' Bernie's the owner of the company: not the boss, the *owner*. 'Yeah, the woman called, said you cussed her out.'

"So I called Open Pantry, I said 'This is Burdette Wine calling. What happened down there?' She goes 'That driver called my girl filthy names, and—All the customers were staring!' I says 'Lady, you're talking to the driver.' She goes 'What?' I says 'What kinda shit you tryna pull?'"

"Yeah."

"Get to my next stop . . . guy says 'Burdette called, you better call your company.' Call back there, Jenny's on the phone. Says 'Did you call back to that Open Pantry?' I says '*Yeah* Jenny, I couldn't stand it,' she says 'Now Bernie's *really* pissed; What you do that for?' I said 'Jenny, this whole thing's getting *blown out of proportion* here, I've wasted an *hour* over one case of wine!'"

"Yeah, right."

"So I fucking go to my next stop, I get another call. Fucking Bernie Burdette. 'You motherfucker, she called me again! What the fuck—' I says 'Hey, this's *bullshit,* man.' 'You're in fucking trouble.'

"I took the fucking truck I went back. I went ten miles outa my way, went back to the Open Pantry, right? I walked in I says '*You motherfucking* sonofab—' I gave it to her, I let it all hang out, I says 'You *fucking* pig,' I went on and on, y'know? And she called the fucking cops . . . Cops come down, calmed me down, told me to leave . . . Then I got in the truck—This's like two hours gone now, right? I haven't done a thing in two hours but argue about this one case of wine—"

"*[laughter]* "

"At three-thirty I still got—fifteen stops to go, I'm *totally* pissed off . . . I call Jenny back she goes 'Aw, you're—J—I think Bernie's gonna fire you, you really fucked up, man,' I says 'Hey, fuck this, Jenny,' I went to the Red Dog Saloon, from Berea—I got there at three-twenty, exactly, I sat there and drank triples till fucking quarter to six . . . Come back to the company: there's fucking Bernie. 'Sign these papers.' I said 'What is this?' he said 'You're getting written up for this.' I said 'Bernie I didn't *do* nothing, this whole thing got blown outa proportion . . . This's *crazy*.' He said 'You sign this.' And I was already half loaded by then, y'know? And the union steward who's kinda my friend there, he said 'Go 'head, sign it, he ain't firing you he's just writing you up.' I said 'It's a matter of fucking principle: I didn't do a fucking thing I'm *sick* of this shit. Kissing the customer's ass.' Bernie says 'You sign this,' I says 'Bernie: *fuck* you. Stick that paper up your ass.' Then, once I said it, it was already over, so I really gave it to him. I threw the fucking wine off the truck, busted the fucking wine . . ."

"Yeah, shit."

"I got fired—because this little cunt— All I hadda do was go in there and sign that paper. It's like me saying 'Danny you're fucked up, sign this just to prove you're fucked up and I'll put it in the file.' And they put it in the file, and every time something like this comes up they put it in the file, and eventually when they wanna fire you they say 'Hey, look at all this shit.' You keep signing these things for something you didn't do— I says 'Fuck you I ain't signing it.' All because of this little whore, I lost a fucking thirty-thousand-dollar-a-year job."

SERENADE

All the mansions were dark, now.

This wasn't the Southside. This street slept undisturbed, in a rich darkness where nothing was owed. Undisturbed even by streetlight, which found itself constrained to a vaulted corridor of leaves . . .

I'd brought a pillow.

A breeze from another season played through the backseat of the Buick . . .

I sat awhile, watching the silent slight activity of tree-shadows against the dirty windows of the car . . . watching, and then only pretending to watch them . . . feeling the breeze . . .

And then I pushed the pillow against the armrest and lay down, went to sleep.

I did that three or four nights in a row, for some reason.

I would leave the pressure of my rooms and the complexity of desire it bred, get in my car at eleven or twelve at night and drive up here, to one of these enclosed and peaceful streets, to sleep among the shadows.

On the last night I was awakened by a policeman's flashlight shining, probing through the windows.

"What're you doing here?"

"Huh? Oh. I got drowsy . . . I was driving and I started dozing off, so I pulled over . . ."

". . . Yeah. Well get on home now."

"Yeah."

"You okay to drive?"

"Yeah."

He kept his light on me as I climbed into the front seat.

When I started the engine he walked back to his patrol car. I was below empty. Not a buck in my pocket. I heard his door slam, put the Buick in drive, and pulled carefully away from the curb.

The Southside was a long way, but mostly downhill from here. I coasted home.

REFLECTIONS

"Oh sure, I know who you mean. I didn't know his name, but he comes in here to buy milk and eggs and cigarettes—Camel cigarettes, he buys. He lives two houses down: he drives that big blue car. He drives a cab, or he used to. I don't think he's working now. He pals around with that other one: the big one—his next-door neighbor. He's a nice boy."

"Yeah, that's Junior: Ray's boy. I know his old man—his old man grew up in the neighborhood. Ray lives on the East Side now. Junior comes into Feef's. He give me a ride back from the track one day: fucking car only had one door working: I had to climb in the driver side."

"Uh you mean that kid live round the corner in the yellow house? Naw I don't know him. See him around here alla time . . . Drive that '74 LeSabre with the busted grille. I'd like to kick his ass for him sometime: seem like he think he got some kinda attitude, 'r some shit."

"Hell, I don't know who that is. You know how many drivers we got coming in and outa here? I'd probably recognize his face. A lot of these guys come in and drive for a few months and then you never see 'em again. We let a lot of drivers go: there's a constant turnover down here. You sure he drives out of Main and not Noble?"

"Yeah I remember him. That little whiteboy with the leather jacket and them motorcycle boots. Gave me onea his lockups one time. He a freak alright, but he probably okay. I dunno man I hardly talked to the kid. Why? What he do?"

"I say hi to him coming in and outa the yard, but that's about it. He hangs out with the guy downstairs of me. He gave me a chair once: this red chair I got in my kitchen. He pulled up one day with three of 'em in the trunk of his car. I don't really ever see him at the clubs—even the neighborhood bars, really. Once in a while when I'm taking a bath I hear him tapping away at a typewriter. My bathroom's right across from his kitchen."

"Yeah. I knew his ex-girlfriend, Marie, so I met him a few times when they were together. Then I moved in here, so now I see him around . . . I'm friends with another girl I think he had a thing for—We all went out one night to the Harbor Inn. Once in a while he stops over when he sees me on the porch and we drink a couple beers . . ."

FLAT TIRE

We're driving to the track, Ed's talking about Uncle John.

"I went to see him yesterday, dropped off a hundred bucks I won playing cards—towards the three hundred? Which it broke my heart to do, I need that fucking money, but . . . I told him I lost the rest in a game. And—I noticed he ain't shaved in a while . . ."

"Yeah?"

"He says he's growing a beard in protest."

"In protest?"

"Yeah I told him he looked pretty good with it. He says he's growing it in protest until I pay him all his money back."

"*[laughter]* "

"He's gonna look like fucking Rip Van Winkle by the time I pay him back."

"Was he serious?"

"He said it was either that or burn the house down, or bury me in a box with enough air and water for six days, so . . . he's taking the mild route, uh . . ."

"What a fucking nut."

"And—I'm over there, right? For some reason he starts tryna impress me how thrifty he is, right? He's wearing these shoes: old paira shiny pointed shoes. He's going 'Looka these shoes! I'm the only guy I know who—I've had these shoes since I was eighteen! They're still in good shape: looka the soles on 'em! They never wear out!' I felt like saying John, you ain't fucking *gone* anywhere since you was eighteen; they'll probably last forever! Those shoes outlasted four presidents—"

"Aw fuck . . ."

"—Am I getting a flat?"

"Yeah."

"Sounds like I'm getting four of 'em."

". . . Sonofabitch . . . You got a spare?"

"I'm tryna think . . ."

We go rattling to the top of the Fleet Avenue exit ramp. His car feels like a stagecoach anyway, it's hard to tell. He stops to lean out the door—

"Is it? Is it flat?"

"Yeah it's flat alright," he says, closing the door. "I just don't feel like changing this moth—I can't change it, I got that— bumper on the back's just barely wired on . . ."

"Shit. Gas stations, up there—"

"Yeah, the point is will they do it?"

We're driving up Fleet.

He says "We could drive to the track like this, far as that goes . . . just take longer . . ."

"*[laughter]*"

[. . . rattling, thumping . . .]

"Why do people stare at you, when you drive with a flat? I mean you know you got a flat, right?"

"*[laughter]*"

"—That guy just yelled to me I have a flat."

"He did! Did you hear that?"

"You think I don't know I'm driving like this? I'm going six miles an hour in a forty-mile speed limit, my head's bouncing off the roof my tongue's hanging out— '*Hey buddy, you got a flat!*' '*Ho-kay, Mr. All-American*—*'"

"*[laughter]*"

"They get in traffic accidents, tryna tell you . . ."

The Sohio was a self-service joint and up the block, the Marathon

345

was too.

"I'll keep driving till the fucking rubber wears out, then just drive on the rim."

"No, you can't drive on the rim, you'll—"

"Vince Bruner. Went all the way to Waterford on the rim. He got a flat—He went a hundred miles to Waterford on the fucking rim."

"Are you kidding?"

"On his rim. He's a legend at Stroh's: this guy's crazy. On his way to the track, got a flat and just kept driving."

"They open?"

"I dunno . . ."

"Don't look like they're open . . ."

"Where the hell you *going?*"

"There's another Sohio station, the corner here . . ."

Must be a mile up Fleet now, we pull into a Sohio station with a service bay.

Two guys in the office. In the heat. Gazing at a sleeping dog on the floor between them.

No business.

"'Scuse me, uh . . . One of you guys change a flat?"

Nothing happens.

And then one of them raises his head, looks at me, calmly, and says "Uh . . . Sure . . . bring it in."

By the time Ed pulls in, the tire is just a fuming mess of wires and strings.

The guy wheels out the red hydraulic jack and says "Okay. Which one is it?"

"It's the one still steaming."

He kneels down and sets the jack in place. Ed's behind him, overseeing the operation.

"That tire can be fixed, I know that . . . just put a few patches on there . . ."

The guy doesn't smile.

"That's the trouble with most people, Danny: they discard things as useless that still got life in 'em. These gas stations, they like that, when you leave tires behind: they just patch 'em up and sell 'em again . . ."

The mechanic doesn't seem to notice. *[machinegun sound of the lugnut gun . . .]*

Ed opens the trunk. String is visible all around the outer edge of the spare.

Back on the way. Up Miles Avenue . . . past Calvary Cemetery . . .

"That's where my grandmother's at," I tell him. "And my grandfather."

"That's where my grandfather's buried."

"He's at Calvary?"

"November twelfth, 1961. I was there when he died, I was twelve years old. I remember sitting on the couch, like it was yesterday. I used to go there and play checkers with him, listen to the ballgames, y'know . . . And—my mother come out says 'He's not gonna make it.' And the priest came over and everything—I remember my old man going in there with a bottle of booze, and having a shot, like a toast to him, y'know? And it seemed kinda—Y'know, they had a *shot* together, y'know . . . and he died like an hour later . . ."

I thought about that, saw figures in a room, and then my own grandfolks, I visualized them both . . . my grandfather resolute and stern, my grandmother restless and saintly . . . and then as a sort of composite . . . an idea that seemed like it had something to do with me . . . an expectation . . . an identity . . . But I didn't know what it was exactly, so I let it go, it receded in the light, and I was rolling along . . .

Ed said "That field over there, Woodland Field? When I was sixteen years old I was playing baseball in Beachwood: MVP every year since I was nine. Every year. I got to be sixteen and this is where the Class F was, the closest one to Beachwood.

347

And then it's Class A, then y'know—minor league contract, whatever, if you make it. I couldn't get down here, my old man had totally no interest in me or anything else . . . he's drinking, the house's in turmoil, everything's crazy at home. All that fucker hadda do was take me down here, have any interest in me: I coulda been in the major leagues. To this day I believe that, I believe it with all my heart. I was great! I couldn't get out here . . . And I didn't join no baseball that year—And then it was over with."

". . . Really? So that was who you started out to be?"

"That's—what I was good at, it's what everyone seemed to expect. I was all set. He wanted to send me to umpire school."

"Umpire school!"

"Yeah, y'know . . . umpire . . . good secure job . . ."

"Where'd he get that?"

"I was planning on being a baseball player, I had every hope in the world to be that—Somehow he come up with this umpire stuff and—was pissed—It was in Florida! Just leave home right now and go to Florida and go to umpire school. He gimme this application he got from the waterfront—'Here, go to umpire school.' ' . . . Well it's in Pensacola Florida, y'know uh—eight-week umpire school . . . But I don't *wanna* be an umpire! I mean it sounds nice but I don't wanna be an *umpire!*'"

"*[laughter]* "

"'Even if I could pass the thing I don't wanna *be* an umpire. Where'd you come up with this—don't even know nothing about baseball, I gotta be an umpire now.'"

"*[laughter]* "

"Any encouragement, or just— Nonea that. Y'know what my old man's advice to me was? When you go to a strange men's room put toilet paper on the seat."

"Right."

"That's the only thing I remember him telling me! In thirty-eight years!"

"*[laughter]* "

"And when you take a shit—Make sure your wallet don't fall outa your pants. And always look for a wallet. I've never found a wallet in thirty-eight years of going to Thistledown, Euclid Beach—every amusement park—fucking racetracks, Las Vegas— I'm almost forty, I've never once found a wallet on the floor—yet. So, other fathers musta told *their* sons to watch their wallets. But *me*, every time Ed goes in the bathroom he puts his wallet in his top pocket of his shirt—I ain't losing *my* wallet. He give me two worthless pieces of information. But I do put toilet paper on the seat at the racetrack, so . . . if that's what I was born to do then that's fine."

I stared out the window, it was a bright afternoon. The brightness seemed to contain a falling, like stuttered rain. Something within the brightness was continually falling.

I turned away from it. "What about as an adult? 'S he given you any advice lately?"

He reaches his Newports off the dash, I can tell something's coming and start to laugh.

He shakes a cigarette loose, takes it in his teeth, flips the pack back up on the dash and lights the cigarette.

"Well yeah about—six seven years ago he was living at this Old Soldiers' Home in Sandusky . . . My mom exiled him for about a year and a half, she kicked his butt out."

"How'd he end up there of all places?"

"I don't know how he found out about it, through the alcoholics' ward at the hospital, and he was a veteran, they found out he had no place to go now—And they sent him there."

"The place was for indigent veterans?"

"Right. Not sickly veterans, because it wasn't a hospital—"

"Right."

"They had their minimum jobs, the guys that would take care of the kitchen, cook . . . the guys that would do janitorial duties . . . He went there and took over with the—Watchman. He was the security guard there. He had security guard badge and hat, at night he would like walk around the grounds . . ."

"What was the place like? Did you ever go down there?"

"Yeah I went down there once. Why I would ever go visit him I have absolutely no idea. I think he was on leave. For three days? And somehow—I drove him back."

"Whattaya mean on leave? Weren't they allowed to come and go?"

"No no, it was kinda like an Army thing there, you just couldn't—They didn't want you to use it as a fucking hotel. You had curfews, and, y'know . . . on weekends you had to be back in by nine . . . I mean they ran it pretty strict . . . They didn't wanna just make it a flophouse, they had some kinda strict rules . . . Just like an Army base."

"Uh-huh."

"And so he got a three-day pass . . . come up to my mother's place and I took him back. And we went to his bunk and he had his own locker—just like Army: Army bunk, locker . . . And, y'know, he showed me his captain's badge, his hat and everything . . . he introduced me to his buddies . . . the guy in the next bunk . . . Mostly they just sleep, play cards . . . tell war stories, just waiting out their final years. So I guess he was kinda impressed by it when he got out . . . he figured I should find out about getting in there myself."

"What, like plan that far ahead? He had so little hope for your old age?"

"No: *then*—at the time."

"I don't get it."

"It was confusing to me too, believe me."

"But you mean—"

"Thought it was a good idea, all in all, y'know . . . rest home in Sandusky . . ."

"*[laughter]* Well wait, I mean—"

"I'da been a ten-year man there now, almost. Figure you get some kinda badge or something, y'know. I'd be in the fucking—Civil War Room by now."

"How old were you then?"

"I was like thirty."

"Well how did he—D'you remember when he brought this up to you?"

"I was bitching about work, or—I'm broke or whatever, I've always been a bum in his eyes no matter what I did, even if I was working I was still a bum . . . Y'know: 'Jeeeez, you wanna go out there bust your ass and work, y'know—You're a veteran, you can go.' I go—'Well what'd this come up for, whattaya mean?' 'Just go to this place and live!'"

"*[laughter]* "

"'Well I got an apartment right now I'm working at Coke, I mean what—?' 'It's *free!*' I go 'It's free, I know,' I go 'Well I understand that, uh . . . What's the average age there, eighty? I mean, I'm thirty-one.' 'Then don't go then!' I go 'Thanks, I . . . prefer not to—' 'Can't you get on the list, at least?!' I go 'Well—I really don't wanna be on the list either, to tell ya the truth, I don't really want 'em to call me, what do I do? just . . . pack my bags and go sit on the bed there and that's it? D'you think that little of me that I can't even survive even as a bum? I have to go there and live, at thirty-one?'"

"*[laughter]* "

"And this went on for a couple of weeks, it wasn't like a one-day thing! Every day tryna hammer me 'Why don't you *go* there?' And it wasn't even like I was living with him intruding on his life or y'know—"

"Right right."

"I wasn't living with him I barely even fucking associated with him . . . 'Then *don't* fucking go there!' I go 'Why would I wanna go there?' 'Why *wouldn't* you wanna go there? you get free meals, free dental cov—free hospitalization—' I go 'Well yeah . . . that sounds good . . . ' 'Free clothes!'"

"Yeah, like prison."

"'Free fatigues!'"

"*[laughter]* "

"I go 'Jeez, Dad, I only served two years . . . What excuse would I give these people for going down there? Am I wounded, or—?'"

"*[laughter]* "

"'My wife died or—What do I do?'"

"*[laughter]* "

"Could you imagine? What is this fucking guy doing here? They be like scratching their heads going—Hey Joe, who's this *guy?*"

"He's thirty years younger than any of the rest of us."

"At *least* thirty—minimum! Why are you here? Well my Dad told me to come. And I'm just gonna stay here with you guys. Sit on the bed with you guys and look at the ducks. For the next fifty years. I mean he stayed there a year . . . But to send *me* down, to ship me out? At thirty-one?"

"So your dad was uh—"

"He says 'Look, if you're a watchman you go to the re-frigerator, got *sangies*—anything you want!' 'But Dad I don't wanna live here and get a sangie at three in the morning because I'm a guard—that wasn't my goal when I graduated from high school, I guarantee you that! I may have not made it but I still have a chance!' 'All these sangies in here!' I hate it when he used to say sangies. But he actually told me he had a little bit of pull. I go 'Well Dad then *you* write the letter of explana-tion why *I'm* coming there. Y'know maybe you'll come up with some better reasons than I got. You go in front of the board and say why they're gonna admit Ed Jr.—What did he do in life to deserve to come here?' 'Well my Dad recommended me, I was in Korea. I was a weatherman, I filled up balloons. And it was brutal and I think I deserve to be here now.'"

"*[laughter]* "

"'Yes, I work at Coke right now I'm making two-fifty a week which is good pay at this time, I do have a girlfriend, yeah, and a car . . . ' 'Son why would you want to be here?' 'Officer I don't know, but my old man thinks it's a good idea. Give me bunk number twenty-three-A and my locker and I'll be happy for the next forty years.'"

LONG—*LONG* HOT SUMMER NIGHT . . .

. . . The dry tire-and-hubcap of a pickup truck, parenthesized in a wash of dirty streetlight, below a network of intervening treeshadows . . . Across the street, music beats from an upstairs lightbulb—bottlerockets hiss and bang—something yelps, the hazy quarter-moon above is an embarrassed guest, a breeze tries and falls short. Who knows what my carpet holds, as two girls push a baby stroller by . . . A flurry of two kids—followed by another—running and turning, shrieking past, laughing . . . The green-lit nightbus, empty, carrying one passenger to the projects . . .

—A shadowed 98 which I know to be gold pulls, lightless and reckless, into the glass along the curb; Mr. Jim is home for the night. The gate below clinks—open, and closed— His footsteps on the porch . . .

I feel like I'm stuck to everything.

He gets home from work around twelve-twenty every night . . . drunk . . . Reels into the apartment downstairs and gets out his tattoo needle. I see him in the mornings—barechested, in shorts—former muscles gone to flab, though still carrying himself with a certain bowlegged daring—Marred with inky tattoos . . . A man in his early fifties, he's taken it into his head he wants to be a tattoo artist. He's got no one to practice on but himself, so every night around this time I hear the hot buzzing of the gun . . . and singing . . . and one-sided conversations, disputes . . . and the gun, buzzing . . .

/ Here's a redlight stuck and won't go green.

I'm a sweat machine, like everyone else in the world tonight: something luminous and vague is growing beneath the dishes in the sink and I don't even *think* about the attic.

. . . I'm rolling, tumbling, climbing around, trying to find cooler positions: I wrap around the drainpipe, I hang from the lightswitch, I crawl inside the shoeshine kit . . . I wake up under the nightstand. *Around this time the telephone blew its horn across the room.* The black thing vibrates to the edge and spills over, I grab it—*Hello, said my shaky voice: well how're you doing?/*

I lay on my back on the cot, waiting for the nosebleed to stop, swallowing whatever trickled down my throat . . . And, since I was lying there anyway, I decided to milk whatever excess energy I might've accumulated over the last few hours . . .

It came, finally, and I wiped off with the sheet.

Outside, all stands in copper and smoke. The moon is an old yellowed animal's tooth . . . a dull fang . . . A motorcycle tears past and rips back . . .

JOHN CLAMS UP

"You want a shot of this?"

"Huh? Nah, nah . . ."

"Sure?"

"Yeah, yeah, I—stopped at a bar had a couple shots with the truck."

"With the truck? You go the hall today?"

"Yeah, I figure I go down there, test the water, y'know. Obviously the word got back there about Burdette. The dispatcher likes me so he sent me out today, but he kinda—made it clear the bosses don't wanna see me down there for a while. It's just as well, it was fucking brutal today."

"What're you gonna do?" I said, finishing the bottle.

"Tomorrow I'm gonna go down there and get a withdrawal card from the union so at least I ain't gotta pay the fucking dues for a while, and then I'm gonna sign up for welfare. Single person with no dependents, they give you one-thirty a month, plus eighty in food stamps."

"Huh."

"So, uh . . ."

"How'd you do today? You got five?"

"Here I'm just telling you I'm at the end of my fucking rope and you wanna squeeze me for another five!"

". . ."

"I got ten if you need it, but this might be the last one for a while . . ."

"Naw, five's enough; I just wanna get another pint."

He exhales . . . flicks me a ten.

"At least you still got John," I tell him.

"Naw that fucker ain't called me in three days! I'm sorry I paid him! Last time I talked to him he said he's through with baseball."

"He's hanging up his spikes."

"He said it's taking his attention away from his mother."

"Maybe he's pulling another one of his retreats."

"Yeah I dunno . . . What time is it? I gotta get over to Feef's."

I decide to skip the pint and bet with Feef instead, so we take a walk . . .

The place is packed. One-Leg Frank is there, and a 7-Up driver with his truck double-parked . . . the Mayor shows up in a nice pair of checkered slacks, with one of his aldermen in tow . . . also a guy in coveralls who stinks like a dead horse and three or four guys I don't know, all standing around trying to get the lines from one another and writing bets. Kids come in and buy up candy, stall the proceedings—Feef's in his usual uproar, cradling the phone trying to keep track of the gum-balls and ostracizing bettors—A kid says "Hey Feef: are you a midget or a dwarf?" and runs out laughing as Feef drops the phone and the door goes *slam*. By the time we've squeezed into line, San Diego Russ has convinced Ed to take a flier on one of his look-just-trust-me, this-a-gift-from-me-to-you picks—the Padres, of course . . . Ed tacks the Padres onto his two-teamer and I stick with my original bet, a two-teamer for ten . . .

I borrow a radio from Ed and take it upstairs. And, in the night, I listen for my scores while he, downstairs and next door, listens for his.

In the morning I collect enough to keep me another couple days, and give Ed back his ten.

PORCHES OF SUMMER . . .

The summer heat was omnipresent, omniscient, omnipotent. The Big Embrace, like a laundry room. That copper battleship haze. The streets were blinding—blank. A trickling glass of ice water, fans buzzing and blowing, and ticking flies. I was buying a pint of hundred proof every day from whatever cash I could come up with—Colonel Lee, Old Crow, J.T.S. Brown. Hundred proof hits you in a different way. Five or ten shots in that kind of heat and I'd feel like going out and cracking someone over the head. Hits you angry. I was sitting ensnared in Sear's one day getting the Buick fixed on the taped up remains of an old Sear's card: I got there early and it turned inevitably into an all-day affair . . . So I walked across the parking lot to a State store and broke my last twenty on a pint of Old Crow to pass the time with and then I was on the phone to Ed, telling him I'd meet him in general admission over the first base line and put ten for me on the favored team . . . and I remember pulling into the dusty gravel lot under some kind of sky that was special at the time and I found Ed and watched about half an inning before I . . . /

Yer washed over by illegal semis and midnight icecream trucks—one thousand turns of the same little tune until yer alarms begin to ring . . . a trapezoid of streetlight turns you into a prone skeleton with the bed just out of reach . . . voices on the street and the acoustics of yer room put them right above you—right behind you—right in the room, till yer sleep is full of the gossip of strangers. Is this a place to dream? The days and nights've ground to a halt.

/ At four a.m. Rhonda was lightly snoring. She was a sort of amateur hooker who lived up the street. She'd seduced three generations of a family of vegetable vendors for free tomatoes and bell peppers. Ed had paid her a few visits which she'd defused by talking about me. I went there blind drunk after the ballgame. It was like fucking a skeleton. I pulled my clothes on with a tremendous headache and walked home.

From early morning till well past midnight people were on their porches: whole families, with nothing else to do. The sight of them infuriated Ed, apparently with the sight of himself. The house directly across the street was home to an ever-changing roster whose regular members included a huge muscular black guy and his three-hundred-pound white wife—a tyrant who screamed at the absolute top of her lungs at him and their baby twenty-four hours a day: literally twenty-four hours a day with a lull now and then, giving him time to consider the fallout from her last outburst before she stormed onto the porch again to blast and berate and belittle him into further submission through the glaring afternoons and soiled nights, until one day the guy exploded in tears and started blindly whipping bottles into the street and bellowing and trying to tear the porch off the house . . . There was also a proud and humorless hilljack in a cap made to look like a McDonald's hamburger, with a massive pitbull on a chain. All the long summer days into summer nights these folks were on the porch, and the porches to either side of them were also occupied, with other people bored and slumped and staring at the street . . .

Ed, when he saw a couple of what he termed unsavory characters sauntering by, would find his way out to the edge of his porch and lean against the column, casually dangling his thirty-eight along his leg, letting it catch the sun, just to let them know . . .

There was a dog living in the yard we shared—the landlord's dog: a big dopey sweet-natured shepherd named Dildo. He'd spend his days bounding back and forth in snatches of abandon—running along the fence chasing kids who teased him and called his name—and end up abandoned to the sorrow of separation as the kids continued, shouting on their way . . . Inbetween, he dozed in the shade and scratched himself and lay gazing mournfully off one of our porches . . . But he was infested with fleas, and the more he came bounding with all he was worth of hopeful innocence to meet Ed coming in the gate or out the kitchen door, the more Ed scorned him with kicks and curses, to which the dog responded with ever-replenished hope and love . . .

It was late morning on I think a Thursday during a week of breezeless ninety-degree heat, and the Southside was Dodge City: the porches across the street were loaded. Ed banged out from behind his screendoor, scuffing along the porch to lean against a column, scanning the street and saying aloud to the street in general "Yep! Another *looonng* day on the porch, eh?" folding his arms and achieving a final disgust with the situation. Dildo the Dog came bounding from the other end of the yard in a paroxysm of hope and love and enthusiasm, onto the porch and right into Ed's arms. Ed struggled free of him brushing off imaginary fleas and dashing back to the house—

Emerging with the thirty-eight giving back the sun for all to see, chasing the dog off the porch and up the drive with the spectators leaping forward in their chairs until the dog and the man were disappeared around back of the house and apparently locked in a showdown—

The street was all eyes. And then a gunshot cracked the morning—and another.

And the street was all waiting.

And then the dog scampered tail-between-his-legs back down the driveway and into the frontyard and curled up on my porch, understanding, finally, the meaning of scorn.

RUSS ALERT

Stepping from the feeble diseased air-conditioning of the Spot into the bright wall of August even my eyes're hot; Ed's folding the paper under his arm—

"Fuck," I tell him, "Every meal I eat in that joint shaves a day off my life."

"—Russ Alert," he says, looking up the street.

San Diego Russ is coming. He spots us and slows into the swollen nonchalance of the tout . . .

"Feef got the lines yet?" he says, approaching.

Ed says "We ain't coming from Feef's, we're coming from breakfast. Not everybody's a sick gambler."

"*Okay, okay,*" Russ says, threatening to withhold his pick of the day . . .

But he can't help himself.

"All you gotta make is one bet today," he says. "Cinci."

Ed, agitated, is re-opening the paper . . .

"Don't bother with parlays, just put a hundred on Cinci. They'll be six to five. Tomorrow you'll thank me."

Another minute or two on the bright empty street, going back and forth over Cincinnati and the day's other possibilities, and then Ed folds the paper and Russ walks on.

Stopping again, with "Hey—Eddie—"

We wait while he walks back to us.

"I got my car in the shop. How's yours running?"

Ed backpedals, going "Well, y'know, it's uh—basically running like shit, y'know, uh—"

"'Cause upstate New York they're running duck races for the summer, and—"

"Duck races?"

"Yeah I got a buddy of mine told me they been running duck races up there."

"Duck races, Russ?"

"Yeah. First three ducks to the pond, y'know. I's thinking of taking a ride up there sometime."

Ed says "Yeah, well, y'know . . . Just let me know . . . y'know, uh, I might consider doing that, uh—"

"I'll see what I can find out. We can split the gas. Later."

"Okay, see you around."

We walk a block in silence.

Then: "Russ's married, isn't he?"

Ed says "Yeah, you seen his wife. Nice-looking broad— nice-looking redhead. *Super* cute, matter of fact."

"Yeah . . . Hm."

"What?"

"Nothing."

Alex came by today with a bag of emergency supplies. A jar of peanut butter, two boxes of pasta, two cans of sardines, three cans of soup, a bag of lentils, twenty bucks, and a book he found at a flea market—*How to Win Money at the Track*. Al gets a kick out of doing things like this: he's a survivalist. Unlike me, apparently.

I opened the book when he left and started a list of debts in the flyleaf, "Al—$40; Ed—$280; Folks—$50; Visa—(fuck Visa)." This was probably the closest I'd come in years to attaining an overview of my life.

In the bright blue break between day and night a cool breeze finds its way through the bathroom window. Lukewarm water in a four-legged tub, atmosphere of empty rooms. Caught in a mirror. Ed's not around, all the bills're overdue, and nothing doing here.

In the bright blue nothing-doing, an overdue cool breaks day and night and winds its way around here.

Ed's overdue, I'm lukewarm here. I ain't around here.

Punch me out: punch me out of orbit. The guy beside me—I don't like his haircut. An older guy, maybe fifty, with a strict blond bowl-cut like a Dutchboy which ends about an inch before his red neck begins and which could've happened only by fierce design. Turns and tells me a story how Elvis came to town in the fifties and played some dive at a Hundred-Fifth and Euclid and offered him some money to carry his bags. This guy said "Hell no I ain't yer nigger." And then he waits for my reaction.

Same guy then he is now. He's been telling that story for thirty years. I don't look at him, just drink my shot.

I come to all the wrong places. Caught in a mirror lukewarm water in a two-legged tub; archive of hungry visions, beating down dark tangents. I want someone to sleep beside. Been at me night and day, tidal and insistent. Winds its way through the window, stains the sheets and doesn't dry.

All I want is "Another shot of Kessler here?" Every few

years you fall down inbetween. I should've gone downtown tonight, where the fireflies breathe. Maybe still time—

Slide off my stool leave a quick tip and—as usual, night is waiting at the door.

(IN STEREO)

Something a couple steps ahead of me cocks its head, eyebrows raised, and says Hah? Howboutit? and I get a pinch in the ass, and turning to investigate I get a playful smack in the head, and whirling to protest I get a poke in the ribs and I let out a sigh, straightening up again and brushing the wrinkles out of my dignity while he or she or me unfolds a treasure map with X marks the spot, and leaning forward to peruse I receive a chummy kick in the pants as the voices of him or her or us commence to ricochet around and off of me with *Eh?* and *Aah?* and *Hah? howboutit, eh?*—Ever so amiable, but I'm beginning to be confused when the silver horns rush in with their distracting dances, leaving me a couple steps ahead of what I didn't get ahold of in the first place and no time to look back as the laughter fades like just another song . . .

JUDGMENT CALL

Ed, squinting at me in the morning sun . . .

I must've swayed, slightly.

A couple minutes later, in the cool of his rooms:

"Yerd from John yet?"

"Hah?"

"John."

"No, no . . ."

"Mm. Must be MIA again."

"You're hitting it kinda hard, ain't ya?"

"So?"

"So nothing, y'know. It's just—y'know. That kinda shit catches up with you."

"You mean you gotta pay it back."

". . . Hah? Yeah, y'know . . ."

"What're we up to now?"

"Hah?"

"Where's the tab?"

He squints again, this time in surprise.

Then he goes into the kitchen. I follow.

He turns, we almost bump. "What's the *problem?*" he says.

. . . there we go: the first few pulls always taste like raw hard grain, but then it levels out, sweet and rolling; below the label-top is all happily downhill. no coffee in the house but i brought back two larges from the hot dog inn and i got a full pack of smokes—abdul gave me a pack on credit. so i'm fortified, right?

Someday . . .

Backyard lights flickering through the leaves.

convex/concave: the glass curves, the amber waves of grain. i can be whatever i want to be at this table, in this window. but it don't get me anywhere except morning.

AT THE TRACK

Ed says "You're a troubled young man. —I can see it in your eyes, y'know, you don't know what direction to go in—You wanna do things, you want adventure, and you just— It's like you're in a vacuum or something. You're floating around— You're looking at me for answers! Like right now!"

"*[laughter]*"

"You're looking into my eyes, you're saying *What do I do? Where do I go?*"

"*[laughter]*"

"—You're a troubled young man. I got you figured perfectly. You want the world—but you don't want the world, and you give a fuck but you don't give a fuck . . . It's because of your youth! If you was old like me you just get a big belly, sit around, play the horses: y'know, you take everything in stride 'cause you been fucked so many times, by life, that nothing bothers you: you get a blowout on the freeway so what? you sit there wait for a fucking towtruck. Hose flies off? you just keep driving! Fucker blows up just leave it on the fucking street. But *you*— You're on the borderline! You're like on the brink of being like a—a great author—"

"*[increased laughter]*"

"—millionaire, or—Or being a total *wino,* or a nobody!— smoking Camel cigarettes on a street corner—And you consider that just as exotic as being a big-time author or a playboy or whatever! It's— You're just so troubled that I wish I could

369

help you."

"Well gimme twenty bucks: that'd help."

"No, it's not money. I could give you a million dollars right now, and it make no difference, to you—"

"Really?"

"No. Because you're a troubled young man. Me? I'm a loser, right? I'm a total—nothing, as Dad sai—I'm a *bum*. But—my mind is *straight*. I know exactly what I am, where I'm going . . . what's gonna happen . . . It's cut-and-dry for me. Y'know? The only pressures I got is—winning at a fucking card game—My pressures aren't—'Jeez, in two years am I gonna—?' I *know* I'm nothing. I'm gonna *be* nothing. But you—I can see the look in your eyes—you're sitting here you're hurt!"

"I don't feel hurt."

"You're *hurt*, you're *hurt!*"

"*[laughter]* "

"Believe me—you're hurt. You're sitting here—just looking off into space—"

"Maybe I'm bored."

"No, you're not bored. You want something, you wanna *grab* something—And it ain't there. And when you grab that thing it'll all be straight. I feel like saying 'Danny: go to the factory, get a job,' or 'Go to Chicago,' uh—anything; I wanna give you an answer but I don't have it."

"*[laughter]* "

"You would be content—I really believe this—getting the cheapest bottle of wine you could find, a *pint* bottle yet, and a fucking sack of Bull Durham—And sitting in a beat up fleabag hotel in Kansas City—And be happy, and just feel like you're experiencing life. Or you could be in Vegas, wearing tuxedos, dating fucking princesses— You could go either way! And either way—*frighteningly* enough—might satisfy you!"

"*[laughter]* "

"You're right on the line! You're either gonna be a total success in life or you're gonna be a total bum. And you're just floating around in that between one and the other. But— You could be a great bum! If you're gonna be a bum you're gonna be a good one."

. . . iguana grass, and late sun down the railroad street: the breeze of desire, through exploded cattails and the reeds of a dead crick . . . brown and still, but alive once with what i gave it . . . these eyes were headlights once, in an obscure world . . . these hands, struggling with chickenwire and abandoned plywood, once touched the world. tough blue cornflowers and standing boxcars/ i always expected to be free, forever. somewhere the . . . compass . . . don't talk to me, don't talk to me anymore. i wasn't waiting, once. ?

SOMETHING LOST, REMEMBERED

Thursday was hot as hell, a heavy ugly day. Well the humidity added up. At night, through the windowscreen beside the bed, something whispered *cooler*. And then it whispered *Here:* and I knew there was a vague shine on the street, and then the rain came driven down in big drops. I didn't see it myself; it was a suggestion right beside the shoulders of a dream . . .

And then today: today had the rare brightness of a new world: the clouds, the blue swept sky, the light—all the day freshly emerged from the chrysalis of a rainy night: silver and gold.

Last night, although we've never met, I had this sexy dream about you. And today is like this:

casual silver . . . with a rustle of reeds we begin, pushing off from shore . . . a hollow pluck—a glance ahead and then away, pretending not to have seen the silvery widths. But we're bound, we're bound away—pushing off from the rustling, the hollow plucking . . . across the column of elements, across the mirror widths, below silver breadths . . . look away . . . with notion our canoe is laden . . . look away . . .

All today I've been thinking of you. The way you've tugged at me I've tugged at you, the way the watery night pulls and is pulled by the new day, the way the little boat tugs and is tugged by the shore . . .

*

Early evening Friday.

    I leave the window chair and put a record on the stereo of old, old music, and then go back to the chair.

Lord the smokestack is black and the
buildings shine like
buildings shine like
buildings shine like
buildings shine like gold
Aw the smokestack is black and the buildings shine like gold

SUMMER JOURNALS

IV

I'm parked on the shore of night: a sliver of moon hangs in a clear blue sky. Downtown stands kindled in a gold from the opposite horizon: glowing from a blue more perfect by the moment, until it quivers to a stop, in the caught breath of day.

Trees are tossed in a desire that blows between day and night, and I settle into sharpened silence.

*

"I'm a white razor moon, the Dog Star shining, fire in the sky, hundreds of murders, twenty-three springtimes, a snow-lit room, a flea-bitten bed, and the sparks in a redhead's laughter; voices from the street and the heavy shimmer of a bourbon August, trophies and a little boy's sailor hat, faded pink wallpaper with a rosary on the wall, the smell of pussy and the taste of fever, banks of grass and oily dirt beside the tracks, the call of a goose and the cold smolder of autumn sundown; the Dakota Badlands and aggravated rape, the Lower East Side at dawn and the sagging bodies of old-timers at the Y, two months in Barcelona and a room in New Orleans, Italians as handsome as daggers and smoking trains going nowhere but away, a lean girl in Paris and a lonesome donkey on an island in Greece, a sky of absolute blue, and lights you've got no inkling of and shadows passed down from thousands of centuries of the dark hunt.

"Look hard enough and a crescent moon shows her other half."

*

Night finds me back under the kitchen bulb.

Three steps painted grey concrete.

Light going nowhere, the wide bay of afternoon.

Clink of gate.

"How you doing, Mr. Jim?"

"Marvelous!" he roars.

He lurches and catches himself.

"Hey," he says. "You working?"

"No."

"What're you doing tonight?"

"Nothing. Why?"

"Can't find anyone for this job out Richmond Road. They make bingo cards."

"Yeah?"

"Let me know if you feel like going out there. Sweep up, drink coffee. I'd go out there myself, I didn't have to work the office tonight."

"I'll do it."

"Yeah? It only pays twenty-four bucks—"

"That's alright. I ain't doing nothing else."

"The regular guy's off, I can't find anyone."

"Yeah, I'll do it."

"If you don't I'll find someone else. And if I don't, fuck 'em."

"No that's okay: I'll do it."

"Yeah, okay. You'll be doing me a favor."

"Time's it start?"

"Eleven o'clock, you work till seven-thirty in the morning."

"Where is it?"

"Way out Richmond Road—I'll get the address. Gimme a knock later—I gotta get a drink."

"Okay."

"Marvelous."

*

That first night started as a nervous adventure. I borrowed three dollars for gas and the makings of a slim sandwich from Ed and set off around ten-fifteen.

Driving up a two-lane road I found the place, or rather a small floodlit sign on a lawn. I pulled into a drive that led behind the building to a fenced-in gravel lot. A backdoor was open on greenish light . . . I put out my cigarette and grabbed my lunchbag.

Inside, the place was long and huge like a warehouse, the light was neutral and dim. Nobody around. Aisles of empty metal shelves, a few pallets here and there. A hundred yards away something was happening—a rhythmic noise. I located a machine of some kind—it was distant—far across the floor. I understood it right away—this machine was the heart of the place—the heart of the whole operation. But the body was too big for the heart: like a heart kept alive in some vast abandoned laboratory. Beside the machine a man was slumped on a stool.

It took almost a minute to cross the floor. He must've heard my bootsteps but still, when I approached he jumped on his seat as though startled. He was a scrawny toothless guy with a ponytail, prematurely old, and he eyed me up and down before pointing where I could set my lunchbag, resentful at having to share his solitude and his responsibility to the machine.

His name was Mason and he eyed me up and down again scratching his gizzard, deciding where to place me and whether

I was up to it.

The machine perforated sheets of bingo cards. The cards were printed side by side on big sheets of card stock, and these were fed into the machine. The machine perforated the sheets so they could be broken into individual cards and boxed up and sent out.

My job, Mason decided, was to feed the machine. His job, I decided, was to sit on a stool waiting for something bad to happen, bowed with the gravity of the situation.

There was nothing much to do. I'd push a broom across the floor, up and down the aisles, and come back to flap a stack of sheets onto the stack at the back of the machine.

At three o'clock Mason declared lunch and shut the machine off. I followed him across the floor to an area near the door where there was a desk and a vending machine and a water fountain. We sat on the floor and ate our sandwiches and didn't speak, Mason presiding over the silence in his capacity as senior employee. He intuited that I didn't have money for the coffee machine and poured me a steaming cup from his thermos. I thanked him and offered him a cigarette, but he said he didn't have the habit.

At three-thirty, prompt, I followed his lead across the vast and lustrous concrete floor to the machine.

*

I was sitting on a pallet against the wall when Mason cut the machine off. That chomping rattling roar stood in the air, audible by its absence. A hesitant quiet lingered at its edges, waiting to filter in. Mason eased himself from his roost and stretched. He walked past me, muttering "Seven o'clock." They were welcome words. I stood up, I bent over, stretched, and wandered behind him toward the timeclock.

The red second-hand of the clock on the wall swept freely round as he pulled out desk drawers and found a pen. Carefully and almost grudgingly he signed my time slip and handed it to me. He was sticking around to keep an eye on things until the new shift arrived.

I said "Thanks. See ya," and walked out the door into the air. Day was the grey of the gravel underfoot.

Driving the freeway west, I was buzzed ahead of my ability to comprehend, riding the road. Spread far below a freeway curve, my parents' neighborhood was nearly awake, and the road sped me onward. I felt a sense of accomplishment and also that the preceding hours had been a meaningless dream. On one hand an open, permanent truth and on the other a greenish secret, folded away and forgetting itself as I drove.

Soon the grey lake ran beside me, distantly dissolving into sky. The grey contained a new conception of time, and I didn't like it . . .

I parked on Prospect and walked into the place. Mr. Jim wasn't there. I handed in my time slip and waited for my check among men waiting to be sent out.

I cashed the check at the bar across the street, the Empire, one of the few bars remaining on Prospect, an old free-standing brick building like a tooth waiting to be pulled: sad old wino haunt with rooms available up above. Twenty-four dollars and change and they kept the change. I paid for a shot of whiskey, drank it, and drove home to bed.

What started as a night turned into a week. Mason and I in the green hours. I found myself wide open, at those hours, to loneliness . . . aspirations . . . memory . . . people I used to know . . . Harder than staying awake was *being* awake, alone with your thoughts . . . an astronaut of time . . . prey to sadnesses . . . guilt . . . hopes . . . longings . . . Rhonda like a whore: skeletal and pockmarked and ravenous, available, lightly snoring at four a.m. . . . Sadie hammered bright thin metallic . . . and Marie of course, watching me . . . At three a.m. I step outside and these thoughts hang above me—a reef of cloud, one endless false dawn . . .

You stare up at it, smoking a cigarette, and then go back to the machine.

After work you step into the grey light feeling empty. You cash your checks at the Empire and the scene inside there sloshes like waves. One morning you're watching quarter porn at eight o'clock. The next, you're first into the basement weight room at the Y. Different aspects of yourself pop up, unexpected . . . As the day widens you're putting yourself to bed.

the rain is the sound of silver: falling in sheets, in swells, in curtains . . . strumming down . . . as cruel as sweetness, and vice versa . . . i'm on my way home, i park, i sit in the bus stop . . . fenced and rain-ravaged yards . . . abdul's is lit. the sound of silver in the awesome exhausting grey of the world . . . no one on the street . . .

. . . clinging . . . clinging, with occasional cool puffs of breeze that've lost their way . . . and everyone's on their floors, having slipped off of beds and chairs, having lost their momentum, having given it all away . . . [low-angle view:] . . . puddles of memory . . . stranded between the dying insects of summer and autumn's bicep.

Mr. Jim worked eight p.m. to midnight, a place called Hours Incorporated. A one-story brick building at the empty edge of downtown. Temporary agency. A doorway beside a vacant lot.

I got down there on a Monday morning and parked under a blue queasy dawn. Inside, I found a place to lean against the wall.

Cigarettes and wine breath, coffee stomach fluorescent light a T-shirt pocket yesterday's pants and planet sweat.

"Anybody work a punch press?" and the hands go up.

"You in the green shirt."

"Me?"

"No, the guy with the bandanna."

They asked who was driving and I raised my hand.

"Okay, and take these two with you. You guys give him a buck each for gas."

They sent us out east to a low brick structure fighting off the weeds—forget the name of the place made coffin handles. Me and two guys to whom nothing was a surprise anymore, much less a joke.

Seven-thirty, the day already wide and hot, a foreman found a place for me beside a stack of crates of coffin handles. Each handle was crimped at both ends by the machine which cut them into pieces from long metal tubes . . .

They gave me a screwdriver.

And I spent the rest of the day sticking that screwdriver

into the ends of coffin handles, popping out the crimps and stacking the handles into crates.

Ten o'clock the coffee truck pulled in with a dust cloud and we went to gather around it. I had enough for coffee and I'd brought cigarettes with me.

Lunchtime the truck was back but I drank water from a fountain and sat on a railroad tie till it was gone . . .

I finished out the day and headed back through a fierce and flaring afternoon. Four-thirty we picked up our checks and took them across to the Empire Bar.

I picked up a pint on the way back to the Southside. The windows at the kitchen table were wide on the blank remains of day. I opened the whiskey and took a hit . . . lit a cigarette and waited for tomorrow.

Hours, minutes . . . Time to start catching up.

Rain falling into this network of backyards turns this into a jungle night. The sky is lit an even glow and we are clustered and tribed under dinosaur trees and giant ferns, looking out from darkened kitchens as the rain falls unabashed—factually and quiet, through layers of leaves . . . every surface a sound (washed or splashed or dripped-on . . . guttered . . . ticking . . . trickling), and the night is full of sounds but beyond words: chorused . . . incantatory . . . sober . . . ceremonial . . . Hush, it says: be still: watch and listen . . .

Watching out from kitchen windows . . . This could go on all night . . .

Meanwhile Ed was on a roll. He caught me in the yard mid-afternoon.

"I hit Feef *again* last night: that's four nights in a row! I've taken him for over a grand in the past week and filtered eight-eighty-two of it back out for bills. I paid fucking Jones, the IRS, Master and Visa, Roy . . . I hit him last night I paid the electricity, the phone, paid Mandy at the bar fifty I owed her, I got Wade's hundred here . . . Man I been hitting him *good*, too: he's getting grouchier and grouchier. All the penny candy's up to two cents. I bet the Oakland game today, three o'clock. One-fifty flat, so I got something to listen to this afternoon—"

He caught himself and looked at me.

Said "Nah, I'm just bullshitting you, I didn't hit him again— You kidding? I finally hit the skids."

"*[laughter]* Did you hit him or not?"

"Naw, no way; that'd be impossible."

"I wasn't gonna ask you for nothing."

He tilted his head back, laughing. It was good to see him laugh.

"Yeah, I did hit him. Four fucking days in a row—I'm rolling! You need ten? What're we up to now, three-sixty?"

"Three-sixty, yeah. No, I don't need any."

"You want another ten? I know you gotta be broke . . ."

"Yeah, y'know, uh . . ."

"You want twenty? I can tell I ain't never gonna see this

money again, it's past the point—"

"You got a fin?"

"I can give you twenty-five—"

"No, five's good. Any more than that I won't go to work tonight."

"Here."

"Thanks."

"I got a steak in the freezer, if you want half for dinner."

"Yeah, alright."

"You gotta cook it though. I got a couple tomatoes, half a cucumber . . . you can cook it up there and bring it over. I don't wanna eat in your place. I feel trapped in there."

"Yeah, so do I. I'll see you in a while."

*

Stop at Ed's to pick up the steak, he's pacing the kitchen.

"I'm losing this fucking Oakland game—I finally did it. Oakland ain't done a fucking thing the whole game. I hadda do it: I hadda break the streak. Two hundred, I bet on 'em."

"Thought you bet one-fifty."

"Aah I took a shot . . . two hundred, and I bet eighty tonight on a two-teamer. There's no way I'm gonna pull this one out."

"I'll be back."

*

Eating steak.

"*Man,* I can't believe I hit that game. Really Danny: I must be blessed. Losing three to nothing the whole game, I finally shut it off—Turn it back on just in time to hear 'em smack one over the wall with bases loaded. Incredible! I can't do anything wrong! I'm fucking blessed! I can feel a halo around my head!"

Later Mr. Jim called.

"I got something for you, if you want it . . ."

"Alright. What is it?"

"Place on Solon Road called Trans-Border."

"Trans-Border? I love to travel—what're they doing, running guns?"

"They make coffeepots."

Off the freeway the night thickens, time closes in. Slipping skeins of mist on a backroad . . . clinging to the windshield, floating past . . . I almost miss the place in the dark, in the dew . . . surrounded by trees . . . Get there eleven o'clock.

I walk in, it's just a little place, the usual dim greenish light, big fans blowing—

I get punched in the arm. It's a miniature woman with a giant pushbroom, looking up at me. She has a fierce gleam in her eyes, like she might want to play.

"HA! Where'd they find *you?*"

"Where'd they find me?"

"Someone with a haircut!"

She pushes her broom away, cackling.

In the office three guys are lounging around scratching their beards. One's behind a desk, the other two are against the walls. One of them is walleyed. They're looking at me like trespassing is a serious matter in these parts. They might be dangerous when sober.

"I'm from Hours," I tell the guy behind the desk.

"I'm from Mount Nebo, West Virginia," he says.

We're watching each other, waiting. I nod and smile. A couple of seconds go by. He drums his fingers on the desk.

He says "You be out there, machine with that fucking Porterrican."

One of the others pipes up, says "He ain't no Porterrican,

he's Niggeraguan, 'r some shit."

Out the office window, a tall dark man is wiping his brow. He looks worried. He stuffs a white hanky into a back pocket and turns away.

"Picked him out right away, didn't ye?" says the guy behind the desk.

I get a strange sense of deja vu. Not like this's happened to me, but like it's been happening to someone else, maybe a new person every night for a long time . . .

I approach the Nicaraguan who's finishing his shift at a big green machine. He seems not right for this place, like he was a respected person elsewhere. Busily working, he explains what I'll be doing. The machine molds plastic trays for coffee-makers. It tips them out in pairs connected by a stem. Every thirty seconds he opens the sliding door, takes out the pair, cuts them apart and slips them into a bag. Takes twenty-five seconds; five seconds to kill inbetween.

He steps back, tells me to give it a try.

I hop in, pull out the newborn pair, I'm fumbling with the razor to cut them apart . . .

Solemnly, he watches me. I turn to open the door . . .

It's easy enough, I get the hang of it, I'm working away.

I relax into the pace, but he says "Open door immediately! Close door immediately!"

A wee woman, different from the first, pushes by with a broom and says "Don't worry. I'll keep an eye on him."

When he sees I've got it he turns to go, he's in a hurry.

"Hey, uh—How do I turn the machine off?"

"Off?"

"Yeah, how do I turn it off?"

"Turn *off?*"

"Yeah, y'know in case I gotta take a piss, or I drop something I gotta stop to—"

"Stop?"

"*Yeah: stop.*"

"*No* turn off! Machine don't stop! You call the foreman he take over—machine don't stop! Breaktime ten minutes one o'clock and five o'clock, lunch half hour three o'clock."

And he disappears—makes his escape. A little woman pushes a broom by, alert . . .

On the table is a clock radio. Beat-up and half melted, blaring an AM station. Open the door, close the door, nick the two pieces apart. You've got to pace yourself for these factory nights, protect your energy, keep your detachment. The songs on the radio are a threat—they're bad enough in broad daylight—at this hour they get under your skin, make you irritable, sick. It's a battle between me and the radio. I try to not pay attention, block it out. Keep moving. Why take it so seriously? Stupid songs on the radio, who cares? Don't think, keep working, be automatic.

There's a radio at each machine, tuned to the same station.

Then the commercials come barging in—they up the ante—frenzied—one after another—five in a row—each one louder than the last—more hysterical—scenarios, jingles—boastfully moronic—pleading—outdoing each other—building toward a crescendo. And it doesn't stop there. They keep coming. Another five—twelve in a row . . .

A few more songs, terrible songs, embarrassingly familiar, they drain you a little more, and then the commercials come steamrolling in again. You look to the dim fluorescent heavens—one!—three, five!—more! A symphony of lies! You slip into a crack between what you're hearing and where you are in the roaring factory night. A dozen commercials—one more for good measure. Your soul squirms there—exposed—irradiated! Forty-five minutes of this, no end in sight.

. . . Put two trays in a bag and reach for the radio—two more trays are pushing out, so I grab them, clip them apart, bag them, and hit the radio's off-switch. Doesn't work. Two more trays are coming—I take care of them—hit the AM/FM switch: doesn't work. Grab the trays coming out—fix them up—reach for the tuning dial: it's broken off. Grab two more trays—clip them, bag them—flip the radio over, no other controls. SON OF A BITCH! Now I'm pissed. I let the machine go and walk around to pull the plug.

The machine jams. Overloads! Bells ringing, lights flashing—a buzzer goes off—a plant-wide siren sounds—three toy women start sweeping in tight circles, the office door bangs open—foreman comes running with a wrench, there's white plastic oozing from the machine . . .

Anyway, I shut the radio down.

. . . Back to rhythm, working along fine. I steal glances, try to get a bigger picture. All around the place are these long green machines, a person locked into each of them. At the end of—whoops: two more trays— At the end of each machine is a big nozzle stuck into a cardboard box. That's the plastic. The machine sucks it up and melts it down and out come the trays and the whole process keeps going . . .

*

Behind me is a wall of boxes, up to the ceiling almost . . . two more trays . . . And then I see him up there: a guy with a beard! Hiding up there—peering over the boxes. Watching us! Watching me!

*

On the table is a drawing. Just a few red lines. Two parentheses with a Y inbetween. A pussy. Someone before me has managed between trays to scrawl a tiny cunt—No head, no arms, legs. Was it the Nicaraguan? Exactly enough lines to express an idea, with a dot for a bellybutton. A functional drawing. The functions being protest and hope.

*

There was a big clock on the far wall. Someone's idea of a sick joke. Pretty soon I was checking it every two minutes. My body worked apart from my mind. I'd blown my wad early and now I was loose in time . . . a spirit . . . prey to every thought, lost in memories . . . upheavals, recriminations . . . haunting sorrows . . . fantasies . . . falling toward dawn without really believing it could ever be . . . like playing the lottery . . .

Now and then I'd zoom back into flesh and look around. A faucet dripping inside me. Wide awake at the wrong hour, and the trays kept coming.

*

At lunchtime I found a *Racing Form* in the breakroom and picked out a double and a quinella at Thistledown for later. Wrote the bets on a slip of paper.

And then dropped the slip in front of a broom on my way back to the machine.

*

When I picked up my check for twenty-four dollars in the morning the sky was blue, the sun was bright. I felt like an animal. I went to bed.

I woke with a headache a few hours later, wondering where Jim would send me tonight. The weather was still perfect.

Around noon I was walking to the drugstore I ran into Ed.

"I just come from Feef's, he's in a nasty fucking mood. I hit another two-teamer last night, for like four-fifty, plus that afternoon game for two-forty—I took him for almost seven hundred."

He tried to talk me into betting my money from the coffeepot job on Detroit that night.

"Sure thing," he said. "Believe me, I'm hot as a firecracker."

It was tempting. I decided to make a last bet on him.

He called later, drunk in a bar, to make sure I'd bet.

"I'm *blessed*, Danny—I can feel it in my bones. You gotta be gambling your whole life to know these things. I tell ya Feef is sweating, man—I got him on the ropes."

"He's only a midget, Ed."

"That's what *you* think. Believe me, I'm on a streak here, and they don't come too often. Jump on it and ride with me, we'll make a fortune. Take Detroit tonight—they're six to five—I got five hundred on 'em. They lose, I'm bankrupt. But they won't lose! We'll hit tonight and bet the whole thing tomorrow and just keep on going—"

Working spot labor I made twenty-four dollars a shift. It cost me four in gas to get to the next job and back. I went to Feef and put eighteen on Detroit at six to five. The game would be played at ten-thirty our time.

That night I worked at the bingo card factory. Me and Mason again. He's at the front of the machine and I'm at the back.

He's got a radio going, and I keep changing the station to check the game. Oakland's ahead three nothing in the fourth. I go back to stack the machine.

Next time I check, Detroit has scored two runs in the fifth and the bases are loaded. I do some stacking . . . push a broom . . . I pile some wooden skids . . .

In the eighth Detroit ties it. In the ninth, Oakland comes up last, the score still tied at three, and they leave a man on base without scoring. I start pacing.

Detroit can't do a thing in the tenth, but they manage to hold Oakland. I'm talking to myself.

Mason gets fed up with me switching the station and tells me to leave the game on. Now *he's* talking to himself. He puts me at the front of the machine, close to the radio, so I can watch to make sure the sheets are shooting straight through and stacking right. BINGO, BINGO, BINGO . . .

Eleventh inning Detroit strikes out, puts a man on first, pops out, strikes out. I can't keep still. Oakland puts a guy on second and a guy on third—That's it, I figure, but still Detroit gyps them. The bingo sheets are stacking hard: BINGO, BINGO, BINGO . . . There's nothing to watch for. The machine rolls a sheet per second onto a pile growing perfectly straight—maybe one in a million comes out crooked or bent. I barely hear the twelfth inning: the pressure's gained a momentum of its own. Through the roar of the machine I hear Oakland load the bases again and—incredibly—crap out without a run. BINGO, BINGO, BINGO—There's a porthole in the armored side of the machine so you can stick an arm through to make adjustments. Mason sits there every night with his *head* through the hole, watching crosseyed for that one-in-a-billion crooked sheet. BINGO, BINGO, BINGO . . . Detroit steps into the thirteenth inning and belts a run over the centerfield fence! The score is four to three. Second batter pops out, third guy hits a single, fourth guy pops out— So there we are, looking better, two outs but we've broken the ice—and batter five cracks a double up the middle, brings the other man home. The next guy whiffs, and we move into the bottom of the thirteenth inning with a healthy two-run margin. The A's come up for their last stand and we put them away one, two, three. BINGO!

I had thirty-three coming and I felt like I'd barely escaped with my life. Three o'clock in the morning, after four innings of overtime, just in time for lunch.

Mason was still muttering . . . I took my sandwich outside and sat on the back steps . . . calming down . . . looking into the thick and itchy darkness . . . a few crickets . . . drinking my victory coffee . . . y'know . . .

Ed says "Let me tell you about last night. I know it's boring but I gotta tell this to somebody. I got a two-teamer going, right? Football—exhibition football. So I win the first game—"

"Let's see. You won the first game and lost the second. I've heard this story."

"—So the second game I got the Browns over San Francisco, I'm getting three and a half. The game's back and forth, back and forth . . . Finally San Francisco's winning twenty-seven, twenty-four with a minute forty left. But I'm ahead with the spot, and Cleveland's got the ball on San Francisco's forty-yard line. So I figure I won it, I light my victory cigarette . . . I said The only way I can lose this game is by a total fluke accident—fumble, interception—combined with another series of freak circumstances."

"Yeah."

"I no sooner said that Danny, than Cleveland fumbles and San Francisco gets it on their own forty. I said Well, no big deal: San Francisco's ahead, it's an exhibition game, they're tired . . . They're just gonna run out the clock. Now the second set of mishaps goes into action. Sonofabitch if they don't take it down to Cleveland's thirty. I said No way they gonna try for the field goal, they're already ahead . . . The guy's gotta kick a fifty-yarder—He's a good kicker, but even so, why take the chance? Sonofabitch if they don't kick the field goal—just to fuck me!

"So I'm yelling, scream—I put the cigarette out, broke the ashtray . . . There's like a minute left. Somehow, by some *miracle* the Browns manage to take it all the way downfield—Down to the ten! They got time for one more play, I said Holy shit! I still got a shot here! Quarterback goes to pass—Just about to throw the ball the picture goes blank! Caption says Please stand by. Incredible! So I dive into the kitchen grab the radio, I'm fumbling for the station— Soon as I tune it in the announcer says 'And that's Newsome for a touchdown!' I—*HooHOO!* He says 'Uh—Did he drop it? I guess he dropped it—No touchdown game's over.'

"I was so *astounded*—so frazzled after winning and losing and winning and losing again—down to the last *vein-tightening* second—I'm trembling, my blood's boiling— That comes in it's worth like three and a quarter. And they come back in the end just to twist the knife again—After my blood's on the floor, running outa my veins—I was dumbfounded. I hadda go outside and walk around, I was shaking so bad. I walked in front of the house for half an hour."

Sunday afternoon the neighborhood's drying out, the sky's breaking up. Jimmy D looked suddenly older at the table in Feef's this morning, more forlorn. He's got a magnifying glass for the entries now. He was sipping at some dark liquid. He swirled the last of it around the bottom of the glass, considering it, as though wondering what the hell it was.

"Feef serving breakfast now Jimmy?"

A little fat girl's counting candy, Ed says "Aah jeez, look at this . . . " Fat knees, fat elbows—a potato-faced girl counting penny candy by herself. He shakes his head, suddenly tired. And then gives me a look that is bright and factual. "She'll never have a date; ever."

And now Fast Eddie's at home, transfixed by the blue glow

of the TV, sweating out a C-note's worth of football and dying among the dirty laundry.

September broke breezy and hot. I woke up late on a Sunday, soaked in sweat. My neck had been stiff for two days and I felt groggy. Already I could smell another day rotting with the dishes in the sink.

Aside from existential questions I had thirteen bucks in my pocket, an envelope with eighty of the rent, and a month-old phonebill for thirty. This working thing didn't seem to be catching me up. I owed Ed almost four hundred, Visa's on the phone I'm answering in funny voices . . . the Buick was giving warning signals, maybe the carburetor . . . All in all, it would've been cheaper for me not to wake up.

I pulled my boots on, rinsed my face, and shuffled out to the car. Way too much light outside: just—y'know, gratuitous . . . Ed's car was gone.

I went to the track.

I lost the first race by a neck.

In the second I liked a horse called Residue of Dreams. Nine to two. I bet him in a quinella with Blow for Blow. Residue gets out front and Blow for Blow runs third. I had three bucks left.

I put three to win on Fast Forward. He ran second.

Something snapped.

I drove ninety miles an hour knocking construction barrels home, took the eighty from the envelope and went to Feef's.

I was on the cot, propped against the wall, Ed's transistor was on in the kitchen. As much noise as information. Still no score in the fifth inning. I must've fallen asleep.

The phone woke me, my old man calling.

When I hung up I remembered the game. The announcer was saying *"Final score, here in Anaheim: the California Angels five, the Detroit Tigers three."*

I'd won.

I went downstairs and knocked on Mr. Jim's door.

Soon after dark it started raining. I threw on a jacket and carried a garbage bag to Abdul's dumpster; dropped it off and kept walking. People in the dark on broken porches, and everywhere trees were dripping. There was light from the Puerto Rican church, cars out front. I stopped in a doorway of Lemko Hall.

Parked cars and wet smoke and the dripping trees. Thirty years ago. There was wet smoke, in the night.

The rain came harder. A fat woman and two girls came splashing . . . laughing . . . The rain came even harder till the street was hissing white with it, and the kettledrums came up from behind the houses, and the rain came even harder till it seemed kind of crazy . . . I stood there in the doorway, under the metal awning, looking out . . .

It was hot, in the kitchen. A record I'd been listening to had stopped. I waited to go to work.

Driving to work one night I forgot momentarily about the delicate state of the carburetor and coming off a stoplight I hit the gas too hard. The car stalled. I tried to start it and it almost kicked. I tried again it strained a little longer . . . Tried again and it groaned.

I sat back to wait a few minutes.

I was perched at the top of a ridge behind the post office, overlooking the mills. Third shift had started, second shift gone home. There was no one in sight.

After five minutes I tried again: there was no change, the battery was too weak.

I left the car and walked to a payphone. Ed's line was busy. I called Jim at the office and said I was stuck and couldn't make it out to Americo Rolled Steel. Ed's line was still busy.

I waited there twenty minutes getting aggravated while he enjoyed his conversation—not a soul passed, in a car or on foot—and then I got through.

"(. . . yes?)" he answered, in the voice of a timid old woman . . .

"Ed."

"(. . . who, please?)" he peeped.

"Come on, ya fucker, it's me: my car's broke down."

"(. . . I'm sorry Sir . . . could you repeat that please without using that type of language Sir?)"

"You scumbag," I laughed, realizing I wasn't going to

work.

"Alright what's the problem boy?"

"I think I just need a jump."

"Who-o-o-a, ho-o-o . . ."

I laughed.

He said "The Favor Department closes at dusk. All my ob-
ligations end there."

I told him where I was.

He said "I'm lying here in my fruit-vendor pants, my hair's
standing up—No one'll see me, will they?"

"If there was someone here I wouldn't've called."

"You got cables?"

"No."

"Alright I'll be there in ten minutes."

I started back to the car feeling good. Funny how a little
mishap can change everything for the better. Now the night
was open-ended:

I sat on the hood of the car looking out beyond the wall . . .
The view was smoky and old, the valley was like the source of
all darkness, from here on out. I felt as though I were sitting
on the back porch of the world, looking out over the neglected
backyard of night . . .

Ed slowed past, eyeing me suspiciously. He turned the Pontiac around and pulled nose-to-nose with the Buick.

He got out with the cables. "I want you to know I consider
this a major favor."

We tried for five minutes but the Buick wouldn't take the
jump. The only thing was for him to push me home.

He bumped me into the post office driveway and I got
turned around, and we started back toward town . . . grinding
up the freeway ramp and banging along the outer lane of the
bridge. He gave me a final tap at the top of the exit ramp and
I coasted down around the loop . . . floated through a redlight
and came to a stop in front of the Greeks.

"I's just getting ready to go out when you called, I got—

little mission to run. You feel like taking a ride?"

"Yeah. Where to?"

"I'll tell you about it on the way."

Another freeway curve, and the night takes up again.

"Awright, here's the deal. About a month ago I started up with this chick on the phone, I've talked to her every night, but I've never met her face-to-face. I've seen her, I know who she is, but she don't know me. And—"

"How do you know her?"

". . . That's not important."

"If you're gonna tell me the story tell me the story."

"I seen her working in a gas station. I's coming home from a game I stopped into a Sohio station for two bucks' worth of gas, and I seen her working there alone . . . Nice-looking broad: blonde hair blue eyes . . . I couldn't get a good look at her 'cause she's behind the glass, but y'know. Anyway I get home I call the station as Lisa. She picks up the phone 'Oblanek's Sohio,' whatever—And Lisa says—y'know: 'Oh, I'm so sorry, I have the wrong number—Is this Oblanek Sohio? What a coincidence: I was there just a couple hours ago, you're that blonde girl? You looked cute in that blue top, it must be pretty boring there at night . . . I work at night too, my name's Lisa . . . ' And this Debbie kinda laughed, and Lisa apologized for bothering her and said goodnight. Now—Even if this Debbie never thought about getting together with another broad, that's gotta break up her night a little, she's flattered, y'know . . . somebody noticed her . . ."

"Okay."

"So two nights later Lisa calls again—middle of the night: 'Hi Debbie it's Lisa, I was bored here at work, thought maybe you're lonely there,' y'know, kinda flirting with her, like broads do sometimes—nothing too obvious, just friendly . . ."

"Yeah."

"And it got to be a regular thing: Lisa start calling her every night. And then Debbie actually start looking forward to it, and—y'know, eventually the subject come up and—Lisa kinda mentioned she was into girls a little bit, y'know. Turns out Debbie's married, she's twenty-one, got some young guy works in a factory during the day they both make minimum wage, they ain't got a car, they both ride bicycles to work, she never sees the guy, she's bored—looking for something to happen, y'know: she's just a young girl . . . So eventually Debbie let on, y'know, she—kinda like to get together with Lisa, try it out, y'know. Not that she's a dyke, but it's—something she never really thought about, and she's been thinking about it, y'know. So Lisa offers to show her what it's like."

"This's amazing."

"And—After a couple more weeks Debbie's—She can't wait to get together with Lisa, y'know? And she start asking when they can meet, right? And Lisa's kinda—little bit hesitant—"

"*[laughter]* "

"She don't wanna rush into something Debbie ain't sure of, y'know, and—Debbie's getting more and more anxious but Lisa don't think the time's quite right, she keeps telling Debbie to wait a little while—"

"*[groan]*"

"And now Debbie claims she's in *love* with Lisa, she's never been in love with a woman before, she says she's willing to do anything—"

"Aah you fucker . . ."

"—Says Lisa's her master, she wants to be Lisa's sex slave, she wants to prove herself—"

"So where we going then?"

"—Says she *belongs* to Lisa, every inch of her body—"

"Ed: where we going?"

"Well Debbie was supposed to leave a little package for Lisa under a trash dumpster, Lisa's supposed to pick it up on her lunch hour—"

"A package?"

"Well, just a few—tokens of her esteem, y'know . . ."

Deserted shopping center. We swung around behind Pick 'n Pay.

Guttering along in the big Pontiac to a row of dumpsters . . .

He claimed he was too fat to be bending over, crawling around. I left the door open and darted out. Under the last dumpster I found a large brown envelope. It was stuffed and sealed, with *LISA* scrawled on both sides, in case anyone else was checking there for mail . . .

Sohio goes by: a girl behind glass in a blonde smear.

Riding back to the Southside:

"Open it up," he said.

"It's addressed to you."

He reached over and tore it open, spilled the contents onto the seat.

There was a letter sprinkled with hearts which began "Dear Master" and ended "Love, Your faithful fuck-slave Debbie." Also a pair of panties and a plastic bag containing a lock of blonde hair.

He held it up to passing lights.

I said "She *really* got curly hair, huh?"

"That's cunt hair, you idiot."

"Oh."

Clear September night at a high school football game, in the stands, among bright unnatural colors, noises: blue and gold . . . Across the field is another set of stands, another set of colors: orange and white . . .

Inbetween are the clatter of the two richly equipped teams, and the two marching bands in full regalia, and the two coaching staffs, and the two spangled squads of majorettes, the electric scoreboard . . . a balloon disappears above the jurisdiction of the lights.

Referees: family men in stripes and spikes . . . And other men: teachers by day—men who never made it out of high school, here for the game, to oversee, to uphold . . . to sustain the ritual, with cops on their side, paddywagon at the gate . . . Parents and neighbors and, central to all this, the teenagers. The awkward fringe kids, the whiz kids, the clowns, the angry embers and the just plain dumb, the stiff guys, the somebodies, the nobodies, the insiders and outsiders and the jittery wannabes, the bullies and prey, those who're bored and just waiting for high school to be over with and those who're at their peak now, and girls so bright they look dipped in light—all caught in the desperate vulnerable play-action of existence up on the brave hill: a spotlit noisy stage, under the dark night. (. . . far away . . .)

The cheerleaders jump and flash and tease in a false innocence that really *is* innocence: tempting encounters with the night, as though night is a bowl over this community and not a sky that lies across open distances and hidden hearts. What looks like spring is really autumn.

Gazing at the sky above the lights, from brass and hotdogs and coffee and pom poms, I can see the face of Charlie Starkweather, and, hovering lower, just over the houses, the shadow of Caril Ann.

ED'S KITCHEN, FOUR P.M.

"Oh:" he says, "New character at the track. Get this. I'm walking across the street to the track . . . Here's this guy—old guy, about five foot tall, hunched over, wearing a baseball cap . . . And there's three guys walking in front of us, right? I'm walking with the old guy, he goes—'MAC!' These guys keep walking, he goes 'MAAAC!' And these guys ain't turning around, y'know? 'MAAC!' Finally these guys go into the track, they disappear . . . So I'm behind him at the turnstile, he's paying his way in. He goes 'MAAC!'—to the guy in the booth, y'know? He goes to the men's room, I follow him in there—'MAAC!' Every fifteen seconds he goes 'Mac.' Just like a fucking parrot; he *looked* like a parrot: little hook nose—"

"*[laughter]* "

"So—I'm talking to this guy I know out there, he says this guy's been coming out there for thirty years. I go 'Well I been coming out here for *twenty* years, I've never seen the guy!' He goes 'I been here since 1952 he's been doing it.'"

"Yeah."

"So I follow him around again, right? He's got suspenders, big suitpants . . . he's going 'MAAC!', five guys turn around— So I sit on a bench with him, he's got this cap, y'know? It says—*So Many Women, So Little Time*—"

"*[laughter]* "

"And I'm timing him, like, one minute—'MAC!' I'm going What the fuck is this? Then I—tried to make conversation

with him, I moved over—'Who's gonna win this race?', y'know
. . . he goes '*How the hell do I know who's gonna win this race?*'"

"*[laughter]*"

"Then he goes back to the *Form*, y'know? 'MAAAC!'—Every
fifteen seconds—all day long."

"Wow . . ."

"So—*Get* this: I seen the guy for the first time in twenty
years of going to the racetrack, right? Sonofabitch if I ain't on
fucking Detroit Avenue yesterday, right? Driving up Detroit
. . . I'm stopped at a light . . . *Who's* coming across the street
with a *Form* in his hand but this guy, right? I go out the window,
I go—'MAAC!' 'MAAC!' he yells back!"

"*[laughter]*"

"Didn't look around, just—automatic: 'MAAC!' . . . I hadda
pull over I was laughing so hard . . ."

I made it home from the Yellow Freight Company at eight-thirty in the morning. I climbed into bed with the sun in my eyes and slept until almost noon.

I spent the day in a kind of bewilderment, always just a step behind waking reality.

Evening snapped me out of it and I felt almost human for a couple hours.

By nine-thirty I was sinking again.

Mr. Jim called.

"You wanna go out to Yellow Freight again?"

"Yeah, sure."

"Okay, it's yours."

The shift began at eleven. From eleven to seven-thirty there was nothing to do but sweep. The building was one long dock, T-shaped, with semi trailers backed up to it all the way around. The regulars were Teamsters. For sweeping they used a crew of spot laborers, five or six of us a night. Our supervisor was an edgy little guy in an army jacket, round glasses, combat boots, heavy-duty workgloves. He was beneath the contempt of the people who ran the place, but he had a desk between some storage crates and a whisk broom with his name scratched into it, and he took his position seriously.

There was nothing to sweep in the first place: only a thin black dust—the carbon residue of truck exhaust, along aisles of freight, under sodium lights. The night smelled like diesel. We couldn't tell the difference between what we were sweeping and what we'd swept. We'd lose track.

By two in the morning we were working in pantomime. Every night deteriorated into an abstract exercise—a challenge to sanity.

By four we were fighting over debris.

By six, we were tossing things on the floor in order to sweep them up: scraps of paper, wood chips . . .

Union guys on towmotors went rattling by with a whiff of propane, eating donuts, flicking cigarettes. There was a huge trash compactor that broke up loose boards and pallets . . . there was a watercooler at either end of the dock . . . the bathroom had plenty of powdered hand-cleaner . . . So between piling up skids and standing around listening to the crack and splinter of the trash compactor and stopping for drinks of water and keeping our hands clean, we could skirt the brink of insanity. I'd go from one end of the floor to the other to stop for a drink of water. I'd zigzag down aisles of freight dodging towmotors on a ten-minute hike to scrub some dust off my hands. And twenty minutes before every break you could look down the line and see the six of us—scattered along—winding down . . . checking over our work . . . wiping our foreheads . . . tying our shoelaces . . .

In the breakroom we'd sit well apart. We couldn't stand the sight of one another. We each thought the other five were bums: obviously unfit for any other kind of work. The Teamsters tried to catch ten minutes' sleep, or they played cards, or dug into huge lunches their wives had packed for them: cans of pop, Zingers, Ho Hos, candy bars, cookies, an occasional sandwich, but mostly little treats: cakes and chips, peanut butter and jelly . . . The six of us sat there drinking coffee . . . silent . . . trying not to meet anyone's gaze.

One guy, a Teamster, came in every break and sat down, put his feet on a chair, pulled his cap over his eyes and started burping. He'd lift his cap to check his pals' reaction. Three of his buddies sat at the table with him—they'd laugh and nudge one another. One guy would sit there, deadpan, saying "You're sick, y'know that?" The guy would let loose in reply—two would laugh and the third, playing his part, would say "You're really a sick motherfucker." This went on for fifteen minutes at the first break, and then a half hour at lunch, and then another fifteen minutes on the late break, every single night I was there. The guy had a big belly and a red face. Like most of them, he looked like he'd be dead of a heart attack in ten years. A couple of the spot labor guys would try to join in by laughing conspicuously. I thought it was something he'd come up with for one night, but it turned out that was his main thing . . .

For some reason they made us take lunch at five o'clock. It was a long wait. My second night I was carrying a headache around, falling asleep in my footsteps, leaning on the broom. I looked down the line at three o'clock and saw that everything was under control. The sweeping was coming along fine. I walked to the end of the dock and downstairs to the breakroom. One of our six was there, grabbing a coffee. A beaten hound dog: lean and hunched over, crooked jaw, mop of curly hair . . . I walked past him, out the door, across the parking lot to my car. I crawled inside and went to sleep.

I woke it was still dark out. I dug a pair of workgloves out of the back, walked across the lot and jumped up onto the dock. The clock said four-forty-five.

As soon as I stepped onto the floor the guy with the crooked jaw came sweeping by.

"Go see John! John wants to see you right away! He's in his office!"

John was the supervisor.

I stepped into his office.

He leaned back in his swivel chair, put his boots on the desk. I figure they paid him four bucks an hour—four-fifty, tops. He twirled his keyring on one finger.

"Where in the *hell* have you been?"

"Whattaya mean, where've I been? I been sweeping," I said.

He took his boots off the desk and leaned forward, containing himself.

Give a guy a ring of keys and his own whiskbroom, he thinks he's Napoleon.

"You were seen leaving the building at three-thirty. It is now four-forty-seven. Where have you been for the last hour and seventeen minutes?"

"I went out to my car to get these workgloves. I was gone five minutes I been sweeping ever since."

"I looked for you at four o'clock—"

"I's probably at the trash compactor, or over on city dock, I dunno. What'd you call me in here for? I got sweeping to do."

He eyed me over.

"Don't leave the dock without my permission. Take your lunch at five o'clock with everyone else. That's all."

Interloper. Right then I decided not to come back that night at eleven o'clock.

And I didn't. I bet a ballgame instead.

Shook 'em up a little at the Greeks today. I took Anna in there, must be the first time in decades they've had a woman on the premises. The place wasn't crowded, but there was a noticeable drop in the level of discussion when we showed up. I nodded to Mihale and he nodded back nervously, went back to rinsing glasses. We stepped into the second room—six cardplayers looked up as though caught in the act—I saw Nick Stavros alone at a table and knew he was a safe place to hitch our boat . . .

"Hi Nick. This my friend Anna."

Nick tipped his hat and shot me a confused look, as though he was expecting a raid: a dam-break of wives and daughters and girlfriends—but Anna smiled to reassure him this was nothing more than it looked like. Nick folded his paper and stood up while we sat down and then sat with us.

"How you been, Danny? You working?"

"Yeah, I'm working nights."

Mihale came and we ordered coffee. Nick paid. Mihale brought two demitasse cups of black grainy coffee—He even managed a smile, although he was obviously wondering about its implications . . . He went away, and men at other tables were watching for developments.

Nick said "You live by the grocery, right Anna?"

"Yeah, that's right. Two houses down."

He told her he'd scared off a couple guys who were trying to strip her car.

"I asked 'em 'Is that your car?' 'Yeah,' they said. 'Which house do you live in?' I asked 'em. They pointed to the wrong house, so I said they better take off."

Anna was aghast. "*Really?* When was this?"

We talked about the neighborhood.

A few minutes later Ed slowed to a stop across the street, window down . . . looking for me . . .

"Waitaminute Anna, I'll be right back."

I walked outside and leaned into his window.

He said "What'd I, drag you away from a pinochle game?"

"No, no . . ."

"—Dominoes, or—"

I laughed.

"Get this," he said. "I found out where John's at; I heard from my mother. You know his mother's real old now, she been sick for a long time . . . Not—sick, that she's dying from anything in particular, but just old, y'know? So John's been looking after her, but now the family decided she's better off in a home, right? So they set her up in a home off Jennings Road—Not a nursing home, but an old-age home—"

"Yeah. So what's John gonna do?"

"—She got her own little apartment there, y'know . . . her own stove and everything, but there's doctors and nurses around—"

"Yeah. But what about John?"

"John went down to the Metropolitan Housing Authority, he talked to the welfare people, whatever—he had to fill out all these forms, all this shit— So now, John's *living with her in the old-age home!*"

"*[laughter]* "

"Somehow he convinced 'em, y'know, she can't be without him—"

"Awwww!"

"And he's officially living with her, in her apartment at the home."

"That's perfect for him!"

"Can you believe that? Why *anyone* his age would wanna—He's the only one there under the age of sixty-five—He's like forty years old! It's mostly women there . . . And now: all the golden-agers get these free bus passes, whatever? 'Cause they can leave the grounds to go shopping, whatever—So now John's upset he can't get a free bus pass every month, so he can ride with all the old ladies!"

"He's gone, man. Your dad must be proud. At least someone in the family knows when to call it quits."

"He's launching a protest, so he can get a pass—"

"He's growing another beard?"

"*No,* he's causing a big stir over there, lobbying for this—"

"Doesn't he realize it's amazing he's there in the first place?"

"—And—The place is eighty percent women, as I say—old retirees, widows, seventy-year-old broads without a family—John says—He told my mother he says he feels like a rooster in a henhouse, 'a rooster in a henhouse'—y'know how he says everything twice—"

"*[laughter]*"

"He says all the old ladies are winking at him in the hallways, in the ping-pong room; they try to corner him in the laundry—"

". . . too much. He must be in heaven."

"Well—*practically:* yeah."

"*[laughter]*"

"And y'know he's got a thing about older women anyway."

"Yeah that's not exactly what most people mean when they say older women—"

"No, but y'know like with his mother, and how he likes to sit around playing cards with his aunts and shit—"

"Yeah."

"Incredible. Anyway, uh . . . I gotta go, here, uh . . . supposed to meet this chick out on Rocky River Drive, uh—"

416

"Who's that? Debbie?"

"No, that's kinda on hold for the moment, uh . . . another one of my—"

"Uh-huh."

"I should be back around four. Stop over."

I went back to the Greeks.

Mihale was at the table now, and a few of the other men had moved closer. Mihale was talking more than I'd ever heard him, telling Anna in broken English about how he used to lay tile in Greece. He'd lived on one of the smaller islands with his mother and two sisters. Anna was nodding and smiling, asking questions. With each question Mihale was more eager, more emphatic, more desperate to unburden himself of the beauty of the life he'd left behind. I sat down and lit a Camel. More chairs were moved closer. Soon we were all caught in the mystery of Mihale's past in another place . . .

When he finished it was quiet. Mihale sat there stunned. It seemed he was realizing that his adult life had been lived, and would be lived, far from where he belonged, in a way he'd never expected nor actually chosen, and which had nothing to do with his true identity . . . as though time had played some trick on him.

We finished our coffee and got up to go. Mihale asked if we wouldn't like some lunch and we declined. Anna said she was a photographer and she'd like to take their pictures sometime— five guys volunteered. We said goodbye, and two men were peeking out from the back poker room . . .

AUTUMN SWIRL

The Duke was gone, he'd moved away.

I called his old man one day and got his new address.

"I saw a guy today reminded me of you: short blond hair and wearing shades—sitting in the sun against a factory wall, one leg kicked-out across the sidewalk . . . Something about the way he seemed to be looking out at the world . . . (I think he was waiting for a bus).

"I think about you and yer lizard once in a while."

———

the contained throb of friendship: catfoot, and creeping . . . strike—a pause, and then the familiar flare . . .

"put a girl in the story," she said the other day. if one were here i would.

/ sailing through the woods: curves of guardrail, narrow trunks—caught in the headlights: centrifugal force and forward motion, the Cutlass finds a straight line like finding home for a moment, then leaves it behind . . . the strike, the pause, the flare . . . /

love is the flare and friendship is the glow contained, consciously overlooked, and utilized . . .

———

"How'd you do at TJ's?"

"I won like eighty bucks, I was— Villain was there. And— Y'know, he's so cheap— He won like six hundred bucks. And his wife kept calling, threaten 'I'm gonna divorce you, get home right now . . . ' On the way out the door—Y'know he drinks like eight bottles of Diet Pepsi during the night: brings an eight-pack to the game. So at the end of the night—His wife's on the phone threatening to divorce him if he don't get home *any second*—He's rattling around on the floor looking for that last empty! 'Cause he needs it for the deposit."

"Who gave him that name 'the Villain'?"

"I did. That was years ago. Now everybody calls him that— even his wife and kids. Nobody remembers his real name."

"Mm."

"Roy was at the Finn with us one time. And Villain kept riding Roy, the whole game. Roy was losing . . . And finally he couldn't take it no more: jumps *over* the fucking table starts choking the Villain. Had his hands around his neck, right? And they got a fan plugged in there, right? Kicked the fan out, blows a fuse—now it's pitch black— Me and TJ's tryna grab all the money, right? You can hear Roy bouncing Villain's head on the ground, he's—*[gurgling noises]*"

"Yeah"

"So I'm grabbing money, y'know? So I put my hand on top of this cold clammy hand— It was Villain! Hard as he can with his hand on his money—"

"*[laughter]* "

"Being choked to death—but won't let go— It was like ice: like fucking Death itself!"

Nine-thirty-seven at night.

"Danny this's Jim, from Hours."

"Hi Jim."

"You been out to Trans-Border before, right?"

"Yeah."

"You busy tonight?"

We stand in the pouring September light with leaves blowing down around us and along the sidewalk . . . The little yellow leaves of the honey locusts flutter down like light itself. We stand in the pouring September day as though in our last moments on Earth.

. . . green-lit windows of a nightbus caterpillar far across a bridge . . .

"So I dunno what to do man, I been talking to this Debbie for like six weeks and she's literally *begging* to meet Lisa—she wants to be my slave, she's leaving me packages, writing me notes—I got ten pairs of panties here, two locks of her hair, nude photographs, tampons— Cute blonde twenty-one-year-old willing to do *anything* to try to please me: what more could I want? But I ain't Lisa!"

"What're you gonna do?"

"I dunno, I'll think of something. I ain't gonna call her for a while."

"Whyn't you forget about her and try something wholesome, like a—I dunno . . . computer date or something?"

"I tried that."

"What, recently?"

"No about fifteen years ago. At the time it was like five dollars. They send you three names of girls and three phone numbers. You fill out a questionnaire, right?"

"Yeah."

"So I figure I'm gonna be slick, y'know? Insteada saying I like football, I'll put I like fucking tennis. 'Steada going to the racetrack I'll say I like to read classical books, or whatever. This way I meet a refined broad: someone that's not a dolt like me, y'know? Anyway, I got three names . . . One laughed it off and says 'Well, I don't need any dates, I'm beautiful, me and my girlfriend did this for a lark, they bet me I wouldn't do this . . . ' Then one was a wife of a Northfield jockey—"

"*[laughter]* "

"Another one to blow off. So finally the last one—Some little Jew girl in Beachwood, right? Nowadays I would never do this. I actually went to her house— And her family: like her brother, father, mother—sitting on the couch waiting for me, like—for the handsome prince to knock on the door."

"*[laughter]* "

"Y'know. And—time I realized they're totally scrutinizing me: 'Looka this—*Who's* this guy, come from—?' I didn't even *think* about that! How naive could I be? I was like twenty-two . . . And I walk in there . . . And here she is, sitting on the chair waiting for this blind date, so they could all look at me. Now I wouldn't do it in a million years! *First* thing I'd do I'd punch the old man in the *mouth*—"

"*[laughter]* "

"Say 'Get the fuck—You're not supposed to be here!'"

"Right."

"And I said 'Hello Sir, my name's Mr. Polack,' y'know . . . "

"*[laughter]* "

"'I worked on the waterfront, couple years during the sum- mer, I got a good grip and all that shit . . . ' This girl: she's like five foot tall . . . Not particularly fat, but just dumpy . . . Thick glasses . . . And about nine coats on: she looked like a penguin."

"*[laughter]* "

"Plus a fucking *scarf*, wrapped around her chin: she was in the *house* with this on. And . . . Didn't say a word to me the whole time I was in the house! Didn't even say hello, y'know, just *sat* there. We get in the car, I start talking to her a little bit . . . I go 'Aren't you hot?' 'Cause you could see she had layers of clothing on; she goes 'This for protection.'"

"*[laughter]*"

"And all the way to the show never said a word, y'know, I go This is ridiculous. I felt like an asshole, y'know? We get to the show . . . We sat there for like a half hour, asked her if she wanted anything 'No; no . . . ' I tried to sneak my arm around her a little bit she moved away . . . Just sat there. I go *Holy* fuck, what a personable broad this is—"

"Right."

"Y'know. I ain't no winner, but— So I'm sitting there, and I'm feeling more like the worst asshole every minute, I'm—like an hour and a half, she don't say a word to me—Just sitting there *frozen* like I'm gonna touch her, y'know. And I went to the bathroom I'm washing my face, tryna get my—wits together . . . Fuck this, man, I just fucking—went outa the show and left."

"*[laughter]*"

"Just left her there! She musta felt really stupid, y'know? I can see her calling Dad—'The guy left me in the show.'"

"You bastard."

"That hadda be bad. But I'm sure that happened to her before: it had to. I get goosebumps just thinking about it now!"

---

rosie was one color and sadie was another color and rhonda was just a fleck of color and marie was more like a stain, but i can't laugh at every joke or go along with all these two-bit emotional expenditures i come up with for myself: i'm tired of getting carried away, or pretending to get carried away/ a sun lands with a crash, a train pulls out of the yard—/ over the tracks . . . past the mall . . . through the days—buildings, faces, traffic—y'know, it's—booze, bricks, pills . . . love and hate . . . sun and rain—pass the salt, pass the sugar, pass the noise, pass the weather—what is this, a gag?/ she turns a card you get danger/ a blade of grass from a crack in a railroad tie, the leaves come swirling down, a moon bobs into place, pigeons flock to flight and dawn gets bigger/—turns a card and you get peace/ the night gives a shrill whistle and the moon sails off—/ surface reality has ceased to entertain me/ sunday, monday . . . thursday . . . / rain falls, but does it really?/ —the strike, the pause, the flare of a match—/ rain falls, but it's up to you whether or not you get wet.

"Hello?"
"Danny?"
"Hi Jim."
"Look I got something for you if you want it—"

(okay, herewego—)
They've been sending me out where the UFOs land, loose clouds fool me into thinking they mean more than they do—greenish lights from somewhere sideways up ahead—growling up the exit and grinding down—I'll try to keep this all in mind a few minutes from now when someone says "Here's yer broom."

Duke wrote back.
"My new porch . . . coffee and a cigarette and blood on the tracks . . .
"I won't be back that way for a long time so if you come this way let me know. You got my new # right? You can stay

here if you want. The lizard don't mind. Coffee, cigarettes, coffee, cigarettes, coffee. Coffee wins. I'll put my thoughts on the full moon, you can pick 'em up where you're at."

Down the steps and out of the track:

"Some people come out here with fifty bucks—And it means *nothing* to 'em, but they're crying. And they got fifty grand in the bank, they own a home . . . And then they say 'You lose because you ain't got no guts out here.' I'd like to see them take their life savings and bet it on a race. That's what I do virtually every race, I bet my life savings. Can you imagine somebody doing that? The pressure? Then I go in a fucking card game with fifty dollars' borrowed money—which I have to pay back—And my electric bill's due tomorrow: if I don't win I don't pay the electric bill. Last Thursday I couldn't buy a newspaper. And from Thursday to Thursday I win five hundred dollars, by stealing, cheating—luck . . . I paid four-fifty in bills. Now, this's Friday, I got forty again, plus my food stamps, and I start over again. I have to go through it every fucking week: it's harder than working!"

(Reprise)

. . . A blue moon and a mystery train . . . Out in the Buick this time, beyond the harbor lights . . . wondering about these men, the simple facts of whose lives don't shed any light on the mystery of the music they made . . . A black book and a pint . . . Whose voices carry something of the width and weight of Southern darkness/ I felt how the night stretched from here down over the South . . . Shades of night, smoky and clear . . . Elvis echoing from among the fir trees at night—Don't the moon look good, mama, shining through the trees? Chuck Berry's drummer kicking up dust . . . The lights of the city across the river . . . Great Balls of Fire! Drink up and laugh at the devil . . . Good Golly, Miss Molly—Clean those dishes, Richard! Train, train! Who added a new innocence to what they stole from deeper, darker voices and so created their own salvation (temporary for them but momentarily permanent for the rest of us), their own enslavement. A violent joy and implicit heartbreak. What's Red Hot Riley doing these days, hanging drywall? Doesn't matter . . . Under yet another moon, the night was wide and wild before me:

"Hey!"

"Hey, *Hours!*"
"?"
"What's yer name?"
"Danny."
"There's a spill in front of Dock Seventeen."
"Right."

After almost two months of silence, John turned up at the other end of a telephone line. Ed came to tell me late in the afternoon, a day in October when autumn and therefore winter were suddenly irrevocable, the smell of the lake in the air . . .

"Called me this morning from the home. He got a hundred bucks for his birthday, wants to bet one of tomorrow's games. I went over and picked it up already. One C-note. Boy I can sure use this motherfucker, too. Thank you very much, John."

"How's he like it there?"

"He says there's a fifteen-year-old girl living with her grandmother, y'know? She's in the laundry room in a nightgown, right? And he's in there at six o'clock in the morning he's doing laundry already. He considers himself King of the Laundry now, he's obsessed with it. And he shows me the fucking—they got like a locker? Opens it up, he's got—ten huge boxes of soap. Not the gigantic size, the *super*-gigantic size. Ten of 'em—and about five bottles of softener—the Laundry *King*. Anyway—She's sitting on a folding chair in the laundry room, John walks in—she's got her legs spread with no panties on. She says 'Y'know I had a baby once.' John goes 'What?' 'I had a baby once. Yeah my boyfriend and me made out, I had a baby. My mother says I'm bad, I have to live with my grandmother. —I have a lotta boyfriends, I like boys. My boyfriend used to take pictures of me.' So John goes 'Well I kinda dabble in photography myself . . . ' 'Well you can take some pictures of me sometime.' John goes back to the apartment—But: Honest John—Gets back, folds his laundry, says—'I'm not really a photographer. I cannot tell a lie.'"

"*[laughter]* "

"Then he says—He was outside walking around the other day, he's out by the garbage bins . . . She's sitting on the grass, throwing pieces of wood chips into the bin . . . She goes 'Hey Mister—I'm throwing these wood chips in the bin; if I miss one I'll give you a blowjob.' He expects me to believe that, right?"

". . . Fucking nuts . . ."

Later there was thunder . . . the leftover kind . . .

. . . Pushing the broom last night . . . Americo Rolled Steel . . . sort of a steely green one a.m. . . . Time takes so long you find yourself with plenty of space between the marking posts—the big ones . . . and then space between the little ones . . . Till time opens up and you find yourself lost in a crevice.

I was chasing a piece of popcorn along a row of towering

steel rolls, till it scuttled sideways and lodged itself beneath one of them. I poked the broom at it, sweeping away the wooden wedge that kept the massive steel roll in place, and continued poking—jabbing the broom, determined—

Someone was shouting.

The foreman came rushing up to me, waving his arms.

"What's the matter with you?! What're you doing? Kick that wedge back under there! Do you know how much these things *weigh?* Pay attention!"

I looked at him blankly.

"Whatsa matter with you?" he said. "Are you crazy?"

The phone rings.

"Oh good, get it," he says. "Find out who it is."

"Who do you wanna talk to?"

"Not too many people."

I pick up the phone. "Hello?"

"Hi, is Eddie there?"

"Yeah he's sleeping. Who's this?"

"This TJ."

I cover the mouthpiece: "TJ."

"Tell him I'll call him back, I don't wanna talk to that asshole."

"I'll have him call you back, TJ."

"Okay man, thanks."

I sit back at the table.

"Anyway," he says, "I'm out at Westgate yesterday, right? Here goes Franco, walking down fucking Westgate, right? He spots me, right? *'Fast-a Eddie, Fast-a Eddie—'* I said 'Frank: fuck you: get away from me.' He says 'Fast Eddie I'm inna da big trouble, I'm inna da big trouble. My wife-a don't have no food for da baby, I need-a milk for da baby. My wife send me to the store I have-a no money, I can't tell her. I get-a paid tomorrow

I give you some money. I need-a five dollar for milk.' . . . I go
'Frank, *fuck* you, you don't need five dollars for milk.' He goes
'I need-a five dollars for da baby, my wife's-a gonna be pissed.
She tell me to the fucking store I don't wanna tell her I have-a
no money. I just wanna milk for da baby. I give y—I *swear
to God* I give you the five dol—I need-a milk-a for da baby:
please. I'm inna da big trouble. Milk for da baby, Fast Eddie.
Don't be a bastard.'"

"*[laughter]*"

"I go 'Alright *Frank* you *cocksucker*,' I said 'I know I ain't
gonna see this fucking five,' y'know? I give him the fucking fin
. . . I go next door to Fazio's. Come back out, I forgot cigarettes. Frank's in the drugstore, I go in there? Here's Frank, in
the lottery line—"

"*[laughter]*"

"Frank—'Gimme da five-a lottery tickets.' I go 'Frank you
cocksucker you—' He goes 'I take a chance-a Fast Eddie: I just
take a chance!' 'You son of a bitch,' I said, 'I'll never give you a
fucking dime as long as I live!' 'Need-a milk for my baby, Fast
Eddie.'"

(Letter from the Greeks)

"Duke:

". . . You turn onto the freeway at night, the highway lights
run maybe five miles and then you're on your own and the colors are four: the blue-black sky, the blacker woods, the white
of headlights and highway lines and whatever's up there in the
way of stars etc . . . and the occasional red of taillights and
radio towers. It doesn't change till dawn.

". . . You're driving to work, listening to a tape . . . searching
for an attitude to get you through the night . . .

"I start each week fresh, and that freshness turns to resolve, and that resolve turns grim. A kaleidoscope: the buildup and collapse of hope to determination to suffocation to wild-eyed scheming about money and escape, to hopelessness, to black waves of anger coming and going like sweat: night to night and within each night, fueled by an almost hallucinatory fatigue . . . I cash my checks, I get a few hours' sleep . . . I wake up, but not quite . . . I go to the Greeks, I have a conversation . . . Late afternoon I try to nap and struggle out of it before the phone rings again with another call to action. Once in a while I surface: exhilaration breaks through and runs away with me, burns up whatever fuel I've got for the night ahead . . . leaves me stranded, moving out on my own . . . I don't know how the people who live like this do it.

"It's all part of a picture I'd never glimpsed, and now the picture casts a shadow over everything, for me. All these corners, pockets . . . this subterranean, sub-diurnal thing . . . It's to the point I can't smoke a cigarette without thinking of the guy who had to roll it at three in the morning . . ."

———————————

I've got this black telephone here, and I'm still waiting for its ugly ring. Crazy, isn't it? when I could be flying along in the Buick with the windows down—

Fuck it: I'm gonna duck outa here.

Just as I step on the stairs it rings, like an alarm: I'm escaping! Slam the door and beat it down the stairs with the alarm chasing me—Off the porch and jump the fence: a close call . . .

—Roll down the window, light a cigarette and pull away from the curb.

I go shooting up the freeway ramp million-tripping over the valley's dazzle, past the city's lonely glow, hearing drumbeats and driven by the winds of— Y'know life can be so

———————————

Ed says, "You're hungry I got leftovers from ma's on Sunday, my old man made chicken and dumplings. She forced me to take it. Plus an orange, plus some rolls, plus some cake, plus the newspaper—plus some stew she tried to take out of the freezer, frozen . . . plus she tries to slip me a ten, plus she's asking how come I don't wear a hat. After I leave there I feel like committing a heinous crime."

" *[laughter]* "

"Meanwhile my old man's telling me I'll get myself in a jackpot, I got a busted taillight, what if a cop pulls me over and I had a shot and a beer and they take away my license— Everything's a big deal with him now. I told you that time about the jumper cables, right?"

"No."

"This's from a guy that all his life didn't give a fuck about nothing—a total *lunatic*—would fight any human being, was afraid of *no* one. Threw ten guys out the window of a China joint, took six bullets and lived, punched out three cops . . . I mean—just—did what the fuck he wanted all his life. And I've heard it from enough people, so . . . But now that he's older, it's totally opposite, where now he's worried and senile about everything . . ."

"Yeah."

"I'm at the house, my mother's house . . . it was a blizzard: *freezing*, outside. My car won't start. I need a basic *jump*, from my old man. Which I know, in itself is gonna be a major project. Right away, y'know: 'You got these old cars, you're always broke, you're a bum—' But I knew that would happen, so I's basically prepared for it. So I sit there while he gets fully clothed: y'know, the boots, the scarf . . . all his emergency equipment . . . fucking Japanese kamikaze hat with the flaps for the ears—glasses, with flashers that go *emergency* on 'em, that flip up and down—"

" *[laughter]* "

"—pocket fulla flares—"

"Right."

"—fucking signs: warning signs, a red flag . . . orange coat for both of us, even though we're in the parking lot . . ."

"*[laughter]*"

"—Couplea big cones outa the closet to block our cars—I mean every emergency equipment possible, y'know. First aid kit, the whole bit. To give me a fucking jump. We get out there—and it's fucking freezing; it's cold out there. Can't open the hood of my car: he's out there tryna open it . . . It opens from the inside but the handle's broke, it's just the cord? Doesn't pop open. So I get out there, I'm pushing on it . . . In the meantime he's—'You bum, you never had nothing your whole life—' On and on I gotta listen to this spiel. Finally he went inside got a pair of pliers, I pulled the cord—I mean this's a good twenty minutes of ridicule. Open the fucking hood—I give him one end of my jumper cables: —missing one of the grips. '*You* fucking jerk, can't even get a fucking jumper cables, cost a lousy five dollars—'"

"Right."

"So he's out there freezing while I'm tryna start the car, he's holding the bare wires of the cable against the fucking battery. Wind's blowing—Fucker won't start, he's cussing—'You fucker: even when you're a kid you were stupid—make my balls swell up like grapefruits!'"

"*[laughter]*"

"Then he gets onto Stan, brings my brother into it—I think you even came into the story: you and Dave. He categorizes everybody. Me, you and Dave and Stan are all bums. Never made it. I need a fucking jump for my car, I wanna go home. Whole parking lot's lit up—people looking out their window— Won't start. We go in the house—Him and my mother start arguing about it. And then I feel like a little kid there, my mommy and daddy's arguing over me—I says *Aww* man, why'd I *do* this? And she goes 'You're out there you got a bad heart, it's cold—Put your flaps down on your hat.' Meantime he puts his glasses down on the table, little lights going off *emergency— mergency—mergency—*"

"*[laughter]*"

"Anyway the cones're still out there, the flares . . . There's an American flag raised by the car, the whole bit—"

"An American flag *what?*"

"He put an American flag there to—emphasize the fact that I was in emergency trouble. A veteran, too."

"*[laughter]*"

"So he's fucking in the closet for a half hour. Moving boxes, Christmas tree ornaments—I'm sitting on the couch; I still got all my shit on, I'm sweating—and he's totally nervous now: I mean this is like a major project for him. I went outside to give it one last shot . . . He comes out with these wires. He goes over to his car, he's fucking around there—He hands me this wire through the window. Here he's got something—plugs into the cigarette lighter—A fucking *wire*: thin as a string, with two little caps on the ends of it to plug into the lighters, right?"

"*[laughter]*"

"He's gonna *jump* my fucking car, right? From one lighter to the other. This thing could not start—two brand-new Toyotas in ninety-degree heat—in a gas station—if they left their sig-nals on for ten minutes and their battery's a tiny bit low. Right? Let alone—It's gonna start a *wrought-iron monster* with a fifteen-year-old battery in a twenty-below blizzard—"

"*[laughter]*"

"—with a little string with a cap on the end. I need major *power*, y'know, from a towtruck: *vvrrrrooooom!*—not this *beeeee* . . . 'Put this in your lighter,' he goes in his car and rolls up the window, right? And he's waiting. About five minutes. I ain't got the heart to tell him. He motions for me to roll my win-dow down. Window don't work; I open the door. He's yelling, through the storm—'Plug it into your lighter!' I go Ohh fuck, he's gonna fucking die . . . Open the window, I go 'I ain't got no

lighter in this car: it's broke.' 'JEEEsus FUCKing Christ, you
FUCKing BUM, FUCK you motherfucking—'"

"*[laughter]* "

"Went back in the house, him and my mother started arguing some more—the fucking carpet's wet, my blood pressure's
up, his blood pressure's up— Two-hour fiasco, never got the
car started. After that I said to myself *Never* again, if I am
stranded on the freeway with an hour to live, will I call him to
help me with *anything*."

"Coffee's fifty."

"And gimme two dollars of regular, pump number two."

"Two-fifty."

". . ."

"Out of three . . . fifty's your change."

"Thanks."

"Night."

(October)

The days are a patchwork: pure yellow and the blue flapping
tarps of sky . . . red berries and a carpet of decaying leaves
. . . sunlight that comes and goes like breathing, that pulls like
a scarf across the hills . . . clouds that go from silver-grey to
blind white, branches black and silver bare, and parks filled
with so much color you can hear it . . .

The nights are alive and restless.

Tossing October shadow and light . . . corridor . . . the tree
wind rises and falls . . . the night is full as an elementary school
with scrapings and noises . . . whistles, faucets . . . picked up

and carried—dropped in all directions till you're not sure where they're coming from . . .

What is there to do with an open window but jump out of it?
   —Sailing over the bridge the wind in my chest stirs up in response—my eyes grow fangs and bark, once:
   orange clouds tramping across the sky, one star signaling frantically from white to green to red to white . . .

. . . Here in the breakroom of Yellow Freight . . . trying to go unnoticed . . . although the supervisor tonight probably wouldn't care . . . He doesn't bother you as long as your area looks okay. I swept my area, grabbed my lunch and came down here, bought a coffee from the machine and immediately spilled half of it on the floor . . . my last half a buck. Twelve-thirty now, seven hours to go.

*

I do another sweep, probably one-fifteen . . . I'm walking back with the broom I run into the supervisor, so I ask him some question about plywood—picking up plywood, y'know . . . Nice guy, but he gets annoyed when he sees you: he wants you to disappear. He doesn't want to have to wonder whether or not you're doing your work (and since all the work here is imaginary there's no way for him to be sure). He'd rather you weren't doing it, so long as you're out of sight. As he turned his back I jumped off the dock, between two trailers. It's chilly out tonight—you can see your breath . . .

*

Peeling an orange at two-thirteen—Hiding gets to be harder

than work.

*

When I look in a mirror . . . I don't feel as strong and sure as I look. Maybe it's the mirror that's true.

*

Seven o'clock now, the new shift coming in . . . confusion . . . I drift into the breakroom, I mill around . . . hovering in and out of sight . . . jump into the parking lot for a last glimpse of the moon . . . the sky blueing up to early day . . . two or three stars . . . you get the idea . . .

Walking to the car, geese are flying in sloppy Vs across the dawn.

Finally I saw Ed's car out front. I went to see him but the lights were off so I didn't knock.

In the morning I went again.

"Where you been?"

"Playing cards. Twenty-four hours straight. I got home nine o'clock last night."

"Wow. How'd you do?"

"I broke even."

"*[laughter]* "

"Eight sick bastards trapped in a basement 'cause no one's got sense enough to quit. This one guy—Old Wally: guy's like seventy years old—*over* seventy. Owns a chain of furniture stores. He drank two fifths of vodka, musta smoked a carton of Chesterfields . . . Near the end, every vein in his face was sticking out, his skin was grey, he had big purple rings under his eyes, and his hair was standing straight up. I thought he was dead! He was completely paralyzed—couldn't say a word, his eyes were half closed . . . He won about four hundred bucks he didn't even know it. Twenty-four hours. I smoked five packs of Newports—the whole time I'm eating. Chips, pretzels . . . a piece of pizza, donut . . . a sandwich . . . drinking pop, beer . . . a couple cigars . . . As of this morning I'm on a new health kick. I'm gonna quit smoking, I'm gonna lose fifty pounds. Otherwise I'm gonna die. I'm actually dying: I can feel it."

Mr. Jim doesn't go in on Saturdays, so there was no work for me last night.

It was cold and rainy.

I went to Jack the Cab's around nine and ate dinner with him. He's one of the Duke's friends, and the three of us had spent a couple nights together before Duke left town. We watched a Bogart picture while we ate . . . Bogart was cool but I couldn't get into it.

I woke up the clock said twelve-fifty-seven. Jack was asleep in the chair. I watched the last half hour of another movie, then woke him up and said so long, took off:

The freeway was shining wet—the rain was done, the night was blowing clear. The airport sailed by . . . The mills blinked hard as diamonds, the white smoke rose in columns . . . The old familiar spread, always a revelation, still a challenge. Once again, I thought if I could stop just long enough to figure it all out—the shining road, the valley of lights and smoke, the broken houses and churches on the crest—I could die on the spot, complete.

. . . At home I turned the heater on.

I did some writing at the kitchen table.

I lay on my back on the frontroom floor by the heater and fell asleep. I dreamed I was at the wheel of my car, cruising slowly through a dark street crowded with kids all flowing into the street . . . streaming against the car and in front of it. I was trying slowly not to hit any of them, but someone in the backseat had an arm around my throat—my head was tilting back— It was a chubby little black girl in a winter coat with a hood—she was smiling, and I was trying to free myself and keep an eye on the road . . . all these kids were pouring in front of the car . . . I hit the brakes but they never held . . . this smiling girl had my head tilted back . . .

I woke with light from the kitchen on me. I stood up, looked in at the kitchen clock. Three-forty-five.

I go over to Ed's, he's got *8:32 a.m. October 7* in pencil on the wall.

He says "I'm three days into my new diet. Seventy-five hours, all I've had is a bowl of Farina. I've lost twelve ounces already."

"Good job."

"I went to Feef's this morning, he been asking about you. 'Where's the cabby? Where's the cabby?'—Every time I go in there. I tell him 'I don't know, Feef—All he does is sit on the porch all day.' Feef gets a big kick out of it. Y'know Feef don't get many laughs, but man he cracks up. I been making up a different story every time. 'Last time I saw him he was just standing on the corner, leaning against a pole—just staring off into oblivion . . . It's almost over for him, Feef.' 'But he's just a young kid!' 'Ahh it's bad, Feef—he's a broken man . . . ' Feef can't get enough of it."

That night I saw Feef gliding by on one of his nightly hunting expeditions . . . Brenda, or Kim . . . Wendy . . . "getting some air," as he would say . . .

The dust of St. Louis and beyond . . . looking out of a mailcar with daylight opening up . . . Oh! and all the things you've seen, with the early frosts that tell of winter coming on . . . the dusty stomp, the dusty shuffle . . . trap drums . . . maybe i'll die and maybe i won't. either way, i'm watching . . .

Al called one morning and said he'd seen a help-wanted sign in a porno shop window on 185th Street. I drove out there.

The manager was an odd clean-cut guy with a head like a balloon that tagged and loomed from a skinny neck. He was behind a glass case built on a platform. I filled out an application. The case displayed rubbers and handcuffs, colored oils and creams, novelty items like cigarette lighters, decks of cards, wind-up toys . . .

He looked the application over and said I'd have to take a lie-detector test. He asked whether I had an objection to that. I said I didn't, and he said he'd call me to set up an appointment. I bought a pack of cigarettes, took a book of girlie matches from the counter and drove home.

The next day he called to ask whether Friday morning at nine would be okay. He gave me directions to a place about forty miles east and said he'd call again with the results of the test.

*

Going to work Thursday night was the last thing I wanted to do, but going to work any night was the last thing I wanted to do, and seven bucks was what I had in my pocket, and what I had in my pocket was all I had anywhere, so . . . So I spent a buck on two lottery tickets as a final stab of hope before calling Mr. Jim, and went to the Greeks to eat dinner and watch the number come in.

Seven-thirty rolled around and I was wiping my plate with a piece of bread, talking to Nick Stavros. The girl in the bikini came on—I had 946. As she was explaining the rules and procedures of the Ohio State Lottery Commission I was doing some arithmetic: two-fifty for the straight price, plus forty-two for the box is 292, minus two for lottery tickets tomorrow, minus a hundred toward what I owe Ed is one-ninety, minus twenty-five for the phone and fifteen for the electricity is one-fifty minus ten for the gas company is one-forty minus twenty to fill the tank is one-twenty, minus fifty for Visa and fifty for Sears is twenty bucks, minus thirty for groceries is—whoa, waitaminute . . . Make that fifty for Ed, after groceries leaves forty, minus say fifty for Lige to fix the carburetor, aah shit. Luckily, the number came 011. Walking down Fairfield I was thinking seven minus a buck for the tickets and three for dinner is three, minus three for gas to get to wherever Jim sends me . . .

I knocked on Mr. Jim's door. From inside came the buzz of his tattoo needle. There was a sort of random crashing and banging toward the door, and then he was there in the flesh, wiping blood off his forearm and swaying forward from the unlit kitchen . . .

"How you doing, Jim?"

"Marvelous!"

"You going in tonight?"

"Oh yeah! You looking to work?"

"Yeah, I dunno. Anything at Yellow Freight?"

"No! No . . . Sorry, man . . . They got all they need. But I'll see if I can find you something. You be home?"

"Yeah."

"I'll give you a call, something comes up."

"Okay. Thanks."

By nine-thirty I was struggling to keep awake. Usually he called by ten-thirty.

Ten-thirty crept up like the climb to the top of a roller-coaster and hung there.

Ten-thirty-five I was on my way to the kitchen to light a candle of thanks to the patron saint of idleness when the phone spun me around in my tracks:

"RAT-BASTARD MOTHERFUCKER—Yeah?"

"Danny?"

"Hi Jim."

"Look I got something at this foundry, Lloyd & Turpin. The regular guy called in sick. You interested?"

"Yeah, okay."

"It's out toward Eastlake, right off Route 2—"

I scraped up some loose change, coasted on fumes into the downtown Shell and put my last three bucks in the gas tank. That left half a buck in case Lloyd & Turpin had a coffee machine. I hit the freeway, tired of living like a trapeze artist.

Eleven-thirty I pulled into the gravel lot and parked. The other cars were old, even more beat-up than mine, like dusty shadows . . . the suggestions of shapes . . . The atmosphere was dense and motionless, down here near the bottom of night. One sodium light threw down . . .

It's only eight hours, I told myself.

Inside, there was no one in sight. The place was full of a roaring, pounding silence that was not, of course, the absence of sound, but the absence of any progression or modulation or resolution of sound: like a black hole of sound. The only light was indirect: filtered through office glass . . . bounced off a coffee machine . . . resting in a timeclock . . . dying off an intermittent flame, from around a corner . . . There was an area of this secondhand light for fifteen or twenty yards, beyond which was a labyrinth composed of different densities of shadow.

—Movement from behind a huge machine.

I worked my way over and he showed me to someone else who took my time slip and led me into the dark.

I followed him to a place between two machines which because of their size and weight and blackness could not be glimpsed whole, but only as abstractions, ideas. They didn't seem to be in operation. As though they had served some massive function once, dimly remembered now—the function as lost in blackness as the climbing tangled extremities of the machines themselves . . . He stationed me in front of two iron troughs, one empty, the other loaded with steel nuts. He handed me a shovel and yelled that I should scoop the nuts from the full trough into the empty one. He said I should keep an eye out for nuts of irregular size and drop them into an empty oil drum. He said it like an afterthought and went away.

I stabbed the shovel into the full trough. It was like stabbing a shovel into pavement. I tried again. The nuts were a solid mass: I couldn't get one of them onto the shovel. I tried for five minutes, embarrassed in case anyone was watching, and starting to sweat, and met with the same response. My arms were ringing.

The foreman came back and took the shovel. He placed one foot on the edge of the trough and stabbed. He got a corner of the shovel down along the slanted inside of the trough and worked it deeper and then, stepping down and using the rim as a fulcrum, brought the shovel up, laden with nuts. He sorted through them with a gloved hand, dumped them into the empty trough and handed me the shovel.

An hour later the palms of my workgloves were in tatters from sorting across the shovels of nuts, and one trough had been emptied into the other. I hadn't found an irregular nut. I stood back and leaned on the shovel and took a breath.

A guy drove up and slid the forks of a towmotor under the full trough, lifted it and took it away.

In a minute he was back with another trough suspended on the forks. He set it down.

It was filled with nuts.

I looked around, expecting to find a circle of laughing men enjoying this, but there was only offhand light and pounding and smoke. I dug in.

My neck and shoulders ached. My lower back tingled with a kind of imminent weakness and I was wrapped in sweat. I cursed myself for being weak and unprepared . . . for being a smoker . . .

I stopped more often now to straighten up and stretch and catch my breath. Once in a while a human form would pass . . . pushing something . . . or pulling . . . like an unformed thought . . . dark, and without features . . . covered in smoke . . .

I finished the second trough and the palms of my workgloves were nothing but strings; my palms were oiled and bloody. My friend on the forklift took the full trough away . . . and brought a third. I might have laughed . . . I don't remember . . .

It wasn't just that the work was hard, but that the work was meaningless: without purpose or end . . .

I pulled a bandana from my pocket and tied it around the palm of my left hand.

As I stabbed into the third trough my muscles felt like rotten snakemeat. I wondered how the regular guy did it every night. And then I thought—Maybe there isn't a regular guy! Maybe they get a new guy every night—And then just pile the bodies of the dead outside. Mr. Jim is in on this. Maybe he and the foreman split the guy's pay every night—be twelve bucks each . . . Who would know? The guys who do this work are total outsiders anyway— I should've left a note.

. . . Twenty-four bucks . . . but I was a half hour late—after taxes that'll be twenty-one, twenty-two maybe and change, and they keep the change at the bar for cashing the check . . . twenty-two even, minus two for lottery tickets, minus five at least for gas is fifteen, minus five for eggs and bread and something for dinner is ten, minus ten towards the electricity . . .

My raging mind got me through the third trough . . . I was kind of stumbling in place, waiting for the fourth. The guy brought it and began to set it down—on my foot— I woke up and roared until he lifted it and pulled back and set it down again . . .

I'd dropped a total of seven irregular nuts into the barrel. I decided not to look for more. Thereby depriving the work of any shred of meaning. I tried to rev my thoughts again, but twenty bucks wasn't enough to keep me occupied with subtraction even if I divided it into nickels. I tried adding up five days' pay and starting down from there, but all that did was extend the hopelessness of the moment a week into the future. The fourth trough took forever.

And then the foreman came and led me toward something else.

I followed him, looking for an escape route, through giant pistons plunging through the floor and roof . . . past pits of flame . . . vast machines that began and ended in blackness . . . conveyors . . . here and there a lost soul, hunched over, stranded in the boiler room of night . . . every surface thick with a permanent layer of soot, a burnt fallout, like what was left of time when time crossed over into whatever this was . . . The place was one big cave-lit chiaroscuro of forms suggesting themselves through dead veils of smoke. I lost him for a minute down a tunnel of pipes and furnaces and rusted wheels. He came back and steered me away from the edge of a grease pit, and I stayed on his heels from then on . . .

We found our way to a clearing lit by a cauldron of flames. A man in goggles and elbow gloves was guiding a mechanical arm which dipped racks of metal plates into the flames and lifted them out again. The foreman stationed me with my back to the cauldron, across an empty rack from an old man, and went away.

Beside us were barrels of the metal plates. The plates looked like telephone dials. I never found out what they were—the old guy had no idea. He'd been there ten years. It was our job to hang them on the racks. When a rack was full, one of us would wheel it over to the man at the cauldron. When the newly dipped pieces had cooled and dried, we'd take them off the rack and toss them into other barrels. There was nothing to it.

Nothing at all.

One dial . . . two . . . three . . . four . . .

. . . clink . . . clink . . .

Thirty-three . . . thirty-four . . . thirty-five . . .

. . . 209 . . . 210 . . .

There was a clock on the wall. I tried not to look at it, but there it was with every piece . . .

Each minute was longer than the last.

Two-thirty-nine . . . two-thirty-nine . . . two-thirty-nine . . . two-forty . . .

. . . Two-forty . . . two-forty . . . two-forty-one . . .

I sped up.

The old guy shook his head and laughed to himself.

He said "Ain't no use hurrying. Always more where these came from. And seven-thirty don't come till seven-thirty."

He had his back to the clock.

I guess after ten years they let you stand with your back to the clock.

And each minute was longer than the past. After sixty minutes I'd gladly have gone back to shoveling nuts.

. . . drip . . . drip . . . drip . . . drip . . .

By the end of two hours this work was torture.

There was an open door. It caught my glance with clockwork regularity. Finally I had to stop for a minute. My arms were working independent of my will. I walked to the door and stepped outside, expecting some kind of difference.

The night outside was dead.

. . . Four-thirty-eight . . . four-thirty-nine . . . . . . four-forty . . . . . . four-forty-one . . . . four . . . forty . . . two . . .

Four . . .

I found a water fountain, splashed water on my face . . .
went to the open door . . . back to the rack . . .

Somewhere in there we broke for lunch. I sat on a bench in
the locker room with a couple guys. No one spoke. I got a coffee from the machine and smoked a cigarette, treasuring every
movement that differed from the one simple, maddening motion involved in hanging those pieces. My hands were shaking.
I took deep slow breaths, trying to relax . . . trying to hang onto
this time in the locker room.

Lunch was over as soon as it started.

I went back to the rack.

There was no way to *attack* this work: it was practically in-
tangible . . . through long elastic minutes . . . piece after piece
. . . the same slight gesture . . . after piece after piece after piece
. . . I tried everything: I switched to my left hand, I used both
hands at once, as the old man laughed and shook his head
because I obviously had no idea how to pace myself for a ten-
year stretch . . . each minute a deep rubbery maze, with something building inside my chest . . . after piece after piece after
piece . . . as the seconds and minutes groaned . . . and stretched
. . . until they lightly snapped, and floated loose within their
hours, and I felt like I was drowning—

The old guy worked on, uncomplaining, at a pace that never varied. He was impervious to this—past it—and of course
unaware of the exponentially replicating helix of tension and
denial and outrage and violence and resolve and despair my
sweating mind was putting me through—

With an hour and a half to go, I had the physical sensation
of my mind beginning to tilt, like a carnival ride: my blood was
boiling up my throat into a roar—

I walked outside and looked at the sky for some vestige of
detachment and swore I'd never spend another night like this.

Somehow I finished the shift. I found the foreman at seven-thirty and got him to sign my slip.

Morning outside was heavy and white.

*

I had enough gas to make it to the polygraph test, but not enough to make it back.

I stopped at my folks' place.

My mother was gone to work, my father was stirring about his morning routine. I sat at the kitchen table, streaked with grease and unable to talk about the night just ended, while he fried me a couple eggs. I washed up a little, borrowed a fresh T-shirt and ate the eggs. I swallowed some coffee, he slipped me a ten, and I drove out to the place.

There was a panelled waiting room with diplomas and clippings and photos and letters of thanks on the walls. A woman handed me a stapled sheaf of papers. A questionnaire. The store manager had emphasized that no matter what, I shouldn't lie on the test. Every conceivable question: 'Have you ever disappointed a friend? Are you ever lonely? Depressed? Have you ever considered suicide? Have you ever had transactions with a bookmaker?' The answers were easy. Then there was a chart with empty boxes: 'Please list any drugs or chemical substances you have ingested for other than medicinal purposes.' This was more involved. 'When was the last time you stole from an employer?' Last time I worked for a bookstore.

I handed the papers to the woman and she gave them to the interviewer, who led me to a back office.

He attached electrodes to my wrists and chest and we went over the questionnaire.

When the test was over he wished me luck but gave no indication of the results.

I stopped at a gas station and put my father's ten in the tank and hit the freeway.

I picked up my check, drank a shot of whiskey at the Empire, and then drove home, pulled the shades and put myself to bed.

Twelve-thirty the phone.

"Danny?" It was the store manager.

"Yeah?"

"Well, I have the results of your test, and—It looks like you're the man for the job."

"Great."

"Can you start tonight, eleven o'clock? There'll be a man here to train you."

"Yeah. Sure."

"Great."

"Yeah . . . Thanks."

ASPIRIN & COFFEE

First night at the shop.

The guy training me, Larry— We're supposed to keep the radio on. Larry whistles to every song, melody—guitar solos, horn charts, organ breaks and all. Relentless . . . note for note: even the commercials. He's been whistling for three hours.

Ring up a sale.

It's funny at first, and then it's like selling candy or razorblades or anything else. Apparently the company hires spotters to come in posing as customers, checking up on our performance. We're supposed to act like salesmen: make sure each customer might not secretly want something more than what he brings to the register. "Will that be all tonight? Any cigarettes? Butyl nitrate? Would you care to join our video rental club?" Just like the mall. Larry's doing a crossword puzzle, keeping an eye on me, whistling. Most of the guys are nervous enough: they want their books in a bag with as little eye contact as possible and get out, but I'm supposed to say "*Black Holes*? That be all tonight? Can I interest you in a vibrating butt plug or an inflatable Sally doll? Cinnamon-flavored Motion Lotion? Yojimbo Root Erection Potion? Or perhaps a miniature wind-up hopping penis?" The guy shakes his head, handling money—"Deck of naughty playing cards? Anal Intruder kit?" Larry says "What's a seven-letter name of an Egyptian dynasty beginning with *P*?"

"Duke:

I've got a plan now. Or if not a plan, then a signal . . . an impulse . . . an arrow . . .

Spent half an hour in the steam room at the Y this morning. When I stepped under a cold shower it was like having my windshield wiped. I went home and went to bed. When I woke up the world was still clear, and light, and wired . . .

Now it's after dark—no work tonight, miraculously—and I've found my way to whiskey and cigarettes as though to solidify the deal. Whatever the deal is. Someone brought me a carton of Mexican cigarettes, so I'm smoking those. I don't have much time to do this anymore, feels good.

I got a job in a porno store the other day—Friday and Saturday nights and Sunday afternoons. Somehow it feels like a step up. I'm gonna keep at the factory thing weekday nights. I'll have to spend some more time as a ghost. I need time, I need money, and I need to get out, and all these things have their price. I think I wanna write a novel. I've never felt that *being* was enough. As though if no one's watching it ain't real. There should be someone watching. So I've gotta hang in suspended animation for a while, and try to keep an eye on the horizon.

I been thinking about credit, too, in all its forms: loans, drugs, drinks, etc. Opened the Book of Leviticus today at random, it says everything's gotta be paid in full, plus twenty percent.

I hope you're doing good out there. Application is the key: application to one thing or another. I guess the trick is getting something to apply yourself to. Anyway . . .

Danny"

Eleven-thirty Saturday night . . . been here two hours . . . nobody but me, the radio off . . . no sound but the air conditioner, and an infrequent clack from the device that scents the air, down back . . .

One-fifty. Guy comes to the door a few minutes ago, tries it, can't get it open. I reach over the counter and yank it open—he's going away, thinks we're closed, he's probably relieved. "Hey buddy—" He hesitates . . . floats back and hovers in the doorway—pale, stiff young guy . . . short hair, neat. He enters the store almost sideways: drawn up straight, as though trying to squeeze by unnoticed. Looks like he does a lot of that. He looks over the straight magazines first. Disinterestedly, as though he's tired of pretending but afraid to stop. He grabs a couple—tame ones . . . Looks like it's a real effort for him to come stake the place out. He glances at a copy of *Honcho,* picks it up, puts it back. The fact that it's in plastic is enough to send him to the counter with the two magazines he's already picked. Maybe next time he'll buy what he wants. He stands at the counter tight-lipped, trying to hold together what's left of a dignity I haven't challenged.

Later I find them, still in the bag, on top of a garbage can at the curb.

Two-forty-five. The walls are plastered with images: airbrushed photos, impossible bodies: gods and goddesses . . . Things are plainly doomed to fail for the rest of us. Not an organic color in sight: every surface bright, unnatural, blank. After a few hours your eyes are exhausted. I stare at the fabric of my jeans for relief . . . I look around again. Twelve-inch purple dildos, the swollen faces of inflatable dolls pressed against their window-boxes . . . It's all a lie. It's the same as TV, the same as McDonald's. All this ass—all this pussy, all these pricks—Nothing there.

. . . Three-fifteen . . . kid in a leather jacket looking things

451

over—serious face . . . he's disappointed . . . What could he be looking for that isn't here? *Asian Slut, Shaved Snatch, Sixty-Niners, Dirty Dames, Captured Women, Oriental Cock, Chicks with Dicks, Tied & Tickled, Super Black Milk, Enema Resort . . .* He was here last night. After an hour and a half of looking through everything, he leaves with a shrug.

Three-forty Dave and Al show up with coffee. They're picking things up . . . reading aloud . . . Dave puts on a pair of novelty glasses with a dick for a nose and stands around trying to look distinguished. Suddenly it's all funny as hell.

———————————

"You working today?"

"Yeah."

"See if you can pick me up a couple magazines. I like to have 'em around the house in case I bring a broad back here."

"Okay. What're you doing today?"

"I'm bet a couple games, I gotta go look at this place at Joe's."

"What's that?"

"Joe's going to Vegas in December, he's going out there to live. His brother's out there, says he can get Joe on as a dealer. So Joe wants somebody to look after his house."

"Oh, he owns that place?"

"Yeah, on Sixty-Fifth. He basically needs someone to collect the rent from the downstairs and send his bills in once a month."

"Yeah."

"So he told me I could move in upstairs for seventy-five a month, look after his shit . . . the place's furnished . . ."

"Yeah that sounds good."

"'Cause I wanna get outa here anyway, I wanna change my address, change my phone—"

"Oh yeah: what's going on with that Debbie?"

". . . Well I didn't call her for a while, y'know? 'Cause I'm tryna find a way to get together with her—And then I call her up I said 'Debbie? This's Jack; I'm a friend of Lisa's.' 'Oh!' she goes, 'Where *is* Lisa? How come she hasn't called me's she mad at me?' I said 'No, Lisa's not angry with you, she had to go to California for a couple months, but she wanted me to call you and tell you she's thinking about you, see if you're okay, y'know . . . ' 'But when will I see her?' I said 'Well Lisa doesn't think the time is right yet for you to get together, uh . . . She thinks you're not quite ready yet.' 'But I'm ready—I *wanna* meet her, I'll do anything—' I said 'Well Lisa thinks you're not quite ready yet, she says you need to be trained.' '*Anything*,' she goes. 'Well Lisa says if you're interested I could put you on a training program, and then when she gets back from California you'll be ready to meet her—'"

"*[laughter]*"

"So she's supposed to come over here next week."

Sunday, ten-twenty-two . . . the night rains on, the lights keep blinking . . . Guys come in out of the rain . . . A big fat guy, fresh and clean . . . obese . . . He browses . . . picks out a thick glossy magazine called *Blonde Bitches* . . . full-color . . . thirty bucks. I put his money into the register without ringing up the sale . . . I count him back his change, hand him the book in a bag. He takes it with special, subtle care: his choice for the night . . . or the week . . . careful of it, in the rain . . . probably as close as he'll get to that kind of luminosity . . . / —phone sex . . . or the embarrassed guys trying to look casual in the strip joints: the girl talks nice to them, calls them honey . . . they put money into garter belts—more and more . . . drop quarters into machines . . . as though these nervous red dreams can somehow add up to one solid real experience . . . instead of a thousand throbbing surrogates . . . reaching for limbs that dissolve when the money runs out . . .

The burnt-leaf inhalation of Top tobacco . . . skies're blue or sodden blank. Jimmy D brings the football pool tickets on Tuesdays. Tuesday noons he's calling up the shadowed stairs: the tickets are blue. I don't know where Jimmy gets them, or what his cut is, or why he's decided, at such an advanced age, to start working for a bookie, after spending his life battling bookies. The tickets sit around the kitchen table till Friday or Saturday—some even till Sunday morning . . . considered, overlooked . . . reconsidered. There are usually too many . . . sometimes not enough . . . and then I hand them back to Jimmy D with my selections marked in pen . . . initials in the bottom corner . . . outside Feef's, or inside, at the table, when Feef isn't looking—slipped, folded with the money, under Jimmy's vague wandering absent palm . . . Jimmy's dealing right under Feef's nose, to Feef's customers. Feef's gotta *know*—I mean he must know, but he doesn't start yelling unless you let him catch you. The whole thing's goofy: I don't even *like* football pools.

We're at the track. San Diego Russ spots us and comes to sit down.

"Hey Russ."

He leans forward and eyes us over as though deciding whether we can keep a secret.

Then he says "I'll give you a perfecta here."

"Okay."

". . ."

"Well what is it?"

"Ready?"

454

"Yeah Russ, what is it?"

"Nine/four. Nine's a Detroit horse."

"Yeah?"

"I's up in Detroit yesterday. With Harmon. Harmon says this is it. Nine/four."

"Who's Harmon?"

"Bet the nine/four, one way. Don't bother reversing it. Y'know, 'cause Harmon don't talk much."

"Who the hell's Harmon?"

"Nine/four. I'll see you fellas later."

The nine's the favorite, we look in the *Form* at the four horse. Every race he got stuck in the gate.

So of course, powerless to avoid it, I go to the window and bet a nine/four perfecta for me and Ed.

The four gets stuck in the gate and runs dead last.

Fuck Harmon.

Pulling up to the house, Ed says "Well it's been a pleasure going to the track, dropping forty dollars . . . getting a migraine headache . . . Now I gotta go sit down for half an hour, get dressed and go gamble some more."

---

the soft october skies high above the bus station . . . i know i'm leaving, it doesn't matter now exactly when . . . today, tomorrow . . . a month or two from sometime . . . be good to meet a girl who doesn't need to say too much/ all the trees are almost bare. there's more sky. where'd this red rose come from? i promise not to tell. the breeze blows light, and there's a hammer held upright . . . the day beyond it pale and quiet . . . the tricks of night—the folding shadows and darkening tunnels—they come and go, with night, and are barely remembered in the wide pale light of day. she exists already, although i might not ever meet her . . . i know she's a lot more serious than i could ever be . . . / sunlight now is really just an indirect fact. even one step up and two steps back add up to something, finally, again . . . now . . . there's graffiti in the bus station stalls, but i have a quiet word for everyone.

Saturday night at the store. I've been starting at nine on Saturdays. The nights are so long I've been renting videos and bringing them in: Westerns, gangster films . . . There's a VCR hooked up to a color TV that I'm supposed to keep supplied with skin flicks from the shelves . . . to whet the customers' interest in the store's video club. What usually happens is the guys gather round the TV and watch enough to get hard before going into the booths to finish themselves off. It's that many fewer quarters to spend.

Tonight I popped a movie into the machine and a signal went through the place: five or six men gathered—from every corner, from down back—in an apparently casual huddle around the TV. The movie opens up: a blonde is unlocking the door to her apartment . . . She turns on a bedside lamp . . . starts to unbutton her blouse . . . The huddle tightens. The woman draws back the bedcovers to reveal the outline of a man in bullet holes—Turns with a gasp to find three guys in overcoats, waiting.

"Where is he?" they demand.

"I don't know!"

"Where is he?"

"*Please*: I don't know!"

One of them empties a gun into her, she falls dead on the mattress.

The men at the TV are surprised: shocked. The huddle breaks up, disgusted:

"What the hell's going on?"

"—Kinda picture *is* this?"

"That's terrible!"

And they dissolve, muttering back to their corners . . .

Ed called just now looking for card money. He'd lost the number so he called my folks' place—My mother answers. He didn't figure she knew I'm working at a porno store, so he says "Danny's been working at this uh grocery store on weekends, he gave me the number—"

"Grocery store?" she says.

"Yeah," he says, "I had the number on a book of matches, but I lost the matches."

She's got the same book of girlie matches in front of her, she says "What was on the book of matches?"

"Oh it was uh . . . Carton of milk, I think. And there was one with an apple."

"Oh yes," she says, "I've got one here. The number's 486-4889."

Ed can't scare up any money for the game, so he's resorting to one of his code-red Emergency plans—one that can be pulled only out of direst necessity, and hopefully never twice among the same group of people. He gets his mother to write him a check and then talks one of the guys at the game into cashing it for him. Someone will always do it because most of them are loaded and they need the extra player. So right off the bat Ed's got to win a hundred to buy back the check. He loses, he's got to say—before the guy leaves—

"Hey, uh—Lemme see that check a minute, I wanna make sure it's uh . . ."

The guy gives him the check saying "This check better be good, Eddie."

Ed rips it to pieces saying "Fuck you, you don't trust me?"

"Whoa, whoa, that's my hundred bucks!"

"How dare you accuse me of being a cheat, I'll beat your fucking head in!"

"You sonofabitch—you gimme that hundred!"

"I'll have your fucking hundred, but don't you ever accuse me of passing a bad check! This my *mother* you're talking about!"

Once a guy went to the bathroom near the end of a game and Ed followed him, lifted the check out of his back pocket and burned it in a toilet stall.

He says "I got a check from my mother; that leaves me with a basic two bucks in cash and my tank's on empty."

"You at your mother's now?"

"Yeah, I gotta come past there on my way to the West Side."

"Stop in: I can give you a ten."

He shows up in half an hour. Surveys the shop, apparently impressed by my new position as captain of all this. I give him a ten, and he picks out a *Swingers Classified,* which I let him take.

Then he says "Hey you got any of that uh Stay Hard Cream?"

"Yeah, we got that."

"That basically just numbs you, right?"

"Yeah, I guess. Why, you got a date?"

"No I got a toothache: I was thinking it might numb the pain—"

" *[laughter]* "

"Fucker's killing me."

*

Three-twenty, I'm trying to write a letter here . . . happen to glance down the hall where the video booths are—There's a guy with the door open—with his dick in one hand, waving at me with the other. I squint to make sure . . . run a hand through my hair and go back to writing.

———————

An October Sunday, high and dry and grey from oyster to pearl.

Day waits for evening. I've got the little color TV here . . . no one comes in much until late afternoon. Football, on TV and radio . . . the stadium's packed . . . sweat is pouring city-wide.

Ed knocks on my door this morning, he says "This playing cards six days a fucking week is *killing* me. Y'know: how much can a human being take? I don't eat right, I don't sleep right, I don't do nothing right. When I was working at least I came home—y'know, went to bed once in a while normal hours— If I had a broad to come home to, y'know, someone to say 'Hey, stay home tonight,' uh—'Here: eat these peas, these vegetables,' uh . . . y'know . . . things be different. I'd *love* to have that, a reason to stay home, but—Just the fact that I'm so fat now—I'm embarrassed by the way I look and I *know* what I look like . . . And I just can't get myself to do something about it."

"Well, you make your attempts."

"Nah, I don't make no attempts. I gotta lose some weight. The more I get depressed, the more things go wrong—the less I care about myself. And it's like a cycle, y'know? it's—Like clothes. I don't wanna get clothes, I'm overweight, What good is clothes gonna do for me? Right? I'm still gonna be fat. You don't understand that, 'cause you're not in that position—"

"I get it."

"And the more I lose gambling, the more things go wrong—get home at night—Should I eat this sandwich? Who in the fuck cares? Y'know? If I gain a pound tonight or not—Is there anybody here that cares? So that's the thing I'm getting into. But then it defeats the purpose because—The less I take care of myself, the less chance I got of meeting somebody. Y'know? It just goes on and on and on."

We walk to Feef's, and as always on Sunday there are people milling around on the sidewalk of the Holy Wesleyan storefront church . . . the usual collection of characters . . . quiet and plain . . . blank . . . families . . . You can't put a finger on it at first, it's just a feeling.

"No wonder I lose every Sunday, I gotta pass these jinxes on my way to Feef's. And then I go to bet and Feef's a midget—How can I win?"

Today there's a couple of very short people here too: an old woman, completely round, and her son . . . on the tree lawn . . . mixed in with a crowd of pale, awkward people dressed in vaguely disturbing colors . . . hospital blues and greens . . .

Ed's shaking his head. "Jesus Christ. Danny, what's a class guy like me doing in this neighborhood?"

Walking back, I ask if John's betting anything today.

"He's got Green Bay and Houston for ten."

"How's he doing?"

"Well supposedly there's this—old burlesque queen at the home, y'know—she used to be a dancer or something . . . She's like seventy or something . . . supposedly she looks like Mae West, because she got real big tits, and she wears dark glasses, probably because she's a winehead, and she got real—beehive hairdo, y'know, and real dark red Betty Boop lipstick on . . . dark thick eyebrows, y'know, with the eyebrow pencil . . ."

"*[laughter]* "

"John says—'She took me in the locker room the other day.' I said 'Whattaya mean, John?' 'She took me in the locker room the other day!' I said '*John*: for what?' He said when she opened up her locker she had—Nothing but panties and bras in there—" Ed breaks up . . .

"*[laughter]* "

"They went into the locker room, everybody's got like a big wooden locker? John says he was really on edge. She said 'I'm gonna show you what's in here,' she opened the door, nothing but panties and bras."

"*[laughter]* "

"That motherfucker's on edge alright: he's on the edge of fucking reality."

"*[laughter]* "

"He tells this to me—And he expects me to fucking believe it! *He* believes it! In his head, in his mind—It *happened* to him *somehow* . . . In his mind it happened. Y'know—'Filled with panties and bras!' It's like a little kid thing, y'know—"

"He might as well said candy canes!"

"Yeah. She opened the door and fucking *doves* flew out. Y'know. '*Filled* with panties and bras.'"

"*[laughter]* "

"'—*Big* bras, big bras . . .'"

"*[laughter]* "

"And some woman made him a pie the other day."

"*Who* made it?"

"Some other—centurion, I dunno . . . Some other woman approaching the century-mark . . ."

*

. . . the sinking lift of a Lucky Strike . . . standing outside in the doorway for some air. the all-night mechanical clicking of a traffic signal box . . . the blown glitter and sighing-down of rain . . . a car goes by . . . not a soul in sight . . .

—wet wind is chasing the flame off the match and up the cigarette: blue into yellow and the orange catches up as the match dies/ okay: now what? exterior: night:

life is mostly colons.

Monday night, Anderson Overhead Door. Bright fluorescents . . . conveyors . . . wide sheets of aluminum. They build garage doors.

Soon as I got here the white foreman stationed me at a conveyor in a long double row of black guys—not one of them looked up till he was gone—and he gave me a drill and a rivet gun and a demonstration. When the seam between two sections comes along, you drill a hole here and here and here, and then you hold the rivet gun like so and pop a rivet into each hole. Simple enough. He watched me work for a minute and then he went away.

Pretty soon a guy in an army cap came up the line and said "Uh—I been watching you and, uh, I'ma show you the right way to do this. You got to drill the hole at a *angle,* like this—" He let me try. When he was sure I had the hang of it he went back to his spot. Once in a while he'd glance down at me to make sure I was getting it right.

He went to the water fountain and a guy with a gold tooth came down.

He said "I'ma show you the *easy* way to do this. You hold the drill like this here, and then you pop a rivet like *this.*"

I tried it his way. Satisfied, he went back to his spot.

A few minutes later he got a phonecall. The guy in the cap came back.

"No, no, no," he was saying. "You doing it all wrong."

I gave him the drill and the gun and he showed me again, and then went back to his spot.

When the guy with the tooth came back I alternated between both methods until the foreman came by and stopped me.

"You're making this hard on yourself," he said. "Do it like I showed you. Hold the gun straight up and down."

I looked him in the eyes, nodding, and he left me there.

I worked for twenty minutes looking over both shoulders and alternating between three methods until the guy with the tooth caught me on the offbeat and came over.

"Here, man—Gimme that gun."

I pretended to watch him carefully, and then repeated what he'd done.

"*No,* man," he said, mustering patience. "It *ain't* that simple. I been here five year—Take my 'vice. *Now*—"

I did exactly what I'd done before. This time he nodded.

"*That's* right, man."

The only thing worse than learning too slow was learning too fast. Either way they got aggravated.

Of course the guy in the cap caught me again, just before break. He came over.

"Look man: I'ma show you *one more time*—"

I laughed, shaking my head . . .

I said "What're you guys, breaking my balls or what?"

He gave me a fierce look.

"Ain't no joke, man."

And then the buzzer rang for the first break.

*

Three o'clock, lunch. The night's going by quick. The guys are playing cards, a game called tunk. One of them just said "A scared man can't work and a jealous man can't sleep." Can't figure out the game. I get into a discussion about football . . . This place is okay, I wouldn't mind coming back here. The coffee machine's only a dime.

———————————

Yellow Freight.

———————————

"Yeah, sure Jim . . ."
Yellow Freight.

———————————

Yellow vs. grey.
"(exhale . . .) Okay Jim."

*

Six-forty-five a.m., hiding in a toilet stall at Yellow Freight, forty-five minutes to go . . .

———————————

Friday morning eight o'clock a girl's bicycle against the rail of Ed's porch.

Evidently that Debbie's begun her training program. God knows what it might consist of: Ed's a creative guy.

———————————

Phonecall from Duke:

I'm saying "*Happiness* is the wrong word, anyway. Happiness . . . y'know . . . I don't have any idea. As far as uh . . . y'know, like an extended state—like you're gonna one day reach a place where—"

"Yeah. Right . . . The only thing I can see to believe in is energy. 'Cause I know if you get up on the mountain—eventually you're gonna have to go back down to the valley for supplies—"

"[laughing] Right. And then you gotta walk back up the mountain. So much for happiness."

"Yeah, I prefer the desert—"

"*[laughter]* "

"—y'know, a few little ups and downs—but subtle—"

"Uh-huh."

"It's cold at night, it's hot in the day—It makes sense."

"Yeah. Once in a while the moon comes up—but you ain't building yourself up into any holes."

"Mm."

"But I don't know why we should even have to— I mean I don't know where I got that idea about happiness in the first place. I don't think anyone ever sat me down and told me about

happiness . . . Musta been just something I picked up somewhere . . . probably just a misunderstanding."

---

follow the pulling curve of the road: leather collar up, cigarette
hand on the wheel: another prince without a name, another
king without a feeling, cool as can be, discovering for the thou-
sandth time that movement is promise and fulfillment too: the
night strewn and flashed with lights and billboards and black
shapes—eye-level past the swelling night of the lake, gun-shot
over the bright night of the mills . . .

Ed bought the paper this morning. He opened it to find the
sports page blank. A printing mistake. He took it as a sign from
God.

Sunday afternoon at the shop. I pocketed fifty for myself last
night and decided to put it on a game today and give the winnings to Ed, toward what I owe him.

Cincinnati beats Cleveland fourteen to seven. A hundred
for Ed.

. . . Sunlight glares pale from bare branches and smooth
spots on the pavement . . . like a Sunday in memory . . . the light
like inhaled smoke . . .

The glass door: a narrow piece of outside: . . . blue shadow, MARTIN'S MENS W, bicycles . . . briefly an old man
with wisps of blown white hair . . . A van goes fast . . . Joey,
a regular, makes his exit—asks if I want something . . . I tell
him "Yeah, bring me a Coke" and immediately regret it . . . I
go back to check the booths with a flashlight . . . I find a token,

four quarters, and a penny. The others'll be here later . . . some of them businesslike, some of them whispering, floating . . . tapping on the doors: "Let me in, let me in . . ."

Woman comes in tonight—short solid hillbilly broad, built like a mailbox . . . She's looking over the dildos, the strap-ons . . . We've got them all: some as big as horsecocks . . . some that plug into the wall, move up and down . . . some with foreskin . . . one with a crank . . . some with so many wires and protrusions—lights, bells, balls—I can't make head or tail of them . . . In all colors: pink, purple, black . . . lavender . . . So she's examining them—she says "D'you think I could order one of these special?"

"Custom made, you mean? I doubt if they do that . . . But there's a catalog on the wall with some we ain't got . . ."

She goes over to look at it . . . studies it—every picture, every description—for almost an hour.

Finally she looks up, comes up for air. She says "Can you tell me the address of this company? D'you think if I sent them an idea they'd make one?"

I said "I don't think they'd make just one, but it's a shot. Here's some paper."

Joey came back. She had very specific ideas about what she wanted, she was explaining it to him . . .

Joey's been trying for a half hour to get me to show him my dick. He makes a regular circuit of these places—comes from the shop on Vine Street to this one, then maybe downtown, then out by the airport and back . . . hangs around, waiting, trying to pick up guys . . . The regulars share a certain tacit camaraderie, but also a disdain for one another. The last two booths on the left have a hole cut in the wall between them. Glory hole. The regulars resort to one another only late, late at night . . . near dawn, when all other options have fallen through.

I've got a sick headache, seems like I've had it for days.

Some accountant kid comes in he's trying to talk to me . . . I'm falling asleep, I need some air. I feel like a cold cup of coffee with a cigarette floating in it.

And then the phone rings. It's the manager. The guy who's supposed to take over at eleven can't make it. The manager wants to know if I can stay till seven-thirty in the morning. I tell him okay, hang up, swallow a couple more aspirins and take another sip of coffee.

Just after eleven the Doctor comes in. I'm not sure he's a doctor, but he looks like my idea of a retired doctor: clean-scrubbed with fine white hair, comfortably though impeccably dressed . . . red cashmere V-neck . . . discreet . . . the model of humble composure . . . soft hands, as I pour him out his tokens . . . and soft-spoken . . . hardly a word . . . He thanks me with a cautious smile and moves toward the back . . .

By one-twenty the place is empty of customers. I slide off my seat to go check the empty cubicles—for money, tokens, whatever . . . My bootsteps are loud coming down the aisle, the wooden doors hang open . . .

I hear a scrabbling sound: just ahead, from the right. The door's wide open, I glance down . . .

And there's the doctor: on the floor: jammed onto the floor between the bench and the wall: pants and shorts around his ankles, knees bent—among the cumshot and cigarette butts . . . tangled, and reaching for the door, a wild and pleading look in his eyes—

I walked out of the porno place at seven in the morning. It was still dark out; the sky was heavy with cloud. All night, the few leaves remaining to a honeylocust at the curb had dangled in a breeze that seemed to gather itself into stillness now before the light . . .

As I swung a U-turn in the empty street, I saw one patch of silvery light among the clouds, like the eye of a hurricane.

I hit the freeway and headed home. Above, darkness had just barely loosened its grip on the outlines of clouds.

Going into the lake stretch I drove through a handful of rain; I hit the gas. I left the rain behind me and took Dead Man's Curve too fast: I fishtailed a little and swerved back into the groove below the bridges. I hit the gas again hard.

I came spun like a spark from darkness into the steel mill turn and what I saw stopped my heart a beat: a lone black smokestack, giving flame into a deep open gash of sunrise: blood on a bull's neck—

and I went spinning like a wheel into a day still unbroken . . .

"How you set for cash?" I ask him.

"Well I get my welfare check tomorrow, so I's just figuring my budget here, uh . . . I gotta give Keith the rent, so I figure after that—if I don't *splurge*—y'know, if I don't go crazy and buy a paper in the morning, I'll have thirteen cents a day for the next month. If I buy a newspaper I'll be starting each day with a seven-cent deficit."

" *[laughter]* "

"Thirteen cents a day . . . For gas, food, bills . . . household necessities, y'know, clothes . . ."

"Looks like a tight squeeze."

"Yeah, well I wanted to start cutting corners anyway, y'know."

"Yeah."

"I kinda like living like this, y'know. I never know whether I'm gonna wake up dead of starvation or frozen to death or—"

"Keeps things exciting."

"Yeah. Y'know what really keeps things exciting though?

Driving—for the last two years—constantly—with the needle on empty—just below the red there?"

"*[laughter]* "

"—Putting a dollar's worth of gas in at a time, never knowing when the car's gonna conk out, or where—under what conditions, or what time of night, y'know . . ."

"*[laughter]* Yeah. Well anyway here's a hundred toward what I owe you."

OctoberNovember's a boxcar with an open door, rolling up—right on track into a land without boundaries.

I'm sitting in my car outside the A-Brite Plating Company. It's midnight. Twenty minutes ago the phone rings. I promised myself I'd never work in another plating company, but here I am . . . stalling . . . the steam of a Dairy Mart coffee rising onto the windshield. Cold night, below freezing. I can hear the buzz of machinery from inside, and I'm waiting to get out of the car and take that fatal step into another spectral factory night.

*

They've got me working at a rattling blue machine—three city blocks long: bubbling cauldrons just taller than I am, with metal arms moving above, dipping racks of plastic parts into churning solutions of every color—boiling, sulphurous . . . pipes running amok, leaking, steaming, disappearing . . . The plastic pieces on the racks are different shapes and sizes—parts for faucets, it looks like—being dipped in chrome. After they're chromed they're silvery, and the racks are green, so it's like flat stylized Christmas trees with ornaments moving all around. It's

my job to lift the racks off the arms after they've completed
a dipping and rinsing process covering an area the size of the
Southside and hang them to dry on a conveyor system behind
me. The origins and endings of this process are lost in a maze
of pipes and circuitry and a boiling roar like Niagara Falls. Every sixty seconds I grab two racks.

Now two girls have come along behind me and they're picking
the dried ornaments off the racks like Christmas is over and
tossing them into boxes. It's mostly women working here.

—Now one of the racks has fallen into a cauldron: They shut the
machine down—they're running around with poles and nets—
hooks—harpoons—They're fishing around . . . They pull out a
body! An employee missing for years! I take the opportunity to
light a Camel, my hands dried with chemicals . . . I got one hand
the color of iodine, and I'm smoking a chrome cigarette . . .

*

After break. I'm working away . . . Here comes this old woman:
grey hair, cropped short—good two hundred, she weighs. She
hangs a rack behind me and some parts fly off. I stoop to pick
some of them up—I help her stick them back on the rack. She's
muttering—I can barely hear with all the noise. I go "*What?*"
She says "I'm old enough to be your grandmother! Show some
respect!" I go "*What?*" She says "There's plenty of cuties on
the other side for you to have sex with! Now leave me alone!"
And she walks off—leaves me standing there.
     So I ask this guy I'm working with "Hey Darryl, what's with
that old woman in the yellow sweater?"
     He says "Aw man, don't pay her no mind, she a little bit
off. She get in fights with them racks! Everybody know about
her!"
     He's yelling at the top of his lungs—women are turning.

470

"Okay Darryl, uh—"

"YEAH, LIKE YOU SAY, SHE A CRAZY FUCK AL-RIGHT! SEE ALL THEM CLOTHES AND SWEATERS SHE GOT ON?"

"Yeah, yeah—"

"SOMEBODY MUST RUNG HER BELL GOOD ONE TIME! CRAZY OLD BITCH, YOU GOT THAT RIGHT! MAYBE SHE THINK YOU CUTE!"

I get a lot of funny looks at lunchtime.

Ed says "Guess who I seen today."

"Who?"

"I'm coming home from a game, right? Seven in the morning, I pull into McDonald's on Broadway? I's just gonna get a coffee. And—I'm walking past the window, who do I see but Angelface."

"Angie?"

"Yeah. She's sitting at a table with all her possessions piled around her in the booth. And—I was— I's gonna talk to her, see if she needs anything, but . . . AahI didn't even go in there man, I . . . I couldn't do it, was . . . too sad, it was just . . ."

(Reprise)

Just got back from a walk. I left around eight-thirty and now it's a quarter past ten. Didn't think I was gone so long.

Something opens up, and runs on—untranslatable . . . and/

It's been raining four days now . . . lightly . . . off and on . . . steadily . . . Tonight is like a dripping mist. Houses riding waves of smoke, downhill to the river . . . streets dead-ended by the construction of the highway down below—a highway

never used . . . a lot of churches left behind . . . changed hands
. . . The sky a soft and breathing glow . . . the strung march
of telephone poles . . . a moisture like soot . . . the strung vigil
of streetlights: pendant . . . cottoned . . . lights in the puddles
. . . branches, curbs . . . the quiet wet ravage of autumn . . . I
stopped into a red place on a desolate corner of Jefferson for
one shot of whiskey, and then walked out . . . sunken cars . . .
the blue of TV . . . torn curtains . . . hives, enclosed below the
river sky . . . transient, abandoned . . . re-inhabited but never
renewed . . . /

—then the walk closes on itself when you hit the stairs: lost,
like a dream . . . whole and sparkling in memory, but buried too
deep to recover . . .

I fell asleep here on the cot.

Open my eyes feeling dazed and thick, a slight taste of whiskey in my mouth, and the light seems brighter now—intrusive.
The clock says ten-fifty. Jim hasn't called.

And he doesn't.

I go into the bathroom to rinse my face and mouth.

Every morning now, a girl's bike against the rail of Ed's porch.
A curtain moves.

A different "we" stand in the pouring but paler november light,
as though in our last moments on Earth . . .

TRUCKS

Sweeping the apron . . . still of night . . . (a privilege no one else wants, because it keeps you outside in the cold all night. I usually volunteer for it first thing, checking in with my time slip and workgloves. There's less to do inside on the dock but you make up for it trying to look busy. A few of these men have been coming out here every night for two years, hoping Yellow Freight will notice them and hire them at a regular wage with benefits and security. The two who've been coming out longest are known to the Teamsters who work here driving the fork-lifts, loading and unloading the trailers. The union men don't call either of them by name, but will occasionally acknowledge one of them with a nod, or by making him the butt of some small joke at breaktime, or with a word at the sinks, if the union guy's in a good mood at quitting time . . . After coming out here night after night, most any spot laborer develops a sense of belonging to this place . . . based on a vague fragile web of remembered nods, offhand remarks, accidental smiles . . . Maybe one reason they don't like to be sweeping the apron outside is that it keeps them away from the warmth of some kind of fellowship they see themselves as having established on the inside. Maybe they feel that if they spend a night out-side, the union men and whoever's watching down will forget their faces . . . But I'm—)

Out between the looming trailers, in the long nonlinear stretch of time after midnight. All these trailers have been emptied, or are being emptied, or swept, or stacked again—All of them are in some stage of readiness toward being sent out again, to somewhere, in the night . . . in the early dawn . . . Even, I suppose, in broad daylight, though I can't picture it. I can only imagine this place at night. The men working inside can't see me, though I'm only a few feet away, just below them: the dock is almost my height, and the space between trailers is narrow, and deep in shadow. The trailers are so close together that almost none of the coppery light inside escapes, and peering into there from out here is like watching through a keyhole into another world . . . but just another world.

Around midnight the sky had been clear, but now . . . near three . . . the dead smokiness that settles every night was here. I left pushbroom, shovel, and trashbarrel, and stepped out from between two trailers. I leaned against one of them and looked around, taking in for the first time in hours a night wider than the boundaries of this place . . .

Fifty yards away, at the edge of the lot, were four trailers in a row, unhitched, unused . . . unreflecting . . .

I walked across the lot and around the other end of them. All four were open-ended. I lifted myself up into one . . . walked through the resounding empty blackness of it, and sat against the back wall.

. . . I found a pack of cigarettes in a jacket pocket and pulled it out . . . I fished matches from that same pocket.

The open end of the trailer framed a square of night: a few yards of grass leading to a barbwire fence . . . beyond which, a wide stretch of marshy ground, and then the black wall of the woods. Above them, in the distance, the red lights of two radio towers, blinking . . . as . . . far . . . away . . . as . . . home . . .

SUNDAY NIGHT

I reached under the table and brought up the typewriter cover, snapped it in place and slid back my chair. Caught my reflection in the night and was caught by it. The window rattled with the wind.

I watched him: expectant . . . conspiratorial . . .

I found sudden approval there and stood up quick, embarrassed, and grabbed my jacket, cigarettes, matches . . . keys . . . I picked up the neat stack of pages and counted them again, though I knew how many were there. Twenty-three.

The wind hit the Buick broadside as I plunged over the bridge and into the scattered pearls of downtown. Never had the Terminal Tower looked so squat. It stood alone and aglow. I felt like I was seeing it after having been to a bigger place.

The campus of Cleveland State was dark, but the copy shop on Euclid Avenue was open.

Inside, the light was bright, fluorescent.

The girl who turned away from the big machine was Marie.

We surprised each other.

"—Hi," she said, coming to the counter.

"Hi. I completely forgot you worked here. Did I know you worked here?"

"Well you should: I've been here almost a year."

"Yeah, that's right."

She smiled.

I said "In fact, you're exactly right. You've been here almost

475

a year. Right you are."

She laughed.

"What's up?"

"Well I just got, uh, need a copy of something here."

I handed her the clean slim sheaf.

"What's this?" she said, knocking it straight on the counter.

"Story I wrote."

"Really? So you're a writer now?"

"Just make the copy."

"Can I read it?" she said from the machine.

"Yeah, I'll show it to you sometime."

"It's not about me, is it?"

"No."

She brought the sheaf back, doubled.

"How much?"

"Don't worry about it."

"Okay. Thanks."

"Where you working?" she said.

"Here and there. Wherever they send me."

"Are you going away?"

". . . Um—Yeah, I'm thinking about it. How'd you know?"

"I dunno. Where to?"

"I don't know yet. I'll drop you a note."

"I'll write back."

I said "Anyway, uh . . . I dunno . . ."

She laughed, shook her head.

I said "Good to see you."

"It's good to see you too."

Ed was playing cards above the Variety Theater.

I hadn't seen much of him lately, and in a few days he'd be moving out of the neighborhood to the house owned by Chicago Joe. Ed had been talking about a change; he said he was fed up with the Southside, meaning he was fed up with himself on the Southside, with the pattern of his days there. The new place was only ten minutes away, but it marked a change in the weave of our lives. I was leaving too, but the urgency I felt to see him was more to do with the pages which caught and surrendered streetlight on the front seat. I'd taken Lorain Avenue instead of the freeway.

Kim was there, a girl I'd picked up once or twice—adjunct to shadows now, walking with a cane . . . and there were boarded storefronts . . . a guy in a station wagon at the curb, windows up . . . a laundromat, open but empty . . . a Korean massage parlor, open all night . . .

I drove casually, gathering final impressions.

Sodium frieze, slipping by . . .

At a Hundred-Seventeenth I saw the Pontiac across the intersection. I hit my brights and he shot me his; I signaled right. He turned left and pulled alongside me in a car wash lot. We left our engines running. He said "I just called you—game's cancelled. I was just heading home."

"What's up? You hungry?"

"No, not really . . . I get a coffee, you wanna—"

"No, I don't care. Let's get a drink. Meet me at Myron's?"

I followed the scarred Pontiac, the brights and dimmings of its taillights, down Detroit Avenue. Ed would be here all his life. His driving was preoccupied but expert. I dreamed of glory while he surveyed his precincts.

Perched at the bar, we ordered shots. He didn't ask about the pages I'd set on the stool beside me.

"Where you been?" he said. "You don't stop over just to hutniak sometime?"

"Working. How you been?" I said.

"Ahh I'm fucking broke, as usual—I's looking forward to this game tonight. Sap usually gives me a buy-in, I coulda walked outa there with a few bills, but his wife's sick, the game's called off."

The bartender set the shots.

"I got 'em," I said.

"What the fuck? You're broke too—"

"I got some money. And I'm leaving."

"Whattaya mean?"

"I'm leaving town, I gotta pay my way out, y'know . . ."

"Where you going? leaving town . . ."

"I told you that a couple months ago."

"What, you're taking a trip, or what?"

"I'm gonna go see my friend Duke out West, and then I got a friend in New York. I's thinking of going to New York for a while, check it out."

"The fuck," Ed was saying.

I could feel the movement of clouds above the bar. Whole continents of cloud, across the night.

A dog—an old black Lab—gathered himself from the shadows and barked at us. Ed's drink jumped in his hand.

I held out a fist and the dog came to sniff it.

"Fucking thing's dangerous," Ed said. And then, to the bartender: "This your dog?"

"That's right."

"He do any tricks?"

"Yeah, he acts retarded."

Bored with us, the dog retired to the shadows.

We sipped our whiskeys.

I said "So what's up?"

"With me? I dunno, what do you want me to say? I'm broke, I'm fat, I'm dying . . . you're abandoning me . . ."

" . . ."

"Lately I been feeling really nervous, y'know? Nervous alla time, like something bad's gonna happen, but I don't know what it is."

"Maybe you got too much time on your hands."

"Hah? I dunno. I been having fucking nightmares, too. Almost every night."

"Like what?"

"All kindsa shit. I dreamt the other night my old man was lying on top of me!"

"What?"

"Scared the shit outa me: he's just lying on top of me looking in my eyes."

" *[laughter]* "

"And I'm always worried about the place catching on fire while I'm asleep, y'know? 'Causea that old heater, or—maybe one of these lunatics I owe money to, coming to burn me down, or someone from my past . . . So the other night I wake up, and I see this orange glow from the other room—I said Holy shit—place's on fire!—jumped outa bed—"

"What was it?"

"Nothing. I's just half asleep, confused, y'know . . ."

"Hm."

"Weird shit, that I think Now why the fuck would I dream that? Y'know? Open up the refrigerator and a bunch of canaries fly out—"

" *[laughter]* "

"And sleep is the only escape I got, now I gotta torture myself with these stupid dreams. I owe so much money to so many places, Danny— But it's more than money. It's being alone all the time, and—It's everything. I got no elevation, y'know: it's all tooth and claw. My whole life is catching up with me. I thought I could escape it by moving to Joe's, but I can see it ain't gonna be no different over there."

"Well it might. Be cheaper, for one thing."

"I'm paying cheap rent as it is. It ain't me in one place or another place, it's me in the world. Y'know what I did today? Just to show you how scared I been feeling."

"What?"

"I called the Society for the Blind, see if they need any volunteers."

I laughed. "What brought that on?"

"I's downtown the other day, I saw this blind guy waiting for a bus. And I's thinking Jesus Christ, all the problems I got, and here this guy's blind, y'know? Kinda stopped me in my tracks a little. How would you get through the day? Why would you even bother? Y'know? So I called, see if they need someone a couple days a week, go to someone's house, read 'em the paper or whatever."

"What'd they say?"

"They said they need a driver on the West Side, they're gonna send me an application."

"Good for you," I said. "You want another shot?"

"I'll get these," he said, nodding.

We were quiet for a minute or two.

"What's on your mind?" he said.

"I was thinking about that questionnaire they gave me for the polygraph test. All those questions. One of 'em was Have you ever considered suicide?"

"Strange question for them to ask."

"Yeah."

"What'd you say?"

"I said yeah. No reason to lie."

"You got no reason to commit suicide. I do, but you don't. You ain't earned it."

"Well the question wasn't *do* you ever, it was *have* you ever. I used to think about it a lot. I didn't worry about whether I'd earned it."

"When?"

"My last year of high school."

He sipped his drink, paying only enough attention to be polite.

I said "I was convinced I knew what life was, and what it was gonna be. It didn't feel like self-pity, it felt realistic. Like I was the only one who wasn't pretending."

"So then what?"

"Well I planned the whole thing out. I wrote letters to a few people, then tore open the envelopes and wrote the letters again . . . I included photographs—"

We had a laugh at this.

I said "I nurtured it. I carried it with me like it was all I had. Then one afternoon when no one was home I put all my possessions into separate piles for whoever I was bequeathing 'em to—records, books—And then I went out to the apartment garages—just a calm quiet afternoon in late spring—and I pulled down the garage door, turned the ignition on my old man's Impala, and lay down under the exhaust pipe. For like a second. Then I got up and turned off the car, lifted the garage door and stepped outside."

" . . . "

"That's all it took! One second. It's like I had to get it out of my system. And I ain't thought about it since."

We sipped our drinks. I lit a cigarette and blew the smoke to one side.

Saying "It was like looking too hard in one direction."

"Hm."

" . . . "

" . . . "

"What about you?" I said.

"What?"

"You want another drink?"

I motioned down the bar.

"You got a position on suicide?"

"You'll burn in hell if you commit suicide. I was raised Catholic. I don't agree with them on every point, but I do believe in God."

"So it's just purely a religious thing with you."

"Yeah. God says you cannot kill yourself."

"But it's gotta be more than that."

"Whattaya mean—for me *personally?* I can't commit suicide 'cause my insurance policy won't let me for two years."

"*[laughter]* "

"I don't have the luxury of killing myself. It's in the policy."

"But aside from the insurance thing, aside from the religious thing—You don't have any other reservations? Your family, your—"

"No, no, no. There's so many ways in this life to get bumped off or die— I'm probably gonna get a heart attack from fucking cholesterol in the next two years, or get shot by an irate bookie or someone in a card game, or get AIDS from one of these hookers . . . It's too late for me to kill myself. Be kinda beside the point. I got too much of an investment of effort and aggravation and fucking—time, and blood. Defeat the whole purpose. Whatever the purpose is. Even if it's only some make-believe God that's watching."

The bartender poured our drinks and took my ten off the bar, came back with the change.

"I brought something for you," I said. I slid the story off the stool and gave it to Ed.

"What's this?"

"Story I wrote."

"No shit. Is it about me?"

"Yeah."

He said "I'll sue you. If you said anything bad about me I'll sue you."

"Okay."

He left his drink untouched and leafed through the pages. My heart raced like an engine straining for the next gear. I sipped whiskey and tried to keep a straight face, as Ed let go bursts of brief dark laughter in recognition and approval, saying "Yeah, that's right" and "That's exactly how it happened . . ."

I said "Don't read it now. Save it."

"Can I keep this?"

"Yeah, that's your copy."

"That's amazing, that you remembered all this stuff. You must have a photographic memory. I always said you were a great writer."

"I thought you were talking about my handwriting."

"I was, but that's gotta be half the battle."

I smiled, and watched my dreams begin.

He said "What're you gonna do with this?"

"I dunno. I was thinking it could be a first chapter of something."

"Maybe we should talk about royalties."

"You'll get paid when I get paid. I'll give you twenty-five percent."

"Twenty-five percent! I should get half! I had to live this shit!"

"Yeah but I gotta live through writing it."

"I feel exploited."

I counted ten twenties from my pocket and tossed them on the bar.

"What's this?" he said.

"There's the deuce I owe you. Thanks."

"You sure you can spare this? Don't give me this now—"

"Take it."

I could feel the night blown clear above the bar. Leaving us to our futures. I walked to the bathroom and watched myself in the mirror above the toilet.

Zipped and went back to the bar.

I was restless, Ed could tell. He said "One more story."

"Okay."

"I wake up at like six today, I can't sleep . . . Get in the car to get a paper, right? Go to Dairy Mart, I'm driving around . . . I got the sports open on the seat, I got a pen—Kinda— looking at it as I'm driving, right? I hit Detroit— It takes a long time to dope this out, 'cause there's like twelve games, there's all these possibilities, y'know . . . Stop and get a coffee, I'm driving up and down—figure I'll look for a hooker. Turn the radio on, nothing but religious stations . . . And I'm cruising around, keeping one eye open for a hooker, circling teams in the paper . . . Meanwhile there's a priest on the radio, reciting the rosary, y'know? And I'm looking around, here's a broad standing on the corner, y'know, I'm looking back at the paper, I'm going 'God the Father—aah that fucking team, the quarterback's hurt—Our Lord who art in heaven, they ain't got no TV coverage,' uh—"

"*[laughter]*"

"'Hail Mary full of grace, threw three interceptions last week,' uh—'Minnesota's plus seven, Give us this day a possible parlay—'"

"*[laughter]*"

"Finally I realized what I'm doing, here I'm reciting the *rosary*—circling gambling bets and looking for a whore—six o'clock Sunday morning— I hadda pull over, I go Wow, this is a—"

"Right!"

"What more *sinful* thing than—Sunday morning going over the sport page, reciting the rosary and looking for someone to suck my dick—"

"*[laughter]*"

"Plus I coulda killed somebody—"

"Or you coulda killed *yourself*, which woulda been perfect timing, with the rosary . . ."

"Yeah. Right as I smack into a utility pole I'm saying 'Hail Mary—'"

"*[laughter]*"

"That mighta been my one shot! 'Cause you don't get too many opportunities like that. My one shot to get to heaven—with the fucking sport page over my face, and some hooker between my legs . . ."

I said "You blew it, man," slipping on my jacket.

And then I laughed again.

We saw ourselves in the backbar mirror, and shadows froze.

He said "Good luck, buddy."

"Good luck, Ed."

I hit the street, still in the glow of his peculiar spell of experience and faith. The night was clear as laughter, and sparkling like loss.

MONDAY

I go into Feef's to bet the Monday night game, Jimmy D's at the table.

"Jimmy."

He hasn't seen me in a while. He turns to look up, eyes wide. I could be anyone. A tout . . . a telegram, a birthday cake . . . his father . . . the law . . . Eddie Arcaro, St. Peter, Walter Johnson . . . Mr. Death . . .

Finally my face clicks, for him. "How are you?" he asks.

"I'm good."

He's searching for a meaning to this encounter . . .

"You working?" he asks. As though this is a question he remembers people ask . . .

"Yeah, I'm working."

". . . You seen your old man?"

"Yeah. I'm going out to see him now. I'm gonna eat lunch with him."

". . . How's Big Eddie?"

"He's . . . y'know, he's—staying above water . . ."

"Yeah . . . The water's pretty deep. Especially when you hit that ocean."

A little after this was over, I was at the table after midnight. I rinsed the coffee cup, slipped on a jacket, locked up, and went downstairs. Dave had moved in, behind Mr. Jim.

I knocked on his door. The night was rolling and blowing. He came to the door without a shirt.

"Hey. C'mon in."

I stepped inside.

"What's up?"

"Nothing; I'm going for a ride."

"Yeah? Sounds good—lemme get dressed."

He didn't ask where; it never mattered.

I pulled out and around the corner.

"Damn, I forgot to get cigarettes."

"I figured you'd have one," he said.

I searched my jacket pockets and came up empty.

"Look around," I said.

He checked the glove compartment, under the seats, above the visor . . . The streets of the neighborhood were deserted.

"Check in back. Look in that taxi jacket back there."

He leaned over the seat and rummaged around . . . "Yeah." He came up with an old squashed pack. ". . . might be one left . . ."

I glanced over, cruising up Literary: he tore open the pack.

"Nope: two left."

"Excellent."

He handed me one. I dug a book of matches out of the seat and gave it to him. He struck a light, protecting with cupped hand the tiny flame that kindled his face, and I leaned over, rolling past Lincoln Park, and he lit mine with the same match. We were all set.

The taillights of an old Caddy brighten to slow, and then dip, diminishing into a turn, surrounded by the black of night. Gives you that sinking feeling . . .

I kept driving and the night sky went from glowing to glowering . . . winter blew in, wrapped itself like a bedsheet around the rear window of an old Pontiac . . . I left town.

CPSIA information can be obtained at www.ICGtesting.com
Printed in the USA
BVOW01s0708090614

355701BV00001B/1/P